Operation Cobra

A novel

By Dave Hedger

First published in e format and paperback
by Sarlat & Stafaidh
2014

ISBN 978-0-9928470-0-5

Produced by Shore Books and Design
Blackborough End, Norfolk PE32 1SF

For friends departed

A special thanks to Linda my proofreader for giving me encouragement and support throughout the writing of this book

Chapter 1

On the first floor of the American Forces Hospital, Master Sergeant Michael Lenihan paced up and down outside the intensive care unit. Behind the curtained doors his wife Carol was fighting for her life after suffering a massive internal bleed.

Lenihan had last seen Carol just before he left for training with the 5th Special Forces group based at Bad Tolz in Bavaria. She had been fit and well and looking forward to a visit stateside to see her mother and sister in a few weeks time. As he killed time in the waiting area, smoking continuously, he reflected their life together. They had married fourteen years earlier in Atlanta Georgia. The one thing that was missing in their lives was a child, this possibility being ruled out by army doctors after extensive tests revealed Lenihan's very low sperm count. Nothing could be done they were told and adoption was out of the question because of his service career.

Carol had a brief affair while they were based in Kure, Japan but this ended when her lover was posted to the American embassy in Athens. They settled down to a comfortable life and although without sex playing a leading part, they had a regular circle of friends and attended parties and functions within the American community.

Although attached to the 3rd British Parachute Battalion as an instructor in close quarter combat, Lenihan never went into their sergeant's mess or socialised with them at all. He never really liked the British; he thought they were a class-conscious nation that always boasted about their military victories of days gone by. The one thing he detested most of all was the way in which the officers looked down on the Americans as a second rate army, constantly criticising their performance in Vietnam.

'Sergeant Lenihan, would you please come with me?' said the nurse, indicating the way along the hall leading to the doctor's office.

'How's my wife doing?' he said in a tense voice struggling to contain his emotions.

'I think it would be better if the doctor explained the details to you sergeant,' she said, adding that she had only just come on duty and not seen any of the patient's notes.

The name on the brass nameplate attached to the door said Colonel J Peters MD USAF. The nurse knocked quietly and a voice said, 'Come in please.' The nurse introduced the two men and left the room closing the door quietly behind her.

'Sit down, Sergeant Lenihan,' said the doctor pointing to a chair. 'I'm afraid I have some bad news for you, your wife Carol died a few minutes ago in spite of all our efforts to save her. We would have called you in to see her in her last moments but the room was packed with staff trying to save her, we really did do our best, I'm very sorry.' Lenihan was shattered and speechless, the doctor pressed a button on his desk and the nurse appeared immediately in the doorway. 'Nurse, would you please bring us some coffee and then see we are not disturbed'.

'Right away, yes sir,' said the nurse.

After lighting a cigarette, in spite of the no smoking sign hanging on the door, Lenihan said, 'How did she come to die, what happened? She was fine before I went to Bavaria'. Colonel Peters was surprised at this question; he thought staff in the emergency room had briefed Lenihan when they phoned his unit after Carol had been brought in by ambulance.

'Sergeant Lenihan,' said the doctor, 'your wife was pregnant and was undergoing an illegal abortion in a downtown area of Frankfurt. It appears she started to bleed heavily and the quack that was performing this operation phoned for an ambulance and left her to her own devices with little more than a pad to stem the flow. When such a bleed takes place surgical intervention is required quickly under clinical conditions. This did not happen; even the paramedics who arrived in the ambulance quickly could do little. I can assure you however that we did all we could to save her. She had lost so much blood that her brain became starved and her other vital organs started to shut down beyond recovery. I am very sorry sergeant.'

'What son of a bitch has been screwing Carol whilst I've been away'? Lenihan went on to explain to the doctor about his sperm count tests and the years they tried for a baby. When it was confirmed that children of their own would not be possible Carol lost interest in the physical side of their marriage.

Lenihan's mind was racing when the doctor said the air force would be able to arrange for Carols body to be returned to America for cremation. 'Is her body in any state to be left for medical research doc,' said Lenihan.

The doctor replied that it was, but certain legal documents would have to be drawn up first, and then her body would be taken to the Kennedy research institute in Dallas, Texas. In the meantime the West German police would be carrying out a full investigation into the matter, it seemed they had already had some leads and an arrest might be possible in a few days.

'I'll drop by in the morning and sign any papers that I have to, if that's alright sir,' said Lenihan getting up from his chair and saluting the senior officer.

'In the meantime can I give you anything to help you get some sleep?'

'No thanks sir, I don't need any drugs, all I want is a bottle of whiskey,' replied Lenihan moving towards the door. 'But thanks anyway sir, please pass on my appreciation to all your staff for what they did. Good-bye, Colonel.'

After leaving the hospital and going out into the dark, wet night Lenihan hailed a taxi to take him to his flat in the American quarter. The journey seemed a long one but in reality was no more than ten kilometres. His mind kept going back to the thought of Carol having an affair; could it have been a one-night stand? Maybe it was something that had been going on for a long time, he may never know. Lenihan decided to talk to Jane in the morning. Jane Casey was the wife of Captain Rod Casey, a close friend of the Lenihans for many years.

When he got home to the flat he went straight to the drinks cabinet and poured himself a large slug of Bourbon whiskey, followed by several more and chain smoking his way through a pack of Lucky Strike. Later

Lenihan staggered into the bedroom and collapsed onto the bed fully clothed falling into a deep sleep instantly. He awoke with a start when the doorbell rang, it sounded like a drill going through his head. When he finally opened it, there stood Jane and Rod Casey both looking very white and shaken. Lenihan had not realised he had slept all night and that it was now almost noon. Jane burst into tears and tried to explain that she and Rod had only just heard the news from a friend who worked at the hospital.

'Mike, why didn't you phone us last night, we would have come straight over, you look terrible.'

Lenihan nodded and motioned for them to come in. Jane went into the kitchen to make some coffee, still sobbing. Rod Casey said he would try to arrange some extra compassionate leave so as to allow Lenihan time to come to terms with his grief.

'No, Rod, I don't want any leave, but I do intend to find the bastard who was screwing Carol. When I do I will make fucking sure he never goes near other women again, I'll kill the son of a bitch.'

'I quite understand, Mike, but please don't make things any worse than they already are at the moment,' replied Casey.

The Master Sergeant, whose attachment to the British airborne unit was due to end in five weeks time, would then be posted back to Fort Bragg in the USA to join his own special forces group, the famous Green Berets.

'Rod, could I ask you a favour?' said Lenihan.

'Sure go right ahead,' replied Casey.

'Could you delay my return to the states for a while to give me time to find Carols lover?'

'I don't know, Mike. That will have to be approved by the general, but I will see what I can do but as a mere captain I don't have much say in the matter. What will you do if you find him?' asked Casey looking concerned. 'Mike, you can't take the law into your own hands, do you understand? That is an order!'

Jane arrived with some coffee and toast and after settling down began to talk about the good times they had all had as a foursome, the dinner parties and trips to the mountains and the skiing.

Lenihan said, 'Not now, honey, please. I can't cope with all that at the moment, my mind is in turmoil and I need to think things through.'

'I'm sorry, Mike,' said Jane beginning to sob, spilling her coffee down the front of her dress and onto the carpet. 'It seems such a waste of life and I've lost a good friend and you, a devoted wife,' she cried.

'Don't worry, honey, I'll be OK. I have asked the colonel if her body can be used for medical research. I'm not sure I can face a funeral back home in the states. You know I don't get on with her family at all well, except maybe her mother. They will all blame me anyway for what has happened. Her sister is the worst, particularly after I spurned her advances when we visited her in New Orleans a few years ago. Carol never knew.'

'She sure as hell did you know because she told me,' replied Jane, now beginning to compose herself.

Rod said they would have to be going soon because he had a meeting at the base at three o'clock that afternoon. As they left the apartment Rod winked and said he would try and talk to the Commanding General as soon as he could.

After he watched the Caseys drive away, Lenihan ran a bath and soaked in the luxurious foam, shaved and dressed. He began to write a letter to Carol's mother; her father died some years previous. The words did not come easy but after an hour he had composed a letter that gave details of a burst ulcer and death in the operating theatre in the local hospital near the base where he and Carol lived.

At the American army headquarters Captain Casey waited in the anteroom of Major General Samuel Price, Commanding Officer of the 9th American Infantry Division in Germany. The door opened and a lieutenant showed the captain in.

'Good morning, sir.'

'Morning, Casey. Sit down. What do you want? You know I'm a busy man. Things are not going well in the division at the moment and I'm getting pressure from above to improve our performance as a fighting unit. This new corps commander is a real taskmaster, wants to make it to the top I suppose, got his sights on the supreme commanders job I suspect. Now what's the problem Captain?'

'Sir, as you know, Master Sergeant Lenihan's wife died yesterday in the US forces hospital in Frankfurt and he is due to return to the states soon because his tour of duty is almost finished.'

'So what!' interrupted the general.

'Well sir, Carol has a big family back home and whilst Lenihan is a tough soldier he simply can't face them all at the moment,' replied Casey.

'But he will have to attend the funeral some time and

surely the family are bound to be present then so what's the difference?' said the general, arranging some papers on his desk and reaching for a cigar. 'Look Captain, what exactly do you want me to do about this situation? Get to the point. In case you have forgotten, I've got a division to run and too much dammed paperwork to process,' he said lighting his cigar sending a great plume of smoke into the air.

'Sir, I have come to ask for a deferment of Sergeant Lenihan's posting back to the states on the grounds that he is emotionally unable to cope with the relatives. The second point is that there will be no funeral because his wish is that her body is to be left for medical research. This will not be popular with the relatives at all. The details are at present being worked out by Colonel Peters and the Catholic Padre along with the army legal department. I have been assured that there will be no legal problems and I can usefully employ Lenihan for as long as you may wish to grant this deferment. Sir, these are my reasons with Master Sergeant Lenihan's welfare in mind, bearing in mind his long and excellent military career'.

'Well I suppose you have put up a good case, Captain so I am prepared to grant a deferment for one month to start on Monday next. That is all I can do without referring to higher authority and you know what a performance that can be I am sure, Captain Casey. He will remain directly under you, let's say on liaison duties. Remember, Casey, one month only. Now if that's all, you are dismissed.'

'Thank you, sir,' said Casey rising and saluting the general.

After he left the office and made his way back to the training section where his own office was situated, he began to worry what Lenihan might do if he found out the identity of Carol's lover. Meanwhile, back at the apartment, Lenihan started to sort out Carol's clothes, jewellery and other personal effects that she had collected over the years. He even found some old love letters that he had written to her while he was serving in Vietnam before they were married. He decided not to read them now but save that till later. The clothes might fit Jane Casey and if she wanted them she could have the lot. Her wedding ring he would keep, but other items of jewellery he would sell to a good buyer in Frankfurt.

The telephone began to ring. 'Hi, Mike, I've got some good news for you. I managed to persuade the old man to defer you for a month, but only a month, then it's stateside I afraid. Look I must go. I'll talk to you later. 'Bye now.'

'Thanks, Rod, or should I say, Captain,' replied Lenihan with a smile.

'Just one thing, Mike, you are assigned to me for this period so be in my office at 0900 tomorrow morning and I will give you some duties. These will allow you some time off base. See you then.'

'Thanks again, sir. See you in the morning, bye for now.' As he put the phone down there was a knock at the door.

'Hello, Mike,' said Padre Flaherty, the Roman Catholic Chaplain to the American 9th division in Germany.

'Hi, Padre, come in. I'm just about to make some coffee or would you prefer something stronger?'

'If you have a little of the firewater I wouldn't say no,' replied the Irish American priest.

During the visit they discussed many things about Carol's life but no mention was made of the circumstances of her death. The Padre offered a requiem mass but Lenihan, who had not been inside a church for years, settled for her name to be read out during a regular mass at the American garrison church on the following Sunday. The Padre said Carol's body would be ready for transportation to the USA the following Thursday and if he wished to view her in the chapel of rest he would be happy to accompany him there that afternoon. Lenihan declined saying he would prefer to remember her as he had last seen her before he left for Bad Tolz.

That evening Rod and Jane came round and Jane cooked dinner for them all. During the course of the meal it became obvious to Lenihan that Jane knew of Carol's condition before the abortion attempt, and he decided that she must have known about her lover as well. He was sure that Jane would not break Carol's confidence even though she was now dead, so decided not to say anything to Jane now but let things settle a little, but ask Jane he would.

Towards the end of the evening he asked her if she would take all Carol's clothes away, sort out what she wanted and dispose of the rest. Although it was a pleasant evening Lenihan was on edge and could not relax, he had to find out what Jane knew. After they left he poured out a large whisky and started to read the old love letters he had written to her all those years ago. Tears welled in his eyes as he worked his way through them remembering their early times together, inside he was festering revenge. As he opened the last letter he noticed a small piece of blue writing paper tucked into a fold of the notepaper. Written on it was the name James P, and a local military telephone number and extension. On a sudden impulse Lenihan dialled the number and was put through to the British Royal Tank Regiment barracks. This camp being situated some twenty kilometres away. As the orderly sergeant answered Lenihan hung up.

If the telephone exchange worked in the same way as they do on American bases all calls out of normal office hours would go to the orderly room or guardroom. Lenihan was sure this was the case. He decided to call again tomorrow using a female friend he could trust to keep her mouth shut. The last thing he wanted was his plan discussed on the camp bush telegraph. The person he had in mind was Christine Ellis, a corporal in the regimental headquarters. Ellis was a friend to both the Lenihans and like Carol came from the town of Oak Ridge in Tennessee. He felt he could trust her with his plan if she would agree.

The following morning Lenihan reported for duty in Captain Casey's office.

'Good morning, Mike,' said Casey.

'Good morning, sir' replied Lenihan.

'While we are on duty it would be better to remain formal in our dealings with each other, don't you agree?'

'Yes, sir, I agree entirely. It would be best for both of us, you being an officer an' all,' smiled Lenihan with a grin.

'Now what I want you to do today is to look through

these training exam papers and give me your comments with regard to changes that could be made to improve things and raise the standards. I had an ear-bashing from the General the other day because the divisional standards are not what the new corps commander expects. A fair amount of the improvement works fall on me so I need your help with this Mike,' said Casey handing Lenihan a sheaf of papers.

'I'll do my best, sir, but I'm a practical soldier not a paper warrior,' countered Lenihan.

'See what you can do and we can talk about it later because I've got to see the colonel at 10am'.

'Not in trouble are you sir?' smiled Lenihan.

'No, not this time, just the weekly meeting of the training staff, very boring, same old things discussed with no real outcome. Half the time it's a paper exercise, in short it's a fucking pain in the arse.'

'Now, now, sir, that doesn't sound like an officer and a gentleman. I'll get stuck in right away if you will show me to my desk.'

'Sure will,' replied Casey. He pressed a button on his desk and a staff sergeant came in.

'John, would you show Master Sergeant Lenihan to the desk I have allocated him and see he has all he needs?'

'Sure thing, sir, come this way please, Sergeant.'

'The name's Mike,' said Lenihan with a grin.

'Just before you go, Sergeant Lenihan, when I get back later we can have a chat and discuss your future duties,' said Casey.

'Sure thing, sir, and once again thanks again for your help,' replied Lenihan leaving the office.   When Casey returned three hours later he called Lenihan into his office.

'Well, Mike, how are you getting on with the paperwork?'

'Quite well, sir, it's far more interesting than I thought it would be and your staff has looked after me really well. I have made my comments on a separate piece of paper, it's almost complete and you can have it very soon sir,' replied Lenihan.

'Good I'll look forward to that, Mike,' said Casey removing his tunic and hanging it on an old-fashioned hat stand in the corner of the room.

'Now, Mike, come into my office and take a seat, this will be informal and we are talking as friends, not as soldiers. I'll make sure we are not disturbed,' said Casey moving towards the door.

He called out to Staff Sergeant Smith. 'John, will you make sure that the Master Sergeant and myself are not interrupted unless something urgent crops up. I'll be conducting a personal interview.'

'Will do, sir, I'll also hold any telephone calls for you. If they are important I'll buzz you through.'

'Fine and thanks, John,' said Casey shutting the door. The captain moved slowly to his desk as if deep in thought.

'Mike, I know it's none of my business but we have been friends for a long time, OK.'

'That's right,' said Lenihan frowning.

Casey continued. 'I'm concerned as to what you might do if you find out who Carol's lover was, you might do something stupid and ruin your career and the rest of your life.'

'My life has already been ruined by this son of a bitch, Rod.'

'Do you have any idea who it might be? For instance, could it be anyone in this headquarters, Mike?' said Casey.

'I've got a feeling it's a Brit stationed near here because of a little note I found. Let's say I'm investigating this line of enquiry at the moment. But not to worry, Rod, I'm not about to do anything rash, I just need to know who he was,' lied Lenihan. 'I do need to know, you understand. I must know, Rod!'

'OK, but just be careful, I mean that, Mike. Anyway let's have a look at those test papers.'

The next few days were filled with routine office work and Lenihan began to get quite involved with this and enjoyed the change from normal military duties.

Corporal Christine Ellis was about to leave the 9th infantry Headquarters when Lenihan phoned,

'Hi, Mike,' she drawled. 'I was going to call you when I heard the news about Carol but I decided to wait a few days until things settle down a little. How are you?'

'I'm OK. Look, Chris, can we meet because I want to ask a favour of you, a favour that requires you to keep you're pretty little mouth shut if you will pardon my crudity.'

'Yes of course, honey, do you want me to come round to your apartment or would you like to meet somewhere neutral, away from prying eyes?'

'I'll pick you up. To be seen together at the moment will only start the tongues wagging,' said Lenihan. 'Could you meet me at the bus station on Grubenstrasse, say outside the ticket office at 1900 tonight? Take a taxi and I'll pick you up from there.

'Sure, Mike, see you then,' she replied nervously replacing the handset of the phone.

It was cold and dark when Lenihan pulled up in his VW Golf. 'Hi, Chris, jump in,' said Lenihan opening the door and trying to adjust the heater controls at the same time.

'I know this seems like something out of the movies, but you are the only one I can trust.'

'What have you got up your sleeve, Michael Lenihan?' she said in a mocking Irish accent and with a smile that lit up her face.

'I'll tell you when we get back to my place. There should be no one about on a cold night like this and we shouldn't be seen going into my apartment.' When they arrived at Lenihans place it was warm and cosy inside.

'What will you have to drink, honey?' asked Lenihan taking off his coat.

'Oh, a brandy and lemonade if you have any. This is such a nice flat, Mike, and I see you done it up recently, I bet Carol chose the wallpaper and colours, Oh I'm sorry, Mike, I forgot'.

'That's OK, I'll settle for a whiskey myself', said Lenihan pouring the drinks. 'Make yourself comfortable.'

As they began to drink he put all the recent events to her and also said that he intended to find the man who was responsible for Carol's pregnancy and punish him. He went on to explain what part she would play if she were to accept his request for help. After carefully listening to the plan she agreed to help but said she did not want to know what Lenihan was going to do after that.

'Thanks, honey, I could kiss you,' he said going to the drinks cupboard to refill the glasses.

'I wish you would,' she said blushing and thinking of the boyfriend who ditched her some months ago for another woman. 'I'm sorry, Mike, I'm not thinking straight with what you have just told me.'

'That's OK,' replied Lenihan handing her another drink. 'Just sit back and relax.'

They talked late into the night. Christine started to get tired and mentioned it was time to go.

'Sure I'll call you a taxi. I can't afford to drive with all this drink inside me. I'll get pulled in by the cops. That's for sure,' he said.

'Before I go, can I use your shower? My apartment is so cold I'll freeze to death!'

'Sure you can. I'll get some clean towels and a bath robe out for you,' he said with twinkle in his eye.

Christine went into the bathroom and got into the shower cubicle. The hot powerful jet of hot water was soothing and warming on her naked body. In the lounge Lenihan poured yet another drink and sat back in his armchair content with his plan so far. After about ten minutes Christine appeared in the doorway dressed in the robe, her long hair hanging below her shoulders. Lenihan motioned to her to sit down, indicating he would dry her silky blonde hair with the dryer and comb it for her as she relaxed. As she walked over to him the robe that was only loosely tied came undone. He could see she was completely naked underneath, her breasts firm and inviting, the slim waist and long legs made her look like a model. She sat on his knee and stroked the back of his neck; he put his arm around her waist and with the other hand cupped her right breast.

She said, 'I hope you don't mind, Mike, but I've fancied you for a long time, I never said anything because of Carol. I know you were devoted to each other and I would not have wanted to spoil your relationship for anything. You do realise that don't you, Mike?'

'It's OK, Chris, I never really thought you were interested because you had a guy for some time, didn't you? Boy you are beautiful. I have always thought you looked great in uniform. You know, a lot of guys are attracted to women in uniform.'

She bent down and kissed him full on the mouth, her tongue exploring inside. He slipped off her bathrobe and she undid his shirt, running her long thin fingers over his chest and down to the belt of his jeans. With one smooth action the belt came undone and her hand moved onto his manhood. He started to caress the area between her legs. Gently he pulled her up and led her into the bedroom.......

Lenihan awoke around 6.00am, Christine was still fast asleep. He swung out of bed and went into the kitchen to brew some coffee.

'Wakey, wakey, honey,' he said as she came to. 'Have some coffee darling. It's a cold but beautiful morning and the sun's up already.'

'I hope you don't think bad of me, Mike, I didn't intend last night to happen,' she apologised, sitting up for her coffee and running her fingers through her bedraggled hair.

'Have you heard me complaining?' he said with a wink. 'Anyway it's been a long time you know. You were doing things last night that Carol would never have dreamed of. When this is all over can we see each other on a regular basis, Chris?'

'I was hoping you might say that, Mike. I know its early days but we could be good for each other.'

Lenihan didn't see Christine over the weekend because she went on a pre-arranged visit to Berlin with a friend. On the following Monday night Lenihan phoned Christine and said to her that he wanted to activate his plan to identify Carol's lover as soon as possible. She agreed at once.

The following morning at 9.30am Christine rang the number supplied by Lenihan, was put through to the British military exchange then asked for the extension number. After a short delay a male voice answered.

'Good morning, regimental admin, Lieutenant Phillips.'

'Can I speak to James please?'

'Yes speaking,' he replied.

'You don't know me but I'm a friend of Carols. She can't ring herself because she has just started a new job and can't use the office phone.'

'I see,' he said sounding cautious. 'I thought Carol was not into working, but I would much rather speak to her myself,' said Phillips.

'As I said, she cannot call you through the day but she wants to see you very soon, this is why she asked me to phone on her behalf. She's asked me to ask you if you can come over to her apartment on Saturday. She really is missing you so much James.'

'Very well, but I can't get there until after 3pm. I'm

tied up in the morning with military duties and I have a difficult wife. I take it she will be alone, what about her husband?' replied the lieutenant, clearly nervous.

'Of course she will. He is away in Bavaria at the moment playing soldiers and won't be back for at least three more weeks. Look, I'm a good friend Carols and we confide in each other you know, so don't worry, it will be OK, but you behave yourself,' she said with a chuckle.

'Yes, fine then, you can tell her I will be there on Saturday about four in the afternoon. Thanks for ringing, Miss er...'

'Mary. My name's Mary,' lied Christine.

'Thanks once again, Mary. Perhaps we can meet sometime in the future. You sound like a good friend. Goodbye for now then and take care.'

'Goodbye, James,' said Christine ringing off.

That night as arranged Christine went to Lenihans apartment and explained how she had set Phillips up for next Saturday afternoon.

'That was very well done, honey. I'll have to make it up to you in my special way.' said Lenihan leading her by the hand into the bedroom.

'Sergeant Lenihan you will wear me out at this rate,' said Christine with a chuckle.

On Saturday Lenihan was up early, unable to sleep the night before in spite of several large bourbons. Christine arrived at about 10am and they went over the plan yet again.

'What are you going to do, Mike? I'm frightened you know.'

'Nothing much. I just want to meet this guy and tell him what happened, that's all.'

'I don't believe you,' said Christine with a shiver going down her spine.

'Now don't worry, darling, nothing's going to happen, you'll see.' replied Lenihan running his hands over her firm breasts and giving her a peck on the cheek. Just then the phone rang, it was Rod Casey.

'Hi, Mike, how are you fixed for coming over this afternoon and staying for dinner?' he said cheerfully.

'Sorry, Rod, but I'm just going out and won't be back till late, how about tomorrow?'

'OK I'll ring you then,' said Casey.

'Great, talk to you then, give my love to Jane. Bye now.'

Phillips arrived just after 4pm. Lenihan saw him pull into the apartment's car parking area, his dark blue Volvo still covered in frost. In the flat, Lenihan, heart pounding with a mixture of apprehension and excitement, waited in the front bedroom. Christine was in the lounge smoking nervously. When the door bell rang she answered it with a smile.

'Hello, James, come in. Carol won't be a minute. Go through into the lounge and take a seat.'

'Thanks,' said Phillips unbuttoning his coat.

'Anyway I'm off now. No doubt I'll see you again,' said Christine. 'Bye bye.'

'Bye, Mary and thanks for everything,' replied Phillips.

As he moved towards the armchair near the window, a sudden movement startled the lieutenant. He froze! Lenihan grabbed Phillips around the neck dropping him to the floor before he had time to react. The more he struggled the harder Lenihan applied the strangle hold.

'Who... who... what...?' he gasped.

'Shut up you limey bastard,' shouted Lenihan, turning round and punching him hard in the face several times.

'Why are you hitting me? screamed Phillips, spitting out several teeth along with saliva and blood.

'Because of you, you fucking arsehole, my wife has died of a backstreet abortion, I'm gonna make sure you never screw anyone again, you bastard.'

Lenihan kicked Phillips hard in the testicles and hit him again in the face, his nose exploding in a bloody mass of bone and tissue. Shaking with rage, Lenihan then dragged the almost unconscious British officer along the hall and out onto the balcony outside his apartment and kicked him down the stairs.

Someone must have heard the disturbance because in no time at all the sound of sirens could be heard in the distance. Lenihan was past caring, he had now extacted his revenge. Back inside his apartment he had almost finished the bottle of whiskey when there was a loud banging on the front door. As he opened the door two American military policemen, both holding nightsticks, confronted him.

'Master Sergeant Lenihan?'

'Yes that's me.'

'I'm arresting you on suspicion of the grievous bodily harm of an officer of the British army,' said the captain in charge.

'Just keep me away from those fucking Brits,' shouted Lenihan, as the other military policeman started to put on the plastic handcuffs. He was escorted to the police car. 'I'll kill the English bastards if I get a chance,' he screamed.

'Shut up and get in the car,' said the provost captain.

Lenihan was bundled into the back of the car with two military police officers sitting either side of him. Within ten minutes he was in the charge room of the American garrison provost Headquarters.

Chapter 2

Liam Reagan walked slowly across the cobbled quadrangle, called Parliament Square, of Trinity College of the Irish Capital. Elizabeth 1, with the intention of furthering the reformation in Ireland had founded the college in 1592. The history of the college was the last thing on Reagan's mind at this moment in time because the dean, on the recommendation of the board of governors, had just expelled him. He had been accused of expressing his views on republicanism and trying to recruit for the IRA within the university. Having just completed the first year of a four-year degree course on the classics and political history, his idea was to join Sinn Fein at the end of his studies and fight the cause on a political level. That had now come to sudden end and he knew he would never be allowed to join another university, certainly not in Ireland at any rate.

The sun shone brightly as he followed the crowded streets leading by a roundabout route to the Ballsbridge district of Dublin, and an IRA safe house. Reagan, a native of Monard, County Tipperary, had come from a middle class family and had left St Mary's grammar school with three 'A' levels. His parents were both dead, killed when their North West Orient airlines DC9 crashed on an internal flight between Baltimore and New York, whilst visiting relatives who had emigrated to the USA. Reagan would have been with them on the flight, but his course started six weeks before they were due to travel.

As he crossed into Westmoreland Street and feeling hungry, he decided to go into Beshoff's famous fish and chip shop, there was a long queue but it was worth the wait. As he stood in line he carefully noted the people around him, in particular, those that had followed him into the shop. Knowing full well that he was on the Garda files, almost certainly the Republics Special Branch took an interest in him as well. It was possible that he was under surveillance from either. It was then he noticed a tall thin man wearing a green-waxed cotton jacket enter the shop. Reagan was not sure why, but he had a gut feeling this man was no ordinary customer. Something told him he could be a member of the Irish police or security forces possibly even British Intelligence.

In spite of the crowded sitting area there were still a few high stools available for customers to sit and enjoy their meal. After Reagan had collected his food he selected a stool near the door and began to eat. While the man in the waxed coat was being served he slipped out of the shop and crossed the road quickly, mingling with the crowds on the opposite pavement and slid into a small shop doorway removing his outer coat. He waited no more than a minute before he saw the man come out of the fish and chip shop, looking in both directions. Reagan quickly made his way along the road towards the O'Connell Bridge. He was sure the man was alone, because if he were part of a surveillance team he would have stayed in the shop and let his colleagues continue the pursuit without arousing suspicion. However he decided not to take any chances and risk the safe house being discovered by the Garda, or anyone else for that matter. He would try to outsmart them.

He entered a tiny shop that sold knitting yarns and patterns and asked the old lady if she had any patterns for Aran jumpers?

'To be sure I have. Many of them, young man,' she exclaimed, opening a drawer under the counter.

'Madam, could I ask you a favour? While you're looking, could I use your toilet? You see I have a stomach upset, and I'm feeling the need rather badly.'

'Certainly you can. Just go through to the back of the shop and out of the door into the yard, the toilet's on the right. Don't worry about the dog, he makes a lot of noise but he's harmless really,' she replied without looking up.

'Thanks a lot, I won't be a minute' said Reagan, slipping past the counter.

As he stepped into the yard he noticed a wall along the left hand side of the property standing about six feet high, he was sure there would an alley on the other side of it. The dog came running up to him barking and snapping at his heels.

'Fuck off you mangy thing,' muttered Reagan, looking for something sturdy to stand on.

It was then that he spotted an old chair, which he grabbed and propped up against the wall. Before he had a chance to climb up the dog again snapped at him, this time pinching the skin on his calf causing it to bleed. This was the last straw for Reagan; he bent down extending his hand as if to offer food to the animal. When the dog came into reach he grabbed it by the scruff of the neck and turned him over onto his back. Gripping the hind legs he swung him round with such force that when his head hit the wall it killed him instantly. He dumped the limp body behind the toilet building, leaped over the wall and made his way along to Kildare Street. The whole operation had taken less than two minutes.

When Reagan reached St Stephens Green he hailed a taxi and gave directions towards the Ballsbridge area. After about a mile he told the driver to stop, paid the fare and got out. He began to walk fast along Anglesea Road, passing number five, which was formally occupied by Brendan Behan, a former IRA activist and famous playwright, before dying in a Meath hospital at the age of 41 in 1964. When he arrived at the safe house he continued past and entered a telephone box about 200 hundred yards along the road. He dialled a number and let it ring six times before replacing the handset. He then dialled the same number again and when it was answered the code words of the day were exchanged. Reagan walked down the road and up to the front door of the house. When it opened he was greeted by Sean O'Rourke.

'Cead mile failte, Liam,' he said in Irish, knowing that Reagan could speak the Gaelic tongue. O'Rourke, the deputy chief of staff for the Dublin area, was pleased to see him again.

'It's good to see you, Sean, how's business these days?'

As they entered the living room, O'Rourke said, 'Well we have been busy in the north with several attacks on the English, including an ambush on the Royal Green

Jackets just over the border from Dundalk. In London two bombs caused some trouble and an attack on the Parachute Regiment barracks in Aldershot has made sure that we are not on the Prime Minister's Christmas card list. What will you be drinking?'

'Bushmills if you have any, Sean' replied Reagan.

'It's about time I had a crack at the Brits. What would you say about me having some special training and then letting me loose on active service, Sean, how about it? I'm sure I could do it, but at the moment I don't know much about guns or bombs.'

'Well, Liam as you know we had it in mind for you to run the political campaign, with your education an' all, not getting into the shooting war,' replied O'Rourke.

'I know all that, Sean, but I want to take a more active role in the struggles, at the sharp end if you know what I mean. It's important for me to be fully involved. I can still give intellectual support when required.'

The phone began to ring using the coded number of rings. When it rang again O'Rourke swapped the coded words and hung up.

'Pour yourself another drink, someone is coming that I want you to meet,' said O'Rourke indicating the drinks cabinet.

A few moments later Reagan heard the front door being opened and words of greeting exchanged, this time in English. O'Rourke came into the room with a middle aged man who he introduced as John O'Hagan.

'John, this is Liam Reagan, one of the newer members of our organisation and a very educated young man at that.'

'Pleased to meet you, Liam,' said O'Hagan offering his hand.

'Good afternoon, John,' replied Reagan noticing at the same time that O'Hagan had an English accent with an adopted Irish brogue.

O'Hagan had been born in South London of Irish parents and had served in the British army for twelve years. He had seen active service in Aden and served with the UN forces in Cyprus, it was here that he met up with soldiers of the Irish contingent. During his service he became a weapons instructor at the British School of Infantry at Warminster in Wiltshire.

It became obvious to Reagan that O'Hagan had more than been accepted into the IRA and enjoyed power and influence, his exact position was not clear to Reagan but he decided not to ask at this time. When the conversation got round again to Reagan's request for a more active role and involvement, O'Hagan said their general level of training must be improved and that this could only be achieved with outside help. He went on to say that he almost managed to recruit an ex SAS man in London who had the skills the Republicans wanted. At the last moment the retired soldier backed out, whether it was fear or conscience was not known. He was now dead following an accident, run down by a car outside a school whilst waiting for his child. The driver did not stop and was never traced.

The next possible candidate was an ex Belgian Para Commando who had been trained along the same lines as the SAS and agreed to work for the IRA to help with his delicate financial position. This came to an abrupt end when he was arrested following a bank raid in Brussels, for which he received an 18-year prison sentence.

'I would be prepared to consider you for such work if the Chief of Staff agrees, and only when we can get an ex-Special Forces man to train us to the level required to help us improve our record. I say this because we do have a rather special task in mind we intend to pull off but it will require a certain type of person with a high level of training and commitment to pull it off successfully,' said O'Hagan with an enquiring look.

'Thanks, John, I can assure you I won't let you down, I'm more than ready to do my bit for the cause and further our aims through military action,' replied Reagan.

At this point O'Rourke said the Reagan should go back to his flat on the other side of Dublin and await further instructions. He should however continue to write press releases and statements for Sinn Fein, the political wing of the IRA.

Liam Reagan realised his presence was no longer required and bid farewell until he was called for in due course. He retraced his journey back to his flat using standard anti-surveillance techniques he had been taught previously from a contact in the Garda.

O'Hagan asked O'Rourke, 'Can we trust this fellow Reagan to keep his mouth shut, because as you know, we are in the process of setting up a training camp in the mountains of Connemara and nothing, nothing at all, will be allowed to interfere with this Sean. Anyone who tries will leave this planet by our usual methods.'

'I can vouch for him, John. He has served us well so far and has been under constant surveillance for some time. He knows our security system well and can cover his tracks and is very discreet. I think he knows full well that if he steps out of line he will be severely punished. Yes, John, I'm certain he's our man,' concluded O'Rourke.

'I'll tell you now that we intend to assassinate a big fish in the Royal Ulster Constabulary. This will require a special type of man and not the usual sort of idiot we have used in the past,' said O'Hagan.

'Given the right sort of training I'm sure we won't be disappointed with Reagan's performance,' replied O'Rourke.

'OK, I will convene a meeting with the general council and recommend Reagan's appointment to the training camp and subsequent operation if he's successful on the course,' said O'Hagan.

'Good' replied O'Rourke; 'now have another drink and tell me about the little birdie you're screwing down in Cork these days.'

Chapter 3

The giant USAF Boeing 707 thundered down the runway of the large American airbase on the outskirts of Frankfurt bound for the United States. Among the passengers was Master Sergeant Michael Lenihan, under close arrest with a military police escort. As the plane soared up into the clouds over Germany Lenihan began to think back over his career in the army.

After enlisting in Los Angeles and undergoing basic training in New Mexico, he was posted to the 2nd Infantry Division at Fort Worth in Texas. As a rookie soldier he became top of his intake and was a natural for the job. Almost before his first year was over he was promoted to PFC (private first class) and it was soon after that he applied for parachute training, having just been awarded the combat infantry badge. In a matter of weeks he was sent to Fort Benning in Georgia, the airborne school. The course proved to be uneventful and after completing the required number of jumps he was awarded the silver wings of a trained parachutist. The wings mounted of his left breast made him feel proud and glad to be in the one of the most efficient armies in the world. His father, Patrick Lenihan, killed in Korea, would have been as equally proud that his son had made something of himself. Within three months came his posting to the famous 82nd Airborne Division with a training program that included visits to Alaska, Panama and Hawaii. It was only a matter of time before Lenihan was sent to Vietnam to play his part in the Asian war.

Based at the massive base of Da Nang, he soon experienced his first rocket attack that killed several of the garrison and damaged stores and equipment. This came as quite a shock but because it was a combat area one quickly became used to it and Lenihan was no exception.

During the year that followed Lenihan was involved in many long combat patrols and raiding parties on the Viet Cong and their villages. He was wounded in a forced helicopter emergency landing after it was hit by machine gun fire close to the border with North Vietnam. The fire fight that followed on the ground left him with a large hole in his left buttock. The successful casevac back to base and subsequent hospital treatment left him fully recovered and awarded the Purple Heart for injuries sustained in combat.

Soon after his return to the combat zone he was called to the office of Lt Colonel Taylor the commanding officer of his regiment. When he received the order he was not told the reason by his company commander, Captain Reynolds, but just to be in the CO's office at 1400 hours wearing his best uniform. Lenihan was puzzled because normally you only went to the CO when you were in trouble; surely the fight in a girlie bar in Saigon was not going to be held against him. After all, he was only defending himself from a drunken marine. It was pity, thought Lenihan that the marine's jaw had been broken and several teeth knocked out. At 2pm precisely Lenihan presented himself at the office of the CO and knocked firmly.

'Come in,' came the reply and Lenihan marched in and saluted his superior officer standing to attention.

'PFC Lenihan reporting sir as ordered.'

'Stand easy, Lenihan. You have come to my notice on more than one occasion over the past year especially that ugly incident in Saigon, but that aside, you're a damn good soldier. I have discussed your record with the Divisional Commander and I am to promote you to corporal with immediate effect. Further I want you to consider a secondment to the Special Forces for training because of your apparent natural ability in the jungle. Well, what do you say, Lenihan, yes or no? Don't stand there with your mouth open man,' concluded the CO with a smile.

'Yes, sir, I mean thank you, sir. This has all come as a bit of a surprise, you caught me off guard. I will of course follow your recommendation for the SF and go as soon as you can release me from duty here.'

'Don't think this is going to be easy, Corporal, the SF standards are high and many candidates fail the selection tests. If you come back here failed, I will kick your arse, do you understand, Lenihan? This recommendation is mine and mine alone, don't let me down, OK?'

Lenihan left the CO's office in a daze and went straight to the quartermasters store to get his stripes sewn on and make arrangements to return some kit prior to his departure to Fort Bragg in North Carolina for the Special Forces selection course.

The course was hard and demanding but Lenihan

passed with flying colours and he was told that he would be placed on the full SF training course straight away. When the course finally came to an end Lenihan was posted to the 5th Special Forces group based again at Fort Bragg. This type of soldiering was the top for Lenihan, nothing could compare with this in his mind.

He was posted back to South East Asia but this time operating from bases in Thailand and Cambodia carrying out strikes across the Vietnamese border. The raids were aimed at supply depots and Vietcong camps and training bases. There was one failed raid on a prisoner of war camp; the camp was empty when the SF group arrived. When his group were sent to Saigon for rest and recuperation Lenihan and his fellow soldiers frequently sampled the delights of the brothels and bars. The army supplied plenty of prophylactics for the men but still some became infected. Not Lenihan however; his weakness was fighting. Towards the end of his second year in Vietnam Lenihan was posted to the new 'A' team and became its sergeant. This coincided with movement to a new camp in Laos.

Six weeks later a raid was planned on a Vietcong training camp deep inside Vietnam well away from any back-up forces. Sergeant Lenihan was to be the second in command under Lieutenant Sowerby. During the raid several soldiers were killed and injured, among the dead was Sowerby. Suddenly Lenihan became the commander of the group; it was a tremendous responsibility, a great weight on his still young shoulders. In the fierce fire-fight Lenihan destroyed a machine gun emplacement and shot some Vietcong, which allowed his own men to escape safely, back to their rendezvous point including himself.

His actions were reported to senior officers during the debrief later and as a result the details passed to the Commanding Officer South East Asia Military Assistance Command, General Crichland, in Saigon. Lenihan was called to the Pentagon and awarded the Silver Star and promoted to staff sergeant three months later. Two weeks leave followed and he was expecting to be sent back to his unit in Vietnam but alas this was not to be. His posting to Fort Bragg came as an unpleasant surprise, for he was to be an instructor. Before his arrival he had already become something of cult figure in the Special Forces, but an instructor he did not want to be. He was a man of action, not a classroom warrior.

The first year in the training unit was uneventful and surprisingly enjoyable; at least he slept in a bed each night and had regular meals and leave. Not at all like service in Vietnam. Lenihan along with three other colleagues was sent to Great Britain for training with the famous 22nd Special Air Service Regiment, the SAS, at their base in Stirling Lines near Hereford, in the west of England.

This proved an interesting time for Lenihan, in particular the training in the storming of aircraft and buildings using stun grenades and plastic explosives. He was also invited to take part in an exercise with D Squadron and parachuted into Denmark at night to test that countries defences against attack. They had to make their way across country without the detection of the Danish forces or the local population who are mobilised for this annual exercise. This proved to be very interesting because there were several close calls where they could have been captured. He found the SAS great guys to work with; they certainly had a good, but sick sense of humour. He felt they were holding something back from their well-proven methods, but could not put his finger on it. They were almost certainly acting on orders from their own command. Every country likes to retain its military secrets and they were no exception. They certainly are the finest Special Forces regiment in the world.

When the course ended Lenihan and his colleagues moved to the USAF base at Upper Heyford for a short leave that included a trip to London and Oxford to enjoy some sightseeing. On his return to the states he had to report back to Fort Bragg and continue in the training wing until his new posting came up; he desperately wanted to get back to Vietnam. Nine months later he was called to the administration offices and given his new posting. He was disappointed at what the Colonel said.

'Sergeant Lenihan, you are to report to the British Airborne Headquarters in West Germany to take up the position of exchange training sergeant, I am glad to tell you this carries the rank of master sergeant. You have good record here and elsewhere in the army and I'm sorry to lose you but you have a career to follow.'

'But, sir, I'm tired of training; I want to go back to 'Nam and do the job I'm trained for. I've done my bit surely. Please, Colonel is there any other way I can get back to real soldiering?'

'I'm sorry, Lenihan, the decision has been made and you will report to Andrews's Air Force base next Monday for the flight to Frankfurt. I would advise you to prepare for the journey and tie up any loose ends here, your replacement arrives tomorrow and you will need to do a handover, that is all.'

Lenihan left the office in despair. 'What are these bastards doing to me? I don't deserve this,' he muttered aloud. If he had not been sent to Germany, Carol would not have met Phillips and be alive today; he would not be in this mess and a career in ruins. Fuck those Limey bastards, and fuck the American army with all their armchair heroes, he thought.

The long flight across the Atlantic from Germany was uneventful and Lenihan slept for several hours. When he woke he suddenly became nervous about the forthcoming court martial in Fort Bragg. The charge of grievous bodily harm to a British army officer was serious one that could lead to prison. The British military authorities were happy to leave the punishment to the Americans provided they could have an officer present for observation at the court martial. When Lenihan arrived at Fort Bragg he was kept in a locked cell in the military police headquarters. The staff respected his rank and he was well looked after with a number of privileges extended to him that he was probably not entitled to under the circumstances.

The day arrived for the court martial and Lenihan made sure his appearance was first class with a freshly cleaned and pressed uniform, his medal ribbons stood out on his chest along with his silver master parachutist wings. At 1000 hours sharp he was marched into the courtroom. He stood to attention and saluted smartly to the military panel. The senior officer in charge of the proceedings was Major General Chesterfield, to his right sat Brigadier General Howard and to the left was Colonel Harrington the Special Forces liaison officer. At a small table to the right of the panel sat the prosecuting officer and nearby the officer for the defence. At the back of the courtroom was the British military representative, Major Herriot of the Parachute Regiment. Before the court convened Lenihan had a long meeting with his defence officer. The officer warned that there was little he could do in the circumstances, but plead mitigation and fall back on Lenihans military record and awards to gain sympathy with the court.

The questioning went on for hours during which time Lenihan explained what took place and the circumstances that led to the assault on Phillips. He made it clear that he did not regret his actions and was not about to apologise. The senior officers took copious notes and finally instructed Lenihan to return to the cells and await their verdict.

When Lenihan was recalled to the court he again stood rigidly to attention: after a short pause the General Chesterfield began to speak.

'Master Sergeant Lenihan, this court martial has reached its verdict. You have been found guilty of a serious assault on a British military officer that will require him to take a long period of convalescence. We have taken into account the provocation that led you to take this action and we are truly sorry at the death of your wife as a result of her liaison with Lieutenant Phillips. It will be of no comfort to you that Phillips has been dismissed from the British army. Also included in our deliberations is your war record in Vietnam. For this reason and your service to the American nation we are not going to impose a custodial sentence. You are to be stripped of your rank down to corporal and dismissed from the United States

Army. There is a right of appeal should you desire it and Colonel Harrington is available to explain the details to you. It would be up to you to implement the procedure and all the paperwork required will be supplied to you on request. You are free to leave this court room and report to the administration office immediately.'

'Thank you, sir,' said Lenihan saluting; he then did an impeccable about turn and marched out of the room.

Outside in the hallway Lenihan waited for transport to take him back to the admin block to sign the multitude of papers concerning his discharge; he had decided not to appeal against the sentence. The main court door opened and out walked Major Herriot who then came up to Lenihan and tried to shake his hand.

'Fuck off, Major, I don't want to shake the hand of any Brit. I'll see you all in hell first, you Limey Bastards. You sons-of-bitches screw my wife, she dies and I get punished for it, fuck off before I deck you - you bastard.'

'Steady on, Lenihan, take it easy,' said the provost sergeant closing on him with a nightstick.

'If you want to hit me with that stick go right ahead and try it, I'll kill you, now you can fuck off, where's my transport?' he shouted.

Major Herriot decided to leave, it would not be possible to talk to Lenihan whilst he was in this frame of mind, and his sorrow for the man was genuine and sincere. A good career wasted by an incident not of his initial making but as a result of understandable action which almost any man would consider, including himself in similar circumstances.

A week later, Lenihan now a civilian with a reduced

pension, getting work became a priority. He decided to go up to New York and call on a friend that Rod Casey had recommended. He was told that he could stay there until he sorted himself out. As he had no skills outside the army, he drifted into club door-security work. It provided him with a living but he was bored in no time at all. Throwing drunken customers out of night clubs could in no way compare with his previous career and the army he had so dedicatedly served.

In certain parts of New York there is a large Irish community and because of his family connections with the old country, his family had emigrated and became Irish Americans, so he was offered work on the door of an Irish drinking club. After about three months he was called into the manager's office.

'Come in, Mike, sit down, and what will you be drinking? I want a little chat with you,' said Patrick Hanlon, a native of Sligo.

'Thanks, I'll have an Irish if you have any, but just a small one as I'm on duty, Mr Hanlon.' Hanlon poured a large Jameson's and gave it to Lenihan. 'Thanks, Mr Hanlon.'

'Now, not so much of the Mr, my name's Pat. You are among friends now so relax, Mike,' replied Hanlon taking a seat. 'Mike, I know all about your army background in the Green Berets including the unfortunate way in which your career came to an abrupt end. The type of work you are doing here now is a waste of your skills. I could be in a position to offer you something much more interesting if you wish. Something that will help my friends back home fight the British and boot them out of Ireland. Are you interested?'

'Before I answer that I need to know what you have in mind, Pat?' replied the ex-soldier with obvious interest.

'Of course, Michael, I understand, but I must warn you, that what I'm about to tell you must be kept strictly confidential,' said Hanlon pouring out some more drinks.

'You have my word on, Pat, not a word to anyone, I promise.'

'The job is to train members of the IRA in military tactics and the use of weapons, including all that goes with it. This would not involve you in direct confrontation with the enemy. You will of course receive accommodation plus all air fares to and from Ireland and of course payment. Well, what do you say Mike?'

'I don't know, Pat. I'm not sure I have any real interest in Irish affairs against the British, although my parents were born there.'

'Well think about it, Mike, and let me know in a few days, but I can tell you there is some urgency involved in this and again to remind you it demands strict secrecy. I cannot guarantee your safety if it becomes known that you have discussed this with anyone outside these walls,' said Hanlon sternly.

'Let me sleep on it, Pat and I'll let you know in the morning.'

'OK, Mike, see you then. Remember, not a word to anyone!'

That night Lenihan was unable to sleep but by the early hours he had made up his mind; he would see Hanlon first thing and agree to help. The following morning in the club's office the ex-patriot Irishman was extremely pleased at Lenihans decision to go to Ireland

and run the training program for the IRA. Progress could at long last begin.

'Just one point I want to make to you, Pat, and it is this, if any of the men I have to train are not suitable I want them taken off the course. I will not waste time with idiots especially with weapons and booby traps being used,' said Lenihan firmly.

'I quite understand, Mike. I will pass this on to the right people before you depart for Ireland. I want to give you some money, let's say for expenses and oh, take the rest of the week off,' said Hanlon handing Lenihan a large brown envelope. 'One last thing Mike, stay at home each night because that's when I'll ring you, and be ready to move at short notice, mind. You are now in the employ of the Irish Republican Army.'

'If it's OK, Pat, I will go now because I want to do some shopping and tidy a few loose ends and I must go to the bank,' said Lenihan stuffing the envelope into his jacket pocket.

He left the club and went for a walk in Central Park. It was warm in the sunshine and he decided to sit under a large oak tree and count the money he had just received. The envelope contained $US 2,000 in used notes. Clearly some shopping was called for and on the way home he dropped into a large department store for clothes and shoes along with toiletries. The phone rang at 8pm that evening.

'Hi, Mike, it's Pat. How are you?'

'Not bad but I'm getting bored at home though.'

'Now listen, I want you in the club tomorrow morning at 11o'clock sharp, you will meet someone who will take the arrangements a step further,' said Hanlon briskly.

'Fine, Pat, see you then, bye for now,' replied Lenihan, his pulse racing.

The house where Lenihan was staying belonged to Mrs Jacobs. A widowed friend of Jane Casey, they had known each other for many years. Mrs Jacobs had a daughter Angie who lived at home while taking her final exams at high school, expecting to go to college in the fall. At 17 Angie was tall and slim with a good figure which was further enhanced by the tight jeans and tee shirts she wore. As she walked around the house, obviously proud of her good looks, Lenihan frequently became aroused. That evening just as the ex-soldier had come out of the bathroom he noticed Angie's bedroom open as he made his way to the living room. Mrs Jacobs was out at bible classes and normally got home around 9pm; she had taken up religion after her husband was killed in a mining accident the year before.

'Mike, are you busy for a moment?' she called.

'No I'm only going to watch TV, Detroit's playing the Chicago Pirates, should be a good game,' he replied.

'Could you come and help me for a minute?'

'Sure, on my way honey. What can I do for you? It's no good asking me to help you with those maths; I was never any good at school.'

'Mike, you're a man of the world aren't you?'

'Well I suppose so. I guess I've been around a bit in my time, why do you ask honey?'

'I want you to screw me. I want you to do all those things you have done to other girls,' she said, now feeling embarrassed.

Lenihan was taken aback by the directness of her

approach. 'Haven't you got a boyfriend who can take you to bed? I'm a lot older than you.'

'Oh sure I've got John but he's a wimp. He's kind and caring but no good at anything like sex.'

'I'm not sure your mother would be very pleased if she found out about this conversation you know.'

'I wasn't planning to tell her. Are you?' snapped Angie getting annoyed. 'Well are you going to teach me or not?' she said, starting to remove her Levi's in front of him.

A moment later, her tee shirt was off revealing small but firm breasts. She was now completely naked; a real beauty. Her nipples were hard and she started to breathe more heavily and lean towards him seductively.

'Right! Let's get one thing straight young lady. I'm a guest in this house and it would not be right for me to make love to you for a whole lot of reasons. Now get dressed and get on with your homework and nothing further need be said on this subject,' said Lenihan firmly.

'I'm sorry Mike, I didn't want to embarrass you or put you on a spot but I thought it must be a long time now since you had a woman. No hard feeling OK?'

'Sure, honey, no hard feelings, but you must realise the position I'm in, living here. I am very grateful to your mum for putting up with me and giving me a roof over my head. This has been a difficult time for me as I'm sure you know. Anyway, I think I'll turn in now and leave you to continue with your homework. I'm sure you have plenty to do. Good night baby.'

'Good night, Mike, pleasant dreams.'

Saturday morning Lenihan reported to the club office at 11am as ordered and was shown into Hanlons office.

'Good morning, Mike. Come and have some coffee. My guest will be here soon.'

'Morning, Pat, it's been a long week waiting for your call but I'm ready now,' replied Lenihan with a smile.

A few minutes later the door opened and in walked middle-aged man. 'Good morning gentlemen,' he said taking a seat.

'Mike, I would like to introduce John O'Hagan, an old friend of mine from way back.' said Hanlon

'Hi, John,' said Lenihan offering his hand.

'Hello, Mike, Pat has told me a lot about you, we can certainly use your expertise and experience in our organisation and we will give you every assistance we can, including a monthly salary. I must say the wages are not high because we run on a tight budget but you will find there are several advantages in working for us.'

'John, I will help you all I can but as I told Pat I require total obedience from the trainees because what I teach is a serious subject as I'm sure you know. I want only your best men for my courses,' replied Lenihan.

'The type of men you will be teaching are all specially selected and are of the highest calibre. All have military minds,' said O'Hagan sipping his coffee.

'When do you want me to start? I have no ties and my army pension is paid into my account, for what it's worth.'

'Do you have a passport that's in date, Mike?' said Hanlon.

'Sure do. I've just renewed it. It's right bang up to date.'

'Good. I can book you on a flight to Dublin next

week. I'll call you when I have the tickets. When you get to Ireland you will be met and taken to a safe house. I shall see you in Dublin after you have passed through our anti-surveillance procedure which will be explained to you when you collect the tickets from Pat later this week,' added O'Hagan with a smile.

'Well with business completed I think a drink is called for,' said Hanlon heading for the cocktail cabinet in the corner of the room. 'What will you both be having gents?'

Lenihan stayed in the office for another hour during which time O'Hagan educated him in IRA doctrine and its aims for the future. His final instructions were to be at home every night at 9pm and await a phone call from Hanlon. When Lenihan left the office he decided to walk home the long way and have a last look at the sights of New York City. The things that had always impressed him were the Statue of Liberty and the Empire State Building. As he walked through the sunshine he began to think of Angie and the incident that took place the other night. He decided that if she made another offer he may well take her up on it. Why not? he reasoned. He would soon be thousands of miles away with no prospect of coming back, at least to New York anyway. Lenihan thought that when he had finished with the IRA he would settle in one of the mid-west states where he would feel more at home than in the big cities. When he arrived home Angie was trying on some new clothes she had just bought.

'Hi, Mike, how's your day been then?'

'OK I suppose, I'm a bit tired, been walking around town taking in the sights. Where's your mother?'

'Oh, she's gone over to Greenwich Village to stay the weekend with my aunt and they plan to go to a bible convention tomorrow, very boring. You know she wanted me to go with her, I ask you.'

'Hey you look great in that dress. How did you get into it? It's so tight.'

'Well I'm just about to take it off, so you can help me with the zip if you don't mind.'

'Sure thing, turn around and I'll see what I can do.'

As he started to pull the zip it stuck and it took several attempts to free it. At that point Angie turned around and let the dress fall to the ground. She was completely naked, her nubile body inviting.

'I seem to remember being in this situation the other day, honey, I must say you are a real beauty, it's very difficult for a guy to resist.'

'Why bother. I'm all yours if you want me,' replied Angie stepping out of the dress and leading Lenihan over to the sofa.

The next two hours provided the 17-year-old girl with the most comprehensive sex education she could ever hope to get and at the end, both she and Lenihan were completely exhausted. As they lay cuddled up on the sofa Angie asked him about his background and what he had planned for the future. He lied that he expected to stay on at the club and perhaps get some promotion in the years to come and buy himself a house. He had no intention of telling her that after next week he would not be around any longer.

Chapter 4

The long flight from New York's Kennedy airport to Dublin gave Lenihan plenty of time to think about his position. He was now in the employ of the IRA and to back out now could bring very unpleasant consequences. He decided to make the best of what was to come.

The aircraft was full of Irish Americans, some going to trace distant relatives, others on vacation, plus the usual businessmen with their conventional uniform of dark suit and leather briefcase. As the Aer Lingus 747 touched down smoothly on the tarmac at Dublin airport right on time, the sun was shining without a cloud in the sky. Lenihans brief in New York before leaving was to proceed to the American Airlines desk at Dublin airport and stand reading a copy of the New York Times, positioning his bag down by his right foot. He was also to wear a black leather jacket and a cheap black plastic watch on his right wrist. The American had to be in position exactly 30 minutes after landing. Included in the plan was a provision for flight delays and other airport difficulties that could cause a timing lapse.

When he was approached he was to do exactly as instructed on the piece of paper that would be handed to him. Feeling extremely apprehensive, Lenihan approached the rendezvous on time. He could not help noticing his hands were clammy and his heart beating so much he thought his chest would burst. He started to read the newspaper making sure that his sleeves were just clear of his wrists to reveal the watch. Just then a group of men approached him talking loudly about golf and giving the impression that they had done most of their playing in the bar of the golf club rather than on the greens. As they chatted about a forthcoming tournament in Dublin and because the area around about was very crowded, Lenihan was soon surrounded by these armchair golfers.

At once he was thrust an envelope with a verbal instruction to go at once to the men's toilet, enter a cubicle, lock the door, read the note and then flush it down the loo. The group moved away and merged with the milling crowds, making it clear that another round of golf was imminent along with, but not before, a pint or two of Guinness. After a minute or two Lenihan strolled into the toilet, acting as calmly as he could, found a cubicle and locked the door as instructed. With hands shaking he tore open the envelope and read the typed instructions. After digesting the information he began to tear the paper into tiny shreds and disposed of them as directed. He realised that this was done so that the IRA could make a positive identification. He also knew he was under constant observation the whole time from persons as yet unknown. The IRA had to be sure that the American was not being tailed by the Irish Special Branch or anyone else. No one must know he was to be working for them.

On leaving the toilet he walked slowly back through the arrivals lounge and out into the sunshine towards the taxi rank. A taxi pulled up almost immediately and

Lenihan got in telling the driver to go to Connelly Station in Amiens Street. The roads were busy and progress was slow due to the rush hour.

'How come the sun's shining? I thought it always rained in Ireland,' said Lenihan to the driver.

'Well we do get good weather occasionally, particularly this time of year. Is this your first trip here?

'Yeah it sure is, I've come over to try and trace my distant relatives,. My folks emigrated to the States years ago from the south of Ireland, somewhere near Wexford as far as I can make out. I'm gonna start at the records office tomorrow and see what progress I can make. Tonight though, I'm gonna take in some traditional pubs and then sleep it off at my hotel,' replied Lenihan as casually as he could.

'If you would like me to pick you up anywhere tomorrow just call this number.
I'll show you all the good pubs and if you like, the ladies of leisure as well,' said the driver offering Lenihan his card with a smile and a wink.

'Gee thanks, I'll remember that buddy, great.'

The cab pulled up on the forecourt of the station in a line of other discharging cabs and Lenihan got out and paid the driver in Irish Punts. It seemed odd being in a country that spoke the same language as him but was very different in many other ways, the accents, the cars and strange money. During the journey he had noticed the cab was being followed by a blue Ford Grenada but this had now disappeared. He walked into the station and up to the information board pretending to read the details.

Within minutes a voice said, 'Come with me, Mr Lenihan, please.'

He followed the small man out of the station and down a side street onto Custom House Quay where the waiting blue Ford was parked. Sitting in the back was John O'Hagan.

'Hello, Mike, welcome to the Emerald Isle. I hope you had a good flight. Aer Lingus are good aren't they? Get your backside in here.'

'Hi, John. Yeah, they looked after me real well, slept most of the way,' drawled Lenihan settling himself in the back seat. 'I take it I was watched from the moment I stepped off the plane?'

'You were indeed, even before you boarded in New York, and of course we have friends in the airline business, you were never alone at any time. We can't be too careful these days, the Special Branch are giving us a hard time lately. On top of that the British MI5 is active here as well. An insider in the Garda told me that it's possible that MI6 also operate with our governments nodding approval - these are the real spooks. Many of them apparently speak our native Gaelic language, which is something you will have to get used to pretty quick. Don't worry though, you're not expected to learn it,' replied O'Hagan giving the driver instructions to move off and out into the traffic.

After they had been going for a short while O'Hagan said, 'Don't be offended, Mike, but I'm shortly going to put a blindfold on you because we are taking you to a safe house where you are to hole up until you move to the training camp, which incidentally, is not quite ready yet.'

'OK I understand, John, but I hope you have plenty of beer and food at this joint. Oh! and a TV because I get bored pretty quick.'

'We do indeed, my boy. I can assure you that things are well and truly taken care of. If fact our massage girls will ease away all your aches and pains in the most pleasurable way you can imagine, if you know what I mean soldier.'

'Sounds great to me, John, but I can't wait to start work and get back into the military frame of mind, I hope your guys are good as we discussed in the states, I'm sure you remember. I won't train idiots.'

'I don't think you will be disappointed, but if you have doubts about anyone tell us and they will be removed or reallocated to other duties. We have a very important task ahead and we do not want another failure through poor operatives. Remember, Mike, the Irish are a very proud people and our colleagues in the Republican Movement are dedicated to the cause. Just be sure that if you do have to get rid of anyone from the course it is for the right reasons only, and not personal in any way. We will not allow personal feelings to interfere at all with our plans,' warned O'Hagan.

As the car made its way to the southern part of the city O'Hagan said, 'I'm afraid its blindfold time, Mike, I'm going to put it on and then you must get on the floor, it will be uncomfortable but it won't be for long.'

Lenihan did as he was told and when he had settled on the floor he asked, 'John, what the hell is the Garda?'

O'Hagan chuckled, 'The Garda, my American friend, is what the English call the old bill, and you yanks call the cops. It's our national police force. The scourge of our lives at times but we have friends there as well.'

'I'm sure in a strange country,' replied Lenihan.

By the time Lenihan was told to remove the blindfold and regain his seat it was almost dark.

The moment the car pulled up at the address, the door opened and they were inside the house in a matter of seconds. The Grenada moved off immediately. In the living room O'Hagan introduced Lenihan to Sean O'Rourke.

'Happy to have you with us, Mike, would you like a beer?'

'Sure that would be fine, but first I must use the toilet - if you can tell me where it is?'

'Up the stairs and the first door on the left,' indicated O'Rourke.

After Lenihan had left the room O'Rourke said to O'Hagan, 'Are you sure we can trust this yank, John? You know I'm suspicious of these patriotic Americans. All this crap about helping the old country, as soon as the going gets tough they fuck off back to the country of Uncle Sam. We've seen this before John, you remember the one that was going to help us make bombs, supposed to be an expert from military ordinance, he was just a nutcase and a petty crook out to make a few pounds,' reasoned O'Rourke.

'I do indeed remember. I also remember blowing his head off at the camp in Kildare when he wouldn't play ball. No, Sean, this fellow has no problem about patriotic causes, his main aim is to hit back at the British in any way possible, plus he needs the money. We have checked his background and his military record is excellent, been awarded the Silver Star for service in Vietnam you know, a real live hero. Pat Hanlon in New York has given us his personal recommendation as to his skills and reasons; fuck all to do with causes. For that reason I think he's the man we want. In any case if he doesn't live up to our expectations he will pay the ultimate penalty in the true traditions of the IRA,' said O'Hagan with a confident look.

'A little test for Mr Lenihan will begin very soon as to whether he can keep his mouth shut. I've already contacted Ann to come and spend the night with him soon. As you well know she can be very persuasive in bed,' continued O'Hagan.

Minutes later Lenihan entered the room and took the drink that O'Rourke had poured for him.

'Now sit down and make yourself comfortable, dinner won't be long,' said O'Hagan switching on the TV for the early evening news.

'Now, Mike, I must remind you, as I said before, you must stay in the house at all times. We have prepared a room in the basement that is very comfortable with everything you need. A little lady will be along to keep you company, that's if you wish of course. I take it you are a normal heterosexual male like the rest of us here?'

'I sure am. A little lady, as you say, would certainly help me while away the long nights. I do understand about your security and would be surprised if it was any other way. Now about the other little matter of food, is that dinner I can smell cooking? I hope so because I'm starved,' said Lenihan.

'On its way, Mike, now make yourself comfortable and I'll see you in a few days. In the meantime Sean will look after you, and by the way don't forget the lady cook, her name's Maria,' replied O'Hagan making a move to leave.

After a good meal and a shower Lenihan decided to have an early night and as he made his way downstairs O'Rourke said, 'Mike, can I have a quick word with you before you take to your bed?'

'Sure you can, Sean.'

As they both settled into armchairs Lenihan said, 'What can I do for you? What would you like to know? I'm here to help in any way I can.'

O'Rourke picked up a biro and a pad ready to take notes of their imminent conversation.

'Mike, I want to talk about rifles, you know the sort of thing, hitting power and reliability etc. What in your view is the best sort of weapon for our marksmen to use? You see, Mike, we have suppliers all around the globe and we can get almost anything including communist weapons like the AK47 and Czech scorpion sub machine guns. We have had some rubbish put our way from South America in the past and it's been an expensive mistake, so what do you think? What's the best for us?'

'Well in my service it's been almost exclusively the Colt Armalite M16 using a .223 or 5.56 NATO round. It's a good light rifle and fairly short but it does like a little looking after; it can be prone to jamming if it gets too dirty. In most cases it is very reliable, even the British SAS use them quite a lot. I know because I've trained with boys in England. My main criticism is that the small light round of .223 calibre lacks stopping power and it is easily deflected by foliage etc. When it hits a body though, it makes a real mess. It's best used by a method called a double tap, that means two rounds fired in quick succession at the target. You might say two for the price of one, this can be very effective.'

'What about European rifles?' said O'Rourke still writing on his note pad without looking up.

'I have used the British L1A1 SLR 7.62 and the German G3, both are excellent and come as standard with a 20 round magazine. The round is larger and heavier than the Armalite which means the stopping power is better and it has a longer effective range. Basically it's a 'one-shot-drop' weapon. The last one I have had personal experience of is the AK47 Kalashnikov 7.62x39. I used one of these in Vietnam. They are a little crude in manufacture but if you can get the ones produced in Russia or Czech Republic you won't go far wrong. I know these rifles are made in many of the communist states including China but the Ruskies and Czechs are the most accurately engineered, and the most reliable. The updated AKM in 5.56 is even better, again Russian or Czech manufactured is the better option. If our M16's packed up in Nam we would use Vietcong AK's if we could get hold of them.'

'What does the 39 mean regarding the AK47 rounds, Mike? I've never heard of that before,' asked O'Rourke.

'It's to do with the case size. The calibre of 7.62, - that's the bullet size by the way, is the same for both the SLR and the AK47. The difference is the length of the case, the AK is shorter and thicker, and therefore they are not interchangeable. In other words an SLR round will not fit into an AK47. East and west rifle ammo is simply not compatible,' replied Lenihan, now in his element.

'May I ask where, in the main, your weapons come from?'

'You may, but I'm not at liberty to tell you. In any case that is handled by someone else anyway. It's not my concern, I have enough to do without all that as well,' smiled O'Rourke.

'Now moving on to handguns, what are your favourites in that field, and why?' said O'Rourke still writing on his pad.

'Well without a doubt it's got to be the .45 calibre Colt ACP semi-automatic pistol. Being hit with one of these is like being slugged with a sledgehammer, not a lot of range but boy, do they stop people in their tracks. Unfortunately the US Army have now gone over to the standard NATO round of 9mm, and one of the best pistols in this calibre is the Browning Hi Power, but another very good pistol is the Italian Berretta, again in 9mm. The British SAS favour the SIG 9mm of Swiss manufacture. One point in the .45's favour is that it's very easy to hand-load the ammunition using easily purchased equipment. The elements such as bullet heads, cases and primers including the powder could come from a variety of sources and be very difficult to trace. I can set up a small manufacturing process quite easily if you like; a lot of private shooters make their own hand-loads in the states because it saves them money. The .45 bullet heads can be made into a dum-dum type of projectile quite simply and by doing so increase its effectiveness. You wouldn't like to be on the wrong end of one of these I can tell you, Sean.'

'I will talk to the people concerned about what you

have just said regarding the .45 ammunition, it sounds interesting to me. We do in fact have a number of pistols of this calibre. Revolvers, Mike. Your thoughts on these lovely weapons my friend.'

'With this type of handgun, the best makes in my opinion are Smith and Wesson model 686, the Colt Python and the Ruger, not to be confused with the German Luger which is a pistol. Use nothing less than a .38 special. Better still, a 357 magnum with a four or six inch barrel for a positive kill. There is a variety of ammunition available for these calibres and they are very reliable, little chance of jamming like a semi automatic pistol. The snag is they only carry a maximum of six rounds in the chamber, but you can get speed loaders for a quick reload. However still not as quick as changing an automatic pistol magazine. The advantage of using a revolver is that of course they do not eject the cartridge case after the shot and less for the police to use their forensic skills on, and they tend to be more accurate, particularly with a six inch barrel'.

'Finally, I know you've had a long day and must be tired, but shotguns. What do you recommend in this line of equalisers?' said O'Rourke pouring out some of his favourite Jameson's whiskey for them both.

'Well I would use an automatic or pump action in 12 gauge loaded with SG shot. This consists of a cartridge loaded with seven or eight 9mm steel balls and is devastating. In fact it can blow a hole in you the size of a dinner plate. Don't use a double-barrelled shotgun, at least not in a shoot-out because of the constant reloading they require. In pump or auto shotguns my recommendation would be a Remmington or Ithaca and the most rugged of them all, the Mossberg Slugster, all American and excellent. I can teach your guys to be fully proficient in all the weapons we've discussed tonight, Sean, including booby traps and other nasties they might need.'

'I know that, Mike, that's why we chose you. Believe me our boys really need some modern training, it's been lacking for years now. Anyway that's all for tonight, do you want some coffee before bed?'

'No thanks I'm pretty bushed right now, all I want is to hit the sack, so if it's OK with you I'll say goodnight.'

'OK. Goodnight, Mike. Oh by the way, breakfast is at 8 o clock and you'll get a good Irish blow-out here,' replied the Irishman putting his notebook away in a drawer.

Lenihan laid awake in his bed that night thinking about the events of the last few weeks and trying to imagine what the future would bring. If the police caught him for instance would he be deported or face a long prison sentence, he had been told that private ownership of firearms was not allowed by law in the Irish Republic. The next few days were spent doing very little except reading and watching TV. There were several visitors during this time but none had been introduced to Lenihan and when they were present he was asked to stay in his room.

On the fifth day John O'Hagan arrived with other prominent IRA men for talks but again Lenihan was not invited to take part until the very end when weapons and training were discussed. His views were sought on several military topics and the IRA leaders appeared happy with what they heard. At the conclusion of the talks it was drinks all round; these were taken in a much less formal atmosphere with everyone relaxing and engaging in social small-talk. About 9pm that evening the meeting finally broke up and the men began to leave one by one, eventually leaving only O'Hagan and O'Rourke in the house with Lenihan.

O'Hagan poured out some more whiskey and said smiling, 'Well, Mike, what do you think of the lads? Not a bad crowd are they, eh?'

'They sure seem a hard group of guys. Are they the men I will be training later on?' he asked, lighting a cigarette.

'No, but they are connected with them on active service in the north and elsewhere, most of them have been very active at one time or another and are well thought of within the movement.'

Soon after 10 o'clock the door bell rang and O'Hagan let in a dark-haired girl of about 22 and showed her into the living room. Lenihan was stunned by her looks. She wore a short denim skirt and tight black polo-neck sweater with high-heeled shoes. She had a very good figure and nice rounded breasts; it was obvious she was not wearing a bra.

'Mike, let me introduce you to Anne. She is one of us and a fully trained masseuse, aren't you my dear?'

'Hello, Mike, yes as John says, I am, and will be happy to oblige if that's what you want, or anything else that takes you fancy,' she purred in her soft Cork accent.

'Yes I would like a massage please, honey; I think I'm gonna like it here.'

'OK, let's go down to your room,' she said taking his hand and leading him out of the room and down the stairs.

The following morning O'Hagan arrived early and told Lenihan that he would be moving to the training camp within a week but Anne will remain at the house until then.

'After last night I'm not complaining about staying a little longer, but I'm ready when you are, John,' replied the American with a wink.

Chapter 5

Peter Riley, O'Hagan's deputy, drove up the ramp at Fishguard after arriving on the overnight ferry from Rosslare in the Irish Republic. The green Austin Montego bore the distinctive number plates of Eire registration; Riley intended to change them at the earliest opportunity. The clearance through customs and immigration was slow due to the questioning by British officers of Irish citizens following a crackdown on the movement between the two countries in view of recent terrorist attacks in London.

Not long ago four Irish continental lorries were found to be carrying explosives and bomb making equipment on landing at Hollyhead; naturally the customs and police were twitchy.

Riley's journey was to a small Belgian village near the town of Bastogne where he was to meet with Pierre Depuy, a supplier of arms to the IRA and ETA, the Basque terrorist group in Spain.

After clearing the docks he made his way through the town and onto the A40 and eventually the M4 to London. Just before Carmarthen he pulled into a small wooded area and changed the number plates to British registration, he also placed a forged British road tax disc in the near side lower part of the windscreen. The reason for this was that in London, Kilburn to be precise, which has a large Irish population, the Irish plates would attract the attention of the Special Branch and MI5 surveillance teams known to operate in the area. Riley's arrival in Kilburn was timed to meet with Paddy Corcoran at the junction of Kilburn High Road and Victoria Road. He only just made the rendezvous by the skin of his teeth after being held up due to road works at Chiswick. Corcoran is a native of Galway and the man who helps the IRA with accommodation in London without getting involved any further with the struggles other than fund raising locally.

'Hello, Paddy, get in,' said Riley pulling up on the double yellow lines.

'Hello, Peter, long time, no see. You don't know the way to the flat do you? Remember to turn right at the next set of lights.' said Corcoran clicking in his seat belt.

Riley was to spend the night in a room above a pub owned by one of the Corcoran's friends: as usual when he was on duty would not have a drink that night, it's a pity more IRA people didn't copy his self imposed rule he thought as he pulled up in the car park of the pub and turned off the headlights. The only time he would relax was when he returned home to Kildare after his journey and business in Belgium was completed satisfactorily.

The next morning began early; Riley was on the road to Dover by 6am to catch the 9am ferry to Ostend. Using forged vehicle documents and passport the passage through the docks and onto the ship took less than twenty minutes. Once the ship was underway Riley took out his European road atlas and over coffee in the restaurant, worked out the best way to Bastogne. The crossing was choppy, one lasting just over four and a half hours and Riley was glad when the 'Maid of Kent' docked in Ostend. He hated boats at the best of times.

The E5 motorway across Belgium was heavy with traffic and in spite of travelling at 70mph Riley was frequently overtaken by juggernauts causing a lot of spray on the wet roads. He disliked continental driving but over the last few years he had done an increasing amount of it to meet arms dealers who themselves keep on the move and ahead of the police. Just south of Namur he came off the motorway and onto the N4 heading for Bastogne passing through the little towns of Marche en Famenne and Champion. Soon after 8am he pulled into Bastogne and once through the town turned onto a minor road heading towards the Luxembourg border. After about eight miles he turned off the road and down a track into a farmyard, parking behind a barn.

As he got out of the car, stiff from sitting behind the wheel for so long, he was greeted by the booming voice of Pierre Depuy. 'Ah, Monsieur Riley, comment allez vous, un bon voyage, non?'

'No it fucking wasn't, all you foreigners treat the roads like a race track, you're all fucking mad, anyway enough of that frog language OK?' smiled Riley.

'OK, you win, Peter,' said Depuy indicating the way into the old farmhouse. Go straight into the sitting room and I'll get some coffee on the go.'

'I don't want any of that strong French crap you usually make,' said Riley warming himself in front of the glowing logs of the open fire.

'Alors, I despair of you Irish, you don't appreciate

the finer things in life like good, fresh-brewed coffee, just like the English.' After the coffee and sandwiches were brought in both men settled down to business. 'I've a man coming tomorrow who can supply you with the fireworks you want, you may not yet know but our usual supplier is no longer with us. I believe he is now in the concrete foundations of a new hotel in northern Spain after trying to double cross ETA, not a good idea Peter.'

'Has this new gentleman done business with you before?' said Riley noting the veiled warning from Depuy.

'Not with your organisation, my friend but I deal with him often, he is very reliable and from the Middle East, he's never let me down yet,' replied Depuy.

'What about prices? Were not made of money you know,' said Riley pouring some more coffee.

'In the morning, my friend, you will see, I'm expecting him about 10o'clock. He will bring some samples so don't worry, his prices should be within your range and he can deliver quickly to almost anywhere except Britain. They are so security conscious and their intelligence is very effective. France is a good a place as any, they rarely ask too many questions and the cross-border routes are fairly easy to negotiate. Anyway let's wait for tomorrow and see what he has to offer,' said Depuy, adding more logs to the fire.

That evening was convivial and cosy in the farmhouse and Riley wondered why he continued to work for the IRA with all the danger and threats that go with it. He had often thought of disappearing to Spain and starting a new life away from all this. Perhaps one day, he mused.

The following morning and exactly on time,

accompanied by his private bodyguard, Ibrahim Aziz arrived dressed in a silk, handmade suit and wearing Italian pigskin shoes. Depuy made the introductions and the three men sat down to do business, leaving the bodyguard outside to ensure there were no interruptions.

'Mr Riley,' began Aziz. 'Tell me exactly what you require in the way of firearms. I say this because I can supply almost anything in this line from a variety of manufacturers and from several different countries around the world,' he continued in cultured English.

'Well I want 40 rifles and 20 9mm pistols as well as 100 kilos of Semtex and 50 hand grenades. Oh, and 5 RPG 7 rocket launchers with about 50 rockets.'

'A very small order indeed, if I may say so, Mr Riley, but what about ammunition for the firearms? You have not mentioned this yet,' said Aziz taking notes with a very expensive gold fountain pen.

'Of course,' said the Irishman lighting a cigar. 50,000 rounds each of rifle and pistol ammunition, by the way what have you got in stock at the moment?'

'I can let you have, with immediate delivery, .223 calibre semi automatic rifles of Brazilian manufacture along with Taurus 9mm pistols, very similar to the Browning's you use at the moment. The rifles are a copy of the M16 made under licence but using American steel and production methods, their quality control is excellent. I have been to the factory and seen the operation from beginning to end. Mr Riley, I have an engineering degree and know quality when I see it, you can be rest assured.' With this Aziz nodded to Depuy and said something in rapid French which Riley could not understand.

At this point the Belgian left the room and in a few minutes returned with a large leather bag, which he placed, on the floor in front of the settee. After undoing the zip Depuy took out a rifle and pistol of the type described by Aziz. Riley examined the weapons carefully after making sure they were safe and not containing bullets. The method in which the Irishman handled the firearms impressed the Arab.

'Tell me, Mr Riley, where were you trained in the use of firearms, as I can see you know exactly what you are doing?'

'In Libya, trained by the Special Forces that surround Colonel Gadhaffi. In fact at El Aseria south of Tripoli,' replied Riley, still engrossed in the weapons.

'Ah my country, I hope you enjoyed your time with us,' said Aziz, finishing up his notes.

'It was too fucking hot and I didn't like the food but otherwise they looked after us well and we were taught a lot of good stuff. Before we discuss prices, Mr Aziz, how soon can I have a shipment ready for Ireland?' replied Riley getting back to business.

'I have all this equipment in Belgium now, not eighty kilometres from here, including the hand grenades you mentioned. The grenades by the way are made in the Czech Republic and are of the fragmentation type with four-second delay fuses. Standard issue to the Czech forces and supplied to other states in Asia and Eastern Europe. I can arrange transport to any port of your choice other than Britain.'

After some haggling they agreed on a price payable in $US within a few days directly into a numbered Swiss bank account in Geneva.

'Mr Aziz, can you get my order to Paimpol in Brittany? We have the use of a fishing boat out of there to ship the goods to the South of Ireland.'

'Of course,' replied Aziz with a smile. 'I will arrange transport and delivery within two weeks, let's say Saturday 14th at Paimpol. The money must be deposited before Tuesday 10th to allow the deal to be completed.'

'It will be Mr Aziz, you have my word on that.'

'I will arrange transport immediately. Where do you want the driver to go on reaching his destination in France?

'If you tell me the make and registration number of the vehicle you will use for this job, I will arrange for the driver to be met at a large Hypermarket on the outskirts of the town, situated just off the main road,' replied the Irishman.

Depuy and Aziz spoke in rapid French that was much too fast for Riley to understand even though he had some knowledge of the language.

'Peter, come outside with me while Mr Aziz makes the arrangements by phone. My garden is lovely at this time of year,' said Depuy indicating the back door.

As they strolled across the lawn and through the flowerbeds, they spoke of old times. Depuy was a soldier in the Belgian Army and served in the Congo during the Lumumber period. He was later discharged for selling military equipment to the locals in Katanga and dealing in black market money. Although he now ran a successful car dealership in Bastogne and managed quite well financially he enjoyed the excitement of illegal arms dealing, plus of course the extra income it provided.

Depuy had been caught once but the police had been unable to produce enough evidence for a watertight case in court and the charges dropped. For the next two years he went straight and police interest in him ceased, as far as he knew, because they never bothered him again.

Once back inside the farmhouse Aziz said there had been a change of plan and that Riley would have to pay Depuy, who then, after extracting his commission, would transfer the remainder into the Geneva account before the due date of the 10th of that month. On the table was sealed envelope containing the details of the vehicle that was to undertake the delivery to Paimpol including its estimated time of arrival at the well-known hypermarket on the outskirts of the French town. In addition was a telephone number for Riley to ring if difficulties should occur in the meantime regarding the meeting of the driver. Aziz also wanted a reciprocal number should things go wrong his end that could affect the delivery, although this was not anticipated.

Ibrahim Aziz could not have known that Riley had the money with him hidden in a secret compartment in the car. He had come prepared, having done business this way before. After coffee Aziz left the house and drove off with his bodyguard to an unknown destination. About an hour after the Arab had left Riley paid Depuy in full.

Later that evening Riley telephoned Paul Delmond, an ex-French Foreign Legion member who was to arrange the transport from Paimpol to Ireland. Early the next morning Riley said his farewells to Depuy and began the long journey back to Ireland. After arriving at Dover he decided not to stop in London but continue through to Fishguard. The drive along the M25 and onto the M4 seemed never ending. When he came off the motorway, the other side of Swansea, he pulled into a secluded field and changed the number plates back to the original Irish ones and replaced the forged tax disc. He carefully hid these items in a prearranged location for later retrieval. As he approached the town of Haverfordwest a police roadblock stopped him.

'Please pull into that lay-by and switch off the engine, sir,' said a police officer politely. 'This is a routine check.'

'Good evening, officer, what can I do for you?'

'Good evening. I see you are from Eire, where have you been in England?'

'Oh just to London to see some old friends, I usually do the trip about three times a year but it's becoming expensive on the ferry nowadays.'

Just then two men got out of a car and came over introducing themselves as Customs and Excise officers. 'Right open the boot!' said one of the men abruptly. As Riley complied with the order the other man started to search the car's interior. The police officer told Riley to stand facing the car and place his hands on the roof; he was then searched carefully.

'What do you lads want? I've done nothing wrong. What's the matter? All I want to do is to catch the ferry back home,' said Riley getting nervous.

'Shut up, you Irish bastard, you think you are clever but we always catch you lot in the end,' replied one of the Customs men roughly.

'What do you mean? Catch who?' replied Riley thanking God that he had hidden the false plates and tax disc just a little earlier. This was a near one alright but he knew he was clean this time.

'You know what I mean. This route is used by the IRA for smuggling,' said the policeman, 'so we are going to stop all you Micks until we eliminate all you from the face of the earth, do you understand?'

'Well I'm not in the IRA or have anything to with them, so don't start having a go at me for nothing,' countered Riley with conviction.

The officers found nothing on him or in the car and let him proceed to the docks but followed closely to the point of observing him drive onto the ferry. Once aboard he sighed with relief, 'Holy Mary, Mother of God that was close, we can't use this route again.'

After docking at Rosslare, Riley made his way in pouring rain along the N25 through Waterford to the city of Cork. Leaving the city on the windswept R600 past the airport he finally turned off and drove into the little village of Ballymartle and an IRA farm. On arrival John O'Hagan, who had spent the afternoon in bed with his girlfriend, greeted him.

'Hello, my boy, did you have a successful trip?'

'Successful and bloody nerve-racking. The goods will be delivered by boat into Rinneen down near Bantry in the next week, the final ETA to be phoned within a few days,' said Riley as they entered the house. O'Hagan made some tea and they settled down allowing Riley to explain his ordeal with the police and customs officers near the docks in England.

'We must give England a miss for the time being, I think it might be better to use the ferry direct to Roscoff or Le Havre. The police in the UK are getting very jumpy since they discovered that last lot of firecrackers on the trucks near Liverpool recently,' said Riley removing his tie and rolling up his sleeves. 'If we continue to travel through England we won't even be able to have a piss without MI5 knowing, they are really cracking down you know John. I don't fancy a term in a British prison or risk getting a spell of interrogation by the security services in one of their special centres in the country. Those bastards make up the rules as they go along without any regard for the law and human decency and respect or civil rights,' he continued, showing real concern for his safety.

'Right, from now on we use the routes you suggest, but for the time being we should be alright because with this latest shipment in our care, the armoury is looking pretty healthy and the ammo in good supply. You know the Libyans have been a great help over the years, albeit at a price, at least they are reliable,' said O'Hagan pouring two large whiskeys. What you need now, Peter is a few days rest at home with the family so you can get back to normal. Do you have anything planned for next week? Tell you what! Take the week off and I'll be in touch, I'll probably come up to Kildare and see you when we can have a pint and discuss the issue then.'

'I'm beginning the get some severe migraines, John; it could be stress-related I'm not sure. I know my blood pressure is up these days; perhaps I'm getting too old for this lark.

'Well stay the night, have a few drinks and relax. Give Maire a ring and let her know you're back safe and sound and will see her tomorrow after you've rested.'

'Good idea, John. I'll do it now,' said Riley, moving to the phone.

Meanwhile, a week later, the lorry arrived on time at the hypermarket on the outskirts of the quaint old fishing port of Paimpol. Paul Delmond met the driver and directed him to a small warehouse near the end of the quai. The vehicle was parked inside and the building secured with an ex-Foreign Legion friend of Delmonds, sitting in as a guard for the night. The guard had no idea what the lorry contained, but for a 10,000 French Francs, he was not about to ask questions.

Early the following morning the loading started. Delmond and the driver began to load the weapons and explosives into the hold of the 'St Nazaire', a 300-ton freighter registered in Brest. The captain, an old hand at gun running, adjusted the ships manifest to show a full load of French wine bound for the shops of Cork. Just after 0600 hours the ship set sail out of the harbour and into the channel en route for the Irish Republic.

The crossing was uneventful and just outside territorial limits she hove to. Out of the darkness came the flashing lights of the MV "An Cloch". The old 70 foot clinker built boat is a familiar sight along the southern coast of Ireland, often being hired out to local fishing groups and individuals who want to go out far enough for deep sea catches beyond Bantry Bay. The skipper, Patrick O'Donnell, knows the coast well having learned the business from his seafaring father. After 35 years in these waters he could land a cargo in any of the hundreds of small bays and coves that littered the coastline between Crosshaven and Dursey Head. O'Donnell was also available to the IRA and did as he was told without asking questions; his life and family were too precious for him to cross them. The sea was flat calm and the transfer took less than 15 minutes, almost without a word being spoken between the crews.

As soon as the transfer was complete, the 'St Nazaire' continued on its voyage into Cork. Just as she was level with Crosshaven, Irish Customs officers came aboard and finding nothing amiss, allowed her to dock at her allocated berth.

Making steady progress along the southern coast, the "An Cloch" crew of two kept a sharp look out for any Irish Navy patrol boats. Once past Galley Head, the sea turned into a heavy swell and the going became difficult, with the boat pitching and rolling with waves coming over the bow and cascading along the deck.

'I hope this fucking thing doesn't sink,' said O'Donnell to his colleague Martin Connelly.

'Well if it does, we might as well go down with it because if we don't get this stuff to Rinneen intact, our lives won't be worth living, Pat,' he replied, lighting a fresh cigarette. It was a great relief when Castle Haven Point came into view, O'Donnell began the slow starboard turn and into the channel that led to the tiny landing stage of Rinneen. As soon as the fishing boat tied up O'Donnell was approached by two IRA men who were to load and drive the weapons to Galway.

'I think it would be better if we unloaded after dark when the visiting Garda officer has returned to Skibbereen, that way we won't get any interruptions,' said O'Donnell.

'OK,' said one of the men, 'but I want this boat guarded until then. We are armed and no one will be allowed to interfere with this lot, is that clear Patrick?'

'To be sure it is. I'll leave it to you then lads. I'll be back in about two hours to give you a hand, come on, Martin lets be having a pint of the best. I think it's your turn to pay isn't it, me old son?'

When the two seafarers returned to the boat, the two IRA men were below deck playing cards and had clearly been drinking.

'Right then, let's get this gear off my boat and you can be away,' said O'Donnell.

At this point the older of the two got up and left the boat to fetch a Ford Transit van, which had been parked close by. As soon as the van had been loaded, the IRA men left without a word; much to Pat O'Donnell's relief. His telephone call to O'Hagan was to confirm that the shipment had been landed and transferred without a hitch.

The IRA quartermaster was clearly delighted saying, 'Well done, Pat, the usual payment will be with you in a couple of days. Just get on with your fishing, etc and when we need your services again we'll make contact in the normal way. Thanks for your help.'

'Anytime, John, you know where I am,' replied O'Donnell wishing he had never got involved with the IRA in the first place.

O'Hagan immediately rang Sean O'Rourke at the Dublin safe house and told him to get Liam Reagan and the other selected men up to the training camp in Connemara. This was to include the American, Michael Lenihan.

The trip to Belgium was to be Riley's last job for the IRA. He left the farm at Ballymartle the following morning en route for his home in County Kildare, somewhat over the limit from the excess of whiskey the night before. Just outside the town of Fermoy, he drove into the side of a heavy lorry that pulled across the front of him at a road junction killing him instantly. The large Scania continental truck, bearing British number plates, carried little damage; the young, fit cropped-haired English driver managed a wry smile as the ambulance departed the scene with the dead gun-runner aboard. Subsequent police enquiries blamed the driver of the car, who, after blood samples were taken, showed an alcohol limit well in excess of the national maximum allowed.

At the safe house in Dublin O'Rourke was making the phone calls that would mobilise the trainees, including Reagan, and get them up to the training camp. Lenihan was to be taken by car using an indirect route, picking up along the way Alan Conlon, an ex Irish army senior NCO, who would be an assistant instructor on the course.

Just after 8am the following morning the car drew away from the house in Anglesea road and made its way through the rush hour traffic towards Portloise. The N7 was busy with heavy lorries but progress was good until just the other side of Johnstown where the car became embroiled in a hold up due to the new Naas town by-pass construction.

The Garda had set up a roadblock outside the Curragh military camp, the main Irish army training area and Headquarters. A few days earlier, according to the news, ammunition and explosives had been stolen from the armoury inside the camp and routine checks were being carried out. The car Lenihan was in passed through without incident and continued towards the turn-off and into the little town of Ballybrittas, finally pulling up outside Conlons small terraced house. O'Rourke got out of the car and walked up the uneven path towards the front door and knocked loudly.

As Conlon opened the peeling, varnished door he greeted his friend with 'Dia duit cad e'mar ta'tu, Sean (hello how are you, Sean), using the Gaelic tongue.

'Go raibh maith agat, Alan,' (fairly well thanks, Alan) replied O'Rourke. 'I think we should use English from now on because of the Yank we have with us, me old friend.'

'Yes of course. I'll be with you in a few minutes, just got to get my bag and say goodbye to Doreen. See you in the car.' As he walked back to the car O'Rourke wondered how Lenihan and Conlon would get along in the confines of the training camp.

When Conlon got in the car O'Rourke made the introductions and they moved off in the direction of Tullamore. After passing through Galway they continued along the N59 and joined the T71. A few miles before the village of Maam Cross, the car turned off and made its way along a track into the windswept mountains of Connemara.

In the distance Lenihan noticed an apparently empty hut but as the car got nearer a man appeared with a rifle, backed up by two other armed terrorists who seemed to come from nowhere. They stopped the car, and after recognising O'Rourke, allowed them to pass and proceed to the farmhouse that was to serve as the base for the training camp.

The surrounding area was bleak and wet underfoot with rough heather-clad hills and small streams. 'The general conditions and weather around here normally discourage casual walkers,' said O'Rourke during the last few yards of the track. 'From the farmhouse a track leads down to the waters of Lough Corrib, a distance of about a mile. We guard this approach all the time and should get not unwanted visitors. We should also get no interference from the Garda either.' he explained further.

When the group left the car and entered the house there were many greetings passed in Gaelic which Lenihan could not understand.

'Gentlemen, please, I must ask you all to speak in English because of our guest here. Mr Lenihan does not have our ancient tongue. He is, of course, American and formally of the Special Forces until an unfortunate incident robbed him of his distinguished career. Some of you may know the American Special Forces more readily as the Green Berets. They played an important role in the Vietnam War and Mr Lenihan or Mike, as he is known among friends, was much decorated due to his service there many years ago. I must inform you that he will be in sole charge here at the camp and assisted by our old friend, Alan Conlon, who most of you know already, with the exception of Liam there. It will be run on military lines and total obedience to all commands will be expected. Need I say more? Enjoy your training and good luck to you all. Mike, over to you,' concluded O'Rourke.

Lenihan stood up and outlined the training program

that he had devised. This would include weapon training drills, close quarter fighting, concealed movement and escape and evasion techniques and finally unarmed combat.

'The training will begin tomorrow morning at 0600 with a cross-country run and muscle-toning exercises. Fitness is most important in any military training arena and this will take place regardless of weather conditions, so be warned, gents. I will not tolerate any weak-willed students who can't take a bit of hardship. For the first few days Mr Conlon will also take part in these exercises alongside the rest of you. Anyone who wants to bottle out, please come forward now then you won't be wasting my time and that of the organisation. Remember, you could be up against the SAS in the north and they don't play games I can assure you because I have worked with them, so from now on let's adopt their motto "train hard, fight easy". That's all, guys. See you in the morning. Oh! One last thing, no one gets pissed at any stage throughout the training, is that clear? That's all.'

One of the barns had been set out with trestles and chairs so that it would serve as a classroom and lecture hall for theoretical subjects. One of the conditions that Lenihan had insisted on, as part of his contract, was that he would be armed at all times with a weapon of his choice. This was a Smith and Wesson model 686 .357 Magnum revolver loaded with hollow-point ammunition and including four speed loaders containing extra lethal bullets.

Lenihan indicated to O'Rourke that he wanted to see where the shooting practice would take place and what type of range facilities existed for movement under fire.

'To be sure, I'll take you there now. Come with me in the car, it's not far. We've found a little valley that's surrounded by steep hills that should deaden the sounds while shooting is taking place. Also we can easily patrol the area to keep out nosey parkers; we are fortunate that many of our friends around here are farmers and use their shotguns all the time for vermin control. The sounds of gunfire are a normal part of life in this area, Mike.'

When they had walked up the valley and back to the car Lenihan said to O'Rourke, 'Sean, do your men know how well trained the SAS are? Remember I've worked with these guys and they will stop at nothing. They are quite ruthless and don't normally take prisoners you know. They will kill your men out of hand without mercy if they get a chance.'

'Yes I know, Mike, but it's not the SAS we are intending to tangle with. In all due respect to you, my friend, our men cannot be trained to their standards, we neither have the time or money to do it you see. In addition, I doubt if we have the calibre of personnel in our ranks, most of them have never had a military career at all. We have a few who served in the Irish army but that is all. Conlon is an example. Our own national army has no special forces of its own but it does have a ranger unit trained by the Canadians I believe. It would have to rely on outside help in this situation but I believe there are plans to improve on this by the government of the republic.'

'I know you use ex-military people like Conlon to train the lads but why do you want Special Forces training? Are you going to set up a unit for unusual jobs like assassinations or abductions and such like?' asked Lenihan.

'Not really, Mike, but the men here have been selected to have this type of training and will be picked out for a particular task we have in mind for the future. This must remain secret for the time being but I will be looking to you for the best man at the end of the course.'

'Sure, Sean, you'll get your man. Now perhaps you can show me the rest of the camp and the firearms that are here,' said Lenihan as they got back into the car.

It began to rain heavily and with darkening skies, a storm was brewing. After they had visited the rest of the site it was time for supper back at the farmhouse. This turned out to be a massive Irish stew with all the trimmings, along with good coffee and plenty of Guinness. There was also a good supply of Irish whiskey to round off with.

During what remained of the evening, Lenihan was introduced to Irish music and republican songs, which he took to straight away and thoroughly enjoyed. Now feeling tired from the journey and the effects of the drink, he was ready for bed. O'Rourke showed the American to his room upstairs which was fully fitted out with a double bed and wardrobes with wall to wall carpet and centrally heated. When they had entered the room O'Rourke handed Lenihan the Smith and Wesson 357 and the ammunition he had asked for back in Dublin. The stainless steel revolver was almost new and the hollow-point, semi jacketed rounds looked menacing. Lenihan knew full well the awesome power and effect of this weapon when used correctly by an expert. He was such an expert.

'See you in the morning, Mike; I shall be leaving for Dublin about ten.'

'Yeah, good night, Sean, see you later.'

After O'Rourke had gone down the stairs, Lenihan quietly slipped the lock and placed a chair against the door handle as a precaution against unwanted guests during the night. During the briefing he had given the men earlier, he had sensed some hostility against him. Perhaps because he, a foreigner, was totally in charge of them and could in theory have anyone of them taken off the course at any time. He noticed strange vibes from Conlon that he did not like at all, he would need watching.

As he lay in bed his thoughts went back to Christine Ellis still in Germany and of the many friends he now missed. When he left America to come to Ireland he told no one where he was going, not even Mrs Jacobs from whom he had rented the room in New York; it was better this way he thought.

He decided to keep the revolver with him at all times and if the pressure of working for terrorists began to get too much he would slip away, killing anyone who got in the way if need be. Lenihan had the skills to survive almost anything and would use them to their maximum if he had to. Having got hold of a map of Ireland he would make for one of the seaports and cross over to England or France ditching the gun at the last moment.

In the morning it was pouring with rain, but at 6am on the dot he had the men out on their cross-country run of three miles.

The only one who protested was Conlon. 'I don't see why I should have to train with the men. I'm here to teach the use of explosives, so tomorrow I won't be running, do you understand, Mr Lenihan?

'You will be running tomorrow and every day until I decide you are fit enough, is that clear, Conlon? I'm not having any lazy bastards in this camp. If I run, everybody runs, if I crawl through the shit, everybody does the same and that includes you, I don't give a fuck if you like it or not, you better believe it. Now get moving.'

Later that day came the first weapon training session and Lenihan insisted on a 100% performance in the handling and malfunction tests he had set at the end. Towards the end of the first week he noticed some improvement in the general standard of fitness and weapon handling. He could not help in noticing a deepening resentment from Conlon because he had to continue with physical training each day, something that he clearly hated.

Around the middle of the second week Lenihan introduced unarmed combat to the men. This included avoiding punches and kicks and anti-knife techniques. Conlon was still seething inside and when Lenihan invited him to attack with a dummy knife he picked up a piece of steel pipe and charged at full speed towards him. Lenihan stepped to one side and kicked the Irishman hard in the stomach causing him to double up and fall, face down. At this point Lenihan kicked him hard in the ribs, bent down and pulled his head back by the hair turning him onto his back. Conlon, now gasping for breath, tried to kick Lenihan in the testicles but he saw this coming and pressed two fingers into Conlons carotid arteries, causing him to drift towards unconsciousness. He was close to killing the Irishman but decided to release the pressure on the side of the neck.

As Conlon came round, Lenihan said to him, 'If you do that again I will rub you out once and for all, you thick bastard, do you understand?'

Conlon was badly shaken by this whole episode and became co-operative and submissive to all commands and orders that he was given by Lenihan although he was clearly not a happy man.

As the weeks passed Lenihan decided that some of the men were not up to the standards he required and could not go any further on the training programme. This included Conlon whose knowledge of explosives was not as great as he had led people to believe. On telephone advice from the American, O'Rourke had them removed from the camp and placed on other duties elsewhere within the movement. The training moved on to map reading and night movements in hostile country including the selection of laying-up positions during the day. Much of the time now was spent outdoors as part of the hardening up process in readiness of things to come.

Lenihan was impressed how well the four remaining men took to it all bearing in mind they were all civilians with no real military training behind them before the course. On the fourth week O'Hagan arrived with O'Rourke to see how things were going and to get a report off Lenihan on the quality of the remaining men under training.

During the journey from Dublin they had not spotted the car and motorcycle that had shadowed them or were aware of the high-tech microphones in place near the safe house in Anglesea road that monitored their movements and conversations. The British Counter Espionage Service MI5 often operated in Eire without official permission from the Irish government or the official knowledge of the Garda Special Branch.

At a private meeting in the farmhouse that night, Lenihan said to both O'Hagan and O'Rourke that in his opinion Liam Reagan was the man they should choose for whatever special operation they had in mind.

'I've taught him all I can in the time available, but to become really good would now require a lot of constant practice and some operational experience. I could suggest further training if I had some idea of what he is going to be expected to do at the end of all this,' said Lenihan with a shrug.

'Well,' said O'Hagan, 'if I could tell you it would put your own life in danger you see, not only from us but the British also.'

'Why is that, John?' asked Lenihan with a frown.

'Well if there was a leak and the plot came to light, everyone would then be a suspect. The IRA don't give anyone the benefit of the doubt, Mike, so the less you know the safer you are. It's in your own interests really you know, my American friend,' replied O'Hagan accepting a glass of Bushmills from O'Rourke.

'Well the choice is yours, gents, but I'm sure you can see what I'm getting at; I don't want to know any details of your future operations but some ideas of the type of work the men will be doing would help me formulate a better course for you,' countered Lenihan, slightly annoyed.

'Mike, I will talk to the other people involved and get back to you on this one. You do have a point but the final decision would have to come from the Chief of Staff. In the meantime, Mike, I think constant shooting practice, concealment and escape and evasion would be a good thing to work on for the time being.'

'I would go along with that, continue your excellent work and we will be in touch soon,' added O'Rourke with a smile. 'We are most impressed with what we have seen so far and would like to enjoy the benefit of your services for a long time to come if you agree, Mike. Both John and I agree that the organisation will improve its military expertise far beyond what we have achieved so far in the past with your help and guidance. The chief of staff and military council in Dublin are equally impressed with what we have told them,' he continued.

'Sure I'm happy to work with you guys but I must go back to the States from time to time to check on my pension and bank etc.' replied Lenihan.

'Yes of course we understand and only to be expected. Good, then I will inform the Chief of Staff that we now have a full time instructor with us to oversee all our training and military standards,' said O'Rourke, pouring more whiskey for them all.

The training continued with further practice in pistol and revolver shooting followed by pump action shotgun and sniper drills. At this stage Lenihan introduced booby traps, the type that can be left behind to slow a pursuit and maim anyone who tampers with them. Of the four remaining men on the course Liam Reagan was the one Lenihan would now concentrate on, having stated he was the best all-rounder and the most adaptable.

The American and the Irishman would go on long hill walks in any weather with Reagan navigating and giving verbal reports on likely laying-up positions and escape routes off the hills. At night, again both men went out with Reagan demonstrating approach techniques to farms without alerting dogs and other animals of their presence. This was to prove useful later in Reagan's career when he frequently crossed the Ulster border under the noses of British soldiers on patrol.

Two weeks later O'Hagan returned to the camp and gave instructions to the other three students on the course; they were going on active service, one up to Belfast and the other two over to England. Lenihan wished them well and watched them drive away from the farm; he would never see them again. The man who went north was arrested and handed over to the SAS, later being taken to England for interrogation by the security services. The other two were caught in London when the police tactical firearms unit SO19 surrounded the flat in which they lived and operated from. They surrendered without a shot being fired and were later sentenced to terms of 20 years each in a maximum security prison. The IRA strongly believed that the police were tipped off but so far there was no proof.

During the evening O'Hagan and Lenihan had the house to themselves and became involved in a long discussion about the IRA including its aims and future objectives. Lenihan said, 'John, I don't see how you can get the Brits out of Ulster, you can't take them on with force and the politicians won't listen. How can you do it?'

'Well you're right, of course, but ours is a long term thing. By keeping up the constant attacks and bombing campaigns we will grind them down and public opinion will call for their removal from the province. After all they have been here in force for well over 20 years and they haven't beaten us yet. I can tell you we are going from strength to strength and with help from people like yourself we will get even more professional in the way we operate. Now Mike, tell me about Liam Reagan, what kind of man is he?' asked O'Hagan.

'Well he's had a good education as you know and has adapted well to the training I have given him. I think he is psychologically suitable for special operations and would be able to kill without becoming a homicidal maniac. He is a quiet and methodical man who will analyse a situation first and plan a strategy to attain his goal. He is not the type of activist who is all guts and glory with a blinkered view of the cause he is fighting for. He is a realist in a real world and someone who knows the limitations of his colleagues and himself. I don't think for one minute he would put himself at unnecessary risk just to score a few dubious points against the British or impress his fellow compatriots. I would definitely have had him on my team in Vietnam because he is level-headed and a natural for military action. In short he's your man, John, without a doubt.'

'Good, this is very good news indeed, Mike. I will pass on your comments to the military council without delay and then we can move onto other things to progress the cause against Her Majesty's government. Now, what will you be having?'

'Sounds great to me. I'll have a beer if you don't mind as I find the whiskey and Guinness a bit heavy. Remember I must not get pissed as I impressed on the men. I like to lead by example all the time.'

'OK, beer coming up right away. Oh, by the way I've got a surprise for you, tomorrow in fact,' said O'Hagan beaming.

'Well don't keep me in suspense,' replied Lenihan quizzically.

' If I said you look as if you could do with a massage, would that give you a clue?'

'I feel better already, when will she get here?'

'About midday, but I must caution you, not a word of what goes on here. Although she's one of us, the less she knows the better for all concerned, especially for her own safety. Remember our brothers will kill women just as easily as men when they have to, where they suspect a security leak. We also have to keep ahead of the British Intelligence Service, you never know whom they might try and turn or where they might crawl out from or blackmail for information. They are crafty bastards and are up to all the tricks you can imagine. They are not winning this war against us and they know it only too well. So remember, enjoy the massage and anything else you get up to, but keep your mouth shut, Mike, your own life depends on it, anyway, enough of that. Now, about that drink.'

'Don't worry, John, I have worked under security conditions for so long that it has become second nature. This type of work is really no different to the training of guerrilla's that we undertook in Nicaragua for my government some years ago,' replied Lenihan accepting his beer from O'Hagan.

The next day the American had free and decided to go early morning fishing on Lough Bofin that lay under the shadows of the Shannawona hills. It was cool as he walked down the track towards the Lough and there was a hint of rain in the air, something to be expected in this part of Western Ireland. As he set up the rods he wished he were in these parts under more friendly conditions. 'I must be getting old and soft,' he muttered to himself.

The spot he had chosen was completely quiet and peaceful with no one to disturb his thoughts except the odd dipping of the float when there was a bite. Lenihan cast his mind back to the days with Carol and how his life had changed since her death; he could never have foreseen his present position. The training of terrorists was the last thing he would have considered.

If only Phillips had not come on the scene and she had stayed faithful, the rest of their lives could have been happy and enjoyable with a good income and pension to follow. Their plan was to buy a small farm in Virginia when he retired and open a riding school. Carol, he remembered, was a superb horse rider and loved to ride whenever she could. She taught several members of the US garrison in Germany to ride, including the commanding general and his own regimental colonel. All that was now gone and here he was training terrorists for a cause he hardly understood.

The morning's fishing proved to be good with two large trout in the bag for lunch; these should go well with a beer and some vegetables he thought. As he began to pack up his gear and get ready to head back to the farm he caught sight of a small glint of light coming from a hillside nearby. Lenihan was convinced it came from the reflections of binocular lenses but he pretended not to notice. A gut feeling told him he was under observation, but from whom? There was no reason for it to be the IRA because he had not left the camp until today and he had no real knowledge of their operations. Perhaps it could be birdwatchers he thought unconvincingly.

Lenihan walked slowly along the track towards the farm and could feel the comforting bulge of the 357 magnum tucked into his waist belt. After about 200 yards, he decided to stumble on a rock and drop his bait box at the same time. This would give him time to have a quick look around as he began to pick up its contents without attracting attention. In spite of this, he noticed nothing unusual and carried on back to the farm. As he went through the front door he saw O'Hagan sitting at the table writing in a notebook.

'Hello, Mike, did you catch anything this morning?'

'Sure thing, what about these beauties?' replied Lenihan opening the bag and placing the large fish on the tablecloth. 'You should have seen the one that got away.'

The ex-Green Beret decided to cook both for his lunch; as he made his way to the kitchen two men rushed in and started to speak to O'Hagan in rapid Gaelic. As he started to prepare the fish O'Hagan appeared in the kitchen doorway.

'Mike, we have a small problem, a Garda patrol car with four officers has stopped at the track where it joins the road. It seems they are examining the ground and it looks as if they might come up to the farm at any moment.'

'Well what's the problem if they do?' replied Lenihan, deciding to say nothing about what happened down by the Lough earlier that morning. 'If they do come up we can either kill them or invite them in for coffee and pass the time of day, so don't worry. I take it the weapons are well and truly hidden along with any incriminating evidence so nothing can be found that would arouse their suspicions?'

'Yes they are, but what about the car bringing Ann. That's about due isn't it?' replied O'Hagan putting away his pistol.

'If they all arrive together I'll tell them she's my girlfriend and that I haven't seen her for a while. I'm sure they will get the message and leave. As for the rest of us we are on a fishing trip to escape the pressures of work. Stay cool and nothing can go wrong. If we do have to kill them we must destroy the car and dispose of the bodies so they cannot be found, ever. So let's hide these handguns but keep them handy just in case. Come on, chop-chop there's no time to lose. By the way, John, are your local cops normally armed?' replied Lenihan concerned at the apparent panic of O'Hagan, an experienced member of the IRA.

'No. The Garda do not carry arms in the normal course of their duties but they are of course available at local police headquarters throughout Ireland. I understand they can only be issued on special orders from the commissioner,' replied O'Hagan, slightly ruffled.

Shortly after, the Garda patrol car pulled up outside

the farmhouse and three officers got out, leaving the driver behind the wheel.

'Good morning, gentlemen, what can I do for you?' said O'Hagan smiling.

'Good morning to you, I'm Inspector Corrigan from Galway Garda Headquarters. Can I ask you what you are doing here, only I know most of the local population around here but not you chaps?'

'To be sure you can,' replied O'Hagan. 'We're up from Dublin doing a little fishing and shooting although the rabbits are a little scarce. Mind you come into the kitchen and see what we caught this morning, two real beauties.'

'Would you guys like some tea while you're here?' said Lenihan.

'No thanks, we've got to be getting back to Galway, this area is part of a weekly patrol so we thought we would drop in on you while passing,' said Corrigan. Are you an American, Mr...?' said one of the officers.

'Lenihan's the name, and yes I am. My parents were born and bred in Sligo then emigrated to the States many years ago. This is my first visit to your beautiful country and one in which I intend to stay for some time, there is so much to see and places to visit I hardly know where to start. I'll be down in Galway soon for a walk around the town and to see the cathedral and of course the pubs that Ireland is famous for. I may even try some of the Guinness if I'm brave enough. But if you guys are passing again drop in for coffee and a chat anytime,' replied Lenihan with conviction.

'Well, gentlemen, it's been nice to meet you but we

must be off because I have a report to write and it has to be on the desk of my chief tomorrow morning at the latest.

The patrol car bumped its way down the track and out onto the road leading to Galway, finally disappearing out of sight through the hilly country of Connemara.

'That was excellent, Mike. I can see we are going to get along just fine,' smiled O'Hagan. Ann's car arrived well into late afternoon due to a breakdown outside Ballinasloe and had to be towed to a local garage for repairs. When she entered the house she was pleased to see Lenihan and looked stunning in a light blue dress and matching shoes.

'Hello, Mike, it's nice to see you again,' she said in her soft Cork accent.

'Hi, honey, you look great in that outfit. I hope you have brought the massage oils with you as I sure can use it right now,' replied Lenihan, with genuine pleasure at seeing her again.

'Of course I have, I'm at your service so to speak; you had better show me your room so I can unpack my things and get ready for later, darling,' she purred.

Whilst Ann was upstairs unpacking and taking a bath O'Hagan said to Lenihan, 'Mike, I'd like you to stay here a little longer because I want to send some more men up to be trained in illegal border crossing, unarmed combat and cross-country travel in hostile territory including escape and evasion. Do you mind? We need to get our teams across the Ulster border and back safely and quickly, you see.'

'Hell no, I don't mind at all. I like this country. So

long as I can do a little fishing now and then I'm happy to remain on the payroll and do my bit for the cause, but what about Ann?'

I have arranged for her to stay with some friends in Clifden that is not far from here and I'll give you the phone number in a minute. When you want her just give her a ring and she's all yours. I'm also going to give you a car so you can go into Galway with Ann for a drink and dinner when you like. Sean and I will be up again in about two weeks, so just relax and take it easy and enjoy yourself with Ann. Oh by the way, take this to keep you solvent,' said O'Hagan, handing Lenihan a wad of Irish Punts.

'Thanks, John, what have you done with Liam Reagan? How is he getting on?' asked Lenihan with genuine professional interest.

'At the moment he is in one of our safe houses up near the border awaiting further instructions and is in very good health. I'll pass on your good wishes. Well I'm off now and leave you to it. Here's the phone number for Ann and this one if you need to contact me in Dublin, but only in an emergency. Is that clear my friend?' said the IRA quartermaster getting into his car.

'Bye for now and have a safe journey,' drawled Lenihan with a smile and relief.

It was to be at least a week before the new trainees were due to arrive and Lenihan spent the days touring the area with Ann and enjoying her company at night. The weather stayed fairly dry and they had some interesting walks in the hills and down by the Loughs and nearby rugged coastline of Connemara.

One night after dinner as they sat down in front of the fire Ann asked what went on at the farm and why Lenihan had to leave Dublin. He told her that it was used as a rest home for the IRA and they had let him stay there as a caretaker to look after the place. She seemed satisfied by this explanation but he began to wonder if she was being used by the organisation to test him with regards to security, especially in bed. As any Special Forces man Lenihan was automatically suspicious by nature and had no plans to spill the beans and by doing so put his own life in danger. Ann never mentioned the subject again but it became clear that she was falling in love with him, and he with her...

Chapter 6

MI5 had had the safe house in Anglesea Road under surveillance for some time and although they knew IRA activity took place there they did not know to what extent. The high-tech microphones that were lent to them by a major electronics manufacturer proved unreliable and not as effective as first thought. In spite of this failing in technology the British Security Service were pretty certain that something big was being planned. What this might be eluded them for the time being. The constant comings and goings of the IRA hierarchy led them to believe that they had found an important new planning centre and these movements were to be exploited to the full.

John Byrne an ex-army intelligence officer now working for the British Security Service was contacted at his base in Belfast and instructed to travel to Dublin to meet a resident of the city. Their brief was to jointly see what information they could come up with as a team and Byrne was to report his findings directly to the deputy director general in London and no one else.

The MI5 officer boarded the Belfast to Dublin express. The journey was uneventful except for a short delay just north of Dundalk due to the train being searched by the Garda and Irish soldiers. At this point

Byrne decided to visit the toilet compartment and hide his pistol just in case. MI5 officers do not normally carry arms but when on duty in Northern Ireland this rule can be waived. His investigations in the south would be carried out clandestinely without the knowledge of the Eire government. Having the Walther PPK 9mm gave Byrne a sense of security, perhaps falsely.

When the train pulled into Dublin station Byrne was met by Donald Gale, his contact in Eire. The platform was crowded so they went straight to Gale's car and drove immediately to his flat on the other side of Dublin, not far from Anglesea Road. During the journey Gale brought Byrne up to date with his observations so far.

As they settled down in the flat for a drink Gale told his colleague that he had followed O'Hagan as far as Galway on several occasions but dared not go any further in case he was spotted and his cover blown. He had used a hire car and a motorcycle at various times to ensure the IRA was not aware of his presence. Byrne was pleased with what he had been told. The excitement began to mount because they could be on to something big as last. Byrne was considering retirement over the next year and this could well be the big one he so desperately wanted after so many years in the background.

'Well, Don, I'm looking forward to working with you again. You have lost a bit of weight I see, keeping off the old Guinness no doubt,' said Byrne offering his hand.

'Yes I'm on a keep-fit thing at the moment, don't know how long it will last though,' he replied, returning the Masonic grip.

'Let's go out and have a drink in the local later

and then you can have a general look around the area,' continued Gale.

'Don, I intend to get a team over from London so that we can watch the house on a continuous basis; I want every move O'Rourke and his merry men make logged and documented. I am particularly interested in any trips to the west of the country and up north. We must nail these bastards. It's clear the Irish government do tail this lot but their successes are not all that good for some reason. I'm sure the Garda is rife with sympathisers.'

During the short walk to the pub Gale told Byrne his general view of the IRA and some things that had come to light in recent checks. 'We know for instance they use the south-west area of the republic for training mainly due to the remoteness down there. The terrain in County Kerry and parts of Cork are ideal for their needs and they go to great lengths to protect these sites from prying eyes. They used the Wicklow Mountains on a regular basis for a long time but that was stopped a little while ago when the Garda and army raided them. Needless to say there were arrests and imprisonments as a result. The trouble with this type of vermin is that you put some away and a new lot are waiting in the wings to take over so you can never wipe them out.

My view is that they need to be eliminated completely by our special forces or the lads from MI6. Have we been able to find out who has been supplying them with arms and explosives yet? I know the French have arrested a few people after our tip offs,' he continued, with passion in his voice.

'We think it's our old friend Pierre Depuy in

Belgium, but as yet we cannot be quite sure. The Belgian police have been asked to help through Interpol so we are waiting on that one,' replied Byrne.

'Tell me, John, when can we expect the team over from London and will they be bringing some electronics with them? The stuff we have at the moment is not all that good. The reason I say that is because we might be able to tag their transport and then make it easier to keep a tighter tail on them, especially when they go out of town and onto the country roads. A lot of roads in the west are very light on traffic and following a car becomes a bit obvious, electronics might be able to give us some distance.'

'I'm told they should be with us in a few days, and in answer to your question regarding the electronics; no they are not. The deputy director has told me that under no circumstances must we engage in any activity in which we could be caught or exposed by the Garda. The diplomatic consequences would be enormous, so no interfering with their cars or phones. Just plain old-fashioned watching and reporting to me in the usual way I'm afraid. If we ever uncover a camp then it will be taken out of my hands anyway and handed over to the army, probably the SAS,' continued Byrne.

'While I was watching the house several weeks ago, another man came and went on a number of occasions, a man of about twenty-five or thirty, quite small with short, brown hair. I followed him into the north Dublin area and then lost him in the crowds. I haven't seen him since though,' said Gale.

'I've a gut feeling the Micks are up to something big

and training for it right now. Their activities just recently have been low key, a few small bombs and a little shooting but that's all. Judging from the past this could be the lull before the storm Don,' said Byrne deep in thought.

As the two men strolled around the streets, including walking the entire length of Anglesea Road, they carried out normal anti-surveillance procedures to ensure they were not followed. After they had eaten Byrne said to Gale, 'Don, we must not bungle this one; that is an instruction from the top, and I mean the top. They tell me MI6 are also involved but to what extent I don't know yet. It's pretty obvious that the government are very worried indeed because security has been stepped up on all senior ministers and the royal family. Even General Housland, the army commander in Northern Ireland, has been given extra protection much to his chagrin. You know what these military types are like, they hate to admit they could also be a target,' continued Byrne, lighting his briar pipe and emitting clouds of foul blue smoke.

'When do you intend to start intensive observations and what do you want me to do after the teams are in position?' asked the Dublin resident cautiously.

'Well, I want you to behave normally and drink in the local pubs but stay away from Anglesea Road. See if you can pick up any snippets of information from bar talk but for God's sake be careful. If you can chat up any of the known IRA girls and get her into bed this may prove useful. I'll leave it to you to use your discretion in this matter. Oh, by the way, don't forget your french letters just in case, you never know who's been screwing them, it could even have been the lads from MI6, what could be worse than that,' smiled Byrne. 'Another angle you might want to exploit is your position in the lodge; you're in the chair this year aren't you?'

'Yes. I take up the master's collar next week, Wednesday to be precise. I suspect there are some sympathisers among the brethren. I may be able to steer a conversation in that direction discreetly and see what happens,' replied the fellow Freemason.

'The team will handle all the routine stuff but I want you with me when I drive up to Galway looking for leads there. We must find this camp if indeed one exists. If there is one I know the government will order its destruction immediately. The surveillance will start within twenty-four hours of the team's arrival in Ireland,' Byrne muttered between puffs on his briar.

The eight-man team stepped off the plane at Dublin airport and were met by John Byrne. Their leader was Jim Stone, one of the most experienced men in A4 branch, the surveillance unit of MI5. The team were to stay in various hotels around the city to avoid suspicion.

After the briefing from Byrne and Gale, Stone and the team began their well-proven methods of tracking and logging all movements to and from the safe house. During the course of the following week O'Hagan was tailed to the farm at Ballymartle near Cork where he kept a girlfriend. From the moment of his arrival the farm and the outhouses were kept under constant observation. One of the team, an ex- telecom engineer, managed to tap the phone line against all orders from London. There were several visitors to the farm; mostly men in small groups and to follow them all would be impossible with the limited resources of the team. MI5 decided to concentrate on O'Hagan. Of the many phone conversations that were tapped one stood out in particular by the constant use of the words "camp" and "yank", but so far there was nothing concrete to go on. If there was a camp, where could it be? It might even be abroad, possibly even America.

Meanwhile back in Dublin O'Rourke was tailed all over the city including to an apparent legitimate visit to Belfast. In spite of this intensive action by the team nothing of any significance could be reported to London except the existence of the farm near Cork.

The deputy Director General of MI5, Sir James Overton MBE, MC, went into the conference room of Leconfield House in London's Curzon Street, to give his weekly report to the senior officers of the security services and the military Chief of the Defence Staff, General Sir Roger Hardy. The topics covered many issues from Russian activity in the UK to the constant monitoring of the British communist party and the movement of other subversive groups active in the country. The details of the report concerning the IRA would take place at the end of the meeting. The bones of the information would be from the coded messages passed from John Byrne and the scrambled telephone calls from the British Embassy in Dublin. Information also came in from other sources including informants on the security services pay-roll.

'Gentlemen please,' began Sir James. The last item today concerns our friends from over the water, the IRA. We have learnt from our field operative's reports that there could be something in the planning stages, possibly something big. As yet nothing is known for certain and it's all speculation but we are pulling out all the stops at the moment. There have been some useful leads from MI6 and French Intelligence in Paris. You will already know that security has been stepped up on all key people and firearm-carry permits have been issued by the home secretary to certain staff and selected cabinet ministers. Continued surveillance on all docks and airports along with major railway stations are in force as from last Friday and will last as long as necessary.'

'What exactly have we got from our man in Ireland?' asked Brigadier Chalmers, the director of Special Forces at the Ministry of Defence.

'From the coded messages I've received, not very much but it seems the words "camp" and "yank" were picked up from a conversation that was overheard, and Byrne, the man on the spot has a gut feeling about it,' replied Sir James.

'A gut feeling, Sir James, is that all we have got, what is that supposed to tell us? Surely we need more than that to justify all this extra security and the enormous cost of providing it,' said Chalmers with a flourish.

Sir James, now slightly irritated said, 'Byrne is a good man and I am happy to rely on his view of the situation as he sees it. It is only a matter of time before we have something more substantial to act upon. The man whose name has come to light is a fellow called John O'Hagan. Special branch tell us he is English by birth, at the moment they are building a profile on him, which I shall get a copy of by the next meeting. Please Brigadier, bear with me on this one, I'm sure something will turn up and when it does we will act accordingly,' said Sir James, thinking that the Brigadier was trying to impress the Chief of the Defence Staff, albeit not very well. The General was a more experienced man than his subordinate in matters such as intelligence gathering activities. His look at the Brigadier during the outburst made this very obvious.

'Sir, can I add a little on the matter of O'Hagan?' said Commander Collins of the Metropolitan Police Special Branch.

'Of course Commander, go ahead.'

'We are indeed at the moment at an advanced stage in compiling our profile of this man. Briefly, he was born in South London and served in the British Army at various locations including Cyprus with the United Nations Forces. Both his parents were born in the Irish Republic and we believe he mixed with Irish troops in Cyprus and this led to his interest in the IRA cause, or it could be like many, just an interest in violence for the sake of it. His parents lived for almost thirty years in Britain before their deaths and as far as we know, never returned to Ireland during that time. He could hardly have any nationalist sympathies for Ireland being English through and through. There is nothing in his military records to show any leanings of a republican nature, so this must have come much later. We simply don't know at the moment, but we are working on this at present. On the surface he has something to offer the IRA due to his military training, his army record is excellent and he served as a weapons instructor with some success for a total of 12 years. He is however an extremely violent man who, when provoked, would kill effectively and without compassion, anyone who crossed him. He has adopted an Irish accent that he maintains except when he's under pressure and also speaks Gaelic well. We are pretty certain he has killed British soldiers in Northern Ireland on active service during his rise through the ranks of the IRA. He is a man of weapons but not a bomber. As soon as we have completed our enquiries, the full report will be available through Sir James for this meeting, hopefully next week,' concluded Collins.

'Thank you Commander, we look forward to the report on this vile man and then it must be action without delay, even if it means liquidation,' said Sir James, winding up the meeting.

After everyone had filed out of the room, Brigadier Chalmers stayed behind to talk to Sir James who was tidying up some papers and placing them in his briefcase.

'Sir James, I would like a quiet word with you if I may?'

'Of course, Brigadier, what can I do for you?'

'Well, sir, I would like to offer my apologies to you for the apparent hostility I displayed when you mentioned the gut-feeling about the Irish situation. This was not meant as it may have seemed. I know you have a very experienced man over there that you must rely upon. I do accept what you say and my apologies once again on that. Secondly, I have available at Hereford two Sabre Squadrons of SAS although one is away in Scotland on a training exercise but they can be recalled at a moment's notice. The other one is involved in training Police Royal Protection staff and again can be ready in no time if required. Their new CO is Lieutenant Colonel Berryman, a good man who has seen plenty of active service with the regiment and won an MC in the Falklands. He knows his job inside out and is raring to go. If there is a camp over there I'm sure we could have a quiet look at it and take it out if necessary. Alternatively there is a Royal Marine Commando SBS team based in Portsmouth who would like a crack at terrorists.

'I must say, Sir James; I favour the SAS because they are more familiar with this type of operation. As it has to be clandestine with no shooting or whizz bangs, if a camp is discovered then there are two possible courses of action we can take. Firstly, it could be leaked to the Irish government and let them take care of it with their own army and Garda; we could lend a hand if they required it. They have had some success in the Wicklow Mountains a year or so ago when they raided a training camp and arrested some of the lads, finally popping them into Mountjoy prison for awhile. Secondly, let the SAS deal with it in their own particular fashion. These men are very good and I'm sure that success could be guaranteed without any fuss. Should you need any advice on this subject I would be happy to help sir.'

'Well, Brigadier, I accept your apology. I must admit I thought you were being a little unreasonable, but enough of that now. You may have a point as a matter of fact. At the moment my hands are tied until more information is received from Byrne and further details come in from Special Branch. One person I do want to nail is our friend O'Hagan. I feel he is acting like a traitor to this country, his country of birth, and all we stand for in the north. I certainly agree with you about using the SAS because if there is an establishment in existence over there it could be well hidden and my men are not trained in what might turn out to be a cross-country infiltration. If you can bear with me a little longer until all the reports are in, then I will call you and Colonel Berryman in for an action-plan to deal with it. It goes without saying that any such action would require the blessing of the Prime Minister and the Chief of the Defence Staff. So if that's all, Brigadier, I will see you here at 10.00 hours next week.'

'Yes indeed, sir. Thank you for your time and understanding. Goodbye, sir,' said Chalmers picking up his briefcase and heading for the door.

As the Brigadier walked into the main foyer of the building he heard the gruff voice of General Sir Roger Hardy. 'Brigadier Chalmers, where the devil have you been? I want to see you in my office at 16.00 hours this afternoon. You had better be prepared to explain your arrogant outburst during the intelligence briefing earlier.'

'Sir, I have to be at a reception at the Duke of Yorks Headquarters at 15.30 today for a presentation of long service awards with Colonel Berryman.'

'Listen Chalmers, you will do as you are damned well told, my office at 16.00 is that clear? Berryman can cope without you; do you hear? 16.00 it is.'

'Yes, sir, I will be there without fail.'

As Sir James Overton made his way slowly along the corridor to his office he pondered the thought of SAS action in the Republic of Ireland and what would happen if things went wrong. The political repercussions were sure to be of gigantic proportions and could bring down the government, followed by the knock-on effect, requiring resignations of senior members of the civil service and possibly the security services. This whole Irish subject had to be handled very carefully; one thing Sir James did not agree with the Brigadier was about informing the Irish government and the use of the Garda and Irish army. He knew full well that both of the services contained IRA sympathisers. This he decided was to be a British operation.

After lunch at his club near to Curzon Street, Sir James returned to Leconfield House in time for the afternoon meeting with the Director General of MI5, Sir Michael Jones. Their talks lasted until late evening and they both agreed that if the MI5 team in Eire were able to pinpoint a training camp or come up with anything else substantial they would recommend action to the Prime Minister.

On the train home that evening Sir James had a nagging feeling inside. While he had no doubt about the capabilities of the SAS or the SBS, what would they do if they found a training camp? Britain's secret service and military forces are not allowed to go around killing people in cold blood, whether they are terrorists or not, although he knew full well it had happened in the past. If steps were to be taken to eliminate the camp and its entire staff it would have to be total and deniable, a black operation.

In Dublin, John Byrne's team had been very busy and this dedication to duty had brought results. Both the safe house and the farm at Ballymartle had provided useful information that was passed on to London by the usual methods. Either the IRA was getting careless with their movements and phone calls or MI5 were improving and having a run of luck, whatever the reason, results were encouraging. O'Hagan and O'Rourke were both followed to the area near Maam Cross in the Connemara hills of County Galway where the MI5 surveillance team broke contact to preserve their cover. They had no idea that the IRA was on to them. Unbeknown to Byrne, one of the team members had been spotted near the farm. Because of the small local community where everybody knows each other he was picked out as a stranger. O'Hagan had then ordered a constant guard be placed on the house and outbuildings with the instructions that if any stranger is caught snooping around he or she must be eliminated immediately and the body disposed of without trace.

At this stage the IRA thought it was possible that the Garda or Irish Special Branch men were involved, but they kept their options open. The IRA quartermaster was determined that no one would be allowed to interfere with the task Reagan was charged with; that being to assassinate Sir Frank Cooper, the Chief Constable of Northern Ireland.

Meanwhile Liam Reagan had been moved to Newtownards, a town to the east of Belfast, and installed in an IRA safe house to begin his plan of action. It might take months before he could strike and all the skills he had been taught by Lenihan may well be used to the full. Sir Frank, by the very nature of his job was a heavily guarded man and it was extremely difficult to get near him. His route to work from his fortress-like home was often altered at short notice and patrolled by police and army units along with strict security arrangements at police headquarters. All other travel he undertook in the province was usually by helicopter and only a handful of senior police officers knew where he was at any one time. Sir Frank's one weakness was golf and he normally played at least once a week on a variety of courses around the Belfast area.

His favourite though was at Broughshane on the outskirts of Ballymena and a quiet area of IRA activity. It was at this course that he made regular bookings under an assumed name. All the staff at the course were aware of his real name and identity, and a charming man at that, often reliving the last game over a pint in the clubhouse with friends. Reagan knew of the senior police officers love affair with golf and where he played most often. A fringe member of the IRA worked in the bar at the clubhouse and also handled most of the bookings. She occasionally passed information to the republicans regarding influential members and their wives attendance at the club.

If an assassination could be pulled off it would be seen as a major victory for the IRA and give them even more standing in the terrorist world. In particular Libya where many IRA men had been trained in the past and who supplied most of the arms and explosives for action against the British.

The killing would show Her Majesty's government that they have the capacity to strike anywhere and anytime as they did when Lord Louis Mountbatten was blown up in his boat off the coast of Mullaghmore, County Sligo in 1979.

While Sir Frank Cooper was not well known outside

Northern Ireland he did have considerable powers in the province and took a hard line with the IRA. Reagan visited the golf course to get the layout of things and decided this location was feasible for the killing. The area was sure to be well guarded when the Chief Constable was playing and Reagan realised he must be in position well before the start of any match. After extensive touring around the site he reasoned the best time for the kill would be near the end of the course. After a couple of hours of following Sir Frank around, his body guards would be bored and lulled into a false sense of security.

Reagan's chosen weapon was an AR15 automatic rifle fitted with a telescopic sight, this had already been zeroed in with the help of Lenihan back at the camp. During the many hours of practice the Irishman had proved to be a natural shot and scored consistent bulls over a variety of distances. As soon as the list of Sir Frank's fixtures was forthcoming from the IRA agent in the club, Reagan could carry out his mission and escape safely back to the republic.

In London, Sir James Overton had been receiving constant reports from John Byrne. It was now clear that a training camp existed in the area of Maam Cross situated in the west of Ireland. A man who contacted military intelligence in Belfast claiming to be a member of the IRA backed up this information. The details were offered on the understanding that he would be given a new identity and moved, along with his family, to England or somewhere abroad.

The senior Intelligence Officer in Ulster, after discussions with Sir James Overton, agreed, but was told by Overton to get as much information as possible before allowing him passage to the mainland. Once in London he would then be debriefed by MI5 and his future decided. Overton hoped this mole did not expect too much from the government because he was certainly not going to get it. Promises are one thing, abiding by them, quite different.

Alan Conlon, the ex-Irish army NCO was prepared to sell out the IRA for all he could get. His initial phone call to army HQ in Northern Ireland aroused the interest of military intelligence who quickly informed MI5. His reasons were many including the humiliation he received at the training camp and the fact that O'Hagan, who he knew from his UN days in Cyprus, was English and yet managed to rise to the top ranks of the movement. On the other hand he had managed only lowly status in the organisation. Conlon realised that if he were discovered giving information to the British he would be executed, possibly along with his family. He also knew that now his identity was known to MI5 they had him in their grip and could manipulate him as they wanted. He was trapped in circumstances of his own making. The thought of this sent a shiver down his spine but there was no going back now. It was too late.

Based on all the information now at his disposal Sir James Overton decided to recommend military action of a reconnaissance nature to his boss Sir Michael Jones, the head of MI5. The final approval had to come from the Prime Minister. In the meantime he would assemble Brigadier Chalmers and the commanding officer of the 22nd Special Air Service Regiment, Lt Colonel Berryman.

A plan had to be formulated and presented to the Ministry of Defence for approval by the Chief of the Defence Staff General Sir Roger Hardy. Other senior officers would not be involved in the plan because of the very sensitive nature and possible political implications, the less people that knew the better; the essentials of a black operation.

In less than a fortnight a plan was submitted and approved by the Chief of the Defence staff and the Prime Minister. The SAS were activated and took up the challenge.

Lieutenant Colonel George Berriman, commanding officer of the 22nd Special Air Service Regiment sat at his desk in the headquarters at Stirling Lines on the outskirts of the county town of Hereford close to the Welsh border. The camp was named after David Stirling the founder of the regiment during the Second World War and a frequent visitor until his death in 1990 at the age of 74.

Berryman had decided to appoint Captain James Rodd to lead the team into the Irish Republic to locate the suspected terrorist training camp. His reasons for picking Rodd were many but the base line was that he was a superb leader of men and his knowledge of infiltration and observation were second to none. Within the last year Rodd had carried out extensive undercover operations in Northern Ireland including forays across the Irish border.

At 1000 hours sharp there was a knock at Berryman's office door. 'Come in,' he said placing some papers in his desk drawer.

'Sir, I have Captain Rodd to see you as requested,' said the Regimental Sergeant Major, a soldier with eighteen years in the regiment.

'Oh come in, James. That will be all, RSM, thank you,' said Berryman with a smile and indicating a chair. 'Now tell me, how is Mary and the boys these days?'

'They are all well, sir. My eldest son is looking forward to starting his new school soon, he wants to follow me into the army but Mary's not too keen on the idea.'

'James. I have called you in today because I have a special job that I want you to do, it requires the utmost discretion and could be dangerous. At the moment only a handful of people know about it so that alone will give you a clue as to the sensitive nature of the assignment. Consider it a black operation,' continued Berryman standing up from his chair and stretching his back. 'I'm not as young as I used to be you know, James, getting a bit past it I suppose.' A moment later there was a knock at the office door and the RSM brought in a tray containing coffee and a selection of the Colonel's favourite biscuits.

Captain Rodd poured out the coffees and settled down to hear what the Colonel had to say; he was intrigued to say the least.

'James, how would you and three other men of your choice fancy a cycling holiday in the West of Ireland? Marvellous countryside you know.'

'Well, sir, I know that we in the regiment are trained and ready for anything, but taking a bike to the Republic is a little unusual to say the least,' replied Rodd just a little intrigued.

'I know it seems odd, but the reason for this form of transport will become apparent later in the briefing. By the way, if you want to alter anything I am quite prepared to listen as you will be the man on the spot, so to speak,' said the Colonel. Now James, this is for your ears only at the moment OK? I have been requested by the Ministry of Defence to send in a team to try and discover the whereabouts of a suspected IRA training camp to the West of Galway. MI5 have men on the ground over there but this camp is in a remote mountain district and they are simply not trained in our type of work. Both the government and I believe that if they tried snooping more closely in this area they would probably be compromised and give the game away, possibly even liquidated, you know what these people are like. These terrorists will stop at nothing.' continued the Colonel, lighting his briar and filling the room with smoke.

'Good heavens, sir. I'll have to call the fire brigade in a moment. You'll burn the place down with that combustion, it's like a smokescreen in here,' said Rodd pretending to cough.

'Shut up you cheeky young bugger and get on with it, if you've got anything sensible to say of course.'

'Sir, have you thought about aerial photography from Nimrod? I say this because with the equipment they have recently obtained from the States and elsewhere they can take pictures from a very great height yet see the hairs on the back of a person's neck. The aircraft would not be noticed from the ground and the results could be very quick indeed and in real time.'

'Yes I know all that, James; the problem is can we trust the air force and the technical people? I fear not. This is a very tricky subject, James, because if such a camp does in fact exist I imagine we will receive an order to destroy it as soon as possible without the knowledge of the Irish government. The whole thing must not come to light under any circumstances. If it does the Prime Minister will have our bollocks for breakfast. It will of course bring the government down and will certainly cause an international incident.

'The subject of using the RAF was talked about at the Prime Minister's meeting but thrown out for the very reasons we have just discussed, I have the full backing of Brigadier Chalmers, so it is down to us, old boy, I'm afraid. We have the advantage of almost total loyalty within our staff and are best placed to carry this off quietly and efficiently. The nearest rivals we have are, of course, the SBS of the Marines but the regiment has been selected for this little job,' continued the Colonel. 'As the area of operation is in Eire you will have to enter the country as tourists.'

'Yes, sir, now I see the connection with cycling,' remarked Rodd with growing interest.

'The plan that has been drawn up is for you and your team to pose as cycle tourists camping in the region. This will give you considerable freedom to move about without arousing the suspicions of the locals as long as you behave yourselves. The panniers and saddlebags should give you ample storage for small arms, navigation and radio equipment you need. Obviously operating in uniform is totally out of the question and the Irish government is not going to be informed because we don't trust them to keep quiet. We have reason to believe there could be a mole in the Irish cabinet. In any case they would not give us permission at the moment because relations between

London and Dublin are a little strained over an incident a while ago when an MI6 agent caused some trouble in Waterford. So you see, James, we are going to be busy and it must be very soon,' said the Colonel pouring more coffee.

Captain Rodd stood up, walked over to the window and looked out over the parade ground towards the famous clock tower. Carved on the base were the names of all members of the regiment who had failed to "beat the clock"; in other words, killed in the line of duty. There were more than he would have liked, they included several of his close friends.

'Sir, if we do in fact find a camp and the IRA are in situ will we be expected to wipe them out?' asked Rodd.

'As I said earlier, I expect an order to that effect but permission must be obtained before any further action, so give me a full coded report over secure radio and leave the rest to me this end. The initial brief from the Brigadier is reconnaissance only at this stage. If it were up to me I'd kill the whole lot of them without leaving any trace of our presence and try to shift the blame on the UDA by careful disinformation. We have a strong suspicion that they have an American over there teaching military tactics. If he were to get the chop as well it may deter others who may wish to follow in his footsteps. Whether it's for money or some cranky ideological reasons we simply don't know. You and your men must not get caught under any circumstances, James! Do I make myself clear?'

'Yes, sir, crystal clear. You need have no worries about me or the team I will select for this operation,' said the young captain, tingling with excitement.

'Now I want you to choose three men to form the team, I don't care what ranks they are but they must be the best we have. On top of this you must impress upon them to keep their mouths shut for all time, don't discuss the plan with any of them at this stage. In short, no briefing until all the training is completed and you have a departure date and the final plans approved. This will ensure that there are no leaks. From that point onwards I'll leave it to you when and where you give the details of the operation. Naturally, following the regiment's usual practice, you have a complete choice of weapons and other equipment. Just draw from the stores and armoury; should there be any difficulties with the QM just let me know and I'll get the RSM to deal with it.

'My advice is for you to practice infiltration and escape and evasion just in case the Garda get onto to you at some stage. Remember, James, if the civil or military authorities stop you over there for God's sake make sure that whatever you do there is no trace of British involvement. Also get on to the ranges and into a little close quarter combat. Oh, and one final thing, James, don't forget your bicycle clips.'

'I'll get onto it right away, sir. When I've made my selection I will submit the names to you for approval.'

'That will not be necessary, James, you know the men much better than I do. If you're happy, that's fine with me? Don't forget to remember me to Mary and the family; we must have dinner soon. I know Rosemary will like that, gives her an opportunity to get out the family silver and me the chance to eat off the table instead of a tray on our laps in front of the TV.' said the colonel with a smile.

After James Rodd left the office Colonel Berryman thought how lucky this young man was with his family at home and he reflected how his only daughter had died of a drugs overdose following a failed romance whilst at university. He and his wife had never got over it. Just thinking of it brought tears to his eyes. As the clock struck twelve he pulled the file out of his desk drawer which contained the details of the operation and wrote across the front the words, "Operation Cobra". This would be the code name used by the few in the know.

Over the next few weeks captain Rodd assembled the men he had chosen. Sergeant Peter Jones was to be second-in-command, a man with a vast amount of experience in the Special Forces behind him and an excellent senior NCO. The other two men were John Peters and Mike Smith, both troopers, each with over nine years service in the regiment. Peters came to the SAS from the Parachute regiment and Smith from the Medical Corps. In addition to his military skills Smith held a black belt in Ju-Jitsu and would be able to teach the others some of the finer points of unarmed combat. Although all SAS personnel are taught silent killing and knife techniques, Smith was the acknowledged expert in these matters.

Sergeant Jones came to the Special Air Service from the Royal Green Jackets after failing the selection course the first time. All this did was to make him even more determined to succeed next time. He was one of ten men left out of the original eighty that started the course and the day he was "badged" into the regiment would stay with him for the rest of his life. The sand-coloured beret with the winged dagger badge of the SAS is the most coveted in the British army and it represents the ultimate military professional being hugely respected by many other armies worldwide.

Their officer and commander of the team, who they all referred to as "boss", was commissioned into the Black Watch. Being born in Inverness and gaining an honours degree in history at St Andrews, James Rodd, although small in stature, became the highland regiment's boxing champion and managed to claim several knockouts during his career in the ring.

The cell, as they were now to be known, spent many days and nights in the mountains of Wales improving their navigation and infiltration skills. This included approaching local farms at night without alerting dogs and other animals to their presence. As a matter of course the cell often walked distances in excess of thirty miles loaded down with military equipment and weapons. Each time they went out soldiers from the nearby training camp at Sennybridge were sent after them. Although there were several close calls they always managed to stay one jump ahead and never caught.

On one memorable occasion the cell decided to be a little bold and broke into the commanding officers complex inside the camp at Sennybridge. Once inside the building they made their way to the Brigadier's office and entered the room by picking the lock. Rodd decided to place a copy of Playboy magazine between the pages of the desk diary and leave a pair of frilly, pink, female briefs in the drawer along with a packet of condoms, one of which was missing.

The mission was a complete success but a day or so

later the balloon went up when the Brigadier's wife went into the office and in her husband's absence, found all the apparently incriminating evidence of his infidelity.

The incident did in fact bring to light certain security deficiencies at the establishment and in doing so gave the Colonel Commanding an embarrassing time whilst the problem was sorted out. To make matters worse he had only recently compiled a report stating to the MOD that the camp was completely secure and beyond any form of terrorist infiltration.

In actual fact the SAS team had no difficulty whatsoever in gaining access and evading the guards who were part military and part Ministry of Defence police. Much later the SAS suggested that a full electronic surveillance system be installed with closed circuit television and infrared sensors across all apertures and pressure pads in a variety of locations around the camp. The cost would be high but the increased security much more assured. Even the safe in the Brigadier's office was replaced as it was old and to an expert, easily opened. All the windows in sensitive areas were of the sash type and in fact should be sealed units. The rebound from the Ministry of Defence to the Colonel Commanding was rapid and severe.

Because the operation in Eire was to be, in the main, a reconnaissance and not a military attack, the cell would be without rifles or sub machine guns or indeed any C4 explosives. With the permission of Colonel Berryman, silenced 9mm pistols were to be carried by each man.

The SIG Company in Switzerland makes these very expensive and quality handguns. The silencers or sound moderators, as they are more accurately known, are factory fitted and so efficient that when the gun is fired the only sound emitted is the mechanical noise of the slide and a 'plop' where the excess gas pressure escapes from the end of the barrel. Fitted with a 15 round magazine and high visibility sights with luminous outlines the pistols can be used in poor light conditions with deadly accuracy. The bullets, or rounds as they are called, are subsonic to compliment the sound moderator but produced with hollow points for maximum damage on impact. This makes the weapon a formidable fighting tool. In addition every man would carry six fully loaded spare magazines and 150 loose rounds.

Each man in the cell would also carry maps, compasses and a GPS positioning system along with binoculars and a Gerber military fighting knife. For the men's comfort and protection, a disruptive pattern Gore-Tex waterproof over-suit and Bivi bag would also be taken along. The Bivi bag is a piece of equipment that allows the men to place their sleeping bags inside and yet remain warm and fully waterproof when used outside in the elements. Bearing in mind the high precipitation levels in the West of Ireland the Bivi bag would be a very useful piece of kit. During the day the cell would wear normal bright-coloured lycra continental-style cycling clothing and appear to be tourists enjoying the countryside and local hostelries.

Captain Rodd had the men out most days cycling and this proved to be a most enjoyable pastime, not one of the men asked about the reasons for this unusual change to their normal training programme. They were indeed a special breed of soldier.

In London, the deputy director of MI5, Sir James Overton, had assembled Brigadier Chalmers and the Minister of Defence Michael Deakin, along with Sir Claude Foster of MI6, the Secret Intelligence Service, and Lt Colonel Berryman commander of the 22nd SAS regiment.

'Gentlemen,' began Sir James. 'I have called this meeting because of some disturbing news that has come my way. My good friends in MI6 have discovered an American who is helping the IRA. Claude, would you be so kind as to take it from here on? Thank you.'

'Certainly,' began the old Etonian. 'We have been snooping around in the republic for some time now and have turned up an American ex-Special Forces Master Sergeant with Irish connections. This gentleman was discharged from the US army in disgrace following an incident concerning a British officer in Germany. Briefly, our chap, a Lieutenant, was having an affair with his wife and as a result she became pregnant by him. It seems the American was unable to father children and this had caused tension between them for years. Predictably the affair came to light when she died whilst having an illegal abortion. The end result was that he snapped and nearly killed our man, which resulted in a court marshal in the United States and dishonourable discharge from the service. The German civil authorities were happy to leave it to the American army command to mete out punishment as they saw fit within their military conduct code.

'We know for a fact that he worked as a doorman at an Irish club in New York that has a strong connection with the IRA and Noraid, the fund raising organisation. He has since disappeared from the scene in the Big Apple and we have reason to believe he travelled to Dublin.

'Gentlemen, this man is a Vietnam war hero and much decorated being very experienced in all aspects of Special Forces operations. He has even trained with our own SAS. His name, we believe, is Michael Lenihan. We also believe that he is the same man that has been mentioned in the telephone calls that have come from a farm near Cork. Although the IRA has not actually stated his name, the word "yank" has been picked up several times by MI5 through tapped phone lines. Now before you say anything, I know originally the use of phone taps were ordered not to be used but they have provided us with very good intelligence and should continue. We are pretty sure that he is training a group of IRA for an assassination attempt and I don't mean ordinary soldiers on the streets of Belfast or Londonderry. Up till now the IRA have used ex-regular soldiers from various armies to help train them, but not someone of this calibre, at least not as far as we are aware of anyway. It may well be that he is now at the camp we believe exists on the West Coast of Ireland. If I may self-indulge just a little gentlemen, I would like to say to Colonel Berryman, destroy this camp and all the vermin you find in it.' Sir Claude began to hand around photographs of Lenihan taken when he served on secondment with a British airborne unit in Germany.

The minister of defence began to speak. 'Gentlemen, as you may be aware, I was at Number 10 this morning for a working breakfast with the Prime Minister. The result is that I have been given the authority to order that this camp, if found, be destroyed and any members of the IRA likewise when the SAS go in. Let me make it quite clear though, under no circumstances must any action be traced back to HM Government. We do not intend to inform the Irish parliament or enlist their help in any way,' concluded Deakin.

'Are you saying, sir, that my men have a free hand when they reach this camp, assuming of course there is one?' asked Colonel Berryman.

'What I'm saying, Colonel, is that any IRA men found in the process of this operation are to be taken out, or whatever term you use in your profession, but without trace to us. Is that clear?'

'Yes it is, sir, very clear indeed,' replied Berryman, obviously annoyed by the attitude of the minister.

'When will your team be ready to move, Colonel?' asked the Minister of Defence pointedly.

'A matter of a few weeks at the most, sir,' replied Berryman.

'Can't you be more precise, Colonel? What sort of an answer is a few weeks? Is that what I have to tell the Prime Minister?'

'This is a delicate operation, you have clearly stated that yourself, sir. I am not prepared to hurry my team along with the risk of cutting corners and risking failure. They will go when they are ready and not before,' countered Berryman.

'Minister, the SAS has a four-man-team at an advanced stage of training; they are the best we have in the country. Because of this, Colonel Berryman and I are confident of a successful conclusion to this operation,' said Brigadier Chalmers with conviction.

After the meeting broke up the Brigadier decided to travel back to Hereford with Berryman in the car. During the long journey the two men engaged in conversation about the operation, secretly wishing they could each go along. The Brigadier said that if the outcome were positive some promotions would be forthcoming including that of Berryman.

This statement worried the Lt Colonel because if he were promoted to full colonel, it would mean him leaving the regiment he loved most and almost certainly moving to a staff post sitting behind a desk in Whitehall. 'No way,' he thought secretly.

When the two officers arrived at Stirling Lines, they settled into the colonel's office for coffee.

Brigadier Chalmers was then introduced to Captain Rodd and how he envied the young officer, it certainly brought back memories of his own time in the regiment. Rodd told the senior officers that his cell would be ready to deploy in less than a fortnight and then asked how they were to be shipped to the republic.

'Before we get to the transport problem, James, the rules of the game have changed slightly,' said Berryman, again lighting his pipe, threatening global warming.

'Can I ask in which way, sir?'

'The PM has authorised the elimination of any IRA members that you may find within the boundaries of the camp. You must leave absolutely no trace as to who carried out this deed. This is, as I said before, vital to all of us,' continued Berryman.

'Whilst you are in the camp, assuming there is one, you must not speak to each other under any circumstances in case your accents are picked up by anyone who may unfortunately survive. There must be no survivors, James, is that clear? No survivors at all. This simple mistake could blow the whole thing sky high,' emphasised the Brigadier.

'As to the question of transport, you will travel from Le Havre in France to Cork by ship and then take a train to Galway. You will be French cycle tourists camping your way around Ireland. James, I know you speak passable French so you had better be the group spokesman. When you get into the area settle into a campsite and tour locally for a week getting the feel of the place. At the end of this period you are to make your way along the coast to Mace Head. This time find a wild spot as near to the sea as possible and make your camp. As you know the area is wild and remote with frequent heavy rain. It's here that your weapons and other equipment will be delivered to you from the sea. James, I want you and the men to pack all your personal gear, including weapons, in waterproof bags and number them one to four. You will be number one.

'You must be in position at Mace Head on the 29th at precisely 0300 hours to meet the delivery, which will come courtesy of the boat troop. Signal to them in the usual fashion and to give them a navigational bead in shore. Oh, by the way, they have absolutely no knowledge of this operation, so let's keep it that way. A need to know has never been more important,' emphasised the Colonel.

In the north of Ireland, Liam Reagan had visited the golf course on several occasions and scouted the area locally to seek out an escape route. He decided to make for Larne immediately after the killing and catch the boat to Stranraer in Scotland where he would lie low for few days and let the dust settle. His eventual destination was planned for France and a safe house in Dinan and then in due course back to the republic. The rifle and binoculars would be hidden and removed by other members of the IRA later. Reagan reasoned that the security forces would know it was the work of the IRA rather than one of the other terrorist groups who operate in the province. In any case, the usual coded message would be passed to the police and national newspapers the following day by the IRA high command claiming responsibility for the assassination.

The main border crossing points with the south would be sealed and patrols in the countryside stepped up along with extra helicopter observation flights. The whole province would be buzzing. The thought sent a shiver down his spine.

The deputy Chief of Staff of the IRA, Sean O'Rourke, had arranged for Reagan to go to a safe house in Millbrook just outside Larne to wash and clean up before catching the boat to Scotland. The reason for this, apart from the obvious, was to remove and destroy all his clothing and to take a hot bath to wash away any traces of nitro-cellulose from the bullets he had fired earlier. Should the police pick him up he would be subjected to a forensic test to detect any such particles on his skin and in his hair.

Back at the safe house in Newtownards Reagan had received the list of golf bookings of Sir Frank Cooper. Using the assumed name of Mr P. Underwood, Sir Frank had listed eight weekly sessions on the links.

It was Reagan's plan to be in position at least twenty-four hours before the Chief Constable was due to play. Near the tenth hole there was a small wood and dense undergrowth making a good laying up position, ideal for the assassination attempt. From the rear of the copse a track ran its way across country towards Larne keeping clear of the roads. This would be his escape route.

The assassin had the use of a small Honda trials motorcycle to help get clear of the area quickly; the advantage of this form of transport is speed and agility on both road and tracks. His main concern was pursuit by helicopter with armed soldiers on board. He was well aware that the military pilots were true professionals and he would be hard-pressed to outwit them. However, he was determined to be away before any of these flying machines could be scrambled.

From his reconnaissance of the golf course it was clear that the Chief Constable felt safe whilst playing there because the level of security was minimal, almost non-existent. In fact, just recently Reagan had got to within twenty feet of the police supremo in the car park while looking at golf equipment in the shop window. He was amazed that the most powerful policeman in Northern Ireland could be allowed to walk around a golf course as if he were an ordinary member of the public.

At the SAS headquarters in England Captain Rodd and his cell were ready to go, all they waited on was the final order from Colonel Berryman. During training they had covered in excess of three hundred miles on their French-built, high-quality cycles and were in good shape and keen to get underway. The only real concern that

Rodd had was, should one or more of the cell have a road accident in Ireland, what he could do about the military equipment they would be carrying in their saddlebags and panniers. As in most countries, in the case of personal injury, the police would be called and it would be a little embarrassing, to say the least, if they found firearms and ammunition. It would fall to the other members of the cell to remove any incriminating evidence before the police arrived. At a very late stage in the final planning Colonel Berryman decided to order the handguns be delivered with the rest of the team's equipment during the drop at Mace Head and this alleviated the problem immediately.

During training a slight hitch occurred when Peter Jones, the sergeant, injured his arm after being thrown during unarmed combat. He was taken to the sick bay and examined by the medical officer. Following a complete check up, which proved that there was no fracture, the arm was strapped up with the advice to rest for a couple of weeks. The Welshman had no intention of resting at all because he was not going to miss out on this unique military adventure. He intended to prove his fitness at all costs; such is the calibre of men in the SAS.

The following morning Captain Rodd was given his movement orders and was told that once in Ireland he had a free hand to carry out the mission as best he could. But he had to keep in radio contact with Hereford with a burst transmission every second day at 2200 hours Zulu time - this being the military time used wherever in the world British soldiers operate. The cell was taken by truck to Portsmouth where they boarded the ferry to Le Havre, from there on they were on their own. The crossing was calm during the early evening and they were in good spirits after having a meal in the ship's restaurant, all expenses paid.

The sea crossing to Cork however, was a much more uncomfortable affair with the ship pitching and rolling almost from the time it left the French harbour. Many of the passengers were seasick and that included members of the cell. John Peters muttered in between retching, 'Whose poxy idea was this? If I had wanted to spray the side of ships with spew I'd have joined the fucking navy. I'm a landlubber and proud of it.'

This brought about some good-natured bantering from the others. They were all glad when the ship docked in Cork and after clearing customs were soon underway towards the railway station. Almost immediately it started to pour with rain and the men struggled into their wet-weather gear. After fastening the hood of his waterproof, Mike Smith said, 'Good old Ireland, trust it to fucking piss down as soon as we arrive. It's a wonder the Mick's aren't born with webbed feet. How come we didn't get a job in the South of France with all those tits and suntans?'

In spite of the rain the men were in good spirits and keen to get away to the West Coast. The train to Galway was fast and comfortable arriving on time, after which the cell made their way along the R336 for about six miles on a beautiful sunny afternoon and soon found a good, well-equipped campsite. The tents were soon set up and a meal prepared after they had all shaved and showered.

Relaxing beside his tent Captain Rodd thought; all this and being paid for it as well. However the job ahead could have very serious repercussions if anything went wrong. In that peaceful and quiet green location it was hard to imagine that in just over a week they could be killing terrorists and destroying all evidence of their passing. Whilst in training the men had decided to grow their hair longer than normal and look just a little scruffy just as students tend to look during their travelling holidays in the university recess. One even sported a beard.

Over the next two days they broke into two groups and toured in the vicinity of Galway. A long day's ride took them to Maam Cross near where the camp was reputed to be. Rodd knew that MI5 were still following various IRA men around Dublin and Cork and his standing instructions were to telephone Hereford every two days until he received the high-tech radio that was to be delivered to them at Mace Head in a week's time. He phoned the duty room at Stirling Lines and was told that further information had since been received from the security services and the next time he phoned in it would be passed in code.

The next day was the 28th and the time had come for the cell to make their way to Mace Head and be in position to RV with the boat troop. They rose at 6am and had eaten, packed and were on the road by 7am; the early morning sun promised a fine day. Sergeant Jones' arm had been giving him trouble and this began to worry Captain Rodd. When they stopped at Scriob for lunch Rodd called Jones to one side; instinctively the Welshman knew what was coming.

'Look, Pete, I think you will have to back-pedal on this operation, if you will forgive the pun. When we go into action I want you to stay in camp as a reserve in case of trouble. I know that arm of yours is playing up and frankly you could become a liability to us if the shit hits the fan and the lead starts to fly.'

'I don't agree, boss, I can and will be responsible for myself and I don't expect anyone to help me if we run into trouble. I have come this far and I intend to see it through. As you may have forgotten, I leave the regiment in nine months time and this will probably be my last job. I won't be a passenger to the team that I can promise.'

'Actually, Pete, I didn't know you were leaving us, I was not told by company office or the RSM. Look! If you are sure you can manage, let's forget this conversation ever took place,' replied the captain now feeling a little embarrassed about the whole episode. Mounting his bike and turning to the others he said, 'I think it's about time we moved on lads, I want to set up camp early tonight. We won't be using a proper camping site so we can be nice and remote and completely out of sight from prying eyes.'

'You mean we won't have flush toilets and showers tonight, boss? I never joined this outfit to rough it. I'm a man who likes his comfort.' said Peters grinning.

'Come on, Peters, get your leg over your menstrual cycle and start pedalling, you prize prat,' called Jones laughing loudly.

As they moved off towards the headland the going became much hillier and slowed them down considerably. It then started to rain and a short time later they reached the tiny hamlet of Carna. At the main crossroads they took a left fork and headed for Mace Head. Gradually the road became little more than a track with potholes; the tufted grass growing in the centre presented a problem for the narrow wheels of their lightweight bikes. Using their Ordnance Survey maps and compasses, they decided on a direct route across country to reach the headland, carrying their machines where necessary. Finally, a very secluded pitch was found in a shallow hollow giving shelter to the tents from the westerly wind. The cell quickly set up camp and made themselves comfortable, later preparing their evening meal and a brew of tea.

In the late evening Captain Rodd held an "O" group (orders group-military meeting) and explained to the men the method of picking up their weapons and other military equipment early the next morning.

'I suggest we all get some rest now so that we are sharp and alert when the boat-troop arrives with our gear,' said Rodd, suddenly feeling very tired for no apparent reason. It had not been a particularly hard day, little more than a pleasant ride in the country. The men took turns keeping watch while the others slept. There was not a soul in sight and the peace and quiet was total.

A little before 3am and in pouring rain the signals were exchanged between the SBS boat-troop's Gemini inflatable and Rodd's men on the beach. Within minutes the small craft had beached and the waterproofed bags were taken ashore. As quickly as they appeared the two men in the boat slipped back into the water and disappeared into the night to return to their mother ship, a diesel powered submarine. No words were spoken between the soldiers and their marine counterparts. The four-man cell carried their equipment up the cliffs and back to the welcoming comfort of their tents. Within minutes they were back in their sleeping bags and fast asleep.

The early morning sun promised a warm day and the men decided to test their handguns on a secluded part of the beach. Each of them fired ten rounds and was responsible for picking up the spent cases and burying them, to rule out any chance of them being found by fishermen. Rodd had to make the usual telephone call to the base in Hereford the following day. He decided to cycle to the small town of Clifden so that he could take advantage of the direct dialling system, therefore avoiding any chance of being overheard by the local operator. This was a journey of thirty miles and a very pleasant ride in the company of John Peters; it also provided the opportunity to bring back some extra rations for the others.

During the conversation from the public call box Colonel Berryman told Captain Rodd, in coded language, the believed location of the camp. MI5 had established that it was situated just east of Maam Cross, somewhere between the N59 road and Lough Corrib. John Byrnes' team in Dublin had followed O'Rourke and O'Hagan on several occasions to this part of Connemara but dared not go any closer.

When Rodd and Peters returned to the campsite at Mace head, Rodd called an 'O' group to brief the team on the latest information he had received from the CO. The following morning they would move off and make for the wooded area near the village of Oughterard and settle into a well-camouflaged laying-up position. It was decided to scout the woods by day and move in under the cover of darkness to build their hide.

After studying the map it looked like a distance of about six miles of boggy ground and hilly, open country that they would have to traverse to reach the expected camp location at a remote farm; exactly what the SAS are trained for. Along the route there was another small wood and if this proved suitable it could provide a forward operating base and emergency RV point if the worst came to the worst. From this forward location the cell could observe the whole area with powerful binoculars including their night-vision equipment. That night Captain Rodd intended to produce at the 'O' group, photographs of the terrorists expected to be present at the training camp; these had been provided by MI5 and included a picture of Lenihan, courtesy of MI6 in London. These photographs were a welcome addition to the weapons that were delivered to Mace Head earlier.

From now on it was all systems go for the soldiers and they looked forward to the challenge with growing excitement. The next few weeks could well prove very costly for the IRA.

Chapter 7

It took the men four days to construct the concealed laying-up position; the reason was that it must remain undetected even during a possible search by the Irish army and police. In addition to providing a camp and a safe haven for the men, their weapons and military equipment were to be left there after the escape to be collected later. The LUP was built in the time-honoured SAS fashion, underground and invisible from above. All the earth that was excavated being carefully deposited around the woods and some dumped in a small lake nearby.

It was decided by Rodd to carry out a night reconnaissance of the IRA camp and test any defences that may have been put in place. It was possible that dogs might be roaming around the farm to alert the occupants of intruders. Knowing from his experience in Ulster, Rodd knew full-well that a wet and windy night was the best for the recce. Terrorists were almost certain to be indoors during such conditions and not inclined to patrol in such miserable conditions. There was a good chance that most of them would be in one of the local pubs downing Guinness and whiskey to relieve the boredom of staying in. Such is the difference between terrorists and professional Special Forces soldiers.

There followed several days of warm, clear weather

with not a rain cloud in sight so the men made the most of it by touring around as ordinary cyclists. Whenever they entered a shop Rodd spoke to Peters in French giving the impression of Gallic travellers; when it came to buying anything he would speak in English with a heavy accent to complete the guise. This worked very well in local pubs; fortunately a French speaking Irishman never challenged them. Although Rodd and Peters spoke French they were by no means word perfect.

Inside the farmhouse at the training camp, Lenihan and Ann had just finished their evening meal and were draining their glasses of good, French wine. With a few days to go before the new trainees arrived they had time to relax.

Over the last few months the ex-master sergeant's conscience had been worrying him and he wanted out; the sooner the better. Their love affair had blossomed but he had not told her of his desire to quit. One thing was certain though; he wanted her along as well. That evening after their dinner, Lenihan decided to tell Ann of his feelings about the IRA and that he intended to slip away. He was prepared to gamble on her reactions.

Although she was a member of the organisation she only had a fringe role and was never expected to engage in any form of military action except to keep her eyes and ears open in the pubs and clubs for gossip. In the early days this had included bedding the odd soldier and setting him up for assassination or knee-capping if he was a local member of the Ulster Defence Regiment.

During the evening they had a few drinks and made love on the floor in front of the fire. It was after this passionate session that Lenihan told her of his plan to leave. For several long minutes she remained silent and just stared at him before taking a deep breath and asking for another drink. To soften the blow the American told her that as far as he was concerned, he had fulfilled his part of the bargain for the IRA. He had, in fact, trained several men up to a high standard including a further man to Reagan's level.

O'Hagan, on his last visit, had told Lenihan that a high command meeting would soon be held at the farm and he would be personally responsible for the security. It was becoming clear that soon he would be required to take an active service role in the organisation and this was something he would not do at any price. After a long talk about the whole terrorist situation in Ireland, Ann agreed to go along with his plan on the condition that they left Eire as soon as possible after slipping away from the camp. Both Lenihan and Ann knew that to be caught would mean certain execution in the usual IRA method of being shot through the mouth or the back of the head depending on who carried out the task. He had not told Ann of the details of the escape plan he had drawn up in case things went wrong and he had to go alone. The couple talked long into the night and finished a whole bottle of whiskey in the process, making love for the second time in a few hours.

Lenihan was certain the house was not bugged and if fact he had carried out some simple tests soon after he arrived which had proved negative. O'Hagan was due to arrive at the farm within the next week with a month's pay for him and once he had the money he and Ann would flee the country for good. He kept the 357 magnum revolver with him at all times. To satisfy O'Hagan, he told him it was for his own protection in case the farm was raided by the Garda or Irish Special Branch Officers.

On Saturday afternoon John O'Hagan drove up the track and parked his car in front of the 1900s farmhouse. When he saw Lenihan he greeted him like long lost son.

'Hello, me old mate, it's good to see you. How's things been here then Michael?'

'Hi, John,' replied Lenihan with a smile. 'No problems so far. Ann's been looking after me real well. Come into the house and have a drink.'

'Now you're talking my language. I can see you definitely have some Irish blood in your veins, my boy,' said O'Hagan in his adopted Irish accent.

After the two men had settled in the living room Lenihan asked, 'When are the new trainees due here? I'm getting a bit bored. I'm a town boy really and all this fresh air and country living is not for me at all, John. Give me the bright lights anytime.' This was a lie but he intended to give the IRA no excuse to suspect his loyalty and therefore put Ann and him in danger.

'Well now, Mike, it's been put back a short while due to a number of things including increased Garda activity in Dublin and Cork. To make matters worse one of our top men has just been arrested in Monaghan on evidence supplied by the Ulster Constabulary. But we are not looking at more than two weeks at the most I think. The active service units in the north are crying out for more of the calibre of men you have trained so well. You have indeed done us a great service for which we will be forever grateful, Mike. In addition, I want more staff to send over to England to continue the bombing campaign in the major cities,' continued the senior IRA man. 'Now before we go any further let's have another drink and perhaps Ann could rustle up some food, it's ages since I last had a meal and I'm starving. I want to discuss something very important with you but that can wait till later, after dinner.'

Ann was asked to get some food ready and when this was done she was taken back to her lodgings in Clifden, after O'Hagan made a phone call to a local IRA man to come and fetch her in a car; normal procedure when important issues are discussed. During the evening the IRA quartermaster told Lenihan a lot about the terrorist organisation and its future objectives and why the training was so important to them. He also said that Lenihan would be called to give further assurances to the Chief of Staff at the meeting set for next week to be held at the farmhouse.

While remaining calm on the surface, the alarm bells were ringing deep inside Lenihan. He was now certain the IRA wanted him to carry out some special job for them. The American knew they would not take no for an answer. If indeed this was what they wanted, it could provide a means of escape once and for all. That night he spent a sleepless eight hours with the whole situation churning over in his mind. With Ann now in Clifden he felt very lonely in the upstairs bedroom. He decided to delay the escape until after next week's high-level meeting; he wanted to see what the IRA had in mind.

The weather had now started to deteriorate with large,

scudding clouds beginning to come in from the Atlantic Ocean. The rain soon turned into a downpour and then settled to a soft, misty precipitation. That night Captain Rodd decided the cell was to move in and take a good look at the camp. After donning their Gore-Tex over-suits, slipping their pistols into shoulder-holsters and stowing spare magazines, they set their compasses almost due west and moved off into the wet night. The going was hard on the boggy ground and the many potholes added to the difficulties encountered by the SAS men. When they reached the small wood that would serve as the forward operating base and emergency RV they decided to split up and scout in pairs. After the night's work was complete they would return to the LUP to present their findings and a debriefing with Rodd.

Captain Rodd and Trooper Peters were first back to camp, tired and wet though. Smith and Jones arrived 30 minutes later and used the SAS RV approach method in true textbook style. After a well-earned brew and some food they discussed what information they had uncovered. Rodd started by saying that he and Peters followed the track from the farm to the road and found it well-used by cars. There were no tractor or any other agricultural vehicle tracks and no signs of livestock movements along it. There appeared to be no evidence of any form of sentry or perimeter guard.

Mike Smith and Pete Jones managed to get into a locked barn and found tables and chairs set up as if the area was being used as a classroom for lectures and instructional sessions. By a sheer stroke of luck, as they was about to leave, Smith found a .223 cartridge lying in the straw near the barn door. On the desks they also discovered an Irish Ordnance Survey map of the border region around Dundalk, a map case and chinagraph pencil.

Rodd and Peters got closer to the house, which only had a hall light on and from this they were certain that the occupants were in bed, most likely sleeping off the effects of whiskey.

The cell now believed this was, without a doubt, the camp initially identified by MI5 but how many men might be in the house they of course, had no idea. Further surveillance would be necessary to be absolutely sure and to try and get some idea of the numbers involved at any one time. If there were more than six, Rodd would have to request some assistance from Hereford. The plan was now to get into a position overlooking the farm by night and spend a few days observing the premises to get a feel of the place.

Again the weather turned fine and clear in this unpredictable climate, so it was back to cycling through Connemara and enjoying the rugged mountain and moorland scenery. The cell travelled through Maam Cross up to Clifden and down the coast back towards Galway before returning to their camp.

On the second day, as they were riding along the road near the entrance to the farm, they noticed a car pulling out and heading towards Galway. It was fortunate that they were travelling in the same direction but there was no hope of keeping up with it. About five miles further along the road, Mike Smith quite by chance noticed the same car had pulled off the road and was parked in a secluded lay-by. He motioned to the others to continue round the bend and stop. Smith could not be sure if the car had anyone inside but the group decided to cycle back and stop for a snack and pretend to mend a puncture. The green Ford Sierra was empty and there was no sign of the driver. At first they assumed that he might be in the bushes answering the call of nature but after ten minutes or so decided against that prospect. A quick look at the map showed there was a small Lough several hundred yards north east of their position; could someone have gone fishing? Each pair of men had a small, radio hand-set tuned to a special, secure frequency. Rodd decided to ride off with Peters to the small copse about half a mile along the road leaving Jones and Smith to settle into the undergrowth and watch the car. They took some photographs and then made themselves scarce, melting into the greenery along with their bikes. Meanwhile Rodd and Peters made for the wood and did the same. They tested the handsets then Rodd and his colleague donned their dark green, rainproof cycling jackets and began to make their way across the undulating ground towards the Lough. The terrain was full of long, tufted grass and heavy vegetation that gave them a good level of cover and they made quick progress in spite of getting very muddy. As the Lough came into sight they spotted a man sitting alone on a large rock apparently fishing. He was tall and athletic-looking. From the photographs that had been supplied by MI6 Rodd immediately recognised Lenihan through his binoculars. The excitement inside Rodd made his heart beat so fast and loud it was surprising that Peters wasn't deafened by it.

'Rodd whispered to Peters, 'Fuck me that's him, that's Lenihan. You remember the photo's I showed you back at camp?'

'I certainly do, boss, I think you're right. I'll let the others know straightaway,' he replied preparing to use his radio.

Sergeant Jones acknowledged the transmission and confirmed that all was quiet their end. 'At last we have something. Perhaps now we can get on with the action and take these bastards out,' he said to Smith.

'I hope so, Pete. I certainly hope so, mate.'

Both pairs of soldiers stayed in their position for several hours while Lenihan continued to fish with some success before he decided to return to his car with the spoils. Slowly the American made his way back along the track to the Ford and placed the fish in the boot. After changing his footwear he sat inside the car and drank some coffee from a flask, apparently listening to the radio.

'For an ex-special forces man he's not very alert is he? Look at the way he came back into the car park. Never checked the area or the car, just put his keys in an' opened up. Now there's an opportunity if ever I saw one, Mike' whispered Jones.

'Yeah, he thinks he's safe and he's letting his guard drop. It proves one thing though, the IRA don't suspect were on to them yet. I just hope MI5 don't fuck it up by getting too close now,' replied Smith, quietly easing his numbed legs into a more comfortable position.

'No I don't think they will. You remember the boss said they had been called off and out of this area; they're just working in Dublin and Cork. It can't be a bad life they lead you know, swanning around in pubs and the like keeping an eye on people, tapping phones and listening in to government ministers talking dirty to their scrubbers,' smiled Jones with envy.

'Perhaps I'll have some of that when I leave the regiment.'

Suddenly the Ford started up and began to move slowly out towards the road, Lenihan apparently fiddling with the car radio. He turned onto the road and drove off towards the farm.

Within minutes the other two soldiers joined their colleagues in the car park; the whole area was quiet and the only sound was the twittering of the birds and the buzzing of crickets in the hedgerow. Rodd decided to return with his team to the laying-up position, deep underground in the woods several miles away and work out the next course of action. He was suddenly aware of the huge burden of responsibility the regiment had placed upon his young shoulders and the junior officer that he was.

Over the weekend the IRA top brass began to arrive in dribs and drabs and by late Sunday evening they were all present with the exception of Seamus O'Malley, from Londonderry, who had been detained at an army checkpoint at Pettigo on the border. O'Rourke decided that the meeting would commence on Monday evening at 1900 hours and take place in the main living room of the farmhouse. By this time O'Rourke should have all his notes ready and O'Malley would very likely be able to join them. Lenihan had been told to stay in his bedroom and watch television until called for by the chief of staff.

The IRA was playing it very cautiously with the American and Lenihan himself was certain that they never really fully trusted him in spite of the long conversations he had had with O'Hagan. He remembered that the pseudo-Irishman spoke in great detail to him about the terrorist organisation, perhaps more than he should have done. In his room Lenihan could hear muffled voices but was unable to pick out any part of the conversations and he did not see the entire top IRA men arrive.

Back at the LUP Captain Rodd decided to cut the telephone line to the farm just prior to the attack. Telephone failure was not uncommon in this area and it could take a week or more to repair. Rodd was certain that the farm did not have radio communications with the outside world. This was borne out by the fact that MI5 had monitored the airwaves in the area and picked up nothing of importance apart from local radio hams and the odd CB enthusiast. The SAS knew that the IRA didn't use radios very often and when they did it had always been on operational duties in the north of the country. It was comforting for Rodd to know the terrorists did not have the availability of sophisticated communications to add to their arsenal. At least not yet!

Monday morning began bright and clear but by noon heavy clouds came in from the west and early into the afternoon it started to pour heavily with increasing wind. Rodd decided that if this weather continued his cell would strike that night. During the day the SAS team studied photographs of known IRA commanders and that of Lenihan. Although at this stage Rodd had not specifically said so, it became obvious to the other men that this was to be a "seek and destroy" mission.

On Monday evening, just before seven pm, the meeting began with an opening address by O'Rourke. 'Gentlemen,' he began. 'I would like to welcome you all to our special training camp here in Connemara, in spite of the wet weather. Tonight we will discuss many things concerning the struggles and later I will introduce you to Michael Lenihan our guest military instructor. He is of course, an American with connections in Ireland. He has proved himself first class in the job and as some of you know we now have a man in the north ready to strike a blow against the English and more indirectly, that lovely lady, the Queen of the empire and her government.

'Anyway, now to begin. I would like each of you in turn to submit your reports so all of the issues can be discussed to the full. Gentlemen, feel free to add any comments you think will contribute to the overall strategy.

'John, can we begin with you my friend?' O'Rourke pointed to O'Hagan.

The meeting went on long into the night without Lenihan being called. At about 1130pm O'Hagan went up to Lenihan's room and told him he could turn in because he would not be called that night.

When the meeting finally concluded in the early hours the IRA men decided that some serious drinking was in order and a bottle of whiskey and some beer was put on the table for this purpose.

Lenihan wasn't tired and lay on his bed thinking about his future with Ann, if indeed there was to be future away from all this. About 2am Rodd gave the men a last briefing with the warning not to speak to each other during their time at the farm. He emphasised the danger of their English accents giving a clue to their identity to any possible survivors during the expected shootout. He also made the point strongly that as soon as the fifteen minutes allowed for the action was up they must depart their separate ways and make for the RV in the small wood en route to the LUP.

As they emerged from the underground hide the rain fell heavily, making the ground underfoot slippery and in minutes they were soaked. Slowly the cell made their way due west towards the farm across the tufted moorland with the gentle hills rising in the direction of Clifden. There was no moonlight and almost completely dark but the men soon got their night vision and began to make rapid progress towards their goal.

As soon as they had left their LUP, Rodd had despatched Jones to cut the telephone wires near the junction with the main road to Clifden, and then meet the rest of the team at the small woods that was to serve as the RV a little later in the operation. The attack would only begin when Jones confirmed the line to the farm was dead. It took the sergeant just over an hour and a half to complete the work and return to the RV. He was covered in mud and sweating profusely as a result of the journey across country and back to meet up with the team.

Finally, Rodd gave the order to move out in pairs; the rain continued to fall in torrents providing the team with excellent cover. The captain was certain that the terrorists would not have any guards out on a night like this; it was not their style and they were too fond of home comforts for that. It was decided to go straight in after a reconnaissance of the area surrounding the farm and eliminate whoever they could without delay. There were to be no prisoners!

As the team approached the farm they noticed a hall light on but the rest of the house was in darkness. The farmyard and outbuildings, including the barns, were quiet with no sign of life, thankfully not even a dog.

Mike Smith, the unarmed combat specialist and the youngest member of the team, began to get butterflies in his stomach. He and Jones went to the end of the house near the deserted cowshed following the plan devised by Rodd. The soldiers each carried a Heckler and Koch MP5 sub machine gun with a 9mm pistol for back up cocked and ready to fire with additional loaded magazines in their pockets along with stun grenades and powerful quartz halogen torches designed to give a floodlight effect and dazzle anyone in range. It had been arranged that the soldiers would only attack on the signal whistle given by Rodd or if they were directly engaged by the terrorists. Surprise was essential.

Rodd and Peters moved very quietly round to the back of the house and were amazed to find the back door to the kitchen unlocked. It opened without a sound. As they crept into the kitchen the two SAS men could hear loud snoring of different tones and depth but there was no way of knowing how many people were in the house. Rodd, with heart pounding, turned on his torch and blew the whistle loudly. Peters also turned on his torch revealing six men asleep on mattresses on the floor, most of them in sleeping bags. O'Hagan woke and managed to roll over and get behind a large wooden crate in the corner as the first bullets slammed into the wall beside him.

Peters began firing into the bodies on the floor rapidly turning the sleeping men into corpses with blood spurting from headshots. In an instant O'Hagan, remarkably agile for a man of his age, fired from behind the crate and hit Peters full in the face with two shots killing him instantly. Rodd made for the stairs unaware that his colleague was already dead. Smith and Jones crashed in through the front door and began moving down the hallway. As they joined Rodd at the bottom of the stairs there was a loud report from a full-bore handgun from an upstairs room. Smith fired and bounded up the 13 stairs in seconds followed by Rodd. Jones stayed in position at the bottom to guard against any sudden counter-attack from persons who may still be alive. Another loud crash followed by a muzzle flash indicated the position of the terrorist and both Smith and Rodd opened fire instantly.

O'Rourke, who had decided to sleep in an upstairs bedroom, was just dozing when the attack started. He was hit in the testicles and breastbone, the rapid burst by Rodd had reduced the Irishman's groin area to a mass of bloody pulp. O'Rourke died instantly his breast bone shattered with fragments piercing his heart.

Lenihan, who had not slept at all that night, quietly slipped out of bed during the commotion pulling the covers up to make it look as if the bed had not been used. He slipped behind a wardrobe in the corner of the bedroom. As the door of the room burst open he held his breath and said a silent prayer, certain he was next for the final shot. The two soldiers shone their torches around the room and looked under the bed. As they were leaving he heard one of them say, 'We've killed the lot of them, let's go.'

Lenihan clearly heard the flat English accent of Smith, and after a further search of the other bedrooms, bathroom and toilet the soldiers made their way down the stairs. When they met up with Jones, Rodd said quietly and breaking his own orders, 'Where's John? He was behind me when we entered the kitchen.'

Jones replied, 'I haven't seen him, boss. Could he have gone outside for some reason?'

'Let's find him and get out of here, double quick. This noise is enough to wake up the whole of Ireland.' As the men made their way through the kitchen they noticed John Peters lying across the kitchen table, obviously dead.

'Who the fuck shot him?' demanded Rodd in his thick Scottish accent.

'Dunno, boss, it was only you and him that came in this way,' replied Smith.

'One of the bastards must have got him before he slotted them. Let's make sure that there are none left alive in this shit-house, let's go, search this place inside out,' said Rodd now fearing that things had started to go wrong. Smith and Jones went upstairs and again checked out all the rooms finding nothing. Rodd went through all the corpses but found nothing unusual.

O'Hagan kept perfectly still with his pistol ready. It was tempting the shoot but he knew he would not survive if he did. He could hardly believe he had not been noticed. Like Lenihan, the IRA man clearly heard the non-Irish voices. 'The fucking Brits are here he breathed.'

Rodd went into the lounge and motioned to the other men to leave by the front door. When they got outside he said, 'One of them must have got away, but we can't leave Peters behind, let's go and get him and be away sharpish.'

The three soldiers quickly retrieved their dead comrade and made for the RV in quick time; the whole operation had taken ten minutes. They were careful not to leave behind any military equipment except spent bullet cases that had been specially prepared for the operation by the Royal Ordnance Factory. The 9mm cases had been marked with East European stamps to throw off the inevitable Garda investigation that would surely follow the attack. It was well known that terrorist organisations frequently used ammunition from communist countries often obtained through Libya and the Balkans.

When the men reached their RV Rodd examined his friend John Peters whilst the others looked on in silence. He was unrecognisable with his face completely shattered and pulped. 'He must have died instantly lads,' stated Rodd unnecessarily. 'But who shot him, that's what I want to know?'

'With all that shooting going on it's impossible to tell, boss, everything happened so quickly and what with it being dark and all that.' replied Smith obviously shaken.

'Did anyone notice the sound of a different calibre being fired during the attack?'

'Leave it out, boss, it was like a turkey shoot in there,' said Sergeant Jones realising that the mission had not been fully successful. The fact that someone had apparently got away had compromised the whole operation. Rodd was well aware that against his orders he had used voice communication, equally.

John O'Hagan waited for some fifteen minutes before moving from his position and quietly surveyed the scene. All his friends and fellow terrorists were dead. His ears were still ringing from the gunfire earlier. He decided to get away from the farm immediately and was thankful that the attackers had not thought of destroying the car outside. The Ford started instantly and he drove down the track so fast that it was a wonder the suspension didn't collapse. When he reached the road he swung left and headed for Galway.

Meanwhile Lenihan began to move slowly and quietly after he had heard the car drive away. Like O'Hagan, he was sure the British Government was involved, or perhaps an English terrorist group.

On the way back to the LUP the soldiers were glad of the heavy unrelenting rain that provided cover and helped to hide their tracks across the open country. The body of Peters had been covered in polythene to prevent blood dripping and leaving a trail for dogs to follow when the search began. As the soldiers arrived at their underground hide Smith was the first to crack.

'In future I will kill any Irishman who gets in my way, the bastards, the fucking bastards.'

'Shut up and pull yourself together, Smith!' demanded Rodd who could hardly contain his own grief.

'Sorry, boss, but I've known John for long time and I know his wife and kids. We often go out as a foursome. Who will tell Kate back in Hereford?'

'I know, Mike. But we have many things to do before we leave here. I'll get on the net to the colonel as soon as possible and let him know. He will do the rest along with the regimental Padre. Following the regiment's tradition Kate will be informed that her husband was killed on exercise and she and the kids will be looked after. Another one who didn't "beat the clock" I'm sad to say. I'll have his body returned to Hereford as soon as I can but it could be some time before the dust settles here and we can retrieve John for burial,' replied Rodd.

Sergeant Jones remained silent; knowing full well there would be an inquiry as to why it would appear a terrorist could have escaped after killing one of the men and the fact that members of the team spoke against specific orders not to do so whilst the attack took place. This would not look good for Captain Rodd or indeed him as the second in command of the cell.

When the three men were settled in their hide and the body of trooper Peters was fully covered up, Captain Rodd said he wanted to speak to Sergeant Jones outside. As they left the hide Rodd advised Smith to set about cooking them all some hot food. The two men walked away from the hide and Rodd said to the sergeant, 'Pete, as you probably gathered I'm very likely to be in deep shit when we get back to Hereford. If one of them has got away and blows the gaff to the press it will cause an international incident even if there is no proof that the regiment was involved. The Colonel and the Brigadier made it quite clear there must be no trace of British involvement. I'm dammed sure this has come directly from the Prime Minister.'

'Well, boss, I agree you – no, we - have a problem so let's discuss the best way out of it and if it's a case of bending the truth slightly at the inquiry then I'm with you all the way, you can rely on that for certain James.'

Thanks but do you think we can rely on Mike Smith to go along with it? I mean he is pretty upset at the moment.'

'I think I can reason with him, boss, just leave it to me. I mean if you go down so do we. Before we get back to the UK we must all agree on the storyline and not deviate one iota? Boss just leave Smith to me I'll sort it.'

'Thanks, Pete, I don't like telling lies but sometimes a little distortion of the truth can save a lot of heartache. It will probably ruin my career in the regiment but I can always go back to my mother regiment in Scotland hopefully. Failing that I can go into the family business of cattle rearing, if I do, Pete, you can be sure of prime scotch beef for life,' smiled the Captain.

'Let's go and eat, boss, I'm starving.'

Back inside the hide Mike Smith was well into preparing the food and tea for his colleagues. 'What's for dinner chef? asked Sergeant Jones. I'm fucking hungry and so is the boss.'

'Well I'd like to say we are having prawn cocktail followed by grilled salmon and sautéed potatoes with green vegetables washed down with a fine, white wine. Unfortunately it's tinned steak and kidney pie with good old strong British army tea laced with powdered milk. Ugh, fucking horrible but there it is boys.'

Gradually over the next few days Mike Smith came to terms with his friend's death and after a long talk with

Jones fully agreed to go along with the story they intended to tell the inquiry board should this be necessary.

The rain continued for several more days and there was no obvious Garda activity in the area. The soldiers maintained a daylight lookout from a tree position in the woods where their LUP was situated. Rodd was eager to fully brief Colonel Berryman, but although he had spoken briefly on the secure radio and in code to Hereford, he could not convey his true feelings by this method. He decided to find an automated telephone box and make a more complete report by landline but still using key code words.

Smith and Jones were to cycle up to Clifden passing the farm track en route posing as cycle tourists, but keeping their eyes open and avoiding contact with the locals. Rodd meanwhile went to Galway to use an ordinary street telephone box to make his report.

The captain approached Galway City on the N59, turning into University Road and crossing the Salmon Weir Bridge before turning right into Eglington Street where he found a telephone box. He placed his French-manufactured cycle against a railing and locked it up with a combination lock and chain. As he began to dial the special telephone number in Stirling Lines that would connect him directly with the colonel, he noticed his hand shaking and the palms sweating.

The SAS commanding officer came on the line immediately without identifying himself. He was to be brief.

'What the hell happened? Tell me as much as you dare in the circumstances. Things are buzzing at the moment; to say the least the shit has hit the fan.'

Rodd gave a concise report using as much guarded language as he could and the colonel seemed to accept this without asking too many questions; that would come later upon returning to Hereford for a full debrief.

Smith and Jones cycled around the area and noticed Garda activity had increased with a couple of roadblocks and a patrol car across the entrance to the farm track. In Clifden they bought local and national newspapers. The headlines stated the massacre at the farmhouse. The usual press theories abounded from gang warfare to drug dealers but little mention of the IRA. The local Garda Chief Superintendent was interviewed by several papers and stated that he expected to make the arrests soon of the perpetrators of this terrible crime. He'll be lucky thought Jones, a case of playing to the crowd no doubt.

After Rodd had made his call to Hereford he returned to the LUP to plan the return of his team to England.

Chapter 8

Mike Lenihan moved slowly down the stairs with the .357 magnum cocked in his right hand, already there was the smell of death and in spite of the darkness he could sense the scene.

He had just over 9000 Irish punts and 2000 US dollars that he found in O'Rourke's briefcase just before he left the house. The American could not help but admire the professional and clinical way in which the operation had been carried out. 'Jeez, these Brit sons-of-bitches really meant business; I couldn't have done better myself,' he muttered. As he stepped over the bodies he went through their pockets finding several large denomination Irish banknotes and a quality Rolex watch on the wrist of a man he did not recognise; these were placed in his pocket. Curiously he did not notice the absence of John O'Hagan.

Outside, in a barn, was O'Rourke's Vauxhall, with the ignition keys still in the lock. Incredibly the car had not been touched. He quickly checked the contents of the boot and got in, driving off smartly down the track. When he reached the road he turned left onto the T71 towards Maam Cross and Clifden. The small Connemara town of Clifden was deserted at this time of the morning and Lenihan drove straight to the house in which Ann was staying. It took several long minutes before the front door opened after repeated banging and ringing the bell. The owner, dressed in her nightgown, said stiffly, 'What will you be wanting at this hour of the morning young man?'

'Good morning lady, I'm very sorry to disturb you so early but I must see Ann, it's very important.'

'She is in bed go away before I call the Garda!' said the old lady starting to close the door.

'Please lady, I must see her right away because I have some bad news concerning a member of her family, it's her uncle down in Kerry. He's been taken to hospital and is not expected to live; I've come to take her to see him.' lied Lenihan.

'Oh all right you had better come in then, I'll make some tea. I'll get her from her bed, just go into the living room mind and wait there.'

A few minutes later Ann came into the room looking worried and rubbing sleep from her eyes. 'Mike, what's the matter, what's happened?'

'Ann can I come up to your room please I must talk to you in private, it's very important and urgent, - really it is honey.'

'I'm afraid the old girl won't approve, she has very old-fashioned ideas about men in girl's rooms. Look, just give me a minute to get dressed and I'll come outside then we can talk in the car. She's a nosey old cow,' whispered Ann, 'and I don't trust her at all.'

A few minutes later the old woman came into the room with a tray of tea and biscuits telling Lenihan to help himself saying that she was going back to bed. He poured out two steaming cups of strong tea and almost immediately Ann appeared dressed in tight blue jeans and a white tee-shirt. As she sat down on the sofa beside him he could not help noticing her nipples standing out, emphasising her ample figure. How beautiful she was and how lucky he was to have her he thought.

'Let's go outside' she said standing up with her tea. 'We can sit in the car in case she hears what we talk about, in spite of her age she has good ears and loves a bit of gossip. Come on, let's go.'

They went out and sat in the car and Lenihan began his story. He told her he was convinced it was an SAS team that carried out the attack on the farm. The sheer professional brutality of the whole operation had a specialist military signature. He added it was now imperative that they leave without delay because of the imminent danger to both of them. As the enormity of what Lenihan had said sank in, the colour drained from Ann's face and she began to tremble spilling some of her tea on the floor of the car.

'Ann we must get away right now, right out of Ireland. Will you come with me honey?' said Lenihan looking directly into her eyes.

'Of course I will, Mike, but what will I tell the old girl?'

'I've already done that, darling, you have a sick relative down south and that you must visit because he is dying.'

'She never said that when she woke me up, but then she never liked any of my family anyway. Just me, I'm her favourite,' she smiled weakly. 'I'll tell her we are going straight away and that we will be back in a few days. That will keep her happy. I must pack a bag but I don't have much here anyway so it won't take long, just give me ten minutes or so and we can be away forever thank God.'

Ann hurried back into the house and explained to Francis the reason she had to go and that she would be back soon. The old lady said she would pray for Ann's uncle so as to help him meet his maker. 'The two-faced old dragon,' muttered Ann as she packed to leave, still shaking and feeling drained.

As she got in the car she leaned over and kissed Lenihan on the cheek fastening her seat belt as he pulled away. Lenihan drove carefully through the small town and towards the T71, the same route as he came in.

'Where are we going Mike?'

'Well I think we should head for the border and make for Belfast and then fly to London. From there we could go to the States and start a new life together, well away from the IRA and all the troubles in this dammed country,' he smiled.

'But Mike I don't have a passport.'

'Nothing to worry about, honey, you won't need one for London and when we get there you can apply to the Irish Embassy for one. All embassies can issue passports to their nationals. Do you have any identity on you for the embassy? If you have it can save time and trouble in getting your passport.'

'I have my social security card and my hospital insurance certificate. Oh and my driving licence with me that should do, shouldn't it Mike?'

'Yeah I guess so, honey. Just before we get to the border I want to dump the car and cross by foot then get a bus or train to Belfast and then onto Aldergrove Airport for a flight to London,' continued Lenihan driving fast but carefully so as to avoid being stopped by the Garda in spite of the early hour.

As they drove through the lush green countryside Ann became quiet and withdrawn, just sitting there staring out of the window.

'I've managed to get quite a bit of money from the camp and with my IRA pay we should be alright until we reach the States where I have my army pension paid into a New York bank. I also have a gun but I'll ditch that before we cross the border, there's bound to be a lake or river that can take care of the firepower. Can't risk getting caught by a border patrol and being armed so don't worry, everything will be OK, honey,' said Lenihan with confidence.

It was as if Ann had not heard a word because she made no reply but Lenihan just put this down to nerves. When they drove past the track that led up to the farm he thought of all those bodies lying there and about the effect this would have on the IRA. He also wondered about Reagan and where he might be. The thing that worried him most was the fact that the killers, who had attacked the farm, may have a positive identification of him. Certainly if it was indeed the SAS then they would have had a full intelligence briefing from the British Security Service and possibly the Irish Special Branch. He was not to know that the Irish government had not been informed of the operation at all.

The couple drove through Galway without incident then headed up the N63 towards Roscommon. Lenihan decided to keep to the speed limits, difficult as it was at times, because of his hurry to put as much distance between him and the IRA as possible. As they approached Monaghan Lenihan noticed the car's fuel gauge read almost empty and pulled into a garage to fill up. Ann said she wanted to phone her sister in Sligo and made her way to a phone box situated just outside the garage forecourt next to a small post office.

Immediately he became suspicious because Ann had never mentioned having a sister before in any of their conversations. At the same time he noticed that she kept glancing at him from the phone box throughout the short call. When she returned to the car her complexion was sallow and her breathing rapid. Once again the alarm bells were ringing inside him although he did not want to believe she had betrayed him to a local IRA unit. If she had, why?

He decided they should cross the border near Mullan, and headed north on the N2 towards Emyvale. After a few miles Ann complained of feeling ill and asked him to stop the car to allow her to be sick. He remembered telling her where he had planned to cross into Ulster and then onto Armagh and then Belfast. As he was looking for suitable place to stop he noticed a car following some distance behind; it appeared to contain two men. If this was the IRA they were moving fast.

When he finally pulled into a wooded clearing at the side of the quiet road Ann was out of the car in a flash and ran to the woods retching and clutching her stomach.

Lenihan pulled his .357 magnum and in seconds the car that was following them swerved in front of his car with several shots ringing out from the passenger's window. Instinctively the American rolled across onto the front passenger seat and out of the still open car door. Moving fast he went around the back of the car and crouched behind the rear wing taking up a two-handed firing position. Several shots thudded into the car shattering the windscreen and one of the side windows; it was clear to Lenihan that these men were not professionals.

As the driver got out of the car Lenihans .357 cracked into action, hitting the young man full in the chest. Before he hit the ground, a second hollow-point bullet found its mark destroying his abdomen. Two other shots hit the Vauxhall causing Lenihan to move around to the driver's side for protection. The other terrorist was now trying to get into the driving seat of the car to make his escape. The American fired again but this shot missed and harmlessly struck a tree. The second shot penetrated the man's skull exploding the contents over the car's interior; again Lenihan fired his powerful revolver and shattered the spine. With one round left in the revolver he quickly reloaded more hollow-point semi metal-jacketed lethal bullets.

After remaining still for a few minutes he was sure that there were no more gunmen in the immediate vicinity and made his way to the wood where Ann was sobbing uncontrollably.

'Why, Ann?' Why did you tell them about my escape?' said Lenihan quietly.

'If I didn't they would have killed my family and

friends, you don't know them like I do, Mike,' sobbed Ann, 'these people stop at nothing Mike, they don't care who they kill, the murdering bastards.'

'I really thought you loved me, honey as I loved you, we could have had a good life in the States, but now it's all gone, finished.'

'What do you mean, Mike, gone? We can still escape, they are the only IRA unit in this area and now they are dead as well,' said Ann looking terrified.

'How can I trust you in the future when you have just tried to have me killed? No, honey as I said, it's all gone - for good.' The single shot between the eyes ended Ann's young life in that small wood close to the border.

Lenihan managed to get both cars off the road and out of sight; also the bodies, which he hid in the undergrowth. He decided to make for Dundalk by walking across country to avoid the roads and the local population. He crossed the road and started over the fields towards Tedavnet giving a wide berth around Monaghan heading onto Swans Cross Roads. The Irish survey maps he had proved very useful indeed. Lenihan walked all day and night covering some thirty miles before finding a deserted barn to hide up in; he was now filthy and unshaven and very hungry.

The following morning he noticed a small farmhouse that appeared to be empty but not derelict so he decided to investigate. There was not a soul to be seen and the area very quiet. After staking the house for about an hour he knocked on the front door. There was no reply so he went around the back but again, no signs of habitation were to be found. Quietly he forced a window and got into the kitchen. The place was certainly a holiday home for someone in one of the large towns towards Dublin. In the cupboard was tinned food and the fridge was full of dairy produce including bread and fruit. Lenihan had a meal and a shower finding some fresh clothes that fitted him quite well. A shave finished off the ablutions leaving him feeling refreshed and well-fed. He decided to set fire to the place, to disguise his visit from the owners who may turn up later for the weekend. The fire could be seen as an unfortunate accident, an electrical fault maybe.

Chapter 9

Liam Reagan managed to hide the Honda trials motorcycle in a shallow hollow about twenty yards off the road that ran along the southern edge of the golf course. The machine had recently been fully serviced giving Reagan the confidence that it would not let him down during his escape bid. His plan was to be in position twenty-four hours before Sir Frank Cooper was due to play and then lay low until the kill. Over the next week Reagan would use all the skills that he had been taught by the ex-Green Beret Master Sergeant to the full.

After he left the safe house in Newtownards there would be no further contact with his IRA masters until after the operation had been carried out. His other equipment included the scoped .223 Armalite rifle, a 9mm pistol, binoculars, rations and camouflaged clothing. Providing the weather held and nothing else prevented Sir Frank from playing on Thursday, Northern Ireland would be looking for a new Chief Constable. The IRA were determined to prove to the world that they could and would strike anywhere, at any time and at anybody they felt prevented them from achieving their ultimate aims, regardless of the precautions mounted by the British government.

At the SAS laying-up position, the remaining team

members were preparing to move out. They would have to leave the body of John Peters in the hide until it could be retrieved later. He was buried and the hole was filled in, carefully marked for later. After a recce of the roads around the area Mike Smith reported a large amount of Garda and Irish army patrols on the road to Oughterard and Galway. The move out would take a change of direction towards Westport and up into County Sligo and over the border into Ulster near Belleek. The original plan was to make for Dublin and the ferry to Holyhead. For some reason the road north towards Westport had no roadblocks mounted.

It was raining "cats and dogs" as Reagan settled into his hide on the edge of the golf course late on Tuesday night. He had with him, fully waterproofed clothing in disruptive pattern as used by army snipers. The scoped rifle was carefully protected in polythene, along with his other optical equipment. The trained hit man did not relish the thought of staying in position for the next twenty-four hours but this is what his training was all about. If the mission were successful it would strike a powerful blow against the British government and elevate him personally within the IRA. Reagan was certain that there would not be a thorough search of the golf course before the chief constable began his game. The reason for his line of thought was that Sir Frank Cooper did not officially play on this course and any large-scale search would blow the cover wide open.

During the night the rain ceased and the temperature dropped quite suddenly bringing a clear star-studded sky. Reagan shivered, either from the cold or the thought of being caught, he was not sure. Certainly the prospect of a long jail sentence was not an encouraging one. The whole of Wednesday passed without incident except when a stray golf ball landed near the hide and three men came looking for it. Reagan was so well-hidden that one man came to within ten feet of him and yet he was not spotted. The trio of golfers never did find their ball and soon moved back onto the greens to continue their game. The IRA informer who worked at the golf course had told the Dublin headquarters that Sir Frank was due to begin his game at 10am and as usual would be using the name of Mr Underwood.

Just before 10am Reagan had his binoculars with the specially coated lenses to prevent reflections, trained on the first tee. Soon after the man he recognised as the Chief Constable of Ulster played his first ball. It appeared that there were only two security guards with him and one of those was the caddy. On scouring the rest of the links and the southern approach road including the clubhouse, the hit man could see no further evidence of police or army activity. Sir Frank was a good golfer who had played for thirty years and along the way won many cups and trophies in police and open competitions. He liked nothing more than playing against his many PCs and junior ranks within the Ulster police. He progressed along the stages quite quickly; by the time he reached the sixth tee Reagan was ready with his rifle and in position for the kill. Just as Sir Frank was about to play the next hole, a Land Rover drove up and a police inspector got out and spoke to his chief. Within minutes both he and the inspector had driven away towards the clubhouse leaving the caddy and the other security man on the green. Some twenty minutes later Sir Frank was back to resume his game; no doubt complaining to his minders about the interruption.

The tension was rising inside Reagan and his hands became clammy with a slight tremor but his senses were as sharp as a razor. Sir Frank struck the ball at an angle and instead of following the line to the hole it veered off to the left and entered the rough. The Chief Constable swore under his breath and began to walk quickly towards the rough, straight for Reagan's position, followed by his two security men. There was no one else on the course and because it began to rain lightly the people on the clubhouse patio moved inside for shelter.

As the Chief Constable came to within 100 yards, the hit man opened fire; the bullet struck Sir Frank Cooper in the throat killing him instantly. The two security men went for their guns and one got on the radio for assistance. Reagan managed to shoot the caddy but was unsure if he had killed him. The other security man began to panic and ran into a small copse. Reagan had to make his move now before it was too late. He ran for the edge of the golf course, made the shallow hide and onto the trials bike in record time. It started instantly and he sped away leaving the binoculars but retaining the rifle and pistol; the rifle across his shoulders on a sling.

The well-planned escape route took him across the fields towards Buckna and then on to a wooded area near Carnalbanagh. The Honda was hidden along with the rifle and pistol and camouflaged clothes. Reagan was picked up by an IRA car and taken to a safe house in the village of Millbrook. In no time at all the police and army helicopters were all over the skies and all the local roads were quickly blocked by patrols. The port of Larne was completely sealed off. Reagan had a hot bath and washed his hair several times to remove any traces of nitro-cellulose from the spent bullets. He then went to a local hairdresser and had his hair styled into a crew cut. All his remaining civilian clothes were burnt in the grate of the safe house. There were police everywhere carrying out house-to-house checks.

The death of Sir Frank Cooper was not announced until the following day when it became world news with the IRA High Command in Dublin claiming responsibility. The terrorist organisation was jubilant.

In London the Prime Minister wanted to know why this senior police officer was allowed to wander around a golf course without adequate security. The Land Forces Commander Northern Ireland, Lt General Sir Richard Housland and senior Special Branch officers including the SAS commander in Ulster were called to Whitehall for an urgent meeting with the Minister of Defence. Clearly heads were about to roll over this incident. As a matter of course the assistant Chief Constable for the province became acting Chief Constable and took full control of the police action. The Prime Minister called an urgent meeting of all his advisors and made it clear answers were expected within 24 hours. Unlimited resources were put at the disposal of the security services but results had to be forthcoming. Several high-level resignations were also likely.

Chapter 10

Alan Conlon, the IRA informer, was contacted by MI5 and told to stay at home and behave normally for the time being. He was placed under constant surveillance by British counter espionage until they were sure it was not a set-up. Conlon was told to arrange a holiday for the family at a holiday camp in North Wales where he would be contacted. Two days after he arrived he was taken to a safe house in Surrey for interrogation. If he thought he was in for a quiet time he was mistaken. The next week was to be the hardest and most unpleasant of his life.

Reading the papers in Ireland he was convinced that all at the farm had been killed by persons so far unknown and did not realise O'Hagan and Lenihan had escaped. The British interrogators were far from kind and welcoming, but hard and threatening with constant reminders that he could be taken back to Ireland and exposed to his former colleagues in the IRA. This would mean certain death at their hands. Before any form of guarantee could be given as to his safety and future he was going to be bled dry of all information and methods used by the IRA. If he thought he could pull the wool over the interrogators eyes he was sorely mistaken, these men and women were experts in their field and brutal if needed. He had never been more frightened in his life. Meanwhile a watch had been put on his family in the holiday camp.

John O'Hagan made his way to Tralee in the south west of Ireland where the IRA maintained a safe house. When he arrived he was shaking and pale with shock at coming so close to being killed and the ferocity of the attack. He was certain it was the SAS, but how did they discover the location so accurately? In spite of all his attempts to maintain secrecy they had found out and as a result several senior men in the organisation had been killed. Was Lenihan among them? There had to be a leak somewhere, but where? In the papers there was no mention of any form of military action but the suggestion that rival factions of the IRA were responsible for the massacre in the remote farmhouse. The Garda had identified several known members of the Republican movement's high command during subsequent investigations. O'Hagan remembered the English voice at the time, it had to be the SAS he was convinced. This voice would come to haunt him.

Sir James Overton briefed the weekly meeting of all current intelligence on the situation in Ireland and advised the Prime Minister directly, a rare and unusual precedent. No mention was made to the meeting of direct SAS involvement because this had to be maintained as a black operation. This would not be leaked to parliament because to do so you might just as well inform the national newspapers. Many MPs willing to condemn or expose any situation if they thought it would improve their own positions and standing. The deputy director of MI5 mentioned that an IRA informer was helping them with some aspects of intelligence and the Minister of Defence wanted full details of the results written in a report to the defence subcommittee. Sir James resisted this with vigour and was adamant that if this report was insisted upon he would resign. Experience had taught him that reports of this sensitivity always got into too many hands and destroyed years of hard intelligence by people who simply did not understand the importance of maintaining secrecy. It was a constant battle of which he was becoming tired, retirement was 18 months away and it couldn't come quick enough.

Alan Conlon was being held in a state of isolation by the MI5 interrogators who showed absolutely no regard for his comfort or wellbeing. Instead of welcoming him as he expected they were positively hostile. Now they had him there was no going back, that's for sure. Conlon told them all he knew about the IRA and the American, which in this case was very little; he did however managed to confirm Lenihan's name and previous military experience. What he could not tell them was what happened, or where the trainees were sent after their course was completed. The IRA high command worked on a need-to-know basis and he was not included or trusted with this information. MI5 was not convinced with Conlon's explanation and continued to threaten and encourage him for more information. In the basement of the country house the chief interrogator was patient and unrelenting in his quest for information.

'Mr Conlon, you do realise you must tell us everything you know or the consequences for you are bleak to say the least. If you do not help us further we have several options open to us as I shall explain. The first one is we could kill you now. Oh please do not underestimate us, my Irish friend, we do not follow the letter of the law here. We are a law unto ourselves. When we deal with ignorant, selfish bastards like you we have a free hand, with official approval. The second option is torture of the most unpleasant kind with or without drugs and the third is to simply hand you back to your people, need I say more? What I can tell you is we are considering all three options at the moment so you had better decide what you want to do and very quickly indeed. My patience is running out, Mr Conlon. So I will leave for a short while whilst you decide.'

'But sir I have told you all I know. I really have'.

'I don't believe you at all, Mr Conlon, what I think you are doing is holding back certain information or deliberately being economical with the truth in the mistaken hopes you may get a better deal from us. In this you are very much mistaken. Clearly what you expect is a new identity, money and all the benefits that have been afforded the soviet and communist bloc spies in the past. You come nowhere near them with the small amount of information you have passed to us over the last few days. Think again Mr Conlon.'

'I have told you all I know. How many more times do I have to tell you that? The IRA only asked me to help them with the training at the camp. I was not taken on by an active service unit afterwards; I have never been active with the movement, ever. I was asked to help because of my knowledge of explosives, a skill I learned with the Irish army during my nine years service in the engineers. Lenihan was not impressed with my skill and told not only me, but the high command in Dublin as

181

well. I thought they were going to kill me themselves at one point but John O'Hagan is an old friend of mine from back when we served with the UN in Cyprus and this probably saved me from the hard liners. Believe me, sir they would kill their own mothers if they thought it would help the cause or their own future in the republican movement.'

'You're lying Conlon, you are a lying, evil little bastard and I am going to break you and in turn destroy your family so don't expect any favours from us, do you understand? The only way out for you is to tell us all you know and be quick about it.'

At this point Conlon was shaking like a leaf and deathly pale losing control of his bowels and retching violently. The chief interrogator left the room and the light was extinguished leaving the bare basement, cold and eerie, with just the sound of footsteps disappearing up the stone stairs. It had been hours since Conlon had eaten and he felt weak and tired. It was clear that MI5, or whoever they were, were far more brutal than he had been led to believe. Meanwhile Conlon's family, back at the holiday camp, had been told he was unwell but being cared for and not to ask any further questions. This was more of a threat than advice or information.

John O'Hagan had a sleepless night at the safe house in Tralee and had a severe headache, more like the migraines he had had in the past but thought had now ceased. The IRA resident had called the local doctor, a medical practitioner who had attended many republican injured in the past and who was trusted to keep his mouth shut. The additional threat on his family, particularly his daughter at university in Limerick helped to keep his lips sealed.

'Good morning, Mr O'Hagan. What can I do for you? I must say you look a little pale and drawn.'

'Hello, doctor, good morning. Sorry to bother you, but I have the most king size of a headache and feeling very weak and a little shaky.'

'Have you been eating properly lately, indeed have you been overdoing it, working too hard without sufficient rest?'

'Well, doc you could say that but I have also felt unwell for some time.'

'OK let me check your blood pressure and take your temperature.' When the checks were completed the doctor said, 'Well your blood pressure is rather high but the temperature is normal. Are you on blood pressure tablets or any other kind of medication?'

'No I have always been well and as far as I know healthy. This has happened all rather suddenly you see.'

'I'll need you to have some further tests at the hospital to make a better diagnosis, blood and urine tests to be sure. You are a little overweight and I guess you do little exercise. Am I right?'

'I'm afraid so, doctor, but in my line of work I don't have very much spare time or indeed the inclination for exercise.'

'I won't ask what you do for a living. In fact it's none of my business, but I will give you a letter for the local hospital. When you have had the tests please call me at the surgery after about a week, and we can then decide what to do for you. In the meantime rest as much as you can and take plenty of fluids, but not the alcoholic variety do you hear?'

'Ok thank you, doctor. I'll be in touch. Thanks once again for coming. You will be paid in the usual way. Good bye for now.'

The doctor left the house and went back to his surgery thinking why he ever got involved with the IRA in the first place; once they get their hooks into you they never let go. Many years ago his misplaced loyalties made him a useful target for the republicans and of course his medical skills have been well used ever since. If only he could get away from this pressure, perhaps telling the Garda might be a good idea but then he would be charged with aiding and abetting the IRA, an outlawed terrorist organisation. What would happen to his family? This was one subject that did not bear thinking about.

Chapter 11

Alan Conlon woke with a start when the door of his room crashed open and tried to focus his eyes in the sudden light of the powerful torch that shone straight into them.

'Get up, you Irish bastard. You and I are going to have a little talk, or rather you will be doing the talking. Do you hear me, Conlon?' said the chief interrogator turning on the main light.

'Why are you treating me like this when I have told you all I know, I thought we had a deal?'

'We don't make deals with terrorists, Conlon and especially not with snivelling little bastards like you. It's obvious you were not happy with the way you were treated by the American, sort of lost face if I'm right, Conlon, am I right, you fucking low-life? Thought you would get a new identity and a pension from the British Government for life didn't you? Wrong, Mr Conlon, you could not have been more wrong, my friend from across the water. Unless you tell me everything I am going to throw you to the wolves in a manner of my choosing. Either way you will not see you next birthday or the jolly old Emerald Isle again. On the other hand I might just turn you loose in Belfast after putting the word out that you're back in town. It depends on you, Conlon, so what do you want to do?'

'No it's not like that, sir you know that. I have told you all in know. Please believe me. I don't have any more information to give. Please, I am telling you the truth. I'm begging you.'

'How long have you been with the IRA?'

'About fifteen years overall, but only low level, never on active service but training'.

'What training did you carry out and where did you provide this?'

'Mostly explosives and weapons training in the Wicklow mountains until this was discovered by the Garda.'

'Where did you receive your own training and over what period did all this take place? I want locations, time span and how you were recruited into the IRA, Conlon. You had better tell me the truth because I won't just be taking your word for it, I shall check with other sources.'

'I was in the Irish army and initially based at the Curragh training depot. I qualified as an explosive expert and later I took the weapons instructor course and then based in Galway, training the Ranger Company. When we were sent on UN duties I went to Cyprus and served two years there on active duty, you know patrolling the flash points along with other UN troops including the Brits. This is where I met John O'Hagan. He was a sergeant in the British army at the time, I was also a sergeant. When I returned to Ireland they sent me to Kildare and then to Lebanon, again as part of the UN contingent for six months, alongside the Americans based in Beirut. I was later promoted to staff sergeant and based again at the Curragh in the training wing and ended my service there. I came out with an exemplary record and for a time lived in Dublin before moving to my present home. I was recruited by O'Hagan when he found out I had left the army, by this time he was well and truly into the IRA. I believe he had been a member for years whilst still in the British army but I don't know this for sure.'

'Carry on, Mr Conlon. I'm all ears.'

'With regard to the American I know nothing whatever about him except he was Special Forces and served in Vietnam. I believe a war hero, whatever that means in this day and age. The training camp set up in Connemara was very secret and I had no knowledge of it until I was required to assist with the training and recruits.'

'You must have known something, Conlon. You must have known what the training was for and who the recruits were and indeed where they were to be sent. Don't tell me you didn't because I don't believe you?'

'Believe me, sir I didn't and still don't know. All I was told was that my experience was required and that I had no choice in the matter. I was to assist in the training and when it was finished I would return home and carry on as normal.'

'So why did you not finish the training? Why were you sent home early and by whom?'

'The American told me I had to train with the other lads, all this running and physical exercise and all that. I protested and he then said my explosives knowledge was not up to date. He clearly did not like me and wanted all the glory for himself. We had a fight and he nearly killed me. If it hadn't been for the others present he would have done, I have no doubt about that, sir.'

'Who organised this camp, Conlon and what was the purpose of it? You have other training locations in the republic, why was this one so special?'

'I don't know, sir, I really don't, but it's a very remote location in Connemara, an old farmhouse near Maam Cross.'

'Who else was present at the time you were there?'

'Well, apart from O'Hagan, there were visits from Sean O'Rourke the deputy Chief of Staff, and others I don't know, but I think from the Dublin high command and one from the north.'

'Did you know the names of the recruits?'

'No I wasn't given that information at any time, sir.'

'I don't believe you, Conlon. Unless you spill the beans completely I will kill you myself and it will not be pleasant I can assure you. Do you understand?'

'Sir, believe me, I don't know anything else. I swear it on my mother's life.'

'Your mother's life? That's worth nothing to me, you lying, Irish pig. I don't trust you as far as I can throw you, do you understand?'

The vicious kick in the ribs ended the interrogation and the room was again dark and cold as the door was slammed shut. Conlon lay on the floor sobbing and completely drained of all comprehension, feeling his life was to end soon. He started praying to a God he had ignored for years.

Lenihan decided to make for Cork and try to get a ferry to France and eventually return to the States. Because of the clearly professional attack on the farm- house at the training-ground it was better to avoid England altogether. From his previous experience in the military he was sure this attack was carried out by the British SAS or the Royal Navy equivalent, the SBS (Special Boat Service). Making his way towards Dundalk he travelled across country by night and lying-up during the day. At this early stage he did not want to risk public transport but when he finally reached Dundalk the train to Cork via Dublin seemed inviting. The further he could get south the safer it should be by his reckoning. The first thing to organise was some new clothes and shoes as he had again become muddy and dirty during his cross- country travel. As he entered Dundalk he came across small men's outfitters in a parade of shops and thought this might just be the place to fit himself with some new clothes.

He decided to break in during the early hours when the town was quiet; there were no obvious signs of an alarm system but he couldn't be sure. Watching the shop at closing time he noted the owner leave after locking up at 5.30pm and walking away towards the town centre and go into a pub. As he was hungry Lenihan managed to come across a fish and chip shop and as he went to order he managed to disguise his voice to that of a German accent. The shop assistant didn't give him a second glance and served him his meal with a smile and a cheery word. After leaving the shop Lenihan found a park and settled down to eat hungrily.

As the evening drifted into darkness Lenihan decided to find some place to hide up, so as not to arouse suspicion from locals by hanging about the town. He looked a little dishevelled but he could imagine the locals would put this down to him being an immigrant farm worker. What Lenihan did not realise, was that Dundalk was an IRA stronghold with its position close to the Ulster border. The local IRA cell were always on the lookout for strangers as the British army often sent Special Forces units into the republic without the knowledge of the Eire government.

As he sat in the park eating, a local IRA activist noticed him and was immediately suspicious of this somewhat untidy character eating and constantly looking around, clearly nervous.

Sean McKenna, a Dundalk man, phoned his local IRA commander and voiced his concern at this stranger and asked what he should do. He was told to keep the man under surveillance and await further backup from the local active service unit based in the town. For about 20 minutes Lenihan remained where he was then decided to walk around the town to get the lie of the land and find the railway station he would need the following day. McKenna found it strange that just a single man alone would be operating in the town as experience had told him the Special Forces always worked in small groups. Could this man be an agent of the British Security Service?

Although not an educated man McKenna knew his town well and had a feel for sussing out odd strangers, his intuition had served him and the IRA well over the years. Although he would have liked to have risen in the IRA hierarchy he was destined to remain low level. His everyday job as a builder gave him good cover for his fringe terrorist activities and provided him and his family with a provable income. Not always the case with more senior IRA men and women. Living without an obvious form of income attracted the Garda Special Branch and occasionally this brought about an investigation or even a raid on their homes. They were also an obvious target for British Intelligence and when discovered, abduction and possible execution by the SAS when officially sanctioned.

The British Government's cooperation with the Garda was somewhat sporadic and unreliable at times, the

British view was that there were many IRA sympathisers within the Garda and this made them unreliable to deal with when it came to terrorism. The same was thought of the Irish Republic Defence Force and subsequently proven on a number of occasions. For years the British government had asked for support on the Eire/Ulster border but the Irish Army often seemed lukewarm in their assistance.

As Lenihan moved off towards the town centre McKenna started to follow him at a discrete distance. Walking slowly, Lenihan took notice of landmarks and passed the pub where the shop owner went earlier for his homeward-bound drink. A car drove slowly down the main road leading to the town centre and then turned around again and went in the opposite direction; this was immediately noticed by Lenihan and he became suddenly acutely aware of possible danger. In the car were three IRA men including the local commander, Mick Flatherty, a former Irish army private.

'He looks like a farmhand to me, Mick,' said one of the men. 'I can't imagine the Brits using someone like that here. They know we are always watching for strangers.'

'Sean is suspicious and quite rightly informed me a little while ago on the phone,' replied the commander.

'I don't trust the bastards but we don't want to go over the top and clobber one of our people. I don't mean to upset the local people as we rely on them a lot for information and if we are wrong, this could backfire locally on the cause,' continued Mick.

'After all that trouble in Connemara recently we have to be careful because we don't know where the Brits will strike next, assuming it was them who raided the camp,' reflected Mick.

'I think we might well be over-reacting a little. Why don't we just pick him up have a little talk and decide what to do on the basis of that, this could all be nothing and we could apologise to the gent and wish him well, what do you think boys?' said Mick.

'Let's do it,' said the driver, 'and then a nice pint of Guinness or two to round off the evening.'

Lenihan decided to make himself scarce, just in case, as the alarm bells were well and truly ringing now as the car turned yet again. As he rounded a corner he noticed a small alleyway and sprinted down it into a small road that led to an industrial estate and a scrap metal merchants'. Quickly scaling the fence he raced to the far side of the yard and hid amongst the wrecked cars to get his breath. 'I'm getting too old for this crap,' he muttered. 'If the IRA catch me I'm dead meat because they will think I grassed on them,' he pondered, looking for a way out of this predicament. The clothing shop is now out of the question, he thought, getting out of town is the priority and as far away as possible.

'The bastard's disappeared,' said Mick, 'where the fuck could he have gone? This looks pretty dodgy to me, boys, we must get him and quick.' Leaving the car the three men began to search the immediate area including going down the alleyway. They were soon joined by McKenna who told them all he knew and offered to help in the search

Lenihan waited for a while and as all seemed quite in the surrounding area he decided to move very cautiously toward the fence on the far side of the yard. As he began to move he heard the sound of heavy lorry's air brakes hissing from within the industrial estate and this gave him an idea. In the industrial estate there were several warehouses and some had lorries backed up to loading bays, with men and forklift trucks working to load goods, no doubt for a number of locations within Ireland. He had to try and find a lorry heading for the south preferably Cork. He managed to get through a hole in the corrugated fencing and into the estate.

During his surveillance he managed to overhear a conversation between a driver and loader, the driver saying he was looking forward to some fishing near his home town of Crosshaven after dropping his load in Cork docks. He could hardly believe what he was hearing, his luck was in he hoped. As the lorry was only about half-loaded it gave him time to decide how he was going to approach either the driver for a lift or stowaway in the back. Fortunately it was an articulated trailer with canvas sides that are held in place with a plasticised cord passed through loops all along the sides. He decided to climb into the trailer and hide whilst the driver was completing his paperwork and having some tea before the journey to Cork. He hoped it was direct with no drop-off points along the route.

The IRA men were baffled as to where the scruffy man had gone and they could only assume he had gone into a house, but which one? There weren't many houses in this area but there were some small flats and rented rooms mostly for staff at the industrial estate. He could be anywhere. They were in a predicament as to what to do now as he had either deliberately or accidently given them the slip. How could he know they were after him?

If they tried to carry out a full search of the local area it would surely attract the attention of the local Garda. On top of that it would also incur the wrath of the IRA Chief of Staff in Dublin for the unwanted attention. On the other hand if they were found out letting a potential spy or member of the British Special Forces get away, kneecapping would surely follow, possibly even death after an IRA court martial.

Mick gathered the men together and said, 'Look boys we have lost this bloke and we don't know if he is someone who shouldn't be here or not. Why don't we forget the whole thing and go to the pub? What I would say to you all is that we must keep this to ourselves and not mention it to any other cell, otherwise our bollocks will on the meat-grinder for sure. Sean, will you keep your eyes open tomorrow and for a few days to see if he surfaces again? If he does we will get him next time.'

'I certainly will do that, Mick you be can rest assured of that,' said Sean with all the sense of drama he could raise.

Later in the pub and after the beer was flowing, all the supposedly professional standards of the local IRA Active Service Unit were beginning to slip. The owner of the man's outfitters shop nearby had heard all this loose talk before and knew the men by name and their dubious reputations. Perhaps he should inform his brother, who was an inspector in the Garda in Dublin of what he had heard that evening.

Lenihan managed to get close to the truck by slipping under an adjoining vehicle, climbing into the trailer and making himself comfortable for the journey to Cork. After about an hour the vehicle pulled out and started down the motorway towards Drogheda and onto the ring road around Dublin. Soon after approaching Kildare the driver pulled into a cafe for his scheduled break and a welcome relief for Lenihan. A couple of hours later the truck pulled into the docks in Cork and was allocated its unloading bay - number 14.

Ex-Master Sergeant Lenihan had to make his escape quickly before unloading began and became concerned about the number of people about. It was now or never. Still dressed in his dirty clothes he slipped out from under the curtain sides of the trailer and casually walked away towards to the ferry port section of the docks.

Chapter 12

Liam Reagan was restless at the safe house in Millbrook and wanted to get away as soon as possible; he didn't trust fully the family who was charged with looking after him. The port of Larne was well and truly sealed off as were all the ports in Ulster so there had to be another way of getting out of the country, even if it meant simply going into the republic for a while. He could possibly melt into the academic crowd in his old university of Trinity College Dublin, even though he had been expelled by the Dean for his extremist views and republicanism at the end of his first year. He still had many friends in the area. He even had a passing thought he might well be able to get reinstated and continue his original course and leave the IRA behind once and for all. The idea of a Masters Degree followed by a PhD later appealed to him.

Reagan decided to go to a local swimming pool to further his cleansing of gunpowder from the cartridge case residue that could still be on his body following the shooting of the chief constable. He wanted to take no chances in case he was picked up by the police and subjected to a forensic examination. The extended time in the water and the effects of the chlorine all helped to eliminate the chances of residue being found on him. He also wanted to keep fit and this entailed running each day for 5 miles around the local footpaths. He didn't drink or smoke.

The whole province was well and truly under security clampdown with police and army patrols on the entire major roads particularly those leading to the border with the republic. Several stretches of the coastline was being patrolled by the Royal Navy especially around Rathlin Island and the area where it might be possible to cross to the Kintyre peninsula of Scotland by small boat. It was clear to Reagan that any form of movement was going to be difficult until the dust settled. After returning from his latest swim at the pool he decided he must get away from the safe house and travel south.

'Where have you been today Liam?' asked Mrs O'Malley, the landlady of the safe house.

'Oh just for a swim, love, and I must get another run in this afternoon as I like to try and keep fit. All the good food you serve me is no good for my waist line even though it's superbly prepared and cooked,' replied Reagan. 'There is one thing I must tell you though, Mary, can I call you Mary?' Mrs O'Malley smiled and nodded. 'I might have to leave very soon and without much warning, so I hope you'll understand and not take offence. You know how it is?'

'To be sure I understand,' she said with a little sadness in her voice as she had quite a fancy for this young republican from Dublin.

'When you go just let me know and I can always pack you some food and drink for the journey, wherever that may be. But in the meantime there's a good film on TV tonight and I would like to invite you come and sit with me and watch it. It starts at 7.30. My son will be out all evening and I have a bottle of Bushmills, which I know you like,' said the 40-year-old landlady, whose husband left her some years ago and was currently serving time in an English prison.

'I'd like that, Mary and will look forward to it, see you later and thanks.' Reagan knew instantly what her motives were and thought he might as well indulge while he had the chance.

Later that evening, he went into the sitting room and was pleasantly surprised to find Mary wearing a short black skirt with a tight, light green tee shirt that emphasised her ample figure. 'Good evening, Mary, wow! You look fantastic.'

'Away with you now, I bet you say that to all the women, now sit down and I'll pour you a drink and we can watch the film.' Reagan took a place on the settee and Mary sat beside him and handed him his drink. She switched on the television and selected the correct channel moaning about the adverts that seemed to go on forever.

'I don't know what you do in the movement and I don't need to, but please be careful out there, Liam, not all our brothers-in-arms are trustworthy and we have always had informers. The bastards are usually caught and dealt with swiftly by the active service units locally. There was one a little while ago who was shagging a RUC girl in Belfast and passing details of a local unit's activities. He was taken out into the countryside and shot through the mouth; quite rightly so in my opinion.'

'It's an ongoing problem we have to deal with, Mary

and that is why we try to keep these things on a need-to-know basis; limits the chance of leaks.'

'I know, Liam and please don't think I'm prying because I'm not and never would.'

'Don't worry, Mary. That's why you were recommended to me and I'm glad you were because apart from being a really good cook, you are beautiful and very kind with it, my love.'

'I don't know what to say, Liam; I am quite overcome with your compliments'.

'Put your glass down and come here, I need a good woman and you are just that, darling.'

Their love making went on for a couple of hours and the film forgotten. Later Mary went to the kitchen to make some coffee and had a glow of satisfaction on her face and a feeling of total wellbeing at the outcome of her invitation to watch TV. All this and getting paid for it, brilliant she thought.

While sipping their coffee Mary asked, 'Do you have any idea when you will be going? Not that I am in a hurry to see you go, far from it, please stay as long as you like, my gorgeous lover boy.'

'I will have to be away soon but I want to see you again in the not-too-distant future.'

'Oh yes please, Liam, you are really something special, and what a performer, I have never had sex like that before.'

'Well there is plenty more where that came from, darling. Just be patient, my love. If you'll excuse me, love, I have to go to bed now as you've worn me out, but what a way to be worn out, Mary. Goodnight sweetheart.'

'Goodnight, love. I'll have your breakfast ready for about nine.'

'Great, see you then, goodnight.' Reagan went to his room and began to think of an escape route out of Ulster and a greater chance of safety. Did he want to remain in the IRA or not? If he decided to try and leave officially he would almost certainly end up dead in a ditch with a bullet hole in his forehead. The IRA rule was once a member, always a member.

The following morning Reagan sat down for breakfast and read several of the national newspapers. The headlines all mentioned the assassination of Sir Frank Cooper the Chief Constable of the Royal Ulster Constabulary. The IRA had already claimed responsibility by a coded message to the BBC in Belfast and was gloating over their success. Again they stated their ability to strike at the very heart of the British establishment at any time of their choosing. Mary had noticed his keen interest in the newspaper articles and said, 'What a success that was for the cause, don't you think Liam?'

'It certainly was but the province will be hot for some time yet so the units will have to be very careful for a while. The big problem is some of the boys get pissed in the pubs and clubs and can be a bit loose with their tongues, as we have found out in the past, my love.'

'But surely this particular job would be very close to the chest of the Chief of Staff in Dublin and carried out by a professional, not some skinny, spotted youth trying to prove something.'

'That's true, Mary but you never know who else knows and the British MI5 and MI6 have ears everywhere these days. They are not averse to offering money and a safe passage and a new life, free from prosecution, to informers who pass useful information leading to convictions in the high court,' replied Reagan deep in thought.

'I hope you are not involved, Liam. I couldn't bear the thought of you being caught and sentenced to 30 years in jail or being killed by the SAS. Please tell me you're not, my lover.'

'Of course I'm not, love, but I have to lie low for a time because I'm a member of the IRA as you know and there's a witch-hunt on at the moment by the Brits.'

'Liam, I was told by the local commander to house a fellow member for a while until the dust settles but of course, not told the reason. But the more I see you reading every article in the papers concerning the killing; I am getting vibes that you might be involved in some way.'

'Shut up! You are stepping over the mark and if I reported you I think you know what would happen, so from now on keep your mouth shut and concentrate on running this safe house. Do you understand, Mary?'

'Liam, I'm sorry. I did not mean to pry but I'm worried about you, my love.'

'That's as maybe but I don't want to hear another word from you about it, OK? Not another word is that fucking clear?'

Liam, I'm sorry, darling,' she said bursting into tears and running into the kitchen, shutting the door behind her. Reagan decided to leave right away and pondered if he should inform the IRA hierarchy of his concerns about Mary O'Malley. Perhaps he should.

The A8 road out of Larne was heavy with traffic from the port and the Belfast- bound bus Reagan was on was running late; the police and army road blocks did nothing to help. When he arrived at Belfast central bus station he was relieved to find security minimal and a taxi to the station was caught without any problem. The Dublin express was due to leave at 1.30pm so he had plenty of time to grab a cup of expensive but mediocre coffee before boarding. Again he thought of the conversation with Mary at the safe house and decided to call his IRA contact, using a public phone box. He had a feeling everyone was watching him but it was probably just him being over cautious. He made the call and explained the concern without overstating the facts. The person on the other end just said OK and rang off. The whole conversation took less than a minute.

The Dublin train left on time and the journey pleasant but anxious for Reagan, as he felt exposed, even though the security measures by the police and Garda were minimal. The main thing was to act normal, he reassured himself, as he made his way to the main exit of the station. Needing the exercise he decided to walk to the university and do a little shopping at the same time. He needed toiletries and some underwear and socks. He realised the recurring stomach pains he had had for years were now becoming much more frequent and persistent. He put this down to stress and the pressure he had been under for sometime although not entirely convincing himself of this theory. His thoughts went back to his visits to the doctor in Monard, his home town in Tipperary, and the appointments at the specialist hospital in Cork. The doctors had said he should grow out of this and yet were unsure of the cause. Over the years they had definitely got worse and his consumption of painkillers had increased. Subsequent visits to the doctor drew a blank as far as a diagnosis was concerned and he was just advised to continue with paracetamol as required. An hour later he knocked on the door of an old college friend and was welcomed with open arms.

'Sean, where in hell's name have you been? I've not seen you for ages. Come in and sit yourself down while I make us some tea.'

'Thanks, Patrick, yes it's been quite a time since I got the chop from the university. I really would like to reapply for admission. Do you think the Dean would wear it?'

'Well I don't know, my friend but there might be a glimmer of hope you know. We have a new Dean, an Englishman, formally of Christ's College Cambridge and a bit of a radical it would seem. He has made it known he had sympathies with the communist students of the time before the cold war; you know Philby, Blunt and McLean and has clear ideas on republicanism in Ireland. He could be your opening door, Sean.'

'I'll try and get you an interview, but a word of warning, don't try and bullshit him as he is very sharp. Just be up front and pray that he sees it your way. Just one last thing, he's gay so you had better keep your hands in your pockets and your back to the wall unless you have gone over to the other side while you've been away,' smiled Patrick pouring the tea, genuinely happy to see his old friend again.

'That's great, Pat. My next problem is to find somewhere to stay for the time being.'

'Sorted, my friend, I have a spare room but no listening through the wall when Maire comes round for a bit of nooky. You never know we might make a threesome one evening,' said Pat.

Reagan moved into the spare room and made himself comfortable but took another two paracetomols to ease the pains in his stomach before lying on the bed and trying to decide his future in the IRA.

The local active service unit near to the safe house in Millbrook decided to pay Mary O'Malley, the landlady of the safe house, a visit. It would not be a social call.

Liam Reagan got his interview the following Tuesday with the dean of the university. As he made his way to the Dean's office he was apprehensive and unsure how far to go regarding the republican views he held, undoubtedly he would have to explain why, in his view, he was expelled by the Dean's predecessor; it would of course be all in his file.

'Good morning, Mr Reagan nice to see you. Please come in and make yourself comfortable.'

'Good morning, Dean. Thank you for allowing me to come and see you.'

'Now, what can I do for you?'

Liam Reagan explained in great detail how he felt about his dismissal from the university and his overwhelming desire to return and continue his studies. The dialogue with the dean included the state of republicanism that exists in Ireland and it was clear that both the Dean and Reagan shared many common views on this subject.

'Well, Mr Reagan you have put your case to me very well indeed, I need time to consider all the facts, but in the meantime my advice to you is to get stuck into your books and my office will be in touch with you within the week.'

'Thank you, Dean. I will look forward to hearing of your decision.'

Reagan left the office feeling positive and keen to return to full-time study. His immediate problem was how to extricate himself from the IRA. Getting back into university could be the easy bit. Getting out of the IRA would be a whole lot more difficult...

Chapter 13

In Dublin, the IRA Chief of Staff, Colm MacDiarmid was furious with the news of the devastating attack on the training camp in Connemara and the loss of his deputy, O.Rourke. He had his immediate staff gathered in a room above a dry-cleaning shop off O'Connell Street in the city centre.

'We know O'Hagan got away because he is in Tralee getting medical attention but what happened to the yank? That's what I want to know. Reagan obviously completed his task by stiffing the Chief Constable of Ulster and made the safe house but he has now left and we have lost contact with him at the moment. He passed some worrying news about the integrity of O'Malley and she has now been dealt with by the local unit. Alive but somewhat the worse for wear I'm told. We won't be using her services again nor would she want us to. The local boys are keeping an eye on her, just in case.'

'Do you think the yank's blown us to the Brits, Colm?' asked Kevin Dempsey, one of the quartermasters, 'it seems strange he has just disappeared off the face of the earth at the moment.'

'I just don't know, Kev, but one thing is for sure if he has and we get him you know what will happen? The one thing in our favour I think is the fact he hates the British because of that problem he had with one of their officers shagging his wife when he was stationed in Germany. I understand she died following a back-street abortion.'

'If he has done the dirty deed on us he will have been spirited away by now to England and safety, Colm.'

'Another problem we have is Conlon, who has also gone off the radar; you may remember he was a trainer at the camp serving alongside Lenihan. I never did fully trust that bastard,' said Dempsey lighting yet another cigarette.

'Now hang on a minute, Kev. We don't know what's happened yet but we need to be very careful for the time being. It's likely the Intelligence Service will be all over the place including the Republic, MI5 in particular.'

'In spite of all this, one thing is for sure, we were successful in knocking off the north's chief peeler in the most spectacular way, and for that we must thank Regan no matter what,' said Padraig Meehan, an IRA bomber.

'I can't understand why Reagan has gone to ground without telling us where he is. I can understand his leaving the safe house but disappearing completely is a mystery indeed. We can't be certain it's the SAS that raided the camp because as I understand from a Garda friend, they found dozens of spent 9mm bullet cases carrying East European markings, similar to the type we use. You will remember, boys we get a lot of our stuff from Belgium, or at least through Belgium, originating in Serbia but coming via Libya. One of our brave men, you know, had just recently returned from Belgium after negotiating a deal was tragically killed in a road accident near Kildare after spending some time briefing O'Hagan at our farm in Ballymartle,' said the Chief of Staff, pouring out large Jameson's whiskey's for all present.

'We would like to think that was an accident, but I'm not so sure. Unfortunately, we can never prove it, but I wouldn't put anything past the SAS, MI5 or MI6. All rotten to the core as far as we are concerned,' replied Meehan.

'Speculating and wondering will get us nowhere so let's have some constructive comments as to what we do next in this never-ending war, boys,' said the chief of staff.

'I think Conlon's been lifted because not only as he disappeared but so has his family,' said Dempsey. 'That's not quite true, Kev because I authorised a short holiday for him and his family at a holiday camp in North Wales where they are now, at least as far as I know. Let's check to make sure the family are enjoying their holiday. If he is missing, interrogate the family as to his whereabouts. Padraig, organise that straight away will you and keep me informed on a daily basis,' said MacDiarmid.

'Do you think this raid could have been carried out by the Protestants Loyalist Paramilitaries rather than the Brits, Colm?'

'I don't. They don't have the tactical skills and training required for the level of damage that was caused at the time. My Garda contact said the carnage was awful with clear, precision shooting. I'm convinced it's the SAS or similar and they were fucking good and very professional,' said MacDiarmid.

'But not professional enough to allow O'Hagan and Lenihan to escape, Colm,' said Meehan.

'No that's true I agree, so it makes me wonder really who the hell was responsible. I'm still certain it was the

Brits. They have two units who are trained to carry this sort of thing out and that's the SAS and the Navy's SBS. It's very doubtful that either of the Security Services are capable of this, my friends,' said the Chief of Staff, about to wind up the meeting.

'One final thing, boys, contact all active service units and put them on their guard and ask everyone to keep their ears to the ground for anything useful to us here in Dublin. On top of that contact our cells in England, in particular the Kilburn area, to listen out in the pubs and clubs for any gossip or facts regarding MI5 or Special Branch activity locally. I want to know everything that goes on, is that clear, boys? One final thing, there is to be no action anywhere until I personally give the orders,' concluded the Chief of Staff. 'Have a safe journey home, gentleman.'

Alan Conlon's wife was terrified by the two men who woke her up in the middle of the night at the holiday camp in Wales.

'Where's Alan my love?' said one of the men with menace in his voice.

'I don't know I swear. I have been told he's ill and getting medical treatment.'

'Where? What hospital? Did he have an accident? Was an ambulance called? Come on, Mrs Conlon, don't fuck about with us we don't have time for games,' said one of the IRA men giving her a firm smack across the face.

'I've told you I don't know where he is, I swear it on my children's life, I don't know,' she sobbed.

'If you don't tell us where he is both you and your

children won't have a life to swear on. So for the last time, where is he?'

'Some men came and spoke to him two days ago and he seemed worried at the time but said nothing to me but I could tell he was on edge. They came back later and took him away saying he was ill and would get medical treatment. I was told to say nothing and just stay here with the kids and act normally; you know the beach, arcades and candy floss, the sort of things families do on holiday.'

'Were these gentlemen police or army, Mrs C?'

'I don't know. They seemed quite pleasant and polite; they never showed any sort of police badge or anything like that.'

'Do you think they were from the British Security Services, Mrs Conlon? I assume you know of your husband's activities for the cause?'

'I know he is involved but he never speaks to me about it; never has. I just have to put up with it and have done for years. I should have left him ages ago and started a new life,' she said shaking and now looking very pale. 'You know, I'm fed up with all this "cause" thing. I've lived with it for years and I've lived with him all these years. Believe me, when this is over I'm taking the kids and will be gone for good and good riddance to it all - and fucking Ireland!'

'Mrs Conlon it will be over for you when we find out what's going on and where he is, not until; is that clear? In the meantime you will keep your mouth shut and say nothing to anybody. If he returns let us know on this phone number. If you don't, we will kill not only him, but you and the kids as well. Mrs Conlon we are not joking! If there is a good explanation for everything then you and the family will be allowed to return home in safety. Just remember what I am saying, is that clear, my little Irish Coleen?'

'OK, OK, you've made your point. I'll co-operate for the sake of my kids but fuck the "cause" and all who work for it.'

'Very wise, very wise indeed, remember what I said earlier, say nothing to anyone,' said the IRA man.

Both men slipped out of the French windows and away into the darkness of the holiday camp carefully avoiding the lit roads and squares. They quickly found their hidden car and made their way to Liverpool and the safe house in Aintree.

The MI5 A4 surveillance branch man posted to keep any eye on things at the camp and in particular Mrs Conlon and the family finally woke and sleepily gazed at his watch, it was 04:10. All seemed quiet at the chalet. The chalet he was in had a clear view of the area and the Conlons' chalet in particular but he was bored stiff and had read his novel until he could no longer keep his eyes open. He hated night duty and longed to get home to bed and into the arms of his new wife.

Mrs Conlon could not get back to sleep and made herself a cup of tea. Oh, to be out of this entire nightmare, she thought.

Alan, her husband, was still under interrogation at the Security Service's safe house in Dorking, Surrey. The basement had been converted into separate rooms with basic living facilities but the doors were always kept locked and the windows covered in steel sheeting so requiring the light to be on at all times. He was convinced he was not going to come out of this alive and another thought crossed his mind, he might be handed over to the IRA. This would be certain death in the most vile of ways. The senior interrogator came into the room and suddenly became quiet and polite with his prisoner.

'Mr Conlon, I have been thinking about you, my friend, you have had a pretty unpleasant time whilst being our guest here and we would like to put matters right and make up to you for the way you have been treated. How would you like to be given a new identity, not only for yourself but for your family as well? This would include new documents such as passports and other papers to allow you to go abroad and start again. Spain is popular and there are large Irish and other European Communities on the Costas where you could integrate without difficulty. We would take care of all the arrangements and monitor your progress and give advice where needed. Housing is easy to come by but you would have to be sure your family are in agreement and go along with the new identity. Unfortunately, teenagers can be awkward about this, especially if they have close friends at home or girlfriends or boyfriends in tow. I know your children are aged eight and ten so it should be easy enough to overcome this.'

The informer was staggered; he was convinced this interrogation could bring nothing but grief for him and his family. 'I was certain you were going to hand me over to the IRA because you thought I was not telling you all I know and now this. Of course I'm interested in having a new life and sooner the better. When can we start the process? Just say the word.'

'Just a minute, Mr Conlon, to ensure your safety we have to go slowly, but I'm sure you have things at home you will want to attend to before you all go abroad, because I'm sure you realise this would be a one-way journey for all of you. What we propose is for you to return home normally and let the dust settle. Visit your doctor with some fictitious symptoms for him to treat, our doctor here can help you with that, and follow your employment for at least a few months. No one knows you are here so when you return all will seem normal and the bonus for us is that you may get to know of other activities that your countrymen might be up to until we extract you.

'Mr Conlon please believe me when I say we want more intelligence from you. Should you try anything untoward with us you will meet your death without further warning and the future of your family would be in the hands of the IRA; rest assured we would engineer that for you. I would hate to speculate what their reaction would be,' said the interrogator with a cold piercing stare straight at him.

The IRA informer felt a cold shiver run down his spine and his palms became sweaty with fear. 'I knew the Brits were hard but never this hard and ruthless,' he said, his voice trembling.

'Because of people like you, Mr Conlon, innocent members of the public and our military are dying, and believe you me, we will stop it. Whatever it takes and whoever we sacrifice, we will stop it! Any IRA man or woman is expendable as far as we are concerned and you're no exception. Just wanted to make that clear and leave you in no doubt, so what do you say to my proposal now?'

'I have no choice, do I? I'll do whatever you say.'

'Very wise, I'll get things moving this end and you will be returned to your family in Wales tomorrow morning. Not a word of the happenings here do you understand?'

'Yes of course, you can rest assured I will do my best for you.'

'I expect nothing less, you will not see me again but we will be watching you constantly and will contact you when the move is due. Just be normal when back in Ireland and let everything take its course. Goodbye. Oh just one thing before I go, if you are contacted by the IRA, ring this number and pass us the details. It's manned 24 hours a day, your code name is "Eagle." One slip-up by you and your exit from this world will exceed your worst nightmare. Goodbye, Mr Conlon.'

The journey back to Wales was tense and lonely as the two men in the car would not talk to him and made it clear they despised all he stood for. When he entered the chalet he was met with pure venom from his wife who was in no mood for explanations.

'Where the fuck have you been, Alan? You will disappear once too often one of these days.'

'My love you know I have to keep my mouth shut on Republican business but I have some good news for you at last, We are going to start a new life abroad with all expenses paid and be free from the IRA once and for all.'

'Who told you that? You know you can't leave the Provo's just like that, they would hunt you down in no time, you idiot. The next thing you know you will end up in a ditch with your head blown off. Remember what happened to Joe Riley a few years ago? executed in a wood in Donegal and his son kneecapped in Belfast. If you want that go right ahead, what about me and the kids, don't we count for anything, you bastard?' said Mrs Conlon shaking like a leaf.

'It won't be like that, love. I have a plan, at least one suggested by the Brits. They have said they will help us all the way and look out for us until the time we leave Ireland forever.'

'So where are we going, none of us can speak a foreign language and what about schooling for the kids, how do you think they are going to settle into a strange school, not being able to speak the language?'

'They will be ok, my love because kids soon learn to speak a foreign language. Mixing with other children will soon sort that problem out.'

'That's all very well for you to say that, but what about us as well, what will you do for a living?'

'I have told you the British will take care of everything so don't worry.'

'Do you really think those bastards will look after us for the rest of our lives, because I don't? People like us are expendable, Alan. As soon as the dust settles they will leak information to the Provo's and we are dead meat. I am not going to put my children in that kind of danger for anyone, especially you. It's you that got us into this in the first place and for what?' You were never going to be a big fish in the movement no matter what. Look, you were kicked out of the training camp in Galway by that yank. I don't know why you didn't get the message then. When you joined the IRA all you did was make it worse for us all. You really have ruined our lives with all your grand ideas and now we are all going to pay the price.'

'Look, my love all we have to do is to go back to Ballybrittas and carry on as normal for a month or two, then when we get the word from the Brits we go, they will take care of everything, they promised, we have no choice. We are assured of an income for life and other help as we need it. All will be fine, my love, believe me. They have told me we will get a new identity and passports so when all the fuss has died down we will be able to travel elsewhere on holidays and perhaps go eventually to Australia or New Zealand where language is no problem.'

'Why can't we go to Aussie straight away, at least we will be thousands of miles away from the start. I don't fancy Spain at all, it's not far enough for a start, Alan?'

'Let me contact them in London and see if they would agree to Australia with immediate travel rather than go back to Ireland,' said Conlon shaking with fear at the thought of going back to his country of birth.

The following morning Conlon rang the number of MI5 and gave his code name of "Eagle" and was put through straight away to a controller who didn't give his name.

'Hello, this is Alan Conlon and I would like to speak to someone in authority please.'

'You are doing that right now, what can I do for you?'

'As you know I have been offered a new identity and the chance to go abroad. Spain was mentioned but this is not suitable because of language and culture so can we go to Australia instead, and immediately?' asked the former Irish army NCO with an edge of panic in is voice.

'The short answer is no! You have to realise that Australia involves a lot of extra cost and organisation where as Spain in simpler, cheaper all round.'

'But I have been promised full protection and relocation abroad and I want to go to Australia,' demanded Conlon.

'Mr Conlon you must remember that the information you gave us was not high quality and we could have obtained it elsewhere soon enough. It's not as if you were a Russian nuclear spy with really valuable and vital intelligence to give us was it? You must realise the IRA has many leaks and informers and we get what we want sooner or later. The information you gave us was low grade and therefore you will receive help commensurate with that, take it or leave it. Do as you were told and all will be well!'

With that the line went dead. Conlon was left reeling and now panic was really setting in, what was he going to do? When he got back to the chalet from the public phone box his wife was waiting for him anxiously.

'Well what did they say?'

'We have to go back home and continue as normal until they contact us, we have no choice, these people don't mess about and they are not open to negotiation. Basically it's take it or leave it and that's that. Remember they also want me to inform on the movement for as long as we are at home. If I don't give them something they may well get really difficult, they have all the odds in their favour, we have nothing. If we are not really careful we will all end up in a bog with bullets in our heads, make no mistake about that, my dear.'

'Why can't we go on the run now and fuck the movement, we could manage somehow surely?'

'My love don't be daft, we have no money, no prospects and we may well have the IRA and MI5 after us. No it's not an option, we have to go back and do it their way.' The end of the families break was due and the return to the republic was foreboding, especially for Alan Conlon. What sort of reception would he receive in Ballybrittas?

As the family walked down the ramp off the ferry in Dun Laoghaire and through immigration they were met by a man they didn't know.

'Hello, Mr and Mrs Conlon, did you have a good holiday?'

'Yes, but who are you?'

'Ah, now that's a question you don't need to know, but I'm to take you home where someone is waiting to talk to you, my friend.'

'Who's that then? asked Conlon with fear in his heart.

'An old friend, don't worry about it. Come on let's get the wife and family into the car as the traffic is getting worse by the day around here and we have a way to go. Ballybrittas isn't it, Alan?'

The journey through the suburbs and joining the M7 towards Kildare was rapid and trouble free in spite of the heavy traffic at that time of day. As the car approached the R445 turn-off for Ballybrittas Conlon was becoming increasingly anxious at the thought of meeting a senior member of the IRA if that was to be the case. He knew the interrogation methods they could employ and he would not be able to resist their methods. Perhaps he was just over-reacting, but he was extremely worried nonetheless.

As his home came into sight all seemed normal and he noticed even the grass in the front garden had been cut; he trod the pathway to the front door with trepidation. His wife and children were ushered in and the girls went straight to their bedrooms to unpack, his wife to the kitchen to make a cup of tea. Mrs Conlon decided not to tell her husband of the visit she received in Wales from the IRA.

The driver who had brought them from the ferry terminal stood by the car looking around suspiciously as if waiting for something to happen then suddenly, without any explanation, drove off back towards the main road. Conlon could only wait and try to anticipate his next move as the man he expected to be at the house simply was not there. He was sure this was all part of the IRA mind game they had played so well and effectively in the past. Although he was a fringe member of the terrorist organisation and used only for his military skills, he knew there were some very clever people at the top and they did not suffer fools gladly. That evening nothing happened and he retired to bed exhausted with all the worry of the past few days, both with the republicans and MI5.

Part of his instructions from MI5 was to contact

them on his arrival home or at least as soon as he could get to a public telephone without arousing suspicion. As he may be under surveillance he had to be very careful in everything he did for either side. He was certain he could not go to his IRA masters and confess, this would be certain death; on the other hand he could claim he was captured by the security services and threatened by them. The Brits would move when it suited them and not before and their offer being Spain, basically take or leave it with no other options open to him and the family. He discarded the idea of coming clean with the IRA as they would almost certainly believe he was a double agent and would feed him to the dogs in the most grotesque fashion. The only choice was to brave it out and continue with his job locally whilst awaiting MI5s instructions.

In London's Great Marlborough Street offices of MI5s A4 Surveillance Branch, the Conlon case was being reviewed by Counter-Intelligence officers along with their SAS colleagues and Special Branch detectives. As usual a representative of the Secret Intelligence Service, MI6, was present.

'Gentlemen,' said the MI5 man, 'we are sure the Conlon family were not, to coin a phrase, "got at" while in Wales as we had them under observation at all times throughout their stay. Of course you all know the results of his interrogation at Dorking. Low key stuff but it did plug a few gaps we had about this training camp in Galway and enabled a plan of attack to be activated, albeit only partially successful. The military did of course suffer a loss during this action. Did we kill all the terrorists? I'm not sure, not sure at all,' said the case controller. 'Out of interest has the body of the SAS man been recovered yet? I know it was deposited in the hide they were using.'

'It has indeed, and a discreet military funeral will be held in Hereford with Trooper John Peter's name inscribed on the clock tower in traditional SAS fashion. He failed to "beat the clock" as they say in the regiment. There was a delay in extraction from Galway because M Squadron SBS tasked with it was tied up at the time and our own boat troop is in Gibraltar, all now resolved,' said the SAS major present.

'So, gentlemen, where do we go from here?' said the case controller. 'Everything has gone a little quiet, I have reports from our people in both the North and South of Ireland, including phone tapping in both parts of the country, just domestic rubbish really, certainly nothing of interest to us. Even MI6 have nothing although they are working with the CIA to try and see if they can glean any further information on this Lenihan fellow. Our colleagues in Europe are also checking their files for any connections with the Foreign Legion or Basque terrorists and such like.

So, gentlemen, we wait for Conlon to contact us and see where we go from there I suppose,' he concluded.

Alan Conlon decided to go and see his local doctor and invent some medical complaint that would tie up with his sudden disappearance from the chalet in Wales. When he got to the doctor's he decided to collapse outside the surgery waiting room, therefore causing a bit of a commotion. The doctor attended immediately and helped him into the consulting room.

'Good heavens, Alan what is the matter with you?'

'I don't know, doctor this happens quite frequently and without warning.'

'Ok I'll give you a complete check-up and maybe refer you to the hospital in Kildare if necessary, so take off your shirt and let's get on with it, my friend.'

After carrying out a full medical the doctor was a little perplexed as he could find nothing conclusive. 'I can find nothing physically wrong with you so it could be a case of nerves, have you had any problems lately that might cause this?'

'No, doctor not really, just the normal domestic worries that we all have I suppose but I do get these sudden head pains and feel weak, such as I experienced just now.'

'I think I'll refer you to Kildare Hospital to see a specialist and a possible scan to see if there is anything I may have missed. Not to worry, leave it to me and the hospital will be in touch in due course with an appointment date for you. In the meantime perhaps you should not drive.'

'Thanks, doctor for all your help and I'll leave the driving alone.'

Within ten minutes Dr Murphy had briefed the IRA intelligence officer in Dublin about his patient's condition. 'Do you think Conlon's trying it on?'

'It's difficult to say at this point but he is very uptight and anxious at the moment, that's for sure,' replied the doctor.

'Keep us informed,' said the IRA man, 'and don't forget the promise you made to us about keeping all this to yourself. I'm sure I don't have to remind you of the consequences, should anything go wrong, my good friend. By the way, how are your wife and grandson these days?' he added chillingly!

The doctor came off the phone and flopped down at his desk, sweat forming on his brow. 'What bastards they are, he hissed, why did I ever get involved with them in the first place?' He had treated many terrorists with gunshot and blast wounds in the past and was in far too deep to get out now. They had him in a firm grip which showed no sign of easing.

When Conlon got home his wife questioned him on his visit to the doctors and what the doctor said to him.

'Why are you always interrogating me, woman? I'm out for five minutes and as soon as I get home you start, bugger off and mind your own business!'

'Don't you take that attitude with me, Alan, you got us into this mess and you will have to get us out of it,' she shouted so loud that he feared the neighbours could hear everything.

'Shut up, you stupid cow and keep your voice down for Christ's sake.'

'Don't you mention the Lords name in vain in this house, you hypocrite. Mass on Sunday and blowing someone up on Monday, it's all the same with you lot, ignorant bastards. You had better watch your step, Alan Conlon because if you cause me and the family any more trouble I'll shop you to those murdering thugs you're supposed to work for so help me I will!'

'Calm down, my love, everything will be fine, believe me. The Brits will get us out of here soon and we need never see Ireland again or those 'murdering thugs' you mention. I want out as well you know.'

223

'Just make sure you don't mess this up, Alan,' she said quietly with fear in her heart. As she set about cooking the evening meal a fear of impending doom descended on her and she began to weep silently.

Chapter 14

At the headquarters of MI5 in London the deputy Director of the Security Service, Sir James Overton had just started the weekly meeting when he was interrupted by a member of staff. Following a whispered message in his ear he halted the meeting and apologised to all assembled that he would have to leave the room for a few minutes. In another office he was briefed by the head of the surveillance unit keeping a watch on Alan Conlon.

'Good morning, sir, sorry to disturb your meeting but it looks like the Provo's are going to get Conlon and no doubt take him away for questioning, probably in a republic safe house. We know they have several and the one in Dundalk is the most likely, it's been used quite a lot recently and we have it under constant surveillance. How would you like us to act? For instance, just let it go or ask the SAS to intervene? Clearly we can't get the Garda involved.'

'I agree using the Garda is not a good idea as our relationship is not all we would like it to be at present. I think the best way forward is to let the Provo's take him and just keep up the surveillance. The other alternative is to abandon him and his family to the IRA and let nature take its course if you see what I mean. We all know it will be certain death for Mr Conlon and heaven knows what will happen to the family. It's a cruel world, Harold as you well know. I think in the circumstances let him be taken and keep on their tail until further notice.'

'OK, sir will do, we'll give you regular updates as we get them.'

Sir James returned to the meeting and passed this information to the assembled members of the government and military and police representatives. Lt Colonel Berryman, Commanding Officer of the SAS, decided to make his point straight away by saying, 'Gentlemen, I'm glad the decision has been made to let Conlon be taken to the safe house because if my men had to go so deep into the republic to snatch him the risks of detection increases with each mile. We are certainly capable to carrying out such a task but the nearer the border the better and Dundalk is very close to the Ulster border.'

'I understand your point, Colonel but we have to be ready for any situation and if we decide a snatch is necessary when could you be ready?'

'We are ready at one hours notice as I have a team from D squadron in Aldergrove Airport as we speak. If any back-up is needed I can get another team from Hereford to the province within four hours. I also have members of the Parachute Regiment Special Forces Support Group, who we have specially trained within that regiment, in Derry, and so you can see, everything is set to go. It's just we need to minimise the risk of an international incident by sending men into the Republic unless we have to.'

'I do understand the implications, Colonel and will bear in mind all you say. Gentlemen, something I would like you to consider is our old friend John O'Hagan who, it seems, unfortunately got away from the raid we mounted in Connemara. We don't know if he was injured or not but it's likely he was because it was apparently a bloodbath on that farm. Remember he is English by birth and technically a traitor; he served in the British Army under the UN flag in Cyprus. The British Government want him badly by any means possible. I have asked Sir Claude Foster here for any help they can give us as he's certain to be in the republic somewhere and sooner or later he will surface. When he does we will have him bang to rights!'

'Sir, do we have any further information on the American who's obviously done a runner?' asked Commander Collins of the Special Branch.

''Fraid not but my guess is he will want to leave the Emerald Isle at the earliest opportunity. We have all possible surveillance systems in place and have alerted the CIA but as you all know their help can be very selective. French Intelligence has promised assistance and I must say they do seem rather cordial at the moment. It must stem from the information we gave them regarding the situation in West Africa, following which they launched paratroops from the Foreign Legion to rescue French priests and nuns and a few civilians from that mission near Kinshasa,' added Sir James.

'Do we have any updates of IRA activity in and around the pubs and clubs of Kilburn?' asked the Deputy Director.

'Sir, it's been quiet for a bit apart from the usual money collections and republican song nights when they all get pissed. Oh sorry, sir, please excuse my language, it was a slip of the tongue.' replied the surveillance team leader clearly embarrassed.

'Not to worry, old chap I do understand, keep your ear to the ground because we need as many leads as we can get at the moment. I am getting some stick from the PM and Home Secretary over the assassination of Sir Frank Cooper and in addition, the association of Chief Constables' are jumping up and down demanding personal protection. We can't protect all 40 plus of them. Gentlemen please make all possible effort to locate the main protagonists so we can deal with them, the PM has given me a completely free hand in this matter,' concluded the deputy Director.

Sir Claude Foster of MI6 leant back in his chair and stretched before speaking. 'Gentlemen we have had some success in tracking down the IRA arms supplier in Belgium. You may remember their man had a "fatal accident" in Kildare following his return from a purchase there some time ago. A Peter Riley I understand, a family man from Naas in County Kildare. Why apparently decent people get mixed up with terrorists is beyond me. However, the arms dealer was Rashid Aziz, a gentleman of Arab descent, who had dirtied his hands for years in the shadowy world of weapon and explosives supply. I say "had" because he has apparently upset some Basque group in Bilbao over a deal and was found floating in a river near St Jean de Luz in France with two bullet holes in his head. This came from Spanish Intelligence so we are sure it's reliable. The trouble is one door closes and another opens and this we believe will be the Balkans. With the demise of Yugoslavia the whole region is awash with weapons of all types and endless supplies of ammunition, so here we go again. The IRA has connections with the Czech Republic and in turn we know they have a Balkan contact or contacts; we just don't know who at the moment.'

'Thank you Claude, I'm sure you will keep us posted. I know there has always been rivalry between our respective services but it is counter-productive at the end of the day and we must work hard to overcome it for the good of the country and I'm sure we will. That is all for today, gentlemen,' concluded the deputy Director General and the group began to disperse to their various offices.

As Lt Colonel Berryman was about to leave, the MI5 deputy head called him to one side. 'George could you spare me a minute of your time? I would like to have a word in private and this is for your ears only and I didn't want to mention this in front of the others as it's rather delicate. You know how politically correct the police are and with Commander Collins present I thought it inappropriate for his ears. Come to my office and we can speak freely as Julie will keep all intruders at bay. She even frightens me at times, she's not married and perhaps she ought to be; a good man might tame her a bit perhaps,' smiled the DG.

Once in the office the DG got straight to the point. 'George, the PM has given me carte blanche to kill or capture the assassin of the top cop in Ulster and we are pulling out all the stops to locate him. When he is finally located would you be able to liquidate him on a black operation? I wouldn't normally ask this of you but we have to show the IRA we mean business and kill the bastards without mercy. Any operation must look as if the killing is internal and we could provide all the necessary disinformation you need. What I suggest is that once he is taken care of, we leak information that he has informed on his own kind and we will arrest a couple of low-life's in Belfast to back this up. You know the score; bring them to London for questioning.

'The name we have is Mr Liam Reagan; or so we believe, from County Tipperary and quite a brainy type by all accounts. Our friend Alan Conlon has squealed, albeit with a little encouragement and our relocation department is dealing with him now. You may remember I mentioned it earlier in the meeting today.'

'Yes, sir I fully understand, and to answer your question about a black operation, I do have a special unit who can deal with that sort of thing and it will be very convincing using the methods the Provo's use to silence their informers. This will guarantee to cause dissent within the ranks of the organisation to our benefit. Just say the word and we will do the necessary.'

'Thank you, George. By the way, how much longer before your retirement?'

'Oh eighteen months yet but I'm looking forward to it after 34 years in the army.'

'What will you do when you finish?'

'The garden will benefit and we will go on the planned cruise that I have managed to put off for years, but my real passion is fishing and coupled with the beauty of Scotland will see me sitting on a windswept beach on a west coast shore, fishing. Hopefully I may even catch a nice cod for dinner, who knows.'

'Ok, George I will be in touch in due course, take care old chap,' said the DG opening the office door. Oh just one last thing, George, will you be at my masters installation in the lodge next week?'

'Just you try and keep me away,' replied the Commanding Officer of the SAS with a smile and a Masonic handshake.

Chapter 15

Liam Reagan awoke in the night with severe abdominal pains and as he vomited he noticed small traces of what looked like partially digested blood in the contents of his stomach. 'I must get this sorted out before it kills me,' he muttered in between retching.

'What the hell's the matter with you, Liam, you look terrible, my friend?' asked Patrick when he came into Reagan's bedroom after hearing the retching which seemed to resonate right through the house.

'I don't know, Pat but I've had this for years and the doctors in Monard and Cork can't seem to find out the cause but it's getting worse I'm sure.'

'There's a good doctor in the faculty of medicine here in Trinity College. I will get him to give you the once over tomorrow.'

'I don't know about that, Pat. I need to keep a low profile because although you may not know, I have been in the movement for some time and trying to extricate myself and that's not easy. Apart from not being easy it can be fatal as they often remind their people.'

'That belly ache you have will be fatal if it's not sorted, Liam. Let me speak to Dr Connolly tomorrow, he's a good chap and will keep his mouth shut I'm sure, leave it to me. Do you want anything such as a drink or painkillers?'

'Just some paracetomol will do, that usually dulls the pain and if I can get back to sleep I will be OK in the morning, really, Pat.'

'OK but call me if you need anything else.'

'Thanks mate,' said Reagan now feeling weak and exhausted.

The following morning Reagan, now a bit better, decided to just have some dry toast and tea for breakfast. Pat had already departed for the university but left a note for his flatmate stating his intention of speaking to Dr Connolly. Later that day Patrick rang Reagan and asked him to come to the university clinic for a private consultation with Dr Connolly.

Reagan was apprehensive for two reasons, one what the doctor might find, and second he was technically on the run from the IRA with all the consequences that could bring. He really did not need all this complication, but what alternative did he have? When he got to the clinic he went straight into Dr Connolly's consulting room and found the doctor middle aged and very amenable and pleasant.

'Well, Mr Reagan what can I do for you? I must say your friend Patrick is very concerned about you.'

'I know, doctor, I have had stomach pains ever since I was a child and was under the hospital in Cork but they found nothing specific. They said I would grow out of it but I haven't. In fact it seems to be getting worse.'

'OK tell me about your habits and diet, do you smoke?'

'No never have and I drink in moderation and then it's only white wine. I have always tried to avoid fatty foods although I'm not a vegetarian.'

'Would you remove your shirt and loosen your belt and just pull your trousers down about two inches so I can feel your abdomen.' Reagan felt very apprehensive about all this and where it may lead to. What if the IRA found out and where he was staying?

Dr Connolly carried out a full examination and took a blood and urine sample. 'I'm going to get you to have a scan. This can be done tomorrow and the sample results should be back in a day or so, Mr Reagan. I suggest you get dressed now please.'

'What do you think, doctor?'

'Well it's difficult to say at the moment but I can feel something we call a mass, the scan will tell us more and then I can decide what I'm going to do for you. I will have my secretary phone you when I have the results. Try not to worry too much at the moment as I'm sure all will be well in the end.'

Reagan thanked the doctor and went home to the flat, worried out of his mind as to what the test results might show.

When Patrick got home that evening he wanted to know what had happened at the surgery.

'Well, Pat I had a full examination and a blood test then I had to piss in a bottle, but other than that, I now have to await my fate. The doc's secretary will ring me for another appointment and take it from there I suppose.'

'How about we go out tonight and have a few beers, down near the waterfront? It'll do you good.'

'No, Pat I will give this one a miss as I want to keep a low profile at the moment.'

'Liam are you in some sort of trouble with the Garda?'

'No, Pat I'm not, but as I said earlier I was with the movement for a while and I need to keep out of the way for the time being. Now I really can't say anymore, Pat, so please don't press me further, my friend.'

'OK I understand, not a word, now what are we having for dinner tonight, do you fancy a KFC from down the road?'

'Pat, that would be good, thanks mate.'

Reagan had a disturbed night and was glad when the first light of day appeared through the curtains. He got up and went into the kitchen to find Patrick up and dressed. 'Morning Pat, you're up early, what, did you piss the bed?'

'Liam, I'm worried about what happened last night.'

'What do you mean?'

'Well in the bar last night I heard your name mentioned by a bloke who I know, or I suspect is in the IRA and he was talking to a small groups of others I don't know, but it would appear they are trying to locate you. One of them seemed a bit aggressive but then they went on to something else and some more people came in. After that it got a lot noisier so I couldn't hear any more. Liam are you in trouble my friend?'

'Pat, can I tell you something in confidence?'

'Of course mate we've known each other for years haven't we?'

'Well I am a member of the movement, you know what I mean, but I'm keeping a low profile at the moment because of a little job I had to do for them some time ago. I am not at liberty to say what it was and I'd rather you didn't know anyway. The problem is I didn't let them know where I am and of course they would think immediately that something must be amiss, which it's not. I'll be honest with you, Pat, I wish I'd never got involved in the first place but I did and that's all there is to it I'm afraid.'

'What are you going to do, Liam?'

'I suppose I will have to go to them and try to get them to see my predicament, but it won't be easy that's for sure. The fact I did not tell them straight away of my location will ring alarm bells in their tiny minds and they are liable to get very heavy; I've seen this before. If I try to avoid them I'm a dead man, Pat.'

'Fucking hell Liam, this is serious!'

'I'll tell you what I'm going to do, I will contact the high command and arrange a meeting with them and see how it goes from there,' replied Reagan.

The IRA hitman contacted the Chief of Staff Colm MacDiamid, through an intermediary and a meeting was arranged for the following day in a city centre flat. Reagan approached the address with dread knowing full-well he was under surveillance by the movement and would be constantly for some time, if he lived that long. As he entered the block, he was approached by two men and challenged for his identity. Having satisfied them he was Reagan, he was led up to the top floor and into the flat where he was searched thoroughly. The two men, whom he didn't know, never left his side; they were clearly armed. He was kept waiting in the kitchen for about fifteen minutes and although he heard voices from the lounge, the door was shut and he couldn't hear what was being said. There seemed to be raised voices but this could have been his imagination.

The door was finally opened and he was ushered into the spacious lounge and told to sit on a straight-backed chair facing the Chief of Staff. 'Well, Liam, where have you been lately?'

'Just lying low as advised by my instructor in Galway.'

'Your instructor has disappeared, Liam.'

'I had no knowledge of that. When I had carried out my mission which was successful, as you know, I went to ground as instructed and, I might add, followed all the usual procedures that a post operation demanded.'

'Where are you staying now?'

'With a friend, here in Dublin. I am trying to get back into the university to continue my studies, the classics you know. I would like to get a Masters then a PhD. As far as the movement is concerned nothing has changed. I am as committed as ever to the struggle,' he lied.

'You should have let us know your whereabouts, Liam, that way we can protect you,'

'I'm sorry. I simply didn't think it would be a problem. The university course would provide good cover for me.'

'Right, from now on we want to know all your movements. By all means follow your study but do not leave Dublin without express permission from us, is that clear? If you do it will be at your peril, Liam. Do you understand?'

'Yes of course.'

'By the way the Brits are pulling their hair out about the killing of the chief peeler in the north. There have been raids and arrests but they have learned nothing and never will if we can help it. Now go back home and stay close to the ground but remember what I have said. We will not require your services for some time but be rest assured your skills will be put to good use in the future,' concluded the Chief of Staff.

Reagan was escorted off the premises and made his way home; the pain in his stomach was bad and he swallowed some painkillers to ease the discomfort. I have to get away from all this, he thought as he prepared to go the university library and begin some study.

Three days later the letter arrived from the admissions department of Trinity College Dublin formally inviting Liam Reagan to begin a course of study, reading classics. It added that if he wished he could take up accommodation in the hall of residence with immediate effect. This he decided to do and in a way this could protect Pat if something went wrong.

When his friend arrived home he told him of his plan to move the following day and the reasons why. 'You don't have to go, Liam, if you don't want to.'

'I think it's best for the both of us really. Anyway, I will often be up all night burning the midnight oil and I wouldn't want to disturb you, especially when you are shagging that gorgeous girlfriend of yours.'

'Alright, Liam if you are sure.'

'I think it's best all round but we must keep in contact and thanks for all your help with the flat and the doctor.'

'That's a point, what's happening regarding treatment?'

'I'm having a scan tomorrow afternoon and then will see Dr Connolly straight after so I have my fingers crossed.'

'Best of luck, but it must be worrying all the same, Liam.'

'It is for sure but I am confident all will be well. At least I hope so.'

'So do I, my friend - so do I!'

The following afternoon Reagan had the scan and the technician made no comment when she looked at the results.

'Well.' said Reagan, 'What do you think?'

'I'm not at liberty to say but I will pass the results to the doctor and he will see you in about an hour following our discussion.'

'Surely you can give me some idea what the problem is, love. You must see a lot of these each day, I'm sure you know how to interpret them.'

'Course I do but as I've just said, it's the doctor who discusses the results with the patient, not me.'

'Oh alright, I didn't mean to upset you, I hope you won't take offence,'

'No offence taken, Mr Reagan. Have a good day,' she said with a wry smile.

Reagan left the scan department and made his way to the canteen for a cup of coffee as he had an hour to wait until he saw the doctor.

'Come in, Mr Reagan,' said Dr Connolly.

Reagan went into the doctor's office and sat down feeling a little nervous. 'Well,' said the doctor leafing through the notes. 'It seems you have a problem in your bowel, it could be cancer but further tests are required to be sure. You've had a blood test but I will arrange an internal investigation using a fibre optic camera. In fact I

239

will arrange this right now as time is of the essence,' said the doctor reaching for the telephone.

'What about all the investigations I had as a child in Cork, how is it they could find nothing?' asked Reagan.

'I can't tell you because I simply don't know but what we have to concentrate on is the here and now. You will almost certainly require some extensive treatment and soon, so let's get on with it.'

'OK, doctor I'm in your hands.' A week later, the investigation had been carried out and Reagan was back with the doctor.

'It's confirmed Mr Reagan, you have a cancer and this will require an operation in the very near future. Shall I arrange it now if I can?'

'Yes please, the sooner the better I suppose.'

Reagan left the doctors surgery in a haze and went to his room in the hall of residence. He decided to inform the Chief of Staff of his condition to keep them sweet and not give them any ideas for tasks they might be dreaming up for him.

Colm MacDiamid received the news of Reagan's illness without compassion and told him to keep them informed of progress, but he was reminded again to inform them if he was moved to a hospital outside Dublin.

Reagan contacted the dean of the university and explained his predicament which was received with much sympathy. It was agreed to delay his admission to the university until he was fully able to continue the study programme.

Patrick arrived at Reagan's room in the hall of residence to see his long-term friend. 'How did it go with the doctor, mate?'

'It seems I've got cancer in my bowel and I need an operation,' replied Reagan.

'Oh bloody hell, how did that happen?'

'I guess you just get it. They say we all have cancer genes in our bodies; it seems mine has raised its ugly head. There you go. Dr Connolly is going to arrange the op as soon as possible he tells me, so it's a waiting game for the moment I suppose. Who knows what the outcome will be, Pat.'

Chapter 16

Alan Conlon tried to carry on as normal at home in Ballybrittas when one morning he got a message, in a phone call, to ring MI5 in London on the number he was given, and had to commit to memory, whilst in Dorking. His instructions were to go to a phone box about four miles south west of the town to make this call. He was also told he was being watched, so not to screw this up. As he had been told by the doctor not to drive he got his wife to arrange a shopping trip to the supermarket in Kildare and used this as cover for leaving home. At the supermarket there was a phone box and Conlon went in and dialled the number. The phone was answered immediately and Conlon gave his code name as "Eagle".

The MI5 duty officer said without preamble, 'Why didn't you use the phone box we told you to?'

'Because it would have looked suspicious, that box is in a lay-by on a busy road and I may well be tailed by the IRA.'

'Listen, Conlon, from now on you will do exactly as we tell you. Do you fully understand what I'm saying? We are watching you and you were not followed, only by us.'

'Ok you win, what can I do for you?'

'What do you know about a man called Reagan, Liam Reagan?'

'Only that he was in the camp in Connemara with me and the yank.'

'What was his role?

'He trained alongside the others, that's all I know.'

'What training did he receive? Did it include weapons and explosives for instance?'

'It was a standard course, and yes, it included weapons and field craft, usual military tactics. He was good though, a real cut above the rest, what you might call a natural.'

'What happened to him after the training was completed?'

'I don't know because I was dumped off the training course by the yank. You know this because we covered it all in your interrogation centre in England.'

'Mr Conlon, you do not need to remind us what we know. Remember, I ask the questions and you answer them, that is all there is to it.'

'When will we be able to go to Spain as you promised?'

'When we decide the time is right, Mr Conlon; soon I imagine,' said the MI5 man without conviction.

'I don't know how much more my wife can take of all this, or me for that matter, please hurry up and get us away, I implore you!'

'All in good time, now be a good fellow and await further instructions,' concluded the voice on the phone.

Conlon attempted to speak but the line had already gone dead. 'Bastards' all of them! They milk you dry then throw you to the wolves,' he said aloud to himself. As he left the phone box he had the feeling someone was watching him, he couldn't put his finger on it but he was certain. Could it be MI5? 'Please God, not the IRA,' he muttered.

His wife had just appeared with a trolley half-filled with groceries and two bottles of wine as he met her at the car, ready to load the items into the boot. Just as he closed the lid, a man came up to him and said, 'Hello Alan, on the shopping run again? Good day to you, Mrs Conlon, how are the children?'

Mrs Conlon just got in the car without replying but her husband turned and faced the stranger. 'Who are you, do I know you?'

'No, but I certainly know who you are, Mr Conlon! You may have guessed we are keeping an eye on you for your own safety, bearing in mind the services you have provided for us in the training camp and utilising your military skills for the movement. Who were you phoning, Mr Conlon?'

Conlon had a feeling of dread so much so he thought he might collapse with fear. 'Oh! Just my Mother in Kerry,' he lied.

'Is your phone at home faulty, and by the way how is she? I understand she has not been too well lately.'

'She's fine now. I really must get down and see her soon. I assume that's OK with you?'

'We have visited her, Mr Conlon and she is far from well, as you well know, finding it difficult to get out now. I say again, who were you phoning just now?'

'I have just told you,' said Conlon with a tremor in his voice.

'Ok, Mr Conlon, be on your way and keep a low

profile, we will be in touch in due course,' said the stranger with a sinister tone in his voice.

On the way home Conlon's wife asked him what all that was all about. 'Oh nothing, it's just the movement keeping an eye on us for our protection, they do it all the time, love.'

'Don't give me all that bollocks, Alan, keeping an eye on us for our safety, like hell they do.'

'Look, love, don't rock the boat, just keep quiet and the Brits will get us away soon, really they will.'

'If you believe that, Alan you will believe anything, let's just get home and the sooner we leave this so called Emerald Isle for good the better.'

The atmosphere in the car was so tense you could cut it with a knife and the journey seemed never ending. When the Conlon's got home and unloaded the shopping it was clear that Mrs Conlon was far from happy and made it clear she was no longer going to cook and clean for him.

'What is the matter with you, love? I am trying to sort this mess out and get us a better life away from here.'

'Why don't you just piss off on your own and get your own fucking better life. Just leave me and the kids alone.'

'Who would look after you if I were to go on the run?'

'Don't you think you are the only man in my life, Alan because you're not.'

'What do you mean, you two timing cow?'

'While you are off playing soldiers I managed to attract an admirer, a man who has actually got some

245

brains, and guess what? he has some standing in the local community.'

'Who is it? I'll fucking kill him with my bare hands.'

'I have no intention of telling you, so go and leave us in peace. Just get out of this house once and for all.'

'You bitch,' shouted Conlon kicking and smashing the TV set.

The situation calmed down a little during the evening and there was tension in the house that the children noticed; they had been out at a friend's when the row had taken place and was unaware of the situation between their parents. The smashed TV set was explained away by saying that Conlon had stumbled into it accidently.

The following morning shortly after Mrs Conlon had gone out to the local shop the door bell rang and Alan Conlon was confronted by two IRA men from Dublin. 'Top of the morning, Alan. How are you this beautiful morning?'

'Good morning, gentlemen, what can I do for you?' said Conlon without inviting them in.

'We need to have a little chat about recent events and to bring you up to date with the movement's progress, you know the sort of thing.'

'Can we talk about it here?'

'No we can't!' said one of the men abruptly. 'Just get yourself a coat and we will go for a little ride and a chat in the car, make it snappy now.'

The car journey took them through Tullamore and onwards towards Mullingar where it took a left turn in the direction of the small village of Moyvore, where it turned off down a farm track.

'Where are you taking me?' asked the increasingly concerned Conlon.

'As I said we want to have a little chat about your activities within the movement Alan.'

'You know what I do for you already and I have proven my use to the movement for years, ever since I left the army.'

The car pulled up at a barn and the driver got out and opened the door for Conlon. 'This way my friend,' he said.

Once inside the barn it became obvious to Conlon this was more than a little chat. There were six men waiting and three were sitting at a table.

'Welcome, Alan, come and sit down.' In silence Conlon sat and tried to relax but it was impossible.

'The other day when you made a phone call from the supermarket in Kildare, who did you speak to? Think carefully how you answer this question,' said the chairman of the group.

'I called my mother as I told your colleague at the time.'

'I don't believe you. We have spoken to your mother and she said she has not heard from you for weeks. I ask you again, who did you speak to?'

'My mum, she gets confused these days and can't remember much, she is suffering from dementia.'

'We have had one of our doctors take a look at your mum and she is fine, certainly not demented as you claim. Last time, Alan, who did you phone?'

The vicious slap across Conlon's face sent him crashing to the floor. As he stood up an uppercut punch to the abdomen caused him to fall again, winded and gasping for breath.

'Get up!' screamed the chairman. 'You will be shot if you don't tell us what we want to know, Conlon. I have a young and willing volunteer here who needs to be bloodied and you will be the candidate for him unless you start talking.'

'I swear I have done nothing wrong,' said Conlon through clenched teeth and grimacing with pain.

'You're a liar, Conlon. Let me tell you what we suspect shall I? You have been informing on us to the Brits and that could explain your absence when you were in Wales with your family. Am I right, Mr Conlon?'

'No that's not true believe me, why would I inform when I know the consequences I would face?'

Another harsh slap across the face sent him to the floor again followed by a kick to the ribs. Conlon screamed in pain and vomited at the same time losing control of his bowels. 'OK, I was got at by the Brits and forced to pass some details but nothing of importance. They threatened my family and me if I didn't co-operate with them. They told me the SAS would shoot us all, there is nothing more I can say. Please understand I had no choice,' pleaded the former Irish Army NCO.

'You fucking squealer, Conlon. You could well have put many a good volunteer's life or liberty at risk by trying to save your own skin. Take him into the other shed,' said the chairman lighting a cigarette.

Two of the men bundled Conlon away to the adjacent shed and dumped him on the floor locking the door behind them. Absolutely beside himself he started sobbing, certain of what was about to happen.

Back in the main barn the chairman considered his next move and consulted with the others present. 'Well, lads we have a grass and you know the usual punishment for that. Are we all agreed?' To a man they all nodded agreement and the decision was made to execute Conlon there and then. 'We will never know what damage he has done to the movement but even a small amount of information passed to the Brits can only do us damage, as you know they never give up,' he continued.

'Where is the young man who will do the nutting?' asked the chairman.

'He's waiting in a safe house in Athlone at the moment for your call. His name is Michael Adare, a member of the Louth brigade. He's a good and conscientious volunteer, I can thoroughly recommend him,' said Sean O'Hanlon, one of the brigade staff present.

'Ok have him sent over and we can get on with it,' replied the chairman.

The car arrived an hour later with Adare and a 9mm pistol was produced by the quartermaster, loaded with Czech manufactured hollow point ammunition. The chairman greeted the young man and told him he was about to perform a great duty to the movement and that this would increase his standing and commitment to the IRA.

'Right, young man, this is what you do. Go straight into the shed and give him two shots to the head; the Brits call this a double tap. This should kill him instantly then come out straight away and give the weapon back to the quartermaster. After a debrief you will be taken back to Athlone. The important thing to remember is to say nothing to no one and just carry on as usual. We will be in touch at a later date. Good luck, so let's go and get it over with shall we?'

The young man entered the shed with the gun in his shaking hand; behind him stood two others. Conlon looked up and screamed as the shots rang out smashing into his head spraying the wall with tissue and brain matter, death was instantaneous.

Michael Adare could not stop shaking and was given a cup of strong, sweet tea to calm him down before he was debriefed by the chairman prior to his departure. At the end of his talk the chairman said, 'Just remember, not a word to anyone and be particularly careful if you go to the pub and get pissed; many have been caught like this. If we were to hear you have been talking you will be next for the bullet, do you understand? There is no way back for you now. Away you go and take care.'

Conlon's body was placed in a large plastic sack and removed to a boggy area of Connemara in County Galway where other informers had been buried; he was just another one of many...

Chapter 17

Michael Lenihan managed to board the ferry to France by sneaking into the back of another lorry just before it drove on, only just avoiding detection by a customs officer. With his heart racing he hardly breathed until the lorry came to a halt on the vehicle deck and the driver left the cab and went to the canteen on the ship. The crossing was rough and he was sea sick for the first time in his life; he couldn't wait to dock in the port of Roscoff. Getting ashore could prove difficult even though he had a valid passport but luck was on his side.

He managed to just walk off the ship with the other foot passengers and through passport and customs with nothing more than a nod from the officers. With a sigh of relief he decided he would try and make his way to Germany and the base near Frankfurt where he once served and hoping to link up with old friends from the army. He would fabricate a story that he had been bumming around Europe and was now on hard times and looking for a little help to get home to the States. He knew there would be no official help, but who knows?

The American ex-Master Sergeant bought a train ticket for Paris and settled down to sleep for the journey. Several times he was woken as passengers came and went at various stations but the journey was uneventful and he arrived in the French capital mid-morning the following day after changing trains at Rennes.

The confusing train boards in the station were not helped though by his lack of French but he managed to locate the platform for the Frankfurt and Berlin train leaving at 5.30pm the same day. With some time to spare he bought some new clothes and had a shower and shave in the station complex. The steak hache and frites along with strong black coffee made him feel so much better and ready for the next stage of his escape to Germany and hopefully into the arms of friends.

The main station in Frankfurt was thronging with people including a lot of Turkish immigrants looking for a better life but causing long queues at cafes and public toilets causing frustrations with the locals. Lenihan was pushed and shoved by these people causing him to fall and land heavily on his left elbow. He got up and saw the man who had apparently caused this and went towards him to remonstrate. The big Turkish guy just spat in his face and with that, Lenihan punched him square on the jaw and the man fell to the ground. The crowd closed in but being fast on his feet he managed to get away and found his way out of the station and into the side streets. He made quick work of putting as much distance between him and the crowd as possible, finding a small bar in which to mingle with the drinkers. He stayed about an hour before attempting to make his way to the bus station and find the stand for the bus out of town to the US army base. The bus was due in 15 minutes and he felt safe now as he was some distance from the station and standing in a shop doorway to avoid the rain which was getting increasingly heavy.

The journey to the base took just under an hour and the bus stop near the entrance was clear of people at this hour. As he stepped off the bus Lenihan wished he was still in the army and living in the safety of the huge base with all its benefits. 'If it wasn't for that fucking Brit officer screwing Carol I would still be here, probably with a promotion by now. Life's a bitch,' he muttered.

He decided to find some cheap accommodation locally but had to be careful with the remaining money he possessed until he could get some help. A local shop with notices in the window provided him with an address. His basic knowledge of German was tested to the hilt. Lenihan managed to secure a small room in a house run by an obliging elderly widow who was happy to take him in for a peppercorn rent in return for a few small domestic chores around the house. This, at least for the time being, would provide him with somewhere to sleep and lie low whilst trying to locate former military friends at the base. He wondered if Captain Rod Casey was still there, as he was the best friend he had had when the trouble all started following his wife's death and the subsequent court marshal leading to his dishonourable discharge from the US army.

Each day he would take up station near the base and watch who came and went, hoping to spot someone he knew. He had to be careful so as not to attract the attention of the military or civil police. The problem he realised was that all military units rotated through postings and there was no guarantee that any of the men and women who were serving during his time had not been posted elsewhere.

One morning at 8.30am, Lenihan noticed a staff car leave the base followed by two large trucks full of soldiers. Sitting in the back of the car was a Colonel and someone who looked very much like Rod Casey, his old pal. 'Thank Christ for that, looks like Rod's still there,' he muttered to himself. The next challenge was to figure a way of making contact. He decided to wait until the following day and try to phone the base switchboard and ask for his friend.

Soon after nine the following morning Lenihan phoned the base. 'Good morning, could I speak to Captain Roderick Casey please,' he asked the sergeant operator.

'I'm sorry, sir, but it's not army policy to connect you to an officer just like that. Can I ask you the nature of your call and I will see if he can get back to you?'

'He's an old friend and I'm over from the States and want to look him up while I'm here. Basically meet up for a beer and chat.'

'Can you leave me your name and number and I will get a message to him?'

Lenihan had already thought this might be the case and managed to persuade the old lady to let him use her phone should this be necessary. 'Have you got a pen ready Sergeant?'

'Sure have, sir, go right ahead.'

Lenihan gave the operator the phone number adding his first name only hoping that would be sufficient.

'I need your full name, sir to pass this message on. It's our rules you know.'

'OK just say it's Mike from way back. Mention 5th Special Forces Group, he'll know who it is then.'

'Sorry, sir, I still need your full name for the record sheet. I don't make the rules but I have to obey them all the same.'

'I'm Master Sergeant Michael Lenihan, US Army retired. Is that OK now Sergeant!'

'That's fine, sir, sorry, but you know how the army is with its rules and regulations. I'll see Major Casey gets the message today.'

The following afternoon the phone rang and the elderly lady answered it formally, in cultured German.

'Herr Lenihan, gibt es einen telefonanruf fü sie.' (There is a telephone call for you.)

'Danke, Frau Liebermann,' he answered taking the phone.

'Mike is that you?' said Casey.

'Hi, Rod, it sure is, so it's Major now, congratulations.'

'I didn't realise you were back in Germany, are you working or on vacation?'

'No, not exactly, Rod, could we meet soon as I need your help and advice?'

'Sure, could you come to the base?'

'I'd rather not, perhaps we can meet in town. There's a little bar down near the bridge alongside the old church, if you can get away for an hour?'

'I can't I'm afraid, not during the day but can manage the evening if that's OK?'

'OK. How about 7 o'clock? I'll buy you a beer, be nice to catch up.'

'Certainly will, Mike, you sure you're not in trouble or something?'

'No everything's fine, tell you all about it tomorrow.

I'd appreciate it if you would keep it to yourself until we have spoken.'

'OK Mike, but you must admit it sounds a little suspicious, but hey ho, see you tomorrow.'

'OK, my friend all will be revealed then, don't work too hard.'

After Lenihan rang off he admitted to himself it did sound odd. If he had nothing to hide what was there to fear from going to the base?

Major Rod Casey sat at his desk pondering the brief phone call from the ex- master sergeant and wondering what would surface from the meeting tomorrow. He knew Mike Lenihan had a quick temper and this had caused him trouble in the past, in fact he often wondered how his friend had managed to become a senior NCO in the army. However Lenihan did have an excellent active service record in Vietnam with the award of the Silver Star; this was probably the reason he had achieved his rank at a relatively young age. That evening Lenihan went to a local bar and was deep in thought when out of the blue he happened to look round at a group of females who had just come into the bar. Instantly he recognised one as Christine Ellis, a corporal at the base administration office.

When she saw him she gasped. 'Mike, what are you doing here, I thought you were back in the States?'

'Chris! What a surprise, how you doing, honey? You look fantastic as ever.'

'Oh you always were a flatterer, Mike, but you have put on some weight and a little greyer than when I last saw you.'

'Well, aren't you going to introduce me to your friends? I won't bite you know.'

Christine did the introductions and then said she wanted to speak to Mike privately which the girls understood and they all moved away to the far end of the bar area.

'What are you doing here? I heard through the grapevine that you had been court-marshalled in the States and discharged from the military, I was really sad this had happened to you, honey. What a waste of army talent.'

'Well these things happen, all because of that Brit Lieutenant. I should have killed him at the time you know.'

'All that would have got you is a murder rap and life in a state penitentiary or worse and we wouldn't be talking now, would we? I've always liked you, Mike and nothing has changed at all.'

'I bet you say that to all the men.'

'Oh, there has been the odd one from time to time but nothing serious. Anyway, my time is nearly up here and stateside is beckoning. They have offered me a post at Fort Leavenworth in Kansas for the next two years so I am tempted, I have to let them know by the end of the week. By the way you are talking to Sergeant Ellis now you know.'

'Well done, honey, you will be catching up to me soon if you carry on like this.'

'That's enough about me, Mike, how about you?'

'Well my story is a little more complicated but I don't want to go into all that now, let's enjoy the evening. What are you drinking?'

Mike and Christine joined the rest of the group for the next hour or so then he asked her if she would like to go for a walk along the river. They strolled arm in arm along the riverbank pathway and through the old part of the town. It was getting dark now and he was concerned about her getting back to the base safely.

'What's the latest you have to be back in base?'

'I'm normally in by 11:30 these days. The military police start patrolling the town about then and I like to back in my room before that. Where are you staying?'

'Oh I have a room nearby and a front door key so I can come and go as I please pretty well. The old lady, Frau Liebermann, who owns the place, is normally in bed by 10 o'clock and snoring loudly soon after.'

'You still haven't told me why you're here, Mike.'

'It's a long story, honey but it will have to wait till later, then I will give you the full blow-by-blow account.'

'Are you in trouble with the police or something?'

'No not really, but things are a little awkward at the moment and I admit I'm a little short of cash, but coping OK so far.'

'How can I help? I have a little money saved up from my salary.'

'No, honey I can't take your money but your support would be marvellous. I've missed you while I've been away and would like to see you on a regular basis if that's OK with you. I don't know how long I will be in Germany, not too long I hope as I really want to get back to the States.'

'Mike, I will give you all the help I can, just ask, honey,' she said kissing him on the cheek.

Lenihan took Christine back to the entrance of the base and made arrangements to see her in two days time at the bar. As they parted she kissed him full on the lips and hugged him closely.

The following evening Lenihan met Major Rod Casey at the bar near the river as agreed.

'Hello, Rod, long time, no see,' said Lenihan reaching for the officer's hand.

'Hi there, Mike, how are you? What can I get you?' said the major going up to the bar.

'I'll just have a beer thanks.'

Rod Casey returned to the corner table with the drinks and settled down. 'Well now, old buddy, what have you been up to since we last met?'

'It's a long story I'm afraid, and there are some things I have to keep to myself. I hope you will understand, Rod.'

'Try me, Master Sergeant Lenihan Rtd.'

'If only I was still an Msg, I really miss it you know. I'm still sore about the way my military career ended on such a sour note. I will get that bastard Brit you know, Rod.'

'Now that's enough of that, Mike, it will do you no good at all. Christ you have already beaten the shit out of him, just leave it at that. I don't want to hear that from you again!'

'OK, OK I'm sorry, Rod, point taken. Rod, what I'm about to tell you must go no further because it could get a little difficult if the authorities found out. Are you sure you want me to carry on with this, in the strictest of confidence?'

'Mike I am, and if at all possible I will respect your confidence.'

Over the next hour and a half Lenihan went over the whole story of what had happened since he was dismissed from the military and covered all the happenings in Ireland. The only bit that he left out was the killings he had personally carried out whilst there such as Ann, the IRA prostitute and informer, and the two republican thugs who had tried to ambush him near the Ulster border.

Rod Casey was astounded when he had heard the full story and was lost for words for a moment or two. 'Fucking hell, Mike, this is dynamite.'

'I know, Rod, but I was kind of drawn into it when I was working at the club in New York, I didn't realise at the time it was owned by an Irish guy. I was short of money, very short of money and this seemed an opportunity to earn a few bucks quickly. It kind of snowballed from there. I never had any intention of doing the IRA toppings myself but I could see it could quite easily go that way. That's why I decided to get out while I could. When this raid on the camp took place it provided me with an escape route out of that fucking place altogether. I'm sure it was carried out by the British SAS because it was surgically precise and had their trademark stamped all over it. It was just luck I was in another part of the house upstairs and managed to hide or it would have been my arse on the line as well. But you now see my predicament and realise why I want to get stateside as soon as I can. I need to put as much distance between myself and Ireland as possible. So I ask you, Rod, can you help me with a loan for the flight?'

'The loan is no problem, Mike, but this puts me in a very difficult position. As an officer, I should report all of this to the military provost command because as an ex soldier you are potentially involved in terrorism. I am no lawyer, but you must have broken just about every law in the book both domestic and international. If I am caught assisting you in any way at all, we could both be cell mates in the slammer for years. Jeez, Mike, this has really put me on a spot.'

'Sorry, Rod, I do appreciate your position and if there was any other way I would take it but there isn't at the moment. All I'm asking for is your confidentiality and a loan to buy a ticket home. Please, Rod I'm desperate!'

'OK, Mike, this is what I will do. I'll draw some cash but you will have to get the ticket for the flight home. I won't say a word to Jane but if she notices the money gone from our account I will have to be inventive with my answers.'

'Thanks a million, Rod, I will pay you back as soon as I can; you know that and thanks once again.'

Rod Casey had to get back to the base and Lenihan wanted time alone to think of his next move but in the meantime he had arranged to meet Christine the following evening. When he got back to the house where he was staying he noticed an ambulance and police car outside.

'Good evening officer,' said Lenihan in broken German to the policeman on guard outside the house. 'What has happened?'

'Who are you?' asked a detective, who seemed to appear from nowhere.

'I am living here for the time being. What has had

261

happened? Is anyone hurt?' said Lenihan nodding towards the ambulance.

'The elderly lady who lives here is dead. We think she has been murdered and some things stolen.'

'Murdered?' said Lenihan, 'but how? Why? She was old and could not have had much money. The reason I was living here was so it would help with her finances and do little jobs for her.'

'You are an American, your name please!'

'Michael Lenihan, sir.'

'How long have you been living here, and how long have you been in Germany?' asked the detective in perfect English?

'I have only been here about a week and will be going home to the States as soon as I can get a flight.'

'Mr Lenihan, you will not be going anywhere until we have carried out our enquiries. You are under arrest on suspicion of murder.'

Lenihan reeled with horror. 'What do you mean, suspicion of murder? I have been in the Rhine Bar with a friend from the US army all evening. I haven't killed anyone!'

'Mr Lenihan, we are taking you to the police station for further questioning. You will be provided with a legal representative of our choice or you are free to engage your own if you wish.'

At the police station Lenihan was granted one phone call and he called Rod Casey who was now at home in the officers' quarters on the base.

'Rod, it's Mike, I've been arrested on a murder charge and I'm at the local police station.'

'Christ Mike! What's happened now?'

'They have nothing on me. I was with you all evening and although I've told them that, they don't really believe me so I guess they'll be talking to you pretty soon.'

'OK I'll come to the police station right away. You are becoming a fucking liability, Mike, you realise that don't you?'

'I know, Rod but I am totally innocent.'

'OK see you soon.' Rod Casey rang off without goodbyes, incensed with all that had happened in last few hours and the implications for himself and his career. 'This man is becoming a pain in the arse but he is not going to drag me down with him!' he muttered to himself.

Chapter 18

Liam Reagan was admitted to hospital in Dublin for treatment of his cancer and Dr Connolly was on hand when he arrived.

'Hello, Liam,' said the doctor. 'Don't worry, I think we have probably got it just in time and therefore the operation and follow-up treatment should come out positive.'

'I hope so, doctor as I really want to continue with my studies and eventually teach, so a lot rides on the doctors here for me. Will you be doing the operation Dr Conolly?' asked Reagan.

'No I'm a physician not a surgeon. Mr Singh, a brilliant colorectal surgeon, will carry out the procedure the day after tomorrow. He's got a very good record with this type of operation so keep your spirits up and look forward to a full recovery, my friend.'

'Thanks I will and thanks for all your help with this, doctor.'

'I'll come and see you after the operation,' concluded Dr Connolly with a smile and a hand shake.

Colm MacDiamid, the IRA Chief of Staff, was informed immediately about the admission and called a meeting of his most trusted advisors at a safe house in the city suburbs. 'Gentlemen, I have to inform you that

Liam Reagan is now in hospital, for how long we don't know, so the little job we have planned for him will have to be postponed for the time being. Assuming he recovers his health and strength, and then starts his university course, it will provide excellent cover for his movement activities and work for us. I know he wants to get into the political side of things but that will have to wait. He is too valuable in his present role after that successful job in the north. Should things not go to plan with his health he will have to be eliminated once and for all.

'As some of you know, when he went missing after the job in the north, we began to think he had done a runner or been got at by the Brits, many wanted his head then. I will not tolerate a death-bed confession so we need to keep a close eye on his medical progress over the weeks. If he opens his mouth to the Brits or Garda it will implicate many of us here today, so let's stay focused on Mr Reagan and ensure he makes a full recovery; or departs this planet without delay. Padraig, it's your responsibility to visit him daily and take a bunch of grapes or whatever. In fact, see he gets all he needs but the main thing is to gauge his mood and commitments to us. Any doubts report directly to me, is that clear?'

'Certainly, Colm. I have no problem with that.'

'OK men that's all for now, we will meet next week, same place, same time.'

After the IRA men left, Colm MacDiamid sat and pondered all that had happened recently; he couldn't shake off his doubts about Reagan but there was nothing positive to go on. Why did he go to ground without informing his masters in the movement, perhaps it was just caution, who knows?

Padraig Meehan turned up at visiting time and stayed for about an hour with Reagan just chatting generally. Nothing was mentioned about the IRA but Reagan was fully aware about the reasons for the visit and the subtle threat behind it. The IRA never gave up and wiould not let someone off the hook if they thought they had been betrayed. Reagan realised he had to be very careful and not upset the applecart. He had definitely not betrayed the movement and nor did he intend too, but he really wanted out if that was at all possible, one route he hoped would be joining Sinn Fein, the political party of the movement. His intellect, he decided, would be used to further the aims of the movement and work towards a united Ireland.

The operation was a success and during recovery Reagan received another visit by Padraig Meehan, this time offering a period of convalescence in Bundoran, County Sligo, at IRA expense. This resort was a well-known haunt of the movement for rest and recuperation following active service in the north or the British mainland. For the sake of simplicity Reagan agreed readily and thanked Meehan knowing full well he would be under constant surveillance throughout this period. At least while he was recovering he would not be tasked with work.

Reagan was discharged the following week with an outpatient appointment booked for a month ahead. He returned to his room in Pat's house and packed his few possessions in a grip then made his way to Dublin's main railway station for the train to Sligo. One essential piece of luggage was the study material he would cover whilst recovering so as to be able to go straight into Trinity

College on his return. His love of classics was as strong as ever and this would be his future.

The house in Bundoran was comfortable and the views across the bay provided him with a perfect study environment to bring himself up to speed for his impending admission to university. He was not aware of being watched but this would be normal in the circumstances. It was well known within the IRA that the Garda Special Branch and undoubtedly the British MI5 and SAS unofficially visited the resort on the lookout for terrorists. Being close to the Ulster border, the British military undercover units often came over in the hope they may spot someone of interest.

Reagan was not known to them as far as he knew and certainly no photographs had been taken of him for many years so they had little to go on. He felt safe from the Brits but not from the IRA. One false move and it would be terminal. He stayed for two weeks and had regular visits from Padraig Meehan to report on his progress and ensure his wellbeing.

'How you feeling Liam, you look well enough?'

'Not bad, Paddy but I get tired quickly at the moment but then again the doctors said this would be the case; the tablets help of course. I have to go to the hospital soon for my post-operative check-up, then hopefully I will be fully discharged except for an annual appointment to make sure there is no return of the cancer,' said Reagan, still feeling weak but hating these constant checks on him by the movement. He knew this would continue and there was nothing he could do about it for the time being.

Back in Dublin Colm MacDiamid was in the local

pub when he was approached by another volunteer who said he wanted to speak to him urgently. 'What can I do for you, Michael?'

'I have news that John O'Hagan, you may remember he was wounded in the raid on the training camp in Galway, has died suddenly in Tralee. They say it was his heart but the local doctor said he had mentioned things to him that perhaps he shouldn't have.'

'What things?'

'I don't know but I thought you would want to know, Colm.'

'OK thank you, Michael, well done it is appreciated. Just say nothing to anyone; you know the drill.'

'Oh sure I do, not a word.'

The Chief of Staff immediately called an urgent meeting of the staff and brought them up to date with his conversation in the pub.

'I need to go down to Tralee straight away. It might be a case of damage limitation but I need to put the lid on it right away just in case. While I'm away Kevin you are acting for me should anything come up.'

'OK, no problem,' said Kevin Dempsey, the Dublin quartermaster.

The following morning Colm MacDiarmid drove down to Tralee in County Kerry to see the doctor who had been treating O'Hagan. He waited until the morning surgery had finished at 12:30 than went into the waiting room and spoke to the receptionist.

'I need to see the doctor right away please.'

'I'm afraid he has finished surgery and has to go on his visits as soon as he has had lunch, Mister er...?

'My name isn't important, lady just tell him I want to see him now, is that clear?' said MacDiamid with menace in his voice and a piercing look in his eyes.

The receptionist went white with fear and picked up the intercom and spoke to the doctor immediately.

The GP came out full of fury at being disturbed during his lunch. 'What do you want? The surgery is closed until 4.30 this afternoon and you will have to wait for an appointment. Now I suggest you go home and come back later!'

'Doctor, I have just come all the way from Dublin to see you and I will see you now, is that clear?' said MacDiamid indicating the office with a nod of his head. 'Or do you want me to call the Garda?'

Suddenly realising who this man in the reception was, the doctor said, 'No Mary, I will deal with this in my office; come in would you Mister er ...? Oh and one thing, Mary, please make sure we are not disturbed. Thank you.'

Once inside the doctor's office MacDiamid came straight to the point. 'I understand you have been treating Mr O'Hagan for some time and that he has now passed away. By the way, I think you know who I am by now and what I represent?'

'I do now but I think you could have been a little more discreet in your approach.'

'Listen, doctor, diplomacy is not my strong point and I do not intend to improve my technique now, clear? Again tell me about O'Hagan but before you do, just let me remind you that you work for us and how is your daughter doing at university?' said MacDiamid

'OK, OK, I get the message, what do you want to know?'

'Tell me about O'Hagan, what did he die of?'

'He suffered a Myocardial Infarct, a heart attack in layman's terms, which was not recoverable.'

'Where did he die?'

'He became ill here in the surgery and I called the ambulance.'

'Did he say anything to you whilst you were waiting?'

'Only that he regretted all he had done since leaving the British Army and that he further regretted joining the IRA. He was quite certain about that.'

'What else did he say, did he mention any names?'

'No names, but he said he used to work as a quartermaster and trainer for the movement but nothing else; you know, putting his past military skills to good use, here in Eire.'

'Are you sure he never mentioned names?'

'Certain. I am sure he knew he was dying. Some time ago I carried out some tests because he got severe headaches. He was diagnosed following a scan at the hospital. He had a malignant brain tumour which would have been terminal in any case. Dying early did him a favour really.'

'What happened when the ambulance arrived?'

'Just before it came he collapsed and went into cardiac arrest, his heart stopped. I carried out resuscitation but it was no good. The paramedics worked on him also but to no avail. He was certified dead at the hospital by Dr O'Connell, a friend of mine.'

'OK, doctor, thank you for all your help and please pass on my apologies to your receptionist, can I leave it to you to decide what to say to her?'

'Oh Mary will be alright, she has worked for me forever. I'll handle her.'

Colm MacDiamid drove back to Dublin satisfied that O'Hagan had done no damage and that he could rest in peace in a local Tralee graveyard.

The GP thought it best not to mention that O'Hagan had talked freely about the training camp in Galway after they became friends and had a regular game of cards, accompanied by a bottle of Bushmills Whiskey. 'A dead man can't speak from the grave,' he murmured.

Chapter 19

In London the pace was as frantic as ever in MI5 and Special Branch. The security services and police had been under increasing pressure from the Prime Minister for results, following the assassination of the Chief Constable of Northern Ireland several months ago with no arrests being made.

Sir James Overton Deputy Director of MI5 opened the weekly meeting of the Security Services. 'Good morning, gentlemen, I have some bad news for you. We have lost Alan Conlon, code name "Eagle", who seems to have disappeared from his home in Ballybrittas. As of yet we have no idea of his whereabouts in spite of the fact he has been under surveillance by our people.'

'How can you lose a man when you have watchers on him day and night?' asked Sir Claude Foster of MI6, the Foreign Intelligence Service.

'It's not yet clear how we missed him but I have instituted an investigation into this unfortunate occurrence.'

'This really is not good enough, James, your service should be able to do better than that. Do you want some help from us?' said the head of MI6.

'No I bloody well do not. We will handle this in our own way.'

'Well you will have to do better than that, my

friend. "Eagle" has provided us with some valuable intelligence you know and we want some more before he is compromised or taken to safety by your organisation.'

'I am fully aware of all of this and we will find him!' said Overton getting flustered.

'Gentlemen, gentlemen, please!' said Michael Deakin, the Minister of Defence. 'This will get us nowhere, now let's concentrate on our priorities and find "Eagle" as soon as possible, for God's sake. We must nail the Chief Constable's assassin, and at the moment, he is the only one who may be able to help us. Should another killing occur of a senior police officer or a member of the government we will all be looking for another job and that goes for the head of the SAS as well.'

'Sir, you appear to put some of the blame on the SAS but remember the surveillance is not down to us, that's the job of the Security Services. We go in when we have a specified target and, I might add, we pursue that target ruthlessly. MI5 lost "Eagle" not us!' said Brigadier Chalmers, Director of Special Forces with obvious annoyance.

'Brigadier, I am well aware of that, but as I said earlier arguing will not help us here and now.' replied the Minister.

The babble of voices in the room was silenced by the Minister when he raised his left hand. 'Gentlemen, this is what we will do. MI5 will concentrate on finding "Eagle" and continue to keep an eye on the Irish population in and around Kilburn including all ports both on the mainland and Ulster. MI6 and I have the foreign secretaries OK on this by the way, to carry on its good work in France and the USA with the assistance of the CIA. Oh and by the way, James, you might be interested in Paul Delmond. The ex-French Foreign Legion man in Rennes seems to be on the loose again. French Intelligence has been very helpful and is looking for him but he's off their radar currently. That is all gentlemen.'

The meeting broke up and after the Minister had left the room, some of the disgruntled heads of services started the predictable moaning, as their competence had been called into question.

'It's alright for him, Claude, he goes home at 5 o'clock in a chauffeur-driven car when our boys are just starting a 12 hour shift, out in all weathers looking for a fucking Irishman and wiping his arse when he blows the gaff on the movement.'

'Steady on, James, you never spoke like that when we were at Eton, but I know what you mean. These ministers are, after all, only part-timers and as soon as we have another election he will be on his bike like the rest of them, and good riddance I say.'

The MI5 resident agent in Eire, Don Gale, was sent to Ballybrittas to join up with the A4 surveillance operative already there to help in the search for "Eagle".

'What have we got so far?' asked Don, when he met his colleague in a local hotel.

'I can't get a lead at all as his house appears to be functioning normally. Mrs Conlon does the shopping and the children go to school each day. I think we will have to phone-tap at the very least, or gain entry for a look around, Don.'

'Are we absolutely certain he's not in there?'

'No not really, but he definitely hasn't been seen locally especially in his local pub, the "Black Staff" just down the road.'

'OK I will get authorisation for a phone-tap, bear with me whilst I contact head office.'

Gale left the room and went to his car where he kept secure communications for contact with London. Fifteen minutes later he returned to the hotel room and told his colleague to proceed with the phone-tap that night if possible.

In the early hours of the next morning the covert telephone-tap was put in place by accessing the line into the house. The unit was dug into the soft ground at the side of the house under some bushes. All telephone calls, now both in and out, would be recorded locally and patched through to the case officer at MI5 offices in Great Marlborough Street, London.

Mrs Conlon was getting anxious at her husband's apparent disappearance. Had he gone to the IRA or had he been abducted by the Brits? She did not know, nor did she know the MI5 contact number given to her husband. All she could do was wait and see what happened.

No one from the movement came to see her or contacted her in any way so she really was in limbo for the time being. Even the children said nothing. Several phone calls were made and received but nothing of any interest to MI5; really just domestic stuff and calls to her mother and brother.

At the SAS HQ in Credenhill, just outside Hereford, the Commanding Officer and the Brigadier were in conference regarding the whole affair around the disappearance of Conlon. 'George,' said the Brigadier, 'those incompetent bastards in MI5 and their counterparts have lost a key informer named "Eagle". It appears he has just vanished into thin air and although they have now tapped his home phone line there is still nothing to go on.'

'Sir, I wouldn't mind betting he's dead, rumbled by the Provo's and now buried in a bog somewhere rotting conveniently away. He won't be found for years if ever. You know the IRA; they are ruthless with informers and deal out summary justice without mercy.'

'I know that, George, but this one seems different somehow, they usually top informers and leave the body to be found as a warning to others, strangely not in this case it would seem. Between us, my friend I am going to ferret around a little and see what I can find out through our many contacts outside MI5. A bit unconventional I know but so be it; not a word, George but I will keep you in the loop.'

'OK, sir, good luck.'

Brigadier Chalmers began his investigation with a call to the Irish Defence Forces HQ at the Curragh Camp in Kildare. His contact was a former British Army Colonel who had served with the Brigadier in the Parachute Regiment and transferred to the Irish Army at the end of his contract and now in military intelligence of the Óglaigh na h-Eireann.

When the phone was answered in the Curragh, the Brigadier was put through to his old colleague and after pleasantries were exchanged the Director of Special Forces came straight to the point.

'Frank, how about we meet up for a drink and chat about old times?'

Immediately the Irish officer knew what was on the cards and that something was to be discussed outside official and diplomatic guidelines.

'Actually I have some leave coming up and quite fancy some fishing down in Kerry, somewhere around Bantry Bay. Why don't you come over and try your luck. The bass and cod around there make excellent sport and the results go down well with a crisp white wine in the evenings for dinner.'

'You're on, Frank; I could come over this Saturday if that's OK with you?'

'I suggest you fly to Cork and I'll meet you there and we can chat in the car on the way down.'

'OK that's great; I'll let you know the flight arrival time in the next hour or so. Talk soon.'

As soon as the Brigadier put the phone down, Colonel Francis Coogan of the Irish Defence Force arranged his leave for the coming weekend. 'I wonder what that crafty old bastard wants,' he pondered.

The official cooperation between the UK and Irish Governments over the whole issue of Northern Ireland was a tricky one with suspicions on both sides of the border, but fundamentally some mutual assistance did exist between the two countries, including the sharing of limited information. For Colonel Coogan there was the issue of divided loyalties. Although he had served in the British Parachute Regiment for over twenty years, he was Irish born and now a senior officer in the country's Defence Force. He had to be careful.

Mrs Conlon was getting increasingly concerned about her husband's disappearance and decided to contact the IRA leadership in Dublin. She went to the capital city by train and managed to find the last known address of the leadership and went in without an appointment.

'I want to see the Chief of Staff,' she said nervously.

'Why?' asked a tall, muscular man with tattooed arms and smelling of beer.

'Because I want to, so where is he?'

'He's not here, and even if he was you would have to make an appointment. Do you understand darling?'

'Listen, don't you darling me, you thick bastard, just tell him Doreen Conlon wants to see him now, otherwise I will go to the Garda as my husband is missing and I want to know where he is - got it?'

'Don't get stroppy with me, love; I'm just doing my job. I will get a message to him OK?'

'Right I'll wait here then until he comes.'

'You can't do that, I don't know where he is at the moment, but as I said I will let him know you called.'

'Right, you have one week to get him to call me at home, after that it's the Garda.' She then left the office without shutting the door and walked into the pouring rain that Dublin is renowned for.

Don Gale, the MI5 resident, followed her back to the railway station and watched her board the train for home. He reported the movement and alerted his colleague in Ballybrittas on her impending return. The telephone tap still proved unproductive but monitoring was going on continually.

The following morning the phone rang in the Conlon's

home and Mrs Conlon answered it with a shaking hand and a quiver in her voice.

'Good morning, Mrs Conlon,' said the male voice with a Donegal accent.

'Good morning, who is that?' she replied.

'I understand you made some enquiries yesterday and of course we want to help you if we can,' said the caller.

'Where is my husband?' she asked without further delay.

'I have no idea what you are talking about, Mrs Conlon.'

'Yes you have, don't try all that crap with me. I know how you operate so where is he?'

'Mrs Conlon what are you suggesting?'

'I'm not suggesting anything at the moment but if you can't help me I am going to inform the Garda my husband is missing. Is that clear?'

'Mrs Conlon I would like to remind you of your husband's loyal service to us and involving the Garda or anyone else for that matter would be a bad idea and not good for your own and your children's future health. Do I make myself understood?'

'You bastards, you threaten me and my children, well you have gone too far this time so fuck off.' She threw the phone down and burst into tears.

All this was picked up by MI5's monitoring system and immediately relayed to GCHQ in Cheltenham and Great Malborough Street in London.

The head of MI5 A4 surveillance section called an urgent meeting with the deputy Director General and brought him up to date with the latest surveillance they had on "Eagle".

'Sir, following the information we have obtained regarding the subject it's reasonable to assume the IRA have him in custody or have indeed executed him for passing details of their activities to us or so they believe.'

'It certainly looks like it, I agree, but until we have definite proof we need to keep up surveillance and devote all our efforts to make doubly sure. I will again contact our cousins in MI6 and bring them into the loop, who in turn will, hopefully, deploy their resources abroad including the republic. Keep up the good work and I shall be in touch shortly with a plan of action if necessary.'

'OK, sir, I will keep you fully informed of any further developments.'

The Deputy Director Sir James Overton immediately contacted his MI6 counterpart and the head of the Northern Ireland Special Branch calling for all possible assistance in tracing Alan Conlon or "Eagle" to use his code name.

On Saturday morning soon after 11am Brigadier John Chalmers the director of UK Special Forces touched down smoothly onto the tarmac of Cork airport using a scheduled domestic flight from London Stanstead. He was met in the arrivals lounge by Colonel Francis Coogan of the Irish Defence Force and an old friend from way back. Both men were in civilian clothes.

'John, it's nice to see you after such a long time, Have you put on a bit of weight lately?'

'Hello, Frank, yes I'm afraid I have and Janet is always reminding me of it, all those bloody lunches in the MOD. I often wish I was back in the regiment but time takes its toll as you know.'

'I have the car outside and all the fishing gear we will need for a productive trip,' he said, collecting the Brigadier's holdall from the baggage carousel.

The 90km journey to Bantry Bay was uneventful along the N71 through County Cork and into Kerry, the only hold up being a Garda patrol stopping and checking car driver and insurance details near Clonakilty.

The Brigadier was keen to get the conversation around to the matter in hand. 'Frank, I wonder if you can help me clear up a small matter of an apparently missing man in your country. I must add this is strictly off the record and no reference to you will ever be made to anyone in the British Government under any circumstances.'

'I will try to help if I can, John but I may not be able to get access to Garda records or any current investigations they may have ongoing.'

'The last thing I want is to get the Garda involved as I believe this man has been abducted by the IRA. You see he is, or was a mole for us and he has suddenly gone off the radar. MI5 were planning to give him and his family a new identity and move him abroad under their informer's protection system. His family are still at home in Ballybrittas and his wife has contacted the IRA leadership in Dublin and been warned off as far as our surveillance has established through phone-tapping and suchlike.'

'Ah, MI5 up to its old tricks again I see. I thought there was an agreement with the Republic that this sort of thing was to stop and the British should request our Special Branch to undertake these operations, John.'

'Yes I suppose you're right but this is not in my control as you know but there is a panic of sorts going on in London over this issue. I strongly believe this character has been executed and probably dumped in a bog somewhere.'

'Frank I don't want to sound ungrateful but experience has shown us that your Special Branch has not been seen to be very sympathetic to the Brits in the last ten years. It would appear we co-operate well in many things such as drug smuggling and people trafficking etc but not with IRA terrorism for some reason.'

'Oh I think you are a little sceptical, John but I must ask you one thing, did the SAS carry out the raid in Galway some time ago?'

'Not to my knowledge,' lied the Brigadier unconvincingly.

'John, that raid had all the hallmarks of the SAS including the foreign markings on the spent 9mm cartridge cases; it had to be the SAS or SBS of the marines. Several dead IRA men were found, some with obvious double tap bullet strikes to the head, classic Special Forces style, my friend.'

'That's as maybe, Frank; perhaps it was your Ranger Force that your government decided to have trained in Canada in spite of the offer we made to train them in Hereford. The Canadians have no real Special Forces experience, ours is second to none.'

'There is no point in us arguing and we will not resolve the issue this way,' said the Brigadier with a smile but with a hint of anger.

At this point the Irish Colonel knew what he had

always suspected; the raid on the IRA camp in Galway was indeed carried out by the British.

The following morning the two officers launched their boat into the choppy waters of Bantry Bay and set their fishing lines with bait to attract cod, which are known to be plentiful in this area. The conversation continued and the Irish Colonel said he would look into the disappearance of Alan Conlon but on a strictly unofficial basis and with no guarantees of any kind. Although the Colonel had served in the British Parachute Regiment with distinction he was now in the Irish Defence Force and that's where his loyalties lay. He had never intended to return to Britain to live and would retire to his country cottage in County Mayo at the end of his service which has eight months to run.

The two men parted company at Cork airport having enjoyed each other's company and some good productive fishing; a large Atlantic cod had provided a sumptuous dinner for them both the previous evening.

The following week the Irish Colonel made discreet enquiries but drew a blank. Irish Army Intelligence kept some surveillance on the IRA, mostly in the border areas, but nothing was flagged up. Even a routine meeting with the special branch in the Curragh Camp near Kildare proved fruitless. It would appear Mr Conlon had disappeared without trace.

Back in Ballybrittas Mrs Conlon tried to carry on as normal but was finding it increasingly difficult with her children often asking where their father was and when was he coming home. The IRA leadership decided to give her some money as she had no income apart from some social security payments, which were barely enough to run the home and feed the children. Late one night a large envelope was put through her letterbox and when she found it the following morning it contained 100 Irish Punts. There was no note but she knew where it had come from. In her heart she knew her husband had been executed by the IRA and there was nothing she could do about it. All she could hope for was help from MI5 and a passage out of Ireland for good.

The brigadier had had several guarded phone calls from the Colonel in Ireland but no information was forthcoming and he realised there probably wouldn't be. Either he was unable to find anything out or he was withholding information for whatever reason. All the same it was frustrating for the brigadier and unlikely to prove any further use. He was convinced the Colonel knew it was the SAS who raided the training camp in Galway, in spite of his denials.

In London MI5 had its usual weekly meeting with the various heads of department and other agencies during which the subject came up about Conlon and his whereabouts. The Director General rose to speak.

'Gentlemen we have recently recruited a mole within the IRA and so far she has provided useful pillow-talk information on activities regarding their supply chain of ammunition and bomb making facilities. It would appear she has ingratiated herself into the upper levels of the organisation and provides, shall we say, "comfort" for a senior member in Dublin. We are carefully guarding her and nurturing her so no details of her will be provided, not even her code name. If we find another training camp or other facility that needs to be erased from this planet I will request the SAS's assistance in carrying it out. Is that OK with you Brigadier?'

'Certainly, sir, we would be delighted to be of service, it's what we do best.'

'Commander Collins, has Special Branch come up with anything lately regarding Conlon?'

'No, sir, we have drawn a complete blank. I have a contact in the Irish community in Kilburn who is keeping his ear to the ground in the pubs and clubs but nothing so far.'

'One thing that has come to our notice, through another contact in the Garda, is the death of a Mr John O'Hagan in Tralee. O'Hagan served in the British Army in Cyprus under the UN flag and although British born, in South London as a matter of fact, moved to Ireland and joined the IRA, rising to the position of quartermaster and training officer/coordinator. It appears he suffered a wound and settled in Tralee to lie low and was being treated by a local GP for dizzy spells and severe headaches along with his injuries. According to reports he collapsed and died in the surgery, the doctor being unable to revive him. We strongly believe he was wounded during the raid on the training camp and escaped to the far south west of the country to be treated. In fact his presence at the camp was confirmed by Conlon,' added the Director General.

'Brigadier, perhaps you could explain how come some people managed to escape during your men's raid on this camp. We know of at least two, one we have just mentioned and the other, an American, who so far has eluded us,' said the Director.

'Sir if there was an easy answer I would give it to you, nothing is certain in this life and that includes SAS operations. It is very easy for armchair bound members of the establishment with the benefit of hindsight, to criticize military operations but they have absolutely no understanding of really what goes on unless they have served themselves. Unfortunately, most of them have not.'

'Brigadier, that was not meant as a criticism of your forces; just an observation.'

'Sorry sir but it didn't come across as that. We have the finest Special Forces in the world, just look at the many other countries' military we train currently including the US Delta Force. Often we have too many overseas commitments and not enough resources to cope. We do our best with what we have.'

'OK OK, Brigadier point taken, perhaps we can move on.'

'Thank you, Director.'

'I have given instructions for the intense surveillance to continue on the Conlon home and family and for the wire-taps to remain in the hope we get a lead on his whereabouts, it's just a waiting game at the moment,' added Sir James Overton, the deputy Director with a shrug.

When the meeting ended the Brigadier went to the ministry of defence in Whitehall where his office was situated to look at all the latest Special Forces operations that were currently underway worldwide. If an operation came up now he really had no spare capacity and would have to scrape the barrel in Hereford or Poole where the

SBS were based. The telephone rang and startled him from his thoughts.

'Good afternoon, John. How is your part of the army these days?' said Lieutenant General Sir Richard Housland, the Army Commander based at Lisburn in Northern Ireland.

'Oh hello, sir,' replied the Brigadier. 'Dealing with these Whitehall wankers is really hard work, roll on retirement. What can I do for you?'

'Talk like that and you will end up in the Tower of London swinging from the yardarm or wherever they swing people,' laughed the General.

'That might be a fitting end to my army life. Anyway enough of that, how can I be of assistance, sir?'

'John, as you know, we have a sabre troop of your lads here doing what they do best. However, some of my senior officers are a little worried about their presence and conduct at high level meetings. I know they had every right to be there but yesterday a meeting was taking place when all of a sudden a large gust of wind blew open the door. In a flash the six SAS guys had 9mm pistols pointed at the door and frankly some of my blokes nearly shit themselves. I don't allow firearms during closed meetings and was wondering if you could have a word with them about this as I don't really have any authority over them. The other thing is they all seem to dress as they please and wear no rank markings so we really have no idea who are officers and who are not.'

'As you know, sir, Special Forces command come directly under me and ultimately the Prime Minister, so we are really outside the normal army command and do not have to answer to them. I suggest you talk to your officers and explain this to them and just carry on your meetings as normal. The SAS and SBS will take what information they need to function and after passing it through the Special Forces command will be tasked accordingly. I would suggest your officers would be very glad my men are so quick with their weapons if they were attacked because for all their training, ordinary infantrymen and officers can't hold a candle to the SAS. Rank plays very little part in SAS operations and I know conventionally trained officers have difficulty with that but that's the way it is, and will continue, sir.'

'John straight to the point as usual; I'll pass it on. By the way, when are you coming over the water to see how the real army operates?' concluded the General with a snigger, putting the phone down. 'What wouldn't I give to be a young subaltern all over again, out on patrol and miles away from all this Whitehall nonsense,' he said aloud to himself.

Five days later Doreen Conlon went into the Garda station in Ballybrittas and officially reported her husband missing.

Chapter 20

Liam Reagan returned to Dublin and entered Trinity College and although far from recovered, began his course in the classics. In spite of being under constant surveillance by the IRA he just absorbed himself in the curriculum and for once he was happy with his lot. The IRA and active service took very much a backseat in his life and apart from check-ups at the hospital his days were filled with study.

Colm MacDiamid, the Chief of Staff, received regular updates on Reagan's fitness progress and decided it would soon be time for him to carry out another job for the organisation, but some refresher training had to come first. At the end of the summer term at the university, the IRA contacted Reagan and asked him to come to a house in Dundalk for a meeting. This was more of an order than a request.

'Good morning, Liam, how are you getting on at university these days?' asked the Chief of Staff.

'The study is hard but interesting. My health generally improving but I still get very tired and have to sleep in the afternoons on most days. The doctors have told me this is to be expected and will continue for some considerable time to come.' replied Reagan, hoping it may go some way to delay any role they had in mind for him.

'Well I know these things take time but we have a job in the north that needs your expertise; we thought that the winter break would be a good time for you to earn your keep, so to speak,' continued the Chief of Staff.

'I really don't feel up to it at the moment, don't you have anyone else who can do it?'

'No I don't, Mr Reagan! You have had the training and it is you who have had the success following that training. Do I make myself clear?'

'Very clear, Colm, but as I said I still feel very weak and on regular medication, I just don't think I can do it at the moment.'

'Mr Reagan this is not a request. In any army soldiers have to follow orders and the IRA is no different, you will do as you are ordered!'

'And if I refuse?'

'Don't even go there, Reagan. Do I make myself clear?'

'Yes I think you do, Colm. What do you want me to do?'

'There is a training course coming up in Libya soon and you will be on it to brush up some skills that may have faded, OK?'

'OK when do I go?'

'We will be in touch so don't leave Dublin without letting us know first.'

'OK, Colm as you say.'

On the way back to Dublin, Reagan pondered over his fate and could not see a way out apart from an IRA bullet if he messed up or spoke about his up and coming task. Many of his university friends offered him trips to London and elsewhere over the break but he refused saying he had much study to catch up with due to lost time throughout his illness. He could run and go abroad, but where? He had no income or any savings to support himself; all he had was a passport and little else. There was an old uncle in the USA, his late father's brother, who had emigrated thirty years ago, who he might be able to contact for help but it was a long shot. They had not spoken for years; he decided to sleep on it.

Ten days later Reagan was contacted by the Chief of Staff and informed he must be ready to travel to Libya in three days time. The journey would be from Dublin to Paris and then on to Tripoli; he would not be alone. The pickup from his residence was early and the rain was heavy for the journey to Dublin airport. At the airport he was met by two others who would travel with him and also partake in the course. No names were exchanged and very little conversation took place during the entire journey to Tripoli.

When the plane touched down and the doors were opened, the heat was stifling and Reagan felt weak and listless; how was he going to get through this course? The journey to the training camp took over four hours through semi arid desert and the coach contained a mix of nationalities; there was a sense of fear and apprehension amongst those present.

It was getting dark as the coach approached a decrepit-looking cluster of buildings and a dusty administration block, the heat was still overbearing. All the men and women trainee terrorists were ordered out and into the reception. The Irishmen could not understand the Arabic commands and this riled the trainers into prodding them with their batons. The interpreter turned out to be an English-speaking Libyan who had attended Cambridge University and held an MSc in biology; he introduced himself as Abdul.

'Mr Reagan, welcome to my country, I hope you settle in well,' said the Arab.

'Thank you, Abdul, this heat will take a bit of getting used to though and I have not been well for some time, but I'll do my best.'

'Yes I'm sure you will as we really make no exceptions here for poor performance and subsequent failures,' added the Arab with an edge to his voice.

The following morning training began with a 5 kilometre run at 5am while the temperature was still 20°C, then into the crude canteen for breakfast followed by communal showers for everyone.

Reagan was suffering and feeling very nauseous; he was sure he would not be able to carry on for too long. The duration of the course was supposed to be fourteen days yet after the first morning he felt so weak that he was certain he would not complete it. There was absolutely no chance of escape from this God-forsaken hole in the North African Desert. The rest of the day was given over to weapons training with the famous AK47 assault rifle. This seemed a little strange to Reagan as he had previously trained and used a 5.56mm Armalite in Ulster; the characteristics of the AK were quite different. At the end of the day he went into his shared bunkhouse and collapsed on his bed, totally exhausted and sweating profusely.

The following day it was grenade training using a variety of Russian made high explosive anti-personnel fragmentation grenades. Feeling a little better Reagan performed well and the former French Foreign Legion instructor seemed happy with his attempts.

During the evening Paul Delmond, a former member of the elite 2e Régiment étranger de Parachutistes, spoke to Reagan in perfect English.

'Liam, why are you here as you are obviously not fully fit?'

'I'm here because I have no choice in the matter, Paul. In my organisation they don't take no for an answer, once in, always in I'm afraid.'

'Ah, this is nearly always the case with terror groups and often the only way out is by the bullet.'

'I might ask you the same question, Paul.'

'Well I'm really Belgian by birth but lived in France from the age of eleven because my parents moved to Lyon with better job prospects but I managed to keep my Belgian passport. I decided to join the French Army but they stopped me because I had managed to get a criminal conviction when I was 17, for beating up a gay man trying to proposition me in a railway station and was sentenced to six months in prison. I simply went into the Foreign Legion recruiting office in Marseille and applied as a Belgian National. Following a selection process I was accepted in the 2nd Foreign Legion Parachute Regiment and after basic training at Castelnaudary sent to Corsica for parachute training at Calvi joining the 2e REP. I completed ten years service and decided to come out into the civilian world and drifted into petty crime.

Because of the skills I possessed I started training anyone who paid me enough money, a sort of mercenary really I suppose,' added the trainer with a Gallic shrug.

'I'll tell you what, Paul, I'm going to struggle to last the fourteen days that we're supposed to be here, it wouldn't be so bad if I was fully fit but I'm not and won't be for some time to come, if ever.'

'Unfortunately, Liam I can't do anything to help you in this situation. I just have to train people and have no say in what goes on apart from the training role and assessment.'

'I understand that, but right now I feel trapped and don't know which way to turn. I'll just have to do the best I can and see what happens I suppose.'

Reagan managed to keep his head above water for the rest of the course and scraped by, but the work involved really took its toll on his health, leaving him unable to sleep for more than a few hours at a time and constantly thirsty with a throbbing headache. When he arrived back in Dublin he was met and taken to see the Chief of Staff who congratulated him on the completion of the training.

'Liam I hope you had a good time in Libya, you certainly caught the sun that's for sure, my friend. I think you deserve a little rest before your talents are required, so go home and just relax; we will be in touch. By the way if anyone enquires about your tan just tell them you had a couple of weeks in Spain soaking up the sun along with the birds and booze.'

'I need the rest, Colm and I will have to visit my doctor because I feel really unwell; this training came too soon after my hospital stay you know.'

'I know that but operational duties must come first in all cases, we all have our trying times but you will have to accept that, however we are not totally unsympathetic Liam and will do our best for you in the circumstances, OK?'

'Yes OK, Colm, I know you will.'

'Right, away you go now and have a well deserved rest, but don't leave Dublin without letting us know first, is that clear, Liam?'

'Loud and clear, I just want to get to bed right now.'

After he left the office of the Chief of Staff said to his colleague Kevin Dempsey. 'We have to watch him like a hawk; I am not convinced he is going to be much use for some time. Two things worry me, firstly his health and second his reluctance to carry on fighting for the cause. If he steps out of line he will have to go the way of Conlon and the likes, if you know what I mean. I want you to place an around-the-clock watch on Mr Reagan, Kev, but only use reliable people and those who can keep their mouth shut.'

'I will keep you informed of all movement and contact you on your emergency number if anything untoward happens, Colm, you can rest assured.'

'OK, Kev, do your best.'

Reagan was driven home and went to bed following a shower and a cup of strong tea, something he had missed in Libya. The next day he made an appointment to see Dr Connolly.

Two days later he went into the surgery and took a seat.

'Good afternoon, Mr Reagan, what can I do for you?' said the doctor.

'As you know I underwent surgery for cancer recently and I just feel drained and nauseous almost continuously. I am taking all my prescribed drugs along with the occasional painkillers but I still feel groggy.'

'I couldn't help noticing you have a fine tan, where did you get that?'

'Oh, I had a couple of weeks in Spain to try and recover but it doesn't seem to have made much difference, doctor.'

'OK, Liam, take your shirt off and lie on the couch, let's have a look at you.'

The examination took about fifteen minutes and at the end of it the doctor allowed Reagan to get dressed and resume his seat.

'Well, Liam I am not happy with the feel of your abdomen and I want you to go back to the surgeon who carried out your operation and let him take a closer look at you. Are you OK with that?'

'Yes of course, doctor, will you make the arrangements?'

'Yes I'll phone him now.' When the doctor finished his conversation with the surgeon he told Reagan to be at the hospital on Saturday at 9am and report to the oncology department.

On his way home Reagan began to worry that something had gone seriously wrong and what the outcome would be. Would it be another operation? He had to let the Chief of Staff know so he decided to go to the office and try and tell him personally.

When he arrived he was met by an attractive woman in her early thirties, and although she never mentioned her name, she was polite and made him comfortable while she phoned Colm MacDiamid and informed him of the situation. Reagan had never met this woman before and wondered what her role was in the organisation. She seemed to have a degree of authority and presence that he had not noticed in all the other IRA staff he had met; she seemed intelligent as well.

Liam Reagan went to the hospital and was examined by the surgeon who decided another operation would be necessary and with some urgency. He was admitted the same day and prepared for surgery for the Monday afternoon.

Back at the Dublin HQ the Chief of Staff questioned a doctor they used to look after injured volunteers and who carried out medical treatment on an unofficial basis. As usual this doctor was also working under threat.

'Doctor, what could be the problem with our man?'

'Well obviously I can't get to see the notes but my gut feeling is that scar tissue could be the culprit or a leaking blood vessel, or simply not enough recuperation time has passed to allow all the systems to recover properly. This man had major surgery and this type of trauma takes time to recover. In some cases it never does recover and the patient may only live for up to a year or so, it's very difficult to know without reading the notes.'

'Do you know the surgeon?'

'No, only by reputation, he's very good by all accounts.'

'So what should we do in the meantime, just sit and wait?'

'That's the only option as far as I can see, Colm.'

'Just tell me one thing, when he comes out of surgery

what is the recovery time for the wearing-off of the anaesthetic, and is he liable to talk irrationally during this period?'

'The substance used in putting someone to sleep varies depending on the patient's condition; I am not an anaesthetist so I can't be more specific on this issue. There is certainly the risk of a patient mumbling during recovery as there always is. Often it's just disjointed nonsense but one can never be sure and it can't be avoided,' replied the doctor uncomfortably and with sweating palms.

'OK thanks, doc, I'll get someone to show you out, and thanks once again.'

The doctor hurried away and this was noted by the MI5 surveillance officer who had just been assigned.

Colm MacDiamid was a worried man and discussed this with the woman who had become his lover, breaking IRA rules into the bargain. 'My main concern is when Reagan comes out of the operating theatre and is taken to recovery. Will he open his mouth?'

'I suppose it's a risk we have to take, Colm darling,' said Mairead Donovan, stroking his shoulders and running her hand down his chest.

'If Reagan talks we are fucked, my love,' replied MacDiamid thoughtfully.

'Now "fucked" is a word I hope you will put into action later, Colm,' said Mairead, brushing her ample breasts against his shoulder.

That night in bed Colm MacDiamid told her the full story of Liam Reagan and his exploits in the assassination of the Chief Constable of Northern Ireland. Over the next few weeks, as he grew more and more confident of her trust, he included the role of Lenihan and O'Hagan and the training camp in Galway. He stated with quiet threatening that any informer would be executed and cited the example of Alan Conlon.

Mairead Donovan, a native of Kilkenny, got to know more about the IRA's activities than men and women who had been in the movement for years.

Had the Chief of Staff, Colm MacDiamid, said too much?

Chapter 21

The Garda turned up at Doreen Conlon's house in Ballybrittas following her phone call to report her husband missing.

'Maidin mhaith – Good morning, Mrs Conlon, I am Sergeant Dillon of the missing persons office in Kildare and I have come to get a few details of your husband if that's OK with you?'

Oh yes of course, please come in, Sergeant.'

The Garda sergeant took full details of Alan Conlon including his last known whereabouts, any known medical problems, and Mrs Conlon's view of his mental state. He also questioned her as to whether he might have a lover or financial worries that could cause him to disappear off the radar without warning. At this point she never mentioned the IRA or his membership but that was sure to come out subsequently anyway whether she liked it or not. The sergeant left after about an hour giving the optimistic view to Mrs Conlon that her husband would be found safe and well. It was not a view he personally shared. Having dealt with many cases like this his first port of call was the Garda Special Branch in Dublin for any possible known links to the IRA.

The following day Sergeant Dillon had an answer back from Dublin. Alan Conlon had previously served in the Irish army as an NCO instructor and after discharge drifted into membership of the IRA albeit at a very low level. There had not been any convictions and he was not on the special branch watch list. He had been known to travel to Ulster but for reasons unknown. He had done several menial jobs since leaving the army and managed to support his family adequately but certainly not lavishly. He, along with his wife and children, had recently visited a holiday camp in North Wales. It was assumed by special branch that this was nothing more than a holiday so no action was required.

Sergeant Dillon carried out all possible enquiries and later informed Mrs Conlon that although no information was forthcoming he was still on the case and would remain so for as long as necessary.

The IRA command had been very quiet and not contacted Doreen Conlon so she had no idea what would happen next. She didn't really expect any help from them and as far as she was concerned they could all rot in hell. As the weeks progressed she became more and more certain that her husband had been compromised and executed by the IRA. Where were the Brits and all their promises of help?

The MI5 phone-tap produced nothing substantial and the surveillance was the same. Mrs Conlon just went about her daily business as usual; the children went to school and had the occasional sleepovers' with their friends. Jim Stone, of the MI5 A4 surveillance unit, duly reported the Garda visit to the house but had nothing else to add.

London HQ ordered the watching and phone-tap to

continue for the time being. The watch team on the IRA HQ in Dublin also produced nothing of any importance with the exception of a local doctor entering and staying for about an hour before returning to his surgery nearby. The disappearance of Alan Conlon, alias "Eagle ", remained a mystery.

In London, at the Marlborough Street offices of MI5, the weekly meeting of the Security Services called on all their representatives for their input and the question of what to do with the Conlon family came up. The deputy Director General opened the debate.

'Gentlemen in view of the disappearance of "Eagle" we still have the problem of the Conlon family which I understand consists of a wife and two young children. We promised the whole family a new life at the appropriate time when it would be clear that "eagle" had nothing further to offer us. I know she wanted to go to Australia or New Zealand but the level of information he provided was not sufficient to justify the cost of this. I gather we offered Spain, but Mrs Conlon was not keen due to the culture and language problems this would bring. Any suggestions on the way forward, gentlemen?'

'Sir,' said one of the resettlement officers. 'What about bringing them to England and perhaps settling them in Norfolk, say Watton, just 18 miles from Norwich for example? We have a number of ex-military houses available from the closure of an old base there and I believe this could be the cheapest option. No foreign language to learn and no change of culture to worry about. There are a number of schools within walking distance and Mrs Conlon could get some employment locally to help with the income.'

'That seems perfectly acceptable to me. What do you all think? Speak up so we can move on, gentlemen.'

After a short debate the general consensus was to go with the idea and the next stage was to put this to the Conlon family. 'Just one thing, sir,' said the Commander of the Metropolitan Police Special Branch. 'Do we really have to honour our commitment to Mrs Conlon? I say this because if the IRA has indeed executed him and it's certainly beginning to look like it, she would come to no harm from them. After all, as far as we know, she had no part in their activities and her husband's debt has been fully paid up by his death. This of course would be beneficial to my department because we would have to supply periodic security for the family and we are currently stretched to breaking point as you know.'

'Commander,' said the deputy Director, 'you are a hard man but I take your point. Perhaps we should put this whole matter on hold until we get something positive regarding "Eagle". Is there any way you could seek assistance from your opposite number in the Garda SP to ascertain "Eagles" whereabouts, you know, off the record? I say that because Chief Superintendent O'Driscoll has been invited to the police college at Bramshill for a conference on international terrorism next month and that you are one of the speakers.'

'Sir I will do my best,' replied the Commander, thinking that crafty old bastard's into everything, talk about fingers in many pies!

'OK, gentlemen, we will maintain the status quo on the Conlon family until we get further information. If by any chance "Eagle" shows up he and the family must be spirited out of Ireland without delay. That is a direct order without further reference to me. The route could be up to Aldergrove and then to Marham or Coltishall, courtesy of the RAF. I want to be kept fully up to date on progress, and by the way, Commander good luck with O'Driscoll.

The meeting ended and Commander Paul Collins of Special Branch and Brigadier John Chalmers went to the canteen for lunch before returning to their specific offices.

'Have you had any leads on the assassination of Sir Frank Cooper yet, Paul?'

'Not really but we have had a wink that the man concerned is an astute and educated gent and not the usual IRA operative we normally deal with. His escape from the scene was faultless and no doubt his trail was well and truly covered. "Eagle" told MI5 that he was pretty sure he knew who this man was but before he could really determine his identity he was booted out of the training camp by the American who we now strongly believe to be Michael Lenihan, formally of the US Green Berets. Lenihan has disappeared from the scene and his whereabouts at this time are unknown. I understand the CIA has been informed but so far nothing. Even if we catch him the only charges that could brought against him are in the Irish Republic as he has committed no known offences in the UK. That's the dilemma we face at the moment, John. We are keeping our ears to the ground amongst the Irish community in Kilburn and elsewhere along with our colleagues in MI5. MI6 are sniffing around abroad in their inimitable style but they like to keep everything close to their chest and only share information when they really have to.'

'Oh the usual rivalry between the spooks I suppose,' replied the Brigadier.

'Just a question, Paul, what would you do if you were able to catch Lenihan within UK territory?'

'I think we would have to get advice from the attorney general on what legal grounds we would have to detain him. As I said, he has committed no known offences in the UK or Northern Ireland. I imagine eventual extradition to the Irish Republic. As police we could not countenance any other sort of action.'

'No of course, but it would be a bummer to have to hand him over,' said the Brigadier.

'So what are you up to in the ministry of defence at the moment, John?'

'Oh all the usual admin nonsense and trying to keep ministers happy on all things military, I have to visit General Housland, the Army Commander in Northern Ireland, next week and straighten up a few of the senior officers who don't fully understand the workings of the Special Forces. They have been moaning that my blokes don't wear rank markings and dress as they like and have the temerity to carry pistols at meetings. The trouble is, of course, that the entire bloody Sandhurst officer training is all about rank and position and status with everyone in their respective posts. The SAS don't operate like that and are pretty much free to choose their own way of doing things. Calling officers "sir" and polishing their boots and pips are way down the food chain,' added the Brigadier with a grin.

'I know, I have had a little training with them in Hereford. I wouldn't like to be on the wrong end of any of them, that's for sure,' said the Commander, picking up his knife and fork.

In Ballybrittas everything was quiet; with Mrs Conlon now certain her husband had been murdered and would never come home. Unbeknown to everyone she had befriended an old past romance who was her first crush at school and with whom she had recently met by chance in a supermarket in Kildare. He had divorced the previous year and lived alone but worked in Dublin, as an accountant; he was clearly comfortably off with a nice detached house and a new car. Doreen Conlon felt the old pangs of days gone by as soon as she met him. It would seem he felt the same. They met again the following Saturday in Kildare; the children staying with friends.

In the restaurant, over lunch, Doreen told him a little of what had happened in her life over the years and he listened sympathetically and with interest. She told of the IRA period and the fact her husband was never going to rise within the organisation and their family life was being torn apart because of it. With Conlon doing mostly odd jobs the family lot was just above poverty level and showed no signs of improvement.

Aiden Riley felt sorry for Doreen and promised he would do all he could for her; she still looked good in spite of her 40 years and he still quite fancied her. They agreed to meet again soon but decided to keep it from the children for the time being, to allow a decent time to pass following the disappearance of her husband. Secretly Mrs Conlon hoped that her husband stayed away for good as she often contemplated leaving him in the past. They exchanged phone numbers and promised to keep in close contact.

MI5 picked up the phone conversations and passed these through GCHQ to London but nothing in them furthered any clues for "Eagles" disappearance, so the surveillance continued with Mrs Conlon being shadowed.

The Chief of Staff in Dublin, Colm MacDiamid, decided to allow Mrs Conlon to go along with the Garda enquiries and let the passage of time bring it to an open verdict, after all there was no evidence that the IRA had executed her husband nor would there be, of that he was sure.

Chapter 22

On the other side of Dublin Liam Reagan came out of the operating theatre and was taken to the recovery room, still unconscious and full of tubes and ECG attachments. Over the next few hours he started to come round but was often violently sick and had terrible pains in his stomach. The following morning the surgeon Mr Singh arrived to see his patient. 'Good morning, Mr Reagan how are you today?'

'Good morning, doctor, I feel terrible and can't stop being sick. What did you find when you opened me up?'

'Well unfortunately there is still a trace of the original cancer. I was convinced we had got all of it but alas not. I have removed some more of your bowel in the hope that this will do the trick. I feel fairly confident we have got it this time but recovery will take time I'm afraid.'

That evening one of the Chief of Staff's deputies, Kevin Dempsey, came in to visit Reagan. 'How are you Liam?'

'Fucking terrible right now and it seems a long period of recovery will be required to get over this, the surgeon told me this morning during his visit.'

'OK I will pass the message on to the right people, just concentrate on getting well,' said Dempsey.

Within ten days Reagan was discharged and the IRA

provided a car to take him home. They would also be available to take him for outpatient appointments and for that, Reagan was grateful.

The Chief of Staff was not happy about Reagan's illness and enforced absence from duty but there was little he could do about it for the time being. At least one problem had passed, that of Reagan talking under the influence of the anaesthetic. Mairead Donovan, the chief's lover, casually asked him what was going to happen to Reagan in the future and whether he would be available to carry out further work for the movement in view of all that had happened recently.

'As soon as he has recovered he will be employed again on active service, we have a number of potential targets for him. He has proved himself in the north as a good efficient operator, "cool, calm and collected," I think they call it under pressure. He is too good to let go and if he ever thinks he can break away, well, let's say he knows the consequences of that!'

'Oh, Colm, I'm sure that won't happen. That's something I would never do, my love, you know that.'

'I sincerely hope not, Mairead. Now come here and make a busy man happy.'

Liam Reagan was lying on his bed thinking of all that had happened since he joined the IRA and regretted every minute of it but realistically how he could get out of it. If he moved to leave he would end up in a bog somewhere with a bullet in the head. All he could try was to prolong his illness and hope for the best but he wasn't confident, as the IRA would keep a close watch on him.

As the weeks passed he grew stronger and stronger

and was pleasantly surprised at his progress, the nausea and stomach pains had passed and his colour returned to a much healthier look. He received several visits from the IRA to check on his progress and he had managed to contact his uncle in America by phone. During one phone call he casually asked about making a visit and his uncle was delighted at the prospect of this. The big problem was how to get out of Ireland. Although he had a passport he did not have much spare cash for the airfare. The other problem was that he would have to visit the US embassy to get a visa and he might be under surveillance by the IRA. He could probably raise the cash through a loan but the visa would be the problem.

Reagan carried on with his studies at the university but mostly from home and had been allocated a tutor who he could call upon when preparing his assignments and course work. One afternoon there was a knock at the door.

'Hello, Liam,' said Mairead Donovan. 'I've been sent to see how you are getting on and whether you want anything.'

'Well this is a surprise. Come in, love, I was just doing some study, trying to keep the old brain active you know.'

'Your course must be hard, how do you manage it all?'

'Well I suppose it's all a matter of application and bloody graft really. I managed to get a reasonably good education in my teens and this is really an extension of that. Who knows, one day I may be a professor at Trinity College,' he grinned. 'Would you like some tea, Mairead?'

'Oh that would be nice, yes please. It's a nice place you have here.'

'Not bad, it's owned by the university and I pay a small rent which I get from my grant and I just about manage food as well. I'm not a millionaire just yet I'm afraid.'

'Oh, when you are a professor, I'm sure the money will come rolling in and you will be able to take your lady to all the nice places.'

'Actually I don't have a lady at the moment,' replied Reagan a little surprised.

'Well that's a surprise. I would have thought you had to turn them away by the truck load, being so good looking and intelligent, Liam.'

'I should be so lucky, my love. What about you, I bet you don't go short on male company?'

'Oh I have my moments but nothing serious at present, how are you feeling after the operation?'

'Pretty weak but improving daily I think, I like to get out and walk a little and go to the pool, although if I don't do more soon I will struggle to get into my swimming trunks.'

'I bet you look good in them. You will have to wear them for me and let me be the judge of how you look and whether it's a struggle or not, you handsome man, Liam.'

'Do you think you should be talking like this to a sick man, Mairead, you don't know how I might react?'

'Well that's my problem, Mr Sick Man. I might have to nurse you back to full health, you never know. So, are you going to show me your trunks?'

'Well I don't know, love, are you sure you want to have a look at them?'

'Of course but with one provision, you have to be wearing them and nothing else.'

'But you will see my operation scar and it doesn't look very nice.'

'I won't look at that; promise,' she smiled.

'OK, just sit there and I will go and change, don't go away now will you?'

Reagan went into his bedroom and changed into his skimpy swimming trunks and although he was slender in build he was beginning to get a little paunch in his stomach through lack of exercise. As he came back into the room Mairead was standing near the window, her ample breasts prominent and her tight blue jeans displaying her long legs and small tight bottom.

'Well that's better, Liam. Wow, what a beautiful sight, turn around and let me see all of you. All man, I can see! Come over and sit down with me on the sofa,' she said with a slight pant in her voice.

Reagan did as he was told and in no time she was kissing him hungrily and with passion, her tongue searching for his at the same time as her hand went to his groin. Reagan guided her to the bedroom and in moments they were making love, as he had never done before. When they had finished they both showered and went into the lounge for a drink. The conversation got round to the IRA and its campaign against the British Army in the north.

Reagan asked what her role was in the organisation and she said it just consisted of office work and a sort of PA to the Chief of Staff. She did not carry out any active duties nor had any special training. As soon as Reagan realised she worked closely with the Chief of Staff he felt his stomach begin to knot up with fear but tried not to show it.

'I must go now, Liam but not a word of what happened here this afternoon, it's our secret, my love,' she said warmly.

Reagan watched from the window as she crossed the square of the accommodation block and made her way out of the complex towards the bus stop for Dublin central.

'Well that was a turn up for the book, an afternoons reading interrupted by a good shag with a beautiful blonde. Boy what a goer!' he muttered.

The following morning Reagan had an appointment with his GP; a routine check on his medication and progress.

'Liam,' said the doctor. 'I have spoken to the surgeon Mr Singh, and he advises that you have a spell of radiotherapy to boost the treatment and I would strongly advise you go along with this. Shall I set up the appointments for you?'

'Please, if you would, doctor, anything that helps get rid of this thing once and for all.'

'OK, Liam leave it to me and the hospital will contact you directly with appointment dates,' said Dr Connolly with a smile.

Three days later Reagan received a phone call from the hospital just outside Dublin, informing him of the dates and times of the RT treatment and the expected duration of its course.

The next afternoon Reagan went to see the Chief of Staff to explain that the treatment would have to take place at a hospital just outside Dublin. It was to start in a fortnight's time and be regular for six weeks, so this meant he would have to travel. As he was leaving, in walked Mairead

'Good afternoon, Mr Reagan,' she said brightly, 'how are you feeling today?'

'Oh hello, Mairead, yes I'm fine thanks and your good self?'

'Pretty good but the boss here works me hard you know, all part of the job I suppose,' she replied with a wink of her eye.

'Well, Liam, I do understand the treatment you are having as my own mother went through the same thing but I must insist that any deviation from this is run through me first. Do you fully understand what I say?'

'Of course, Colm without a doubt,' replied Reagan, with a shiver going down his spine.

As soon as he left the Chief of Staff's office, Reagan went into a small pub for a stiff drink to calm his nerves. 'What the fuck have I let myself into?' he muttered to himself after the first long gulp of Guinness, albeit against his doctors orders.

Two days later he was in the shower when there was a knock at the door of his flat. 'Hang on I'll be with you in a moment,' he shouted, grabbing a towel and wrapping it around himself. Still dripping he answered the door to find Mairead standing there, looking like a Page 3 model, with her slim figure and long hair down to her shoulders. 'Hello Mairead, what are you doing here?' he asked.

'Well that's not a very nice welcome, Liam. I have only come round to see how you are as you looked a little pale in the office the other day.'

'Sorry, love you took me by surprise, come in, please.'

As they entered the living room Mairead put her arms around his neck and kissed him on the cheek. 'Well it's nice to see you again, my love,' she said, as she gently removed the towel from around his waist and let it drop to the floor.

After they had finished making love Mairead was preparing to leave when Reagan suggested she stay a little longer as he wanted to discuss something with her.

'I can only stay for a little bit longer as I have to pick up my mum from the bus station at three o clock because she's returning from Limerick.'

'OK I won't keep you long but I want to tell you something in confidence and something that could affect my life here in Dublin.'

'What do you mean, could affect your life, Liam?'

'Well I'm sure you know my role in the IRA and what effect it has had on the Brits.'

'Liam I am only the chief's PA and not party to their secrets and operations, they keep all that to themselves you know,' she lied.

'OK I'm sorry I mentioned it. Let's forget it shall we?'

'Don't be like that, Liam, I didn't mean to upset you but I have to be very careful you know. If I ever let anything slip I would end up in the Liffey or a bog somewhere pretty quickly. You don't want that do you?'

'Of course not, my love but you are not the only one in danger because if MacDiamid finds you here or finds out we have been shagging, both of us are for the high jump. You do realise that don't you, love?'

'What do you think we ought to do then?' she asked.

'There's not a lot we can do but be very discreet and not see each other too often, darling.'

'But I don't want that, Liam. Why can't we just run away and go abroad, away from all this?'

'You know we can't. I have all this bloody treatment to go through first before I can do anything. It's supposed to take about six weeks or so and I don't know how it will affect me in the meantime. I've got no choice at the moment, Mairead.'

'Oh, Liam what are we going to do?'

'Don't worry we will sort something out but for the moment let's just keep a very low profile and carry on as normal.'

The IRA Chief of Staff's PA quietly left Reagan's flat and went to pick up her mother from the bus station. She did not notice the MI6 surveillance officer noting all her movements and timings.

The treatment started within the fortnight and Reagan soon began to feel the unpleasant side effects of RT. The nausea was the worst, but he managed to cope with it well enough to lead a near-normal life, still managing to follow his study package from the university.

In the Chief of Staff's office Colm MacDiamid asked Mairead Donovan to visit Reagan regularly to check on his progress and report back. There was an outstanding job that had to be accomplished and Reagan was the only man with the skills to carry it out. After that he was expendable, explained the Chief of Staff to his lover, Mairead, as they lay in bed that evening.

'Colm you should not be telling me all this, should

you?' said Mairead, getting up from the bed and looking for her hair brush.

'Darling, I trust you implicitly, I know you can keep your mouth shut and serve the cause for the long term good of Ireland.'

'I know, Colm, but I think it would be better if you kept the operational details confidential to yourself and to those who need to know. After all, I'm just a PA who looks after the office and indeed looks after you, my good looking man,' she said with a flutter of her eye brows. Mairead knew full well that this response would reap information she could pass on in due course to the right people. The Chief of Staff, as hard as he was, easily fell prey to feminine charm and this was something she could dish out in abundance.

In London, at the headquarters of MI6, the operations Director for Eire called a meeting of his staff on the Dublin job.

'Gentlemen we have, as you know, gained a mole within the IRA in the form of the Chief of Staff's PA, or that's what we believe her role is at present, along with keeping him company in bed. We have, so far, only had a small drip-feed of information but it has to improve as she has been warned of the consequences if it does not now she is in our clutches. She was recruited through her mother, who as some of you know, worked for the Northern Irish office in Stormont until she became ill and had to retire. Although a native of Southern Ireland, Mrs Donovan has strong links through family ties to the UK. She hates the IRA and all it stands for and so it seems does her only daughter Mairead. It appears this young lady has a good education having gained an honours degree in history and economics at Galway University three years ago. She is also a fluent Gaelic speaker and is able to understand the topics of conversation at meetings. This could indeed prove very useful to us as time goes on. According to our contacts at the university, she undertook most of her adult education in Gaelic so has a good technical knowledge of the language. If fact she may well be offered a position with us in the future if all goes well.'

'Sir, what do you want us to do regarding surveillance at the moment? For instance, should we continue with it or back off and let her do the contacting? I am concerned that our efforts may become noticed by the IRA and blow the whole thing possibly ending with her death if they suspect her as an informer,' asked the principle surveillance officer.

'Giles, you're right, we don't want to compromise anything at the moment. Call off the watchers and withdraw quietly and for God's sake don't tell MI5 what we have, you know what goons they are. At the moment let's keep her at arm's length. Her contact procedure is a dead letter box in Phoenix Park and so far this has worked well. That's all gentlemen and good hunting,' concluded the operations director.

Reagans RT treatment progressed well and although the side effects were at times debilitating he coped well enough and was bolstered by the odd clandestine visits by Mairead. As usual her visits were often late at night, Reagan often wondered how she managed to avoid IRA surveillance.

During one of the visits she said, 'Liam, do you think

we could run away from this place as soon you feel well enough, darling? I've had enough of the IRA and that bastard MacDiamid and all his cronies.'

'Why, Mairead what's happened?'

'Oh, I have to service him in bed, as you know, and I'm fed up with it and as soon as he becomes bored with me, who knows what then! He tells me all sorts of things that perhaps he shouldn't and this just gets me in deeper and deeper.'

'Darling I see what you mean; it puts you in a very awkward position.'

'I'm sure sooner or later the Garda will be on to me because I know they sometimes follow known IRA members around and probably tap their phones or whatever, then what do I do Liam?'

'Well hold on a moment, let me think,' he pondered.

'Look just carry on as you are but try not to get involved in conversations regarding IRA jobs or strategy. In a way be the grey man, or perhaps I should say, grey woman, if you know what I mean? I know you will have to carry on fucking him but this can't be avoided at the moment. You'll have to keep up appearances for the time being and until I'm strong enough for us to decide what to do next.'

'Liam, are you in deep? I don't mean to pry but I am concerned for you because they want you to do another job soon but I don't know what it is and will try and find out, my love.'

'Don't, Mairead! because if they think you're digging for information it could get very dangerous for you. They have their ways you know.

'What I suggest is you just carry on as normal and go to bed with him and quite possibly it will all come out during pillow talk. It might be a good idea to pretend you are not very keen on me and this hopefully this will lead him away from any sympathy for me via you. Do you see what I'm getting at love?'

'Has he told you what he wants you to do, Liam?

'No not yet but I believe it's pretty important as my last job was. Boy, what a job that was.'

'Oh, Liam please be careful, I couldn't bear it if anything happened to you, my darling,' she said, her mind racing!

Mairead Donovan left Reagan's flat soon after midnight and made her way home through the back streets and then by taxi to the Stillorgan district of Dublin.

Back in the flat, Reagan was concerned about Mairead and also what the IRA had planned next for him to accomplish in the name of the cause.

When Mairead went into Colm MacDiamid's office the following day she began to tidy up the desk as the premises' had been raided by the Garda during the night but nothing of importance had been found or any files seized. This happened on a regular basis and the chief was well-practiced in keeping all sensitive documents and files hidden elsewhere; even Mairead didn't know the location of the cache.

When Colm MacDiamid came in later in the day he wasn't surprised about the raid although he had no knowledge of it at the time because he had been away in Sligo with his secret lover and was not to be disturbed by anyone.

'Hello, Mairead I see our Garda friends have paid us a visit again. Is everything OK in the office and nothing damaged? because if it is I will make a claim against the bastards yet again for compensation.'

'No, Colm everything seems to be in place and no damage, a little ruffled, but I can sort it all out, no problem.'

'I don't know what I would do without you, love; come here and give us a kiss,' said the chief leering.

During the afternoon Colm MacDiamid again began talking to Mairead about IRA aims and objectives and what he was planning in London and Belfast to injure and kill Brits and soldiers. He even included an operation in Germany at a large British Army base.

Mairead Donovan was dumbstruck when she was told that Liam Reagan was to play a big part in the London job, killing a cabinet minister in the heart of the capital.

'Colm, how do you think you can organize a job like that? London must be as secure as anywhere in the world. How would anyone ever get near a cabinet minister? They must have security guards or police protection with them all the time?'

'Don't you worry, love we can and will do it. Some years ago we blew up the MP Airey Neave outside parliament, we placed a bomb under his car and up it went; him with it. Never underestimate our will to give the Brits what they deserve for occupying our country. We will never give up, do you hear, never!'

'You know, Colm, I don't really like Liam Reagan very much you know.'

'Why? He is OK and has rendered the cause a great service.'

'I know he has but he just doesn't appeal to me as a person.'

'Well I'm glad to hear it, my sexy, young lady. I'd hate to think you might two- time me with him after all.'

'Oh you have nothing to worry about on that score, Colm. You're twice the man he is,' she replied in a cold sweat.

Several weeks later Mairead Donovan made her way to the dead letter box in Dublin's Phoenix Park and left a message for her handler regarding the proposed IRA action including the killing of a cabinet minister. At the prescribed date and time, she returned to the dead letter box to retrieve the response from London. This time she was tailed by an MI6 agent who was waiting close by and who, against directions from the Secret Intelligence Service, decided to keep her under close surveillance.

She went home to her flat in Stillorgan and read the instruction she had been given. She was told to keep intelligence coming and to increase the quality of the information to include locations and possible dates and names of operatives. She was further informed that she would get all the protection she needed if she felt threatened or likely to be compromised at any time.

'It's alright for those spooks in London, sitting on their arses in the safety of their offices and surrounded by flunkeys at their beck and call,' she muttered.

She decided to go and see Reagan again and see if he had improved medically enough to come up with some sort of an idea of what to do. The doorbell of Reagan's flat went soon after 11pm that night and although he was in bed he was not asleep.

'Hello, Mairead this is a surprise, come in, darling let me take your coat.'

When they had settled in the living room she began to shake uncontrollably.

'God, Mairead what's the matter?'

'Liam I'm worried. Colm has told me that they are planning big jobs in London, Belfast and Germany and that you are to play a major part in it, my love.'

'This is news to me,' said Reagan.

'Well I can assure you that they want you to kill a British cabinet minister in London. Liam have you killed anyone before?' she asked, knowing the answer but keeping quiet.

'I can't talk about that, Mairead you know that.'

'Liam just listen to me, have you killed anyone for the IRA?'

'You know fucking well I have, and yes it was someone important! I'm sure lover boy Colm MacDiamid has already told you that while he's screwing you, like he does every day.'

'He doesn't screw me every day, Liam, don't say that to me.'

'Well what do you expect me to say? How do you think I feel with that going on, Mairead?'

She began to cry and sob quietly, falling into his arms. 'I'm sorry, Liam I didn't mean to upset you but I have to know what is going on so as I can keep at arm's length from it all. Remember what you told me, love?'

'That's OK, darling we will work something out soon and put all this behind us. I have decided to abandon my university course as soon as I'm fit enough to flee and I hope you will come with me, my beautiful lady.'

'Oh, Liam you know I will. I have some money saved up that will help us make a fresh start somewhere abroad, right away from this dreadful place.'

'Right, what we must do is this, love,' said Reagan in deep thought. 'Just carry on as normal as I will and don't come near this place for at least a couple of weeks while I sort something out. I know it will be hard but it's for the best darling.'

'Talking of it being hard, darling, do I sense something else getting hard?' she said, running her hand between his thighs...

Chapter 23

Rod Casey and Lenihan spent several hours at the police station being questioned by several detectives about the murder of his landlady, but in the early hours of the morning he was released without charge.

'Christ, Rod, that was a close call but I'm innocent, I swear it, my friend,' said Lenihan.

'Mike, this cannot go on. I have a career to think about and if this gets to the general I'm finished. You have to go home right away and leave Jane and me out of it. Do you understand?'

'I know that but how do I get home without money?' replied Lenihan desperately.

'I might be able to advance you some but I have commitments of my own financially, Mike. In any case I would have to keep it from Jane.'

'Rod, I don't want to put you in an awkward position but could you do me one more favour?'

'What's that, Mike?'

'Could you get Sergeant Christine Ellis to contact me straight away?'

'Sure, I know her; she's in admin at the base. I'll contact her first thing tomorrow, or should I say later today bearing in mind the time now. By the way, where will you be staying now because your lodgings are now a crime scene?' said Casey.

'Oh shit, I never thought of that. If the police will let me get my things I'll have to find a cheap hotel for a couple of days.'

'Mike, as soon as you get settled, phone me at the base and I will get Ellis to make contact and for God sake, stay out of trouble.'

'I sure will, Rod I've had enough drama for a lifetime here and just want to get back to the States as soon as I can.'

Later that day Lenihan managed to find a cheap hotel room and the police confirmed two days later that they had no further interest him, as new witnesses had come forward and an arrest was imminent. They also added he was free to leave Germany and suggested he didn't ever return.

Sergeant Christine Ellis phoned him at the hotel that evening and they made arrangements to meet the following day in the local park.

'Hi, Mike, it's great to see you again, how's it going?'

'Well you don't want to know, Chris. I've had a hell of a time with the police here and was arrested for a suspected murder, but all is OK now as they have found the real culprit and I can leave Germany just as soon as I can, honey.'

'Jeeze, Mike. Major Casey said it was urgent I contact you as there had been some trouble around here. I heard on the news about the murder of an old lady in town. Apparently some local scumbag has admitted the homicide,' said Ellis. 'Anyway, Mike, what now?'

'Chris I want to return home to the States and would like to see you when you get to Fort Levenworth, assuming you have decided to take the posting they offered you.'

'Well now, Michael Lenihan, Master Sergeant retired; you are assuming a lot of things! It so happens I am taking the posting to Levenworth and I am due to go in two weeks but in the meantime I have the weekend off.'

'That's good news, honey how about we get together and have a drink tonight because there is something I would like to discuss with you?'

'Sure, Mike, I hope we do more than discuss things, honey, if you know what I mean?'

'Great, why don't you come to my room at the hotel, number 12, say about 7o'clock and I will have some wine ready cooled?'

'I certainly will my man and looking forward to it, if you know what I mean!' she said with a cheeky smile.

Later that evening Christine Ellis knocked on the door of the hotel room and it was opened instantly by Lenihan, freshly showered and shaved.

'Hi, Chris, come in and sit down,' he said, kissing her on the cheek.

'A kiss on the cheek, Mike is that all I get?' she said frowning but with a subtle smile.

'Oh, honey that's just the start; the best is yet to come,' said Lenihan, pouring the chilled white wine into two glasses.

'Well are you going to tell me what has happened since you left the military as I was sad to lose contact with you after you were court marshalled in the States, apart from our recent meeting in town?' she asked.

Lenihan went into a long made-up history to explain his absence which she seemed to accept although a little suspiciously, but decided not to push it for the time being.

'Honey what I would like to ask you is can you lend me some money for the fare back to the States? I will of course repay you as soon as I'm on my feet.'

'Sure I can, but I would like to see a lot more of you when we get to the States you know, Mike. Where are you planning to go?'

'Well if you're going to Kansas that's good enough for me, honey. I will get some work locally; there are a number of shooting ranges in the area and as I was a trained sniper I should get an instructor's job without any trouble,' said Lenihan.

'That would be great. When do you want the money and how much, honey?'

'There's a flight to Dallas from Frankfurt via Amsterdam in four days time and the fare is about US$350, is that OK?'

'Sure. I'll let you have the cash tomorrow afternoon as I'll have to go to the base, bank cashier to get it. In the meantime I think you should take me to bed to say thank you, my lovely ex-Master Sergeant!' said Ellis, slowly unbuttoning her tight, green blouse.

The following day they met and Christine Ellis passed the money in an envelope to Lenihan.

'Thanks, honey you are a real friend and I will make it up to you as soon as you get to the States.'

'By the way, Mike I have added a few more greenbacks so you have something to tide you over when you get stateside. Don't open it now, save it for later. In the meantime, Michael, let me take care of all your needs this evening, I'm sure you know what I have in mind.'

The next day Lenihan went to Frankfurt airport

and bought a ticket for Dallas/Fort Worth for the flight on Thursday evening; he was dreading any problems at either airport. He arrived three hours before his flight was due to depart and settled into the departure lounge. During his wait he decided to phone Rod Casey and tell him what was happening and the fact he would not be bothering him further. Major Casey was, to say the least, relieved to see the back of the retired master sergeant, hopefully once and for all.

During the long waiting time at the airport, Lenihan was apprehensive and almost expecting a tap on his shoulder at any time. No tap came and the flight was called and he boarded normally. The flight to the USA seemed never ending and when the pilot announced they were starting their descent into Dallas on time Lenihan again became concerned as to whether he might be arrested and questioned by the FBI or CIA regarding his activities in Ireland.

The plane landed with scarcely a bump and taxied to the disembarkation area of the airport and the passengers gradually filed out of the aircraft and into the airport arrivals lounge. So far, so good, he thought. He went through customs and passport control without incident and collected his bag from the luggage carousel making his way to the exit and the taxi rank.

'Where do you wanna go, buddy?' said the cab driver.

'Just take me to a really cheap hotel downtown.'

'You got it, buddy. You did say cheap didn't you?'

'Yeah I'm a bit pushed at the moment, so cheap it has to be, ok?'

'Sure no problem,' he said driving away and narrowly

missing another cab with the accompanying sound of the horn and screeching of tyres. The US$1000 that Christine had given him certainly helped at the moment and he would have to get to Kansas and get settled before she arrived back in the States. 'What a great girl she is,' he muttered to himself

The hotel was certainly cheap but adequate for his purposes; his main priority now was to get to Kansas and close to Fort Levenworth, so he could see Christine Ellis when she arrived. His first task was to get a replacement driving license and social security card but as he was a US citizen this would not prove difficult and he set about this straight away.

Having set the documentation process in action, Lenihan enquired at the railroad station about train times to Levenworth; he would pick up the licence and social security paperwork there.

'No problem, buddy. There's one every day except Sunday, leaving here at 10:00 pm.' The booking clerk also mentioned the fare but Lenihan did not notice what the guy said as he had no intention of buying a ticket.

On Saturday evening he arrived at the railroad station early and took note of the platform for Levenworth; the train was in and being prepared for the long journey. As it was dark he could move about the station with ease and made his way along the track towards the side of the train but out of sight of the platform and entered a carriage without being noticed. His only concern was the guard who would come round once the train was underway to check tickets of all passengers. If all went well he would disappear into the toilets as this was about to happen and wait until the coast was clear.

Once inside the train he noticed that most of the seats were booked with the passengers name and destination on a small card in a holder on the backrest of the seat. The train started to fill up and there were few spare seats left by 9:45pm so Lenihan just kept moving so as not to appear suspicious. At 10:00pm on the dot the train started to pull out of the station and gradually gathered speed. At around midnight the carriage lights dimmed and people settled down to sleep. Lenihan took a spare seat and was wide-awake and alert for the ticket inspector.

The train sped through the night without checks on tickets and the only interruption was the light-refreshment trolley that came round with coffee and snacks. Lenihan bought coffee and doughnuts but remained alert and ready to move if a ticket inspector appeared. Eventually the train approached Levenworth and slowed, coming to a stop in the large station. Many passengers alighted, a considerable number of them obviously servicemen from the army base locally. Lenihan mingled with the crowd and slipped into a toilet, close to the exit which had an electronic gate actuated by the ticket.

'Shit,' he muttered. He turned around and walked along the platform away from the exit and towards the far end of the station in the direction of the marshalling yards. No one seemed to notice and he managed to slip between some sheds and settled down to wait until dusk so he could climb the fence and be away.

Some time later some workmen came along but he managed to hide and was not discovered. When it was dark he climbed the perimeter fence and left the station, using all the stealth skills he had learned in the military.

When he was a young soldier he had to take a course at Fort Levenworth and wondered if any of his old instructors were still local, albeit retired. He found a cheap hotel and settled in but his priority was to get a job and find somewhere more permanent to live, at least until Christine arrived from Germany.

The following day he went to Fort Levenworth camp and asked at the gatehouse if any of his old friends were still there, mentioning a few names he could remember. The young Staff Sergeant consulted a list and said there was but he was unable to help further due to service regulations. Lenihan mentioned he was a "retired" Master Sergeant in the Green Berets and was just looking up old friends; he conveniently forgot to mention he had been dishonourably discharged from the military. The sergeant faltered slightly at this and decided, reluctantly, he would just push the regulations to one side a little and mentioned that Sergeant Major Jim Brackley had recently retired from the army and lived locally. The sergeant added he believed that Brackley was involved in a local survival and shooting school and acting as an instructor. Lenihan thanked the soldier and set off to find this school with the hope of finding a job.

Later that afternoon he found the school on the edge of town and soon tracked down Brackley, who recognised Lenihan straight away. 'Mike, you old son of a gun, it's nice to see you again, what have you been doing, my friend?'

'Jim, it's been a long time with much water under the bridge, how you doing, ol' buddy?'

'I know you left the military under a cloud and

although I don't know the circumstances I'm sure there was a good reason for it,' said Brackley, making some coffee.

'Some fucking Brit officer was screwing Carol in Germany and she became pregnant; she died after having a back-street abortion while I was down at Bad Tolz training some rookies. I gave him the beating of a lifetime and was court-marshalled and dismissed from the service. They reduced me to the rank of corporal; all I get is a pension at that rank so it's hard getting by, Jim.'

'Jeeze, Mike, you certainly have had a raw deal, how can I help?'

'I need a job really, Jim. I went to Spain after I was discharged and worked picking grapes and fruit for the wine industry,' he lied.

'Ol' buddy, you have many skills learned hard in the military, I'm sure I can find you something here. Leave it with me, Mike I'll see what I can do, now drink your coffee.'

The following week Mike Lenihan started work as an instructor in survival skills at the Kansas Survival and Practical Shooting School. At last a regular job and fully legal in every sense of the word; a million miles from the IRA.

Lenihan had managed to find a rented home on a trailer park about five miles from the school and Fort Levenworth military camp. The park was well maintained and his home in good condition with air conditioning and a good heating system at a reasonable monthly rent. Settled at last! Now with a job and somewhere to live he could plan his future with Christine Ellis.

As soon as she arrived at Levenworth, Lenihan met her and invited her to his home on the trailer park, suggesting she move in as soon as possible. As a sergeant, she would normally be allocated a room in the camp accommodation block but she was also allowed to live outside the camp and this is what she chose to do. She moved in with Lenihan immediately and set up home with him, living as his wife.

'Mike I'm so glad we're together at last. I thought I had lost you when you were court-marshalled and disappeared off the face of the earth, where did you go, honey?'

'It's a long story and I will tell you sometime, but not now, let's just get our lives together and move on. I have a job and so do you; by the way how much longer do you intend to stay in the army, Chris?'

'I've discussed this with the personnel department and they have offered me another period of service as I have a good record and fulfilled all my yearly assessments to their satisfaction. They have also suggested that future promotion is likely to staff sergeant in the not too distant future. However if this promotion should happen it would mean a posting away from Levenworth unfortunately, Mike.'

'Sure I understand, honey, but that will probably take at least a year to eighteen months yet, as you know the US army have a time-served policy regarding promotions so it's not an immediate concern to us is it?'

'No that's right, Mike, I just need to get settled in my new post and see how it goes. I mean, if we were to get married in the future I might leave the service altogether and find something else to do. Perhaps we could get that small ranch you mentioned when we were in Germany and raise some horses? That would be nice, honey.'

'That was something Carol had always wanted to do but all that was snatched away by that Brit officer,' replied Lenihan choking up.

'I'm sorry, Mike I didn't mean to upset you, sorry, honey. How about some coffee and pancakes for lunch?'

'I forgot to ask you, did you know Jim Brackley at Levenworth or when you were at Fort Bragg? He has recently retired as a Sergeant Major and got me this job.' said Lenihan.

'No, Mike although I have heard of him; a bit of a bastard by all accounts. They were talking about him in the office the day I checked in; they asked me the same question.'

'He's from the old school and a real disciplinarian, particularly with recruits; nearly cost him his career at one time. I also understand he was involved in some trouble in Vietnam, something to do with throwing Vietcong out of helicopters but I don't know if any of it's true,' said Lenihan, sipping his coffee.

Anyway, honey I am going to make this place into a home for us, somewhere cosy to come home to after a long, hard day, what do you think, Mike? By the way, I heard, through the grapevine, that Major Rod Casey might be posted here soon, as the new provost officer in charge of the detention centre.'

'If that's true, honey, that means promotion to Lieutenant Colonel. Good for him, he deserves it really, he was good to me when I had my troubles and has a super wife in Jane; do you know her Chris?'

'Not really although I have seen her on the base in Germany; I usually keep my distance from officers if I can, although Casey himself was OK. He was always in the colonel's pocket and crawling up his arse, automatically agreeing with everything he said. I suppose that's why he got on so well and climbed the rank ladder rapidly,' she said with a sigh and shrugging her shoulders.

Lenihan settled well into his new job and life with Christine was fun and enjoyable. They had little contact with other military personnel from the base when she was off duty and he didn't want his past court-martial record to damage her prospects in the army; the US army had long memories. He was now definitely an outcast as far as the military was concerned and she could easily be tarred with the same brush by some for living with him and still serving. They decided to try and keep their personal circumstances as private as possible and live quietly.

Chapter 24

Doreen Conlon carried on with her life minus her husband, but content with her new man Aiden who was quite different from Alan, the low grade member of the IRA. Garda enquiries continued into his disappearance without success and were quietly scaled down. Both the Garda and Doreen were convinced he had been murdered by the IRA but this would probably never be proved.

Aiden Riley provided her and the girls with some sort of normality and security in terms of money and wellbeing and she could not ask for more. He made it clear that if her husband ever turned up he would melt into the background but would be there for her, if that's what she wanted.

'Doreen, my love, if Alan never comes back would you be mine forever? I know this would take time legally, something like seven years or so, but we could live as man and wife long before that and I would look after you and the girls and give you the life you have never had.'

'Oh, Aiden, of course, that's what I really want, I know I shouldn't say it but I hope he is dead because he has brought nothing but heartache and trouble to us since he joined the IRA with such big ideas. He was never going to make it big time with them and even if he had of done he would probably have ended up in prison for life so the fact he has disappeared brings no sadness for me. It's you I want now not him and what's more, I would like to move away from Ballybrittas as soon as possible.'

'I think you ought to see a solicitor regarding the legal position, what with him missing and you clearly want a divorce. Of course you can move in with me in Dublin as my house has four bedrooms and a large garden for the girls. I think we could be very happy together and give a stable home for the girls, my love,' replied Aiden warmly.

'That sounds good and the answer from me is yes without a doubt, but let's talk to the girls and see what they say as it will affect them greatly, Aiden.'

The following day, both Aiden and Doreen sat down with the girls and discussed the whole situation, with Doreen explaining that their dad worked for the IRA and had gone away forever. The girls took it surprisingly well and after some tears and hugs finally agreed to go and live in Dublin.

Aiden Riley took Doreen to see a solicitor friend and the legal position was explained that she could start divorce proceedings on the basis that her husband was still alive. If, after a certain length time, he never appeared, she could apply to court for a divorce on the grounds of desertion. If it was proved beyond doubt he had been murdered she was free to marry as a widow. Doreen immediately asked the solicitor to instigate divorce proceedings on the grounds of irretrievable breakdown and desertion. Within two weeks, she and the girls moved in with Aiden Riley and soon settled in with the girls joining a new school and making new friends.

At last Doreen was happy and contented being well away from Ballybrittas and the whole IRA thing. Her life was starting a new chapter.

Meanwhile, in another part of Dublin, Liam Reagan was recovering from the RT treatment and getting stronger daily and enjoying his studies. Mairead Donovan continued her clandestine meetings with him and carried on with her work for the Chief of Staff. She remained under surveillance by MI6 but there was nothing to report to London; of course this shadowing had been officially called off by the director of the Irish desk at the secret intelligence service at their Vauxhall HQ.

Mairead kept up her information to MI6 via the dead letter box in Phoenix Park but there was little to report at the moment, mostly routine stuff of little importance. The Chief of Staff was continuing his pillow talk but Mairead was careful not to ask too many questions so as not arouse his suspicions. If he suspected she was passing on information she would be executed without further ado and she knew it. She could not believe the chief was so free with the things he said, bearing in mind his position at the very top of the IRA. This cannot continue she thought, something has to give soon, what was he playing at?'

Late one afternoon, Colm MacDiamid came into the office, quite obviously the worst for drink, and called her into the back room which was used as a store cupboard. 'Shut the door, Mairead,' he said.

'OK, Colm is everything alright?' she said nervously.

'Yes everything is fine but I want you now, so take off all your clothes and take me in your mouth, you beautiful woman.'

'Of course anything you say, my handsome man,' she replied with quiet disgust. After they had finished she went back to the filing while he made some phone calls and spoke rapidly in Gaelic to his deputy in Belfast, who was visiting a local active service unit on the outskirts of the city.

Mairead overheard the guarded phone call and noted the meeting arrangements that were made for the following week; by this time she knew the coded location codes they used currently. The meeting was set up for the following Tuesday in Killybegs, County Donegal, set for 7pm.

Although she did not know the reason for the meeting she intended to find out if she could and pass this onto to her MI6 contact via the dead letterbox. The following morning she came into the office to find MacDiamid already there.

'Good morning Colm, you're getting off to an early start today.'

'Morning, me darling, yes I have a busy day ahead as I have to go to Donegal and see some people up there, just getting few things together.'

'OK. Have you got it all or do you want a woman to sort it out for you?' she said with a smile.

'No everything is fine but I will be away for a couple of days so you can have some time off if you like.'

'That's very good of you, Colm, thank you.'

'OK, I'll be off then, love see you on Saturday, be good won't you.'

'OK, Colm, have a safe journey and take care, can't wait till you get back,' she lied.

She decided to stay in the office for at least two hours until the chief was well on his way to Donegal and not to give the impression she was in a hurry to get away. She decided to go and see Liam Reagan and make the most of the chief's absence.

When she left the office she went into the city centre and did some shopping for some sexy underclothes. All the time she was on the move she carried out anti-surveillance techniques, that she had been taught by her MI6 contact, to make sure she wasn't followed. No one, it seemed, was on her tail and she called Reagan on his mobile; even doing this she was guarded.

When Reagan answered she said, 'Hello, Liam how are you today?'

'Oh hello, my love, yes I'm fine and yourself?'

This choice of words, which they had agreed on, ensured they were both alone and could talk freely.

'Liam I have a few days off, can I come and see you - now?'

'Of course, darling, I'll be waiting for you but be careful won't you.'

Mairead made her way to Reagan's flat by a roundabout way, ensuring she wasn't followed and received a warm welcome when she arrived.

'Mairead, it's great to see you and what a surprise, where's MacDiamid?'

'Oh he's off to Donegal for some reason. With a bit of luck he might get run over by a tractor or something.'

'Mairead, has something happened, you seem bitter?'

'Oh, the other day he came in pissed and I had to give him a blow job in the office; he couldn't even get it up and it was disgusting. I'd like to kill that bastard; he treats me like an unpaid prostitute!'

'OK, OK, love you're here now so relax, I'll get some tea on and we can have a nice long talk. The sooner we get away from all this crap the better,' replied Reagan. They had their tea and a long conversation about what they could do to get away from Dublin and the IRA.

'Liam, I'm worried about my mum. If I just disappear, what will they do to her to get at me? They'll never believe she wouldn't know where I'd be staying, they might torture her.'

'I know but I don't believe they would harm her, they might just keep her under surveillance in the hope she would lead them to you.'

'You really think so?' she said with tears running down her cheeks.

'What I suggest is that we get her another mobile phone, in addition to her own. She could use her own for all normal use and the new one just for contact with you.'

'Liam, that's a good idea and I could send her some money to pay for the calls. You are so clever, darling, that's why I love you, apart from other things of course.'

'What other things do you mean, darling?' said Reagan with a wicked smile on his face.

'Oh I think you know, your wonderful body and that lovely cock you know how to handle so well, talking of which, isn't it about time we went to bed and practiced?' she cooed.

When she left the flat she again carried out her well tried and proved anti-surveillance procedures to get home safely. The following day she went to the dead letter box in Phoenix Park and passed her latest information to MI6 regarding the meeting in Killybegs for the following week.

A couple of months passed and Lenihan made steady progress towards restoration of full health and his studies brought praise from his tutors at the college. In the Chief of Staff's office Colm MacDiamid remained stoic and determined to have Reagan carry out at least one more spectacular job for the IRA. After that, as he informed Mairead, the hit man would be expendable as he would become too hot and too expensive to provide cover from the authorities in both Britain and Ireland. Of course there was always the possibility of a relapse in his illness and a deathbed confession that would blow the IRA sky high.

Mairead Donovan was aghast at this but could not show it and appeared completely non-committal in her daily work for the chief. She and Reagan had to get away and fast. The thought crossed her mind of killing the chief but she had no knowledge of this sort of thing; it might of course be quite easy as he trusted her so much. The problem was, there were always visits to the office of other IRA men, sometimes without warning. She considered all the possibilities and decided that if it was going to happen at all, then when they were alone in bed would be her best bet. She had to get some instruction on what to do and get it right first time. Should she inform her contact at MI6 or just go ahead and do it?

The next time she met Reagan at his flat she decided to broach the subject and get his advice. 'Liam, I would like to ask you something but I want you to hear me out first, OK.'

'Alright, love fire away,' he said.

'Well it's difficult to know where to begin, but hear goes. Colm has told me that after the next big job you do for the organisation, you might well be expendable. He is worried that you may have a relapse of the cancer and if the worst comes to the worst and you get really bad, you might make a deathbed confession and blow everything sky high,' she said, shaking and tearful.

'That's how all of them think, they are very brave when they are safe but come the time when they are caught many turn Queen's evidence to save their miserable skins. The British Government protects some of them but I'm sure the SAS also take care of the rest in their own particular style. A number of squealers have been found in the countryside of the north after being shot through the mouth and information put out about them being informers; you know, one cell against the other, Mairead.'

'Liam, I'm really worried about all of this and I have an idea to kill MacDiamid when we are next alone but I don't know how to be sure it will work,' she said, deliberately not mentioning her work for MI6.

'Wow, my love, steady on a bit, you sure you know what you're saying, killing the Chief of Staff of the IRA in Dublin!' he said with alarm.

'I know, I know Liam, but I have to do something, with your steady recovery they will be in touch soon for you to do another job, and who knows what will happen after that?'

'The thought has crossed my mind and each time you come here is also increasing the risk of them finding out about us. If they did, God knows what MacDiarmid would do to both of us, darling,' said Reagan deep in thought.

'Mairead, you will have to let me think about this for a few days and it might be better if you didn't come here but we meet somewhere else for the time being. In the meantime do nothing and just carry out your duties as normal,' replied Reagan.

'OK, Liam I will do what you say but where can we meet as I must see you regularly, darling. You know that don't you, my love?' she said, putting her arms around him and hugging him tightly.

'I will sort something out, Mairead, just leave it to me. I'll call you tomorrow on your mobile, when you're at home, in the evening about 7 o'clock.'

'OK, well I must go now as it's getting late and the cabs get so expensive after midnight and there might be bogy men out there after me, darling,' she said with a weak smile.

After she left, Reagan decided to have a Bushmills whiskey with a little ice to calm him down a little after what was said and digest it all. He couldn't sleep that night and got up at 3am to make some coffee and start the formation of a plan to get him and her away from Ireland altogether - well away from the clutches of the IRA.

The following week Reagan was summoned to the Chief of Staff's office for a meeting. 'Good morning, Liam how are you? Come in and sit down, my friend,' said Colm MacDiamid with a smile.

'So how's the recovery going?' he continued, pouring some tea for them both.

'Well I still get pain and diarrhoea on a regular basis but then the doctor said this would be the case for some time to come. It can be a real pain in the arse if you will pardon the expression. I have a full check-up coming soon followed by more tests and then a meeting with the oncologist for the overall results, you know, Mr Singh at the hospital.

'OK, Liam it's clear you're not fully recovered yet but the show must go on as they say. I have a little proposition for you, in the strictest confidence you understand.'

'Of course, Colm I do understand. By the way, where's Mairead today, is she sick or something?'

'Oh she's not been feeling too good lately so I have given her some time off, just a few days to sort herself out, you know the sort of thing, I believe it's women problems. Now to business, we have a job coming up in London and you are the man for it, without a doubt, if anything like your last action in Ulster is anything to go by,' said the chief.

'What is the job?' said Reagan with some alarm.

'We intend to kill the British Home Secretary whilst at a function to raise money for servicemen wounded in action both in Ireland and elsewhere in the world they have operated,' said the chief smiling broadly.

'How will this be possible with all the security surrounding him? Especially after my killing of the chief constable in Northern Ireland, some time ago, Colm.'

'You will become a local living in the area near the Woolwich Army Barracks where the function will be held, by the way that's in South London, Liam.'

'We would never get to within 500 yards of the place

let alone close enough to get a weapon in place for the hit, and what about an escape for me should I be successful?'

'Don't worry, my friend we have already thought of that. The weapon is already in situ in a flat overlooking part of the barracks. As soon as the minister gets out of his car he's yours, albeit it will be a long and difficult shot to be sure but I know you can do it, my friend. To that end we have arranged a refresher course for you up in the mountains of Donegal starting next week. You will be picked up at 7 o'clock Monday morning so be ready to be away for a week at least, maybe more depending how you get on,' said MacDiamid.

'This surely is a suicide mission, I would never escape from the area alive and you know it, Colm!'

'Liam, I can assure you it will be fine as we have arranged a safe house close by for you to hole up in while the search goes on. The weapon will be abandoned in the flat, we have to accept that but it can soon be replaced from our usual suppliers,' replied the chief sternly.

'What weapon will I have to use, Colm?'

'An M60 machine gun with a 100 round belt.'

'Christ Almighty, Colm! I could take out half of South London with that, it would be a massacre; many innocent people would be killed. I can't do that.'

'You can and you will, or face the consequences, Liam. Need I say more?' emphasised the chief of staff. 'You must remember that there are always innocent casualties of war, and we are at war with the British Government, a war we will win in the end. It has all been set up and the weapon has already been smuggled in and stowed securely with the ammunition and an escape plan is in place for you. A number of key people are involved and this will be a great victory for us in the movement. Do you understand?'

'This is fucking madness and I want no part of it I'm telling you now, Colm!'

'Let me tell you once again, Liam, you have no choice if you wish to continue to live on this planet. You are well and truly in, so make no mistake about it. You are going to be shadowed everywhere you go from this moment on so don't even think of trying to escape. Do I make myself clear?' replied the Chief of Staff.

Liam Reagan left the office and made his way home to the flat in shock at the revelation that he was to kill the British Home Secretary and probably take many others at the same time. He still had his mobile and managed to get through to Mairead that evening.

'Mairead, I have been told you are off sick, why didn't you tell me?'

'Who told you that, my love, that bastard MacDiamid?'

'Yes he did because I was told to go to the office today to be given my next job. Do you know what it is, love?'

'No, Liam, I was told to take a few days off because there was very important business to discuss and my presence was not required. I think he is getting bored with me and has probably got someone else in mind to screw next,' she replied.

'Whatever you do don't come near this flat because he said he is going to have me followed everywhere I go and I believe he will certainly do that. I have to go to Donegal next week for a refresher course prior to going to London for the next job so our contact will be very limited, darling, at least for a little while. Be ready at a moment's notice to escape from Ireland once and for all, Mairead; in the meantime just carry on as normal but don't ask him any questions and hopefully he won't suspect a thing, for both our sakes OK?'

'OK, Liam, but try and keep in touch when you can, my love and take care won't you? I couldn't bear it if anything happened to you,' she said crying softly.

'OK, love just be patient, we will get out of this mess, I promise,' he said with as much conviction as he could muster.

When Mairead went back to work she tried to be as normal and chirpy as ever, just acting in her flirty way towards the chief and he responded as he always did by pinching her bum playfully as she passed. No mention was made of Reagan until the chief suggested she make a visit that weekend to see how he was getting on with the recovery from his illness.

'OK, Colm, I will if you insist, you know I'm not keen on him but duty calls I suppose. I draw the line at taking him a bunch of grapes though,' she said with a grimace.

'OK, OK, Mairead I will make it up to you on Monday when our work is done here for the day,' said the chief, holding up his hands in mock surrender.

'Oh another shagging session then, is this really what I got a university degree for,' she mumbled to herself out of his earshot, whilst making some tea in the kitchen of the dingy office complex.

Saturday morning Mairead Donovan knocked on the

door of Reagan's flat as cheerful as ever. 'Hello, Liam, how are you? Colm sent me to see how you were getting on,' she said quickly before he had chance to speak. 'Can I come in then as it's pouring with rain as usual,' she asked, making a move into the flat.

'Mairead what the hell are you doing here? I thought we agreed you would stay away for the time being.'

'It's OK, the boss sent me officially to see how you're getting on. I got the greeting in quickly in case we are being watched and you reacted and said anything we might regret, sorry, love.'

When they sat down Reagan told her what had happened in the office and what he was expected to do in London.

'Liam, you can't do that, you would be killed and you would never get away in one piece. Anyway, how do you know the Home Secretary will actually be there on the day,' she said alarmed.

'It's a tradition that has become the norm for this event and if he didn't arrive, the hit would be postponed for another time. Anyway, it's been advertised in the press as a forthcoming event for July and there's likely to be several military top brass there as well. MacDiamid wants me to take out as many people as possible with a machine gun.'

'Liam, this is outrageous, the man's a lunatic. I bet he wouldn't have the guts to do it himself. You can't do it, darling, please listen to me!'

'I have little choice at the moment and I am looking desperately for a way out but I am being followed, apparently,' said Reagan.

'Oh I'm really worried about you, my love. What are we going to do?'

'Just do nothing at the moment; it might be the case that I go to London and escape from there. What you could then do is to stay put for a little while here then escape and meet me in England. We might be able to emigrate to Australia or New Zealand.'

'Can't we just go now, I mean today? I have some money put by which would tide us over until we get settled with somewhere to live and get jobs. We are both intelligent people and work should not be too much of a problem, we could live quietly in the country and raise a family. Oh, Liam let's do it now, please,' she implored.

Liam Reagan settled into the training camp in windswept County Donegal near to the little village of Creeslough under the shadow of Muckish Mountain. The whole area was very quiet and had scattered farms rearing mostly livestock and little else so the training would not be disturbed, particularly the small valley, surrounded by woods, where the shooting practice would take place. The farmhouse resembled the original one he stayed in during his initial training in Galway under the watchful eye of Lenihan, the disgraced US army NCO, early the previous year. Anyone hearing shots would naturally think it was farmers, shooting rats or pigeons in the area. The local Garda just normally patrolled the main N56 road and were unlikely to venture off road or into the numerous narrow lanes around the village.

When he arrived, Reagan was greeted by a man who refused to give his name and simply said he was in charge of training and that names were not necessary. His first lesson was due to start at 9am the following morning on the dot. It was also made clear to Reagan he was not, under any circumstances, to leave the camp and visits to the village pub were definitely out of bounds. His mobile phone was taken off him, along with his watch, "just precautionary" he was advised by the nameless man with the Cork accent.

'What weapons are we going to be using in training?' asked Reagan casually of the instructor.

'Well now, my friend, the 9mm pistol and an AR15 Armalite rifle, that's all I have been told to include,' said the man, obviously bored with his job.

'Is there anyone else on this course and what about machine guns, surely our organisation use them as well, don't they?' replied Reagan in frustration.

'Let's get one thing straight, Mr Reagan, I do the teaching and you do not ask questions, is that clear?'

'What's the matter with you? It's perfectly legitimate to ask questions surely on any course. On my original one, earlier, I was encouraged to as many questions as I liked and I intend to carry on doing so. OK?"

'No it's not fucking OK, you will just do as I say and like it, otherwise I will let the chief of staff know how you are not co-operating and let him deal with you. Just because you go to university I suppose you think you are something special, well you're not!'

'I'm not claiming that I am someone special at all and you have got the wrong end of the stick and if you don't snap out of it I will let Colm MacDiamid know personally, so fuck you as well, OK!'

Reagan never saw the punch coming that floored

him in the kitchen but he would bide his time here and strike when he was ready. 'I'll plant this bastard in a bog myself,' he muttered, as he cleaned the blood from his mouth in his room later.

The following morning he presented himself in the barn for training and settled into a chair with baited breath.

'Top of the morning, Liam,' said the man with the Cork accent, smiling and jovial, quite unlike the day before.

Reagan just nodded and the lecture began with basic weapon drills and safety of the pistol and rifle. The load and unload procedures including magazine changing took about an hour and then it was time for tea and reflection. The instructor tried to engage Reagan in a light hearted conversation but he was having none of it and just nodded or gave negative answers to all that came his way.

The rest of the week dragged on and Reagan learned nothing he did not already know. In fact, it appeared this so called instructor had very little idea what he was talking about and nothing at all about the methods of approaching a target and setting up a shooting position. Not a patch on the Yank.

In just over 10 days Reagan returned to Dublin and was visited by the Chief of Staff in his flat close to the university. 'Well, Liam old son, how did it go?'

'Colm, do you really want the truth?'

'Of course, because he gives you a very good report and says you were very attentive all the way through but did not ask any questions which he found a bit strange.'

'The man, I never did get his name, is thick and

useless as a trainer, his so- called knowledge is very basic and should not be training anyone until he knows what he's doing. He also punched me for thinking I'm clever for going to university, his words not mine. If we are down to trainers like him, Colm we are in trouble I can tell you right now. He is as bad as the Yank was good, it's the likes of the American we need not that tosser who thinks he's Rambo.'

'Liam, this is serious, if what you say is true, and something I need to look into quickly, as we have new recruits in the pipeline.'

'Well, Colm, that's my opinion and if I get the chance to meet him when I'm fully fit, I'll break his neck for sure.'

'I can see you feel strongly about this and because you have a proven record with us I must do something about it urgently. Leave it to me, Liam and I'll get back to you.'

'OK, Colm, but I had to say it because if the quality of future recruits depend on the likes of him, it doesn't bode well that's for certain, and not a hope of routing the Brits from the north and uniting Ireland.'

'OK, Liam thanks for this information and now just relax and continue your treatment. I will be in touch in due course with further instructions for the big job we want you to accomplish in the cause of freedom.'

After MacDiamid left his flat, Reagan poured himself a large Bushmills, his favourite whiskey, and pondered his next step for freedom; both his and Mairead's away from this nightmare.

In the office, Mairead carried on as usual and never

gave anything away about her relationship with Reagan. To do so would undoubtedly result in her disappearance and certain death at the hands of the terrorist organisation.

Reagan toyed with the possibilities of an escape from Ireland with Mairead via the ferry from Rosslare to Fishguard in Wales or perhaps travel to Larne in Ulster and catch the ferry to Cairnryan in Scotland. Either posed enormous risks for them both and capture by the IRA was not an option. But for the moment, though, he and Mairead would have to bide their time and wait for the right opportunity to make the break for freedom.

Later that evening, Mairead made the perilous journey to Phoenix Park to make a delivery to the dead letter box supplying information to her contact in the British Security Service, MI6. She steadfastly refused to name Liam Reagan in any of her messages, as she knew they would arrest him without delay if they were aware of his active involvement in IRA activities. She intended to keep him safe from the British and Irish Governments and especially the Republicans; he was hers and hers alone. During the journey back to her flat she was unaware of being observed by the small man, dressed in an overcoat and wearing a cloth cap, who followed her away from the park to the bus stop. The car tailing the bus to her to her home was discrete and stopped 100 yards from the address in order not to be noticed. Her suspicious movements were reported to the Chief of Staff the following day whilst she was out of the office shopping for tea and coffee.

Liam Reagan attended his regular out-patients appointments and the doctor was generally pleased with his progress and made a small but significant change to his medication, informing him his next appointment would be in six months time. He was free to return to full time study at the university.

Chapter 25

In London, at a meeting of the Security Services and Special Branch, the Home Secretary asked for the current reports on the whole situation and if there had been any steps towards apprehending the killer of the Chief Constable of Ulster.

Sir James Overton, of MI5, began his report by saying that Alan Conlon had disappeared and was believed dead, in fact, executed by the IRA and surveillance of his home and wife had been scaled down. It would seem that Mrs Conlon had a new man in her life, an accountant by all accounts, with no known IRA connections. He added that this suspicion had been supported by the Irish Garda, albeit on an unofficial level, in an informal telephone conversation to his opposite number in Dublin. Other general surveillance was carrying on as usual in Ulster with the assistance of the military and Special Branch.

The chief of MI6 operations in the Irish Republic added that all was quiet and nothing to report with regard to the killing in the north. They were mainly concerned with gun-running missions from the Middle East into the republic and therefore into terrorists hands. No mention was made of the information being made available through the dead letter box in Phoenix Park.

'Gentlemen,' began the Home Secretary,' we really

must get a move on and find this killer as I'm getting serious flak from the Prime Minister and of course there is fear it could easily happen again. The security on the late Sir Frank Cooper was in my opinion somewhat slack and that is why he was assassinated so easily on the golf course.'

'Sir, I must protest!' said Commander Collins, the head of Special Branch. 'It's all very well to criticise the security arrangements of the late chief constable but he was a difficult man to cover. If he had had his way, there would have been no cover at all. For some reason he could not see himself as a target; God knows why, as he had been a copper in the province for years.

'Whatever we tried to do he would always alter things and in all honesty he was out of his depth in this field. The day he was killed he insisted on minimal security and indeed ordered his close-security detail to remain in the clubhouse so as not to interfere with his golf match. I ask you, what should we have done? Ignored that direct order?' Commander Collins was flushed with anger and sat down reaching for his glass of water, his hand shaking with rage at the cabinet minister's remark.

'Sir, I whole heartedly agree with the Commander on this issue because Lt General Housland tried, on many occasions, to advise the Chief Constable on his personal security risks and he completely disregarded it every time,' said the Army Commander's deputy, Brigadier Rose.

'OK, gentlemen, I get your drift but the situation remains that we have not yet caught the assassin and we had bloody well get a move on. What are the SAS doing these days over there George?'

'Sir we are tasked on many ongoing duties, mainly on the border but not actively seeking the killer as it's not on our agenda. Having said that, if we are given the name and location of the culprit by MI5, or special branch we are, of course, happy to take care of the situation. I assume though you would like him or her taken alive to allow for a trial and subsequent long prison sentence to deter others from this course of action. Am I right, Home Secretary?' replied Lt Colonel Berryman, Commanding Officer of the Special Air Service Regiment.

'At the moment, arrest is our preferred option but that may change and if it does you will be the first to know and action, George.'

'I understand, sir. We will await further instructions on that one,' replied the Colonel.

'Right, gentlemen this is what we will have to do. With immediate effect pull out all the stops, and dare I say it, the budget is virtually unlimited to bring this situation to a successful conclusion. I don't care how you do it and I must stress all services must, and I mean must, work together on this one. There is to be no inter-service rivalry and one-upmanship on this and if there is, I will have someone's bollocks on a plate. Do I make myself fully understood?'

The meeting broke up with mutterings of dissention among those present, particularly the Commander of Special Branch.

'It's all very well for him sitting on his big fat arse in Whitehall laying down the law but in reality he has no idea what goes on in the real world. Let's hope he's next on the list to leap off this planet with a bullet in his head'.

'Now that's fighting talk, Paul which could get you sent to the tower, but you have a point I must agree,' said Brigadier Chalmers, the Commander of Special Forces, with a weak smile. 'How about a drink at my club to settle the dust?'

'Bloody good idea, I need one after all that,' said the Commander.

Meanwhile, at MI6 headquarters, the latest message from Mairead Donovan was being discussed; all she really said was that a big job was in the planning and would probably take place in London. At this stage she could offer no further information as she was ordered from the office during discussions. It was likely she may be able to elicit more information from her regular liaisons with the chief of staff in his bed. The decision was taken to allow her to carry on supplying information for the time being and the unofficial surveillance on her to continue.

Mairead Donovan went to work as normal on Monday morning and was first in the office as usual. She tidied up the desk and began to type up a report on a Sinn Fein meeting in Belfast for the chief's attention later. As soon as Colm MacDiamid came in she knew something was wrong; he was very quiet and not his normal jovial self.

'Good morning, Mairead,' he muttered and went straight to his desk.

'Good morning, Colm and what a lovely one it is for a change,' she replied.

'What have you been doing?' he said without pre-amble, looking straight at her

'What do you mean, Colm?' she said, startled and suddenly feeling very scared.

'You have been followed and I want to know what you have been up to in Phoenix Park late at night?' he demanded with menace.

'Colm, I know it's daft but I need more money than I earn to look after my mum and I thought, stupidly, I might be able to earn a little extra from prostitution to provide the extras my mum deserved. I just couldn't do it in the end and went home. That's the truth, Colm, plus the fact that I'm falling in love with you,' she lied.

'I don't believe you. What do you mean, with prostitution, you fucking slut, and I trusted you all this time with things you should not really know.'

'Colm, it's true. Believe me, darling. It was just a passing thought but there was no way it was going to happen, I swear it, really I do, my love.'

'How can I ever trust you again?'

'It will not happen again and I would never betray you or the IRA ever, I mean it, Colm.'

'Mairead, I just can't take a chance on that, as so much depends on secrecy and discretion with all we do here, and here you are going off and selling your body to any stranger on the streets.'

'But, Colm, it didn't happen I assure you. I just couldn't go through with it and it will never happen again.'

'You're fucking right it won't happen again. I'll see to that.'

'What do you mean?'

'Listen, and listen good young lady. You will go home and stay there until I tell you to come back in. Don't go anywhere because you will be followed and it will be reported back to me and then it will be out of my hands. Do I make myself clear? Now go home.'

Mairead Donovan hurriedly left the office and went straight home, shaking from head to foot and having trouble breathing through the stress of it all. As she went through the front door she grabbed her mobile phone from her handbag and called Liam Reagan.

As soon as Reagan picked up the receiver she blurted out, 'Liam, I have been followed by the IRA minders and they noticed that I had been to Phoenix Park at night.' She purposely decided not to tell him the real reason for the visit.

'But what were you doing there, particularly at night? It's dangerous and you never know who's about.'

'Liam, it's OK, I decided I wanted a walk and thought that was a good place to go and have a long think about all that has happened over the last few months.'

'But at night, Mairead, surely not a good idea, my love. Anyway, what did MacDiamid say to you?'

'Yes basically he told me to go home and stay there until he contacts me. I am not to go anywhere because I will be followed and that it will be reported back to him and from then on it will be out of his hands, the bastard.'

'Mairead, now remember just stay calm and you will be alright, OK?'

'OK, Liam. I will but I want to see you soon.'

'You will, my love I promise, just leave it to me.'

Liam Reagan put the phone down and thought, all this has to end soon or we will both be killed or sent to prison and have the key thrown away.

Colm MacDiamid immediately called a meeting of

his inner council to discuss the whole situation and to try and decide if any possible leaks had occurred through his PA's indiscretion. He opened the meeting with a breakdown of Mairead's known movements which were a bit thin on the ground to say the least.

'Gents, what do we know? Not very much it would seem.'

Paddy Jameson, the man who followed her sat up and addressed the group, ' I followed the young lady from the park to the bus stop and then my colleagues did the same and tailed the bus back to her home. Although she seemed nervous and looked back frequently she never met anyone or spoke on her mobile phone during the journey as far as we know. There were not many people on the bus and the observer in the car had a pretty clear view of her all the time. Why she went to the park is not clear.'

MacDiamid decided not to tell them that she sought out men as a prostitute to further her income; it might reflect back on him for being inadequate in bed as they all knew he was in a relationship with her.

'Well one thing is for sure, gents, our surveillance system works well as it was not discovered and blown by her. Having said that, she is not a trained operator so I suppose we can only pat ourselves on the back a little. By the way, Paddy, who authorised the tail on her, as I was not informed?'

'Oh, I didn't know that, Colm, Kevin Dempsey told me to carry this out and as he is on the council, albeit not present today, I naturally imagined it was official and had your blessing.'

'No it fucking well did not have my blessing; by the way where is Dempsey?'

'I believe he's in Belfast at the moment visiting a sick relative, an aunt I think,' replied Jameson with a smug smile.

'When he gets back tell him I want to see him, in the meantime, all surveillance stops and will only be authorised by me in the future, gentlemen. Is that clear?' replied MacDiamid.

The meeting broke up and Colm MacDiamid was alone in the office when the telephone rang. It was his contact in London. A coded message was passed within thirty seconds and the way it came through, MacDiamid knew he had to go to a phone box near the main railway station in Dublin and ring a number in South London at 9pm that night. This had to be confirmation that the assassination in Woolwich was on and what travel arrangements needed to be made, for Reagan to go to England soon.

That night, MacDiamid got the OK he needed from the London-based contact and the hit was scheduled for mid June. It was now April.

Back in his flat, Reagan pondered several ways to escape. Whatever he came up with, the risks were enormous both for him and Mairead but they had to make a move soon no matter what.

A week went by before the Chief of Staff called in Mairead Donovan for a chat. When she arrived, the chief made some tea and settled down with her in the back office.

'Now, my love I suppose you are wondering why I have called you in today?' he said with a weak smile.

'Well I was hoping I'd be coming back to work for the organisation I have grown to love and respect in its fight for a united Ireland,' she replied.

'Well, that's exactly what I want, Mairead and to start back today. In fact, if you are not doing anything in particular, right away, as I have so much work to do and need your expert help,' he said.

'That's all very well, Colm, but what about all the threats I had about not going out and I would be followed here, there and everywhere?' she said, looking as calm and composed as she could.

'A necessary precaution, my love. I'm sure you understand we have to be very careful and treat every little hiccup.'

'Some hiccup, Colm, I thought I would be put up against a wall and shot like a traitor,' she said with a concerned frown. 'You need have no doubt about my loyalty to you and the movement as I have said for the umpteenth time,' she continued.

'Yes I know, my love and now am I forgiven?' he smiled.

'Yes, I suppose so, Colm, but as a penance, I think you can take me out for lunch in the country soon.'

'Darling I certainly will, but in the meantime come here and be nice to me, like you always have.'

Mairead moved onto the sofa alongside the chief and instinctively his hands moved to her breasts as she nestled into his shoulder, much relieved her ordeal was over. His excitement was obvious and she decided to take full advantage of this, slowly and provocatively untying his belt as she looked him straight in the eye.

Over the forthcoming weeks or months she intended to destroy him and reveal as much detail to the British as she could, at the same time preserving her man Liam. She was aware that something big was being planned, but what? Pillow talk might just provide the answer.

Later that day, Colm MacDiamid announced he had to go out and would be away for about four or five days and that Mairead was to stay and man the office but have no contact with anyone within the organisation. If anyone contacted her, she was to let him know on his mobile phone but not give out any details as to his whereabouts. That was not difficult because she genuinely didn't have this information anyway. After he left the office she waited for about an hour and then phoned Liam Reagan at home. She had been told by MI6 that it was unlikely that the IRA had bugged their own offices but nevertheless it was still a gamble and a risk she had to take.

When he answered, she said it was important they met as soon as possible and that she was going to visit her mother, so perhaps it could tie in with that. He agreed and the arrangements were made for the day after tomorrow. Reagan was intrigued but asked no questions on the phone realising that something was wrong and a face to face meeting was the best option for them both.

Reagan slipped out of his flat and caught a bus into the city centre of Dublin then took a train to Dalkey, on the southern outskirts of the city and then walked for about a mile along the coast road, finally taking a bus back to Blackrock where Mairead's mother lived. Although Mairead told her mother about Liam, she stressed the secrecy and forbade her to tell anyone else, due to her job with the IRA. They had not yet met but Mrs Donovan was anxious to meet this man who was studying at the university and who was her daughter's lover.

He arrived at the house and Mrs Donovan welcomed him in and sat him down in the living room, supplying him with tea and biscuits. Mairead had not yet arrived.

When her daughter got to the house, she was flustered and nervy from all the exertion of her roundabout route to get to her mother's house without being followed. Unbeknown to Reagan she had undergone limited trade-craft training with MI6 regarding anti-surveillance techniques, along with dead letter box methods during her recruitment to the British Intelligence Service as an agent.

'Darling you look tired and I'm sure you're not eating properly,' said Mrs Donovan taking her coat.

'Oh I'm alright, mum, you always fuss when I come to see you. Hello, Liam how are you sweetheart?' she replied, kissing him on the cheek with a grin.

'Oh come now, girl, there will plenty of time for all that smoochy stuff later after we have eaten. I have made a good Irish stew for us all,' replied Mrs Donovan going into the kitchen.

As soon as her mother left the room, Mairead and Liam embraced passionately and held each other tight for several minutes before speaking.

'Liam we need to get away soon before you get to go on this job. Colm has told me what is planned and that you are expendable if you can't escape from the scene. I want to kill that bastard, setting you up like this. It's alright for him, he's not in danger, the most he could expect is a short prison sentence for being in the IRA or something like that,' she said with a shiver.

'I know, love and you're right, we must get away from this country once and for all, how is the question.'

Mrs Donovan came in with the food and they all settled down to eat the delicious stew, served with freshly baked bread and a glass of white wine to wash it all down. Mairead told her mother all about their romance and that they wanted a future together. Liam hardly managed to get a word in; such was the enthusiasm of his girlfriend who by now was in full flow and blossoming about their proposed life together.

Mrs Donovan listened with obvious pleasure and discretely never made any mention of her daughter's involvement with British Intelligence; this would come later when she was alone with Mairead. Later, during the afternoon, Mrs Donovan said she had to go out to get some shopping and would be back about 4 o'clock. This would give the couple some time alone. After she left the house they got down to some serious talking and their immediate future was discussed.

'Mairead my love, have you got any idea how long MacDiamid will be away from Dublin; I assume he's not in the city?'

'He said about four or five days but I have no idea where he's gone. All I have is his mobile number for emergencies or, if I was contacted by anyone in the movement to let him know. It seems a bit strange to me but with him you never know what he's going to do next,' she replied, cuddling up to him and placing her hand on his leg.

'I don't have a lot of money saved at the moment so our travel options are limited but perhaps we could go to England for a time, perhaps getting jobs to earn some more, then go to Canada. What do you say, my love?'

'Yes let's and before he gets back, darling.'

'It doesn't give us much time really. Do you think we can do it?'

'Definitely, Liam, why don't we go to Rosslare and get the boat to Fishguard and then to the south coast of England and live quietly until we can emigrate to Canada.'

'I suppose we could do just that. In fact, we could get to Rosslare in about two hours from here but I don't know the boat-sailing times,' he replied excitedly, even though the killing on the Chief Constable of Northern Ireland was constantly on his mind and the consequences that it could bring about if he was caught.

'Let's do it, Liam, I can get my savings from any bank in England once we are there and find a flat for the time being. Oh let's do it, darling!'

'What about your mum, what will she say?'

'I'm not sure but I will tell her once we are safe and away from here. I'm sure she'll understand, Liam, I'm sure she will.'

'Ok, let's do it right now. Does your mother have a car?'

'Yes she does, it's a bit old but roadworthy I think. The keys are in the hall.'

'What will she do if she finds it missing? Call the Garda I suppose?'

'No I'll leave her a message before we go and tell her

369

I needed it urgently and will phone her later to explain. She's OK and will understand. Don't worry, my love it will be fine.'

'Right then, we had better get on with it. We can take the N11 to Wexford and then the N25 to Rosslare and freedom, love,' he replied.

'Do you want to go home and collect anything before we go?' she said.

'No it's too risky and so it would be for you; on second thoughts we have to get some belongings and documents including our chequebooks. What about we meet here tomorrow and ask your mum to drive us to Rosslare. Do you think she would?'

'I'm sure she would. Then at least she would still have her car after we had gone. Look, Liam I will work on her when she gets home and call you this evening. It might be better if we got back here tonight instead of tomorrow. The sooner the better because I think this whole thing will blow up in our faces if we wait any longer. Leave it to me, darling, I'm sure I can win her round.'

Liam Reagan left the house and made his way home to his flat near the university, to pack a few items he would take on their journey into freedom; his savings were pretty small but it would have to do.

Mairead Donovan did the same but not before leaving her mother a note to say she would be back later that evening and that she had something important to tell her. When Mrs Donovan got home from shopping she read the note her daughter had written and immediately decided that the important thing she wanted to tell her about must be that she was pregnant. Well, she thought, things are different these days, quite unlike her youth when such a possibility was unthinkable.

It was pouring with rain when Mairead got back to her mother's house and immediately Mrs Donovan wanted to know what this important thing was that her daughter wanted to discuss. She was concerned that Mairead was carrying a large grip, obviously fully packed and heavy. Over the next hour, Mairead Donovan explained their predicament without mentioning that Liam was the killer of the Chief Constable the previous year in Ulster. She merely said he was being groomed for a big job on the mainland and that he was having none of it. In addition, she wanted out of her job and because she knew so much and her own life was in danger. She was at the beck and call of a violent and powerful man. Mrs Donovan was aghast at hearing all this and was only too anxious to help them both get away.

Liam Reagan's departure from his flat was slightly more complicated because he had an idea he might be under surveillance, albeit occasionally, because of the job he was earmarked for. He decided to pack his few belongings into a large briefcase and go to the university library therefore giving the impression he was doing some extra study work on his classics course. Fortunately he knew his way around the corridors well and would indeed go to the library and wait for darkness to make his escape. For the next two hours he picked books from the shelves and appeared to read intensively but he could not concentrate and just bided his time. He had no idea if, indeed, he was being watched but he could not afford to take any chances because both his and Mairead's life

371

would be in danger. He had spoken to his lover earlier by phone and told her he would be late arriving at her mothers' and not to worry.

Mrs Donovan gave Mairead some money to get them over the next few days and to buy tickets for the boat journey to Fishguard, with some to spare once they were in Wales.

'Thanks, mum you're a real sport. I'll pay you back as soon as I can and we will stay in touch, so don't worry about us. If the IRA does contact you, just say I have disappeared and you have no idea where I am. Don't make any mention of Liam will you?'

'Oh don't trouble yourself about the IRA. I know how to handle them alright.'

'OK, mum but be careful. I don't want to risk you getting hurt or involved in all this and by the way, do you still have any contact with British Intelligence? I know you once said they had spoken to you when you were at Stormont,' replied Mairead, feeling a little more confident.

'Oh no that all finished years ago after I retired. They knew I was becoming ill with this diabetes thing I have and didn't want to bother me. I suppose, in any case, I had nothing to tell them after leaving the office. I have never kept in contact with my work-colleagues after I moved back to Dublin and have not attended any reunions. That sort of thing is not for me, as you know, darling. Anyway, I'm going to make some more tea. Now, when is that man of yours going to get here? By the way, he's really handsome isn't he?'

'Now, mum, I don't want to hear you talking like

that. The next thing I know, you'll be running away with him instead of me and yes, he is good looking and intelligent, so a pretty good catch I think. I'm sure we can make a great life together after we get away from all this,' she said grinning and continued laying out the cups and saucers on the kitchen table.

Two hours later, Liam Reagan arrived at the house with his belongings in a large briefcase, having successfully got out of the university, so far as he was aware, undetected. Mrs Donovan was delighted to see him again and made a fuss of him the moment he stepped through the door.

'Liam, Mairead has told me all about your plan and I will help you both to get away from here just as soon as you are ready, so don't worry about anything. By the way, you are sleeping in the spare bedroom tonight, young man,' she said with the look of a future mother-in-law.

'That's no problem, Mrs Donovan. I'm very grateful for your help and I promise I'll look after your daughter.'

'Anyway, Liam that's enough of the Mrs Donovan, my name's Julie,' she said with a chuckle, at the same time giving him a hug.

Chapter 26

In London, the senior members of MI5 decided to let the situation lie with regards to Doreen Conlon, as she seemed to have settled into a new relationship and was of no further use to them. Additionally, it was unlikely the IRA would bother her or her family in the future. It was well known that she hated the terrorist movement and played no active part in its operation or knew anyone else who did, apart from her husband who had disappeared off the face of the earth.

Don Gale was selected to pass this decision to her at the earliest opportunity and called before his chief the following Monday, allowing him time to get home from Ireland and back to London. As he knocked on the door, at the arranged time, he was called in immediately by the Deputy Director General, Sir James Overton of MI5.

'Good morning, Don, please take a seat,' said Sir James.

'Good morning, sir,' replied Gale, sitting down and feeling just a little nervous.

'Don I have a small but delicate matter to discuss with you and for you to then carry out my instructions to the letter. The future of Doreen Conlon, who I know you have had under surveillance for some time, has now been decided.

'You may recall, her husband, Alan has disappeared

and is feared dead. In fact we believe executed by the IRA. The Garda unofficially concur with us on this. He and Mrs Conlon, including the family of two small girls, were offered sanctuary in Spain under our protection scheme and although he was keen to go immediately, she was not. Now that it appears she has a new man in her life, we have decided to withdraw this offer and cast her adrift so to speak. Your task, Don, is to visit her and pass this information direct, excluding any mention of her husband's apparent passing,' concluded the deputy Director, leaning back in his chair.

'Sir what is the position if she asks me directly if her husband is still alive?'

'On this you will have to use your judgment and perhaps say we simply do not know where he is or indeed what has happened to him, but due to the passage of time we feel it's time for her to move on with her life. Do you see what I'm saying, Don?'

'I do indeed, sir, but it could be a little sticky as it hasn't been that long since he disappeared has it?'

'No it hasn't, Don but we have enough on our plates without worrying about a terrorist's wife and family as well. Remember Conlon's role was explosives, and many of these devices have killed our soldiers and civilians!' replied Overton abruptly.

'Point taken, sir, I will get on with this just as soon as I get back to Ireland. I can get a flight at 1000 tomorrow morning.'

'Good, Don, and by the way let me know her reaction. In fact, call me directly and do not go through anyone else, as this is not widely known in the service; only by the selected few so to speak. I don't have to point out to you that this is most secret and for your ears only. Just before you go, I have been looking at your record of service and it makes good reading, so it's likely a promotion could well be in the offing, in the not too distant future, if this is successful. Give her this £2000 as a sweetener,' he said, handing Gale a large envelope and standing up to indicate the meeting was over.

'Thank you, sir, I will be in touch as soon as it's been completed,' replied Gale.

Don Gale made his way to the canteen for lunch and during his meal he pondered what the deputy director general had said. This could be tricky, particularly if Doreen Conlon started to ask awkward questions that he could not answer. He would have to play it by ear and his cover would also be blown in Ireland at this point. As for all that rubbish about promotion, how many times had he heard that in the past? All he wanted these days was the quiet life and head towards retirement and long days fishing and playing golf. Since his wife had left him, due to his erratic working hours he had not bothered with women apart from the occasional one night stand and sea fishing had become his main hobby along the North Devon coast.

Gale caught the 10am flight to Belfast and made his way into the republic by train to Dublin and finally his flat in the suburbs. The following day he would travel to Ballybrittas and confront Mrs Conlon. The sooner he could get this out of the way the better, he thought.

The next morning he set off in a hire car for the small town of Ballybrittas and on entering, he thought about phoning her to arrange an appointment but decided to drive past the house first, out of curiosity. As he approached, he noticed a medium sized transit van outside and a man loading small items of furniture into it, along with help from Mrs Conlon. Gale decided to phone her right away and see what was happening. He used his mobile with a digitally protected number so it couldn't be identified and dialled her known phone number. She answered almost immediately.

'Good morning, Mrs Conlon,' said Gale in his adopted Irish accent.

'Who is this?' she replied, without any pretence of politeness.

'Mrs Conlon, I would like a quick word with you as soon as possible to clear up a little outstanding matter that affects your future. I am not from the IRA but an interested party who is trying to help you and your family,' replied Gale, a little breathless.

'Whoever you are, don't bother with the fake Irish accent because you don't fool me. You're a Brit that's for sure, aren't you?'

'OK, Mrs Conlon you win, I am but I want to talk to you with some urgency as I see you appear to be moving,' replied Gale now in his normal London accent.

'Not now, Mr fucking Brit I'm busy. Anyway, what do you want?'

'Mrs Conlon, it's not my intention to hinder you in any way but to assure you, after this meeting that I'm trying to arrange with you, we, or any of the British establishment will not bother you again. That's a promise.'

'Promises, promises, how many times have I heard that Mr Brit?'

'Mrs Conlon could we meet, locally, as I have something to give you as well? You suggest the place of your choice.'

'You haven't found that husband of mine, have you?'

'No, Mrs Conlon we haven't, and we are not looking,' said Gale firmly.

'OK, Mr Brit, meet me outside O'Hanlon's in Kildare this afternoon at 12.30 and let's get this sorted, once and for all, OK? By the way, how will I recognise you?'

'Don't worry I will recognise you and the meeting will be short and to the point.'

'Right, at 12.30 then,' she replied.

'Great I'll look forward to seeing you then. I hope you will be alone, as I will. It's better that way really,' he concluded, ringing off somewhat relieved.

Doreen Conlon was right on time and looked quite stunning in a blue jacket and short, grey skirt; her outfit finished off with black, high-heeled shoes. Don Gale had been in position for an hour before the arranged time to check for any obvious surveillance by the IRA.

'Good afternoon, Mrs Conlon,' said Gale, making her jump a little after being startled by his approach.

'Hello, Mr Brit, now what can I do for you?' she said without a smile.

'Perhaps we could go and have some coffee or perhaps lunch if you are hungry.'

'I'm not hungry but coffee sounds good,' she said, with just a little less hostility.

Once settled in the coffee bar, she again asked what this meeting was all about and mentioned she had to be back home soon, because she was moving to Dublin with her new man.

'Mrs Conlon, thanks again for coming and the information is for you and you only. I understand my department offered your husband, and of course you and the girls, a safe haven in a European country in respect of information passed to us. It has come to our notice that he has subsequently disappeared and is feared dead. I can tell you honestly that we have absolutely no idea where he is or what has happened to him, but his disappearance has nothing to do with us at all.

'What I have been instructed to tell you, is that the arrangement to relocate abroad has now been withdrawn because your husband is nowhere to be found, so the arrangement ceases. This does not mean we cannot help you and the girls of course. I would like to give you some monetary reward to help you with your future and can assure you that we will have no further contact again,' said Gale sipping his coffee.

'Mr..., I also believe my husband is dead, almost certainly killed by the IRA and I am not surprised at their actions. I despise them and you Brits, but you seem to be genuine; and yes I don't want to go to Spain as promised. I never did, but again you probably know that anyway. My life is about to change forever, now I have found Aiden. I should have married him years ago but he and I went our own ways and fate has brought us back together, thank God. Even if Alan did make an appearance I have taken legal action to end our marriage, one way or the other, either by desertion, death or divorce, so there is no going back on that one. I don't know why I'm telling you all this as you are really the enemy,' she smiled, 'aren't you, Mr....?'

'Actually, Mrs Conlon, we are not the enemy, that title is reserved for the IRA and will always be the case. The British and Irish Governments are on common ground and many of your fellow countrymen have served with distinction in our armed forces in both world wars and for that we are profoundly grateful. With regards to yourself, I want to give you this package, which contains £2000, on behalf of the HM Government to help you in your new life and on which I offer my profound congratulations and good wishes for the future.'

'I am almost tempted to say thank you but it seems a little shallow right now but thanks all the same. You have restored some of my dignity which was definitely lost when Alan was with the IRA and all that went with it. To that end, if I had any information regarding the movement I would share it with you but I most certainly have nothing and never did have. Aiden is my future now, along with the girls, and our new house is in Dublin. It's all I ever wanted you know.'

'OK, Mrs Conlon I'm glad we have managed to sort this out amicably and can now go our own ways and, with the best will in the world, never meet again. Take care and enjoy what you now have. Thank you,' said Gale, standing up ready to go, shaking her by the hand.

Doreen Conlon ordered another coffee and slowly sipped the piping hot latte, watching Gale walk through the crowd and out of sight. In another time and place she could quite fancy him,she thought.

Don Gale hadn't, in fact, gone far but managed to select a position from where he could observe Doreen Conlon as she finished her coffee and walked back to her car and drive off in the direction of Ballybrittas. He followed, at a discrete distance, all the way home and watched her go indoors after being met at the door by her new man.

He arranged for the telephone taps to be removed soon after and all MI5 interest was scaled down on the Conlon family, or what was left of them. Don Gale reported to the deputy Director of MI5 personally and relayed the whole story to him over lunch in the private, senior staff dining room in the London Security Service Headquarters.

'Now, Don about the matter of your promotion,' began Sir James with a twinkle in his eye. 'I have the position of senior case officer available, that I would like to offer you, based in Gibraltar. Would you be interested? No need to tell me now, just sleep on it and let me know in the morning,' added Sir James Overton.

Chapter 27

At 1030am the next day, Liam Reagan and Mairead Donovan were driven by Julie Donovan to the County Wexford port of Rosslare to catch a ferry to Fishguard, in Wales, for the start of their journey to England and freedom from the IRA. The crossing was rough and they were both seasick, only being relieved when the ship finally docked. They took a train into London and managed to find a cheap hotel for the night before another train to Brighton and the start of a new life. Julie Donovan drove home to Blackrock, in Dublin, worried about her daughter's future in England and whether the IRA would come knocking on her door asking the whereabouts of Mairead.

If indeed the terrorists did come knocking, Julie decided, she would kick up such a fuss and make so much noise, someone would call the Garda and that should scare the IRA away and leave her alone; this really was her only option.

The next day Mairead called her mother on the new mobile phone they had bought, especially for this reason, and assured her they were alright and happy and to remind her that she must only use it to contact her. For all other calls, Mrs Donovan must use her normal phone, just in case.

Colm MacDiamid returned from his trip early and went into the office to find Mairead missing and not answering her phone. Puzzled, he went to the pub and met up with some friends and had several drinks. A little while later Kevin Dempsey, his quartermaster, came in and joined the group.

'Ah, Kevin just the man I want to see,' said MacDiamid, obviously a little the worst for drink.

'What's the problem, Colm me old mate?' replied Dempsey, sipping his drink.

'The problem is you, Kevin. Who gave you the right to put a tail on Mairead recently without running it past me first?'

'Just because she works for you, Colm it doesn't mean you own her. You might be fucking her but she works for us so don't you forget it OK?'

'You just keep your fucking nose out of my business, Dempsey or I will beat you to pulp, you get me!'

'Oh fuck off, Colm, you're pissed again, but then again that's nothing new is it? Is it lads? We see it all the time,' said Dempsey, looking for support from the others present.

Dempsey never saw the fist coming that smashed into his nose, shattering the bone and sending him backwards into the bar and finally causing him to fall to the floor.

'Get up, you bastard, get up before I kill you, Dempsey,' shouted MacDiamid, now in a rage and frothing at the mouth. The other men present decided to lead the chief of staff away to the other side of the pub and get Dempsey out and away before any more trouble and perhaps the arrival of the Garda.

In the office the next day, Colm MacDiamid again tried to contact Mairead without success. He then tried Liam Reagan but again, there was no reply; something strange was going on, he decided. A personal visit was required and he gathered together a small team of men to accompany him. First he visited Mairead's address but the place was clearly empty. Next on the list was Reagan's flat in the university, again without success. They made some enquiries but no one they spoke to seemed to know anything. Back in the office MacDiamid gathered his team for a meeting.

'Gentlemen,' he began, 'it appears that my PA has disappeared along with Reagan. Does anyone know anything before we organize a hunt for them both?'

'I never did trust her, Colm, although there was nothing specific to put my finger on I just had a bad feeling about her, but I accepted she was your PA and therefore your choice and left it at that,' said Padraig Meehan, a member of the active service team.

'We had carried out checks on her as best we could and she seemed committed to the cause, as we all are, and her work was good and reliable. I never had any doubts about her, Paddy,' replied MacDiamid with a shrug.

'Could it be that she has just run away with Reagan, I know she visited him at home during his illness,' retorted Meehan.

'You're right, Paddy but this was with my permission simply to check on his welfare. I never had any doubts about her reliability,' said the chief.

'Colm, does she know any of our intentions for the future?' said George Collins, head of the Dundalk active service unit and a very influential man in the organisation.

'Nothing, George, nothing at all that would be of use to anyone,' replied MacDiamid with butterflies in his stomach.

'Why did Dempsey order a tail on her recently? You remember she was found late at night leaving Phoenix Park and gave some story about trying to become a prostitute to earn some extra money. Apparently she couldn't go through with it and just went home. She did in fact go home and it never happened again so far as we know,' said Meehan.

'Tell you what I think, Colm, she has done a runner with Reagan and he is properly screwing her as we speak in some hotel. Give it time and they will surface,' said Collins with a grin.

'When they do, gentlemen they will both be for the high jump. I left specific instructions that Reagan must not leave Dublin without first letting us know and as for Mairead I just don't know what to think. Maybe she has just gone to visit her mother who I know is not very well but she should have let us know first,' said MacDiamid, increasingly worried and concerned at what he had told her in bed. She knew far more than she should and if it ever came out he would be executed by his own kind and he knew it.

Over the next week or so the IRA pulled out all the stops to find the pair, without success, and again Colm MacDiamid called another meeting to discuss what to do next. The visit to Mairead's mother proved fruitless as she acted as if Alzheimer's was setting in because she spoke in such confusing terms that the man who visited her decided not to continue his questions and left her alone.

'Gents, it seems we have drawn a blank with our search and therefore I suggest we issue a kill order on both of them if they ever come to light; all our leads have drawn a blank. I have arranged a watch on Mairead's mum for the time being but do not hold out much hope and if we get nowhere in a couple of weeks we might as well withdraw it. No point in wasting resources' on a lost cause. Does everyone agree?' said MacDiamid.

There was general agreement but a key man was missing from the meeting and that was Kevin Dempsey following the altercation in the pub with MacDiamid.

The Chief of Staff asked where Dempsey was and why was he not at the meeting.

'Colm, I think you know why Dempsey is not here after your attack on him in the pub the other night. He needed hospital treatment and is, at the moment, a bitter man and not able to give us his best,' said Collins.

'He should have kept his big mouth shut and he had no right to order the tail on Mairead without consulting me. That is the procedure we all have to follow!' shouted MacDiamid to no one in particular.

'Colm, Colm, calm down this will get us nowhere. I suggest we get him here and thrash this out, once and for all, so it doesn't degenerate into an ongoing feud. Shall I go and get him now? said Meehan.

'Would you, Paddy? I think you're right, you normally are, my friend,' replied MacDiamid, now clearly calmer.

An hour later the IRA quartermaster, Kevin Dempsey, walked into the room with his face heavily bandaged.

'Kevin old friend take a seat. Can someone get him a cup of tea?' asked MacDiamid.

After they had all settled down again, the mood lightened and became much more convivial, just like normal meetings, but never forgetting the seriousness of their purpose.

'Kevin, I just want to apologise for the other night. I was totally out of order and obviously I was pissed and that is unforgivable. I should have known better,' said MacDiamid.

'I guess we were both to blame and let's make sure this doesn't occur again. By the way my nose is really sore and it has not improved my good, youthful looks, boys,' replied Dempsey with a grin.

'If you walk down O'Connell Street looking like that, Kev, you'll frighten the life out of all the girls more than you usually do,' said Collins with a belly laugh.

Colm MacDiamid suddenly stood up and rapped the table with his teaspoon to get attention.

'Right, gentlemen, I have an announcement to make and which I ask for your careful consideration before answering. I would like to stand down from my position as chief of staff; I have served our cause for 25 years and feel it's time to let new blood take over. It goes without saying that I will continue to serve in whatever position is required of me, although hopefully further down the scale of authority.

'The main reason for this decision is that Janice, my wife, is ill and has been for some time and although I have kept it quiet I am sure some of you already know she may have less than a year to live. The doctors are still carrying out tests and frankly I want to be with her much more than I am at the moment.

'I suggest we take a break for an hour and let you men, the future of the IRA, decide what you think is best and who my replacement should be,' concluded Colm MacDiamid, sitting down with heart pounding in his chest.

When the meeting re-convened, the general agreement was to put the job of chief of staff to ballot among the senior members of the organisation. Within the week it was decided that George Collins of Dundalk was to be the new man in charge and the person to take the movement forward. He had considerable experience of active service both in the north and on the English mainland.

Collins called a meeting for the senior members, to lay out his strategy for the future and there was full attendance in Dublin.

'Gents, we have to try and find Reagan and Donovan at all costs, simply because we had planned that Reagan would carry out an important mission on the mainland and although he doesn't know the full details of this, he knows enough to blow the whole thing sky high. Do we have any leads as to their whereabouts?'

In the absence of Colm MacDiamid, Kevin Dempsey spoke up. 'I know we covered my disagreement with Colm the other day but I still have a suspicion that he may have said more than he should have, to Mairead, during their obvious affair. I have no proof whatsoever but I do have these nagging thoughts, it's not that I dislike the bloke, far from it, but I do have my doubts. Could she be working for the Brits?'

'As far as I can see we only have a couple of choices, continue the search for them both or interrogate MacDiamid at the farm in Meath. We must bear in mind Colm's service with us through thick and thin but if he has indeed talked he must be punished in our usual fashion,' said Collins, frowning and looking at each man individually.

'George, just for the moment can we just place Colm under surveillance and see what happens? I can't believe for one moment he would do anything to harm the cause, simply because he's in deep with the rest of us and could be looking at 30 years in the UK if caught,' said Meehan.

'I think you're right, Paddy but we need our best man for this. Who would you suggest?' replied Collins.

'The bloke I have in mind is Peter O'Halloran, based at the moment in Galway. I understand he learnt his trade as a sergeant in the Garda CID until he was caught fiddling his expenses and when confronted, beat a superintendent to pulp. Following a spell in Portlaoise Prison he was released and has worked for us ever since; with some good results I might add,' replied Meehan.

'OK then, I'll leave you to set this up and I'll look forward to any results. Let's give it a try for one month only, starting immediately and then evaluate the results, if any. If indeed anything comes to light in the meantime we will act accordingly and swiftly. Give O'Halloran all the information he needs with regard to Colm's address and car registration number but do not, and I mean do not, give any other details or reasons why we require his services,' added Collins.

'Will do, George, I'll get on it right away,' replied Meehan.

Later that afternoon, O'Halloran was given the details he would require with instructions to start immediately.

When the meeting broke up, Collins sat at the table that doubled as a desk and pondered the possibility that MacDiamid had in fact talked to Mairead Donovan in far more depth than he should have done. The fact that he resigned his position suddenly only added to the suspicion of it all. In spite of these doubts he found it hard to believe that a man of MacDiamid's experience could have been so stupid; he intended to find out. At 6pm that night Peter O'Halloran began his surveillance.

At his sick wife's bedside, Colm MacDiamid became the doting husband and he intended to carry on this way until she died, bitterly regretting his affair with Mairead and wondering why he ever joined the IRA, as it was pretty obvious they would never force the British Army out of Ulster, no matter what they did militarily. The only way forward was the political route and not with bombs and bullets.

After a full month of intensive surveillance, O'Halloran reported his findings at a meeting called by Collins.

'Hello, gentlemen, I don't know most of you here today but I have carried out surveillance on the subject and really there was nothing unusual to report about his movements. He visited several people in the city and once went to Limerick with his wife; I believe to see a healer who is quite famous over there and treats seriously ill people with some success, it is claimed. It seems there is absolutely nothing to worry about, but one thing I was unable to check out was his home telephone as I do not have the necessary tapping equipment or indeed the expertise for this type of operation. From my point of view all seems normal,' said O'Halloran somewhat relieved.

'Thanks, Peter for all your efforts and perhaps we can call on your services again in the future,' replied Collins, in a manner that the choice was not an option.

After the meeting broke up, Collins and Dempsey

stayed behind to have a further talk about the proposed operation in Woolwich, South London, later in the year - the assassination of the British Home Secretary.

At home, Colm MacDiamid was constantly worrying about the reaction of his colleagues if it came out about his pillow talk to Mairead. The idea of taking his wife to England for medical treatment could provide a good cover for his eventual escape from the movement, unless they caught Mairead first and killed her. The problem was that he knew they would torture her first and she would tell them everything, fully implicating him all the way; not only would they kill her but him also. He had to get away from all this forever and soon.

Chapter 28

In Brighton, Liam Reagan and Mairead had some early success in finding jobs, she as a hotel receptionist and he working in the bar of a golf club. Quite ironic, he thought, given his past employment with the IRA. The small furnished flat they rented on the outskirts of the coastal town, provided good accommodation but the strain of being constantly alert soon began to result in arguments.

'Liam, this isn't working, we row constantly and you're so moody all the time. What's gone wrong? We were so in love back home in Ireland,' said Mairead, crying softly.

'I don't know, my love it has to be the fact we are always looking over our shoulders. I wish we were much further away from here. I would like us to go to Australia and get settled over there, perhaps going to university and studying for my degree. Remember, you already have one darling,' said Reagan.

'If we went there I would never see mum again, you know that. You don't have any parents but I have my mum and I want to see her from time to time, especially as she's ill now,' replied Mairead, wiping her eyes.

'Well what do you suggest Mairead?'

'I don't know, but I don't feel safe here that's for

certain,' she said, also worrying about her commitments to MI6 and the fact that Reagan didn't know of her involvement.

'One thing is for certain we can't go back because that would be madness, we would both end up in a bog somewhere with bullets in our heads. We can't go to the British authorities because it would mean a long prison spell for me. In a word, my love we are stuffed,' said Reagan in despair.

'At the moment every Irish voice I hear frightens the living daylights out of me, Liam and I don't think I can stand it much longer. And by the way I'm pregnant!' she said sheepishly.

'Pregnant, Mairead how did that happen?'

'Well I think you had a major part in that, Liam, it's not divine intervention that's for sure. The way we have been going at it lately it was bound to happen sooner or later, darling,'

'Oh shit, this really complicates the issue. When the baby is born it must have a stable home life, not one of constantly travelling to keep out of the IRA clutches. We can't keep running forever Mairead,'

'I know that, darling so let's try and get something more permanent and settled, but what?'

'When is the baby due, love?'

'I'm two months pregnant, so seven months to go according to the doctor I visited the other day.'

'You didn't tell me you went to the doctor, Mairead.'

'I know, darling but I wanted to make sure first before I told you, so now we have it, Liam, we are going to be parents.'

'This really does change things, my love and the way forward has to be even more carefully planned now.'

'Liam you are pleased aren't you?'

'Of course, love but I have to think of a way to keep us all safe from those murdering bastards over the water, plus I have to get ongoing medical treatment for myself. I have to stay fit so as to be able to look after you both, darling.' concluded Reagan, giving her a cuddle and a kiss on the cheek.

After sleeping on the problem, Reagan had come up with a plan and decided to put it to Mairead the following evening when they were both at home.

'Darling I have an idea you might like to consider: what about we go to Portugal? There are plenty of bars and hotels we could work in until we get ourselves settled and the Portuguese are really friendly to the British.'

'That's fine, Liam but you have forgotten one fundamental thing, we are not British but Irish!'

'I doubt that they would know the difference, love. Anyway, Spain is much more popular with the Irish than Portugal so the chances of us running into people we don't want to meet is so much more reduced, my love. The other advantage of Portugal is that because it's a small country, your mum could fly into Faro, from Dublin or Cork, and we can pick her up and bring her to our house easily,' said Reagan with conviction.

'Do you think it would work, Liam?'

'If we settled on the Algarve, not only is the weather good but the distance to Faro airport is not that far, my love. OK, we would have to learn Portuguese but that shouldn't be a problem as we are both fluent in Gaelic; another language should be straight forward, darling.'

'They do understand English in Portugal I know, love, because I went there in my gap year and loved it, Liam.'

'Right, I think what we should do love is for you to have the baby in England and move soon afterwards, in the meantime we could go to Portuguese classes locally to give us a head start, what do you think?'

'That means we have to wait seven months, Liam.'

Over the next few months they kept a very low profile and saved as much as they could which turned out to be more than expected. The local adult education college provided lessons in colloquial Portuguese and their progress was good. Mairead's mother visited once after flying into Heathrow and was met by them for the train journey to Brighton. She seemed pleased and looked forward to being a grandmother. There was still the worrying aspect of the IRA but she had not noticed any obvious enquiries going on, so gradually relaxed about the whole thing.

As a precaution, Julie Donovan casually mentioned to a friend that she was sure the couple had fled to Australia and would not be coming back. As there was a chance that it might get back to the IRA, this was to further cover their trail. Just a young couple in love and looking for a better future she insisted.

Mairead and Reagan began searching for a job in Portugal, for him, on the internet and there seemed to be plenty of choices available; although the wages were not good they should be able to manage. Rented accommodation was affordable and the cost of living a bit cheaper than in England.

Mairead went into hospital and produced a baby girl two days later, after a difficult labour, and although tired and overwhelmed with the responsibilities of motherhood, returned home happy. A phone call to her mother confirmed all was well and that she must come and see her granddaughter soon. Mairead enclosed a photo on a text to her mother but Julie was not sure how to open it. 'Bloody new fangled thing,' she mumbled as she struggled with the options menu, finally managing to see her baby granddaughter at last.

When Liam was at work she decided to get in touch with MI6 and explain her lack of contact over the last months. She had a special number to call and with trembling hands dialled the number which was answered immediately. She gave her code name and was put through to her handler; the call being scrambled.

'Where have you been?' was the stern reply.

'I had to run because I was about to be found out. On my last dead letter box run I was followed and confronted with threats of death if found to be passing any information to anyone,' she replied breathlessly.

'Say nothing else, we have to meet. Where are you now?'

'I'm in England but this has to remain secret because I'm scared of being found, don't you understand?' she stammered.

'Say nothing else on this line. Ring me this afternoon from a public phone box to receive instructions,' replied the man putting the phone down.

That afternoon, Mairead rang the number and spoke immediately to her handler.

'Right I know you are in the Brighton area and we must meet as soon as possible. Be at the main railway station near the booking hall at 10 o'clock tomorrow morning and you will be contacted. When you are approached, the contact will say to you, 'which is the way to the football stadium' and you will reply 'out of the station and turn left' then await further instructions, do you understand?'

'Yes I do, but I must warn you I will have my new baby with me just in case your man doesn't know and is expecting a woman alone,' she replied.

'Right I will pass this information on but make sure you are alone apart from the baby, this is most important,' he said ringing off.

The following morning Mairead Donovan was right on time for the meeting when all of a sudden she was approached and passwords exchanged without preamble.

'Come with me,' said the female agent, walking off towards a parked car on the station forecourt. After settling into the back of the car with her baby the agent drove off without a word. After about a mile the car turned into a side street and parked in a resident's bay with the agent indicating they get out and follow her into the terraced house.

Once inside, Mairead was met by a man in a smart dark blue suit sporting an old Etonian tie and polished brogue shoes.

'Good morning, Miss Donovan,' he said without introductions.

'Good morning,' she replied, frowning and a little scared of what was coming next.

'We need to know what happened in Dublin that made you leave in such a hurry. Were you compromised in any way and if so did you tell them anything?'

'I was followed from Phoenix Park after visiting the dead letter box. I know they never realised what I was up to because I would not be here now if they did. I managed to convince Colm MacDiamid, the Chief of Staff, that I decided to become a prostitute to earn some extra money to look after my sick mother. I also told him that I could not go through with it and went home. After a short period of time he accepted this and we then carried on as normal, with him bedding me at regular intervals. I realised by this time I had to get out of this altogether and came to England without them knowing. I have no doubt that I am on their wanted list and if caught the place I would visit next is a bog in Donegal, along with so many more,' she said, earnestly cuddling her baby.

'Miss Donovan, you really should have told us and we could have helped you in some way. What about your baby, who is the father?'

'He's a long term friend, who I want to marry and start a new life soon.'

'Miss Donovan, his name, please!'

'I don't see that's any of your business.'

'Miss Donovan, please; you are, or have worked for us so it is our business and we will find out if we have to. It is clear you have nothing new to offer HM Government and the information you have passed has been fairly low key but nonetheless helpful. One last thing, do you know who the target is for assassination in London? You will recall you mentioned this in one of your messages.'

'Not really but at one time the Home Secretary was casually mentioned; beyond that I know nothing. I always had to leave the office when sensitive discussions took place.'

'What about when you were in bed with MacDiamid, was he more forthcoming, if you will pardon the pun? Did he ever mention the killing of the Chief Constable of Ulster?' continued the man.

'Nothing was ever mentioned about that at all, that one was some time ago wasn't it? before my time. All conversations were of a general nature, nothing specific. Remember I was well down the food chain in the organisation. I might add I think this dead letter box idea is a bit dated now, don't you? A bit of cold war stuff really,' she replied a little more boldly. 'Surely secure email is much more efficient and quicker with less risk these days instead of scurrying around like a Soviet agent in Berlin,' she added.

'Quite, quite Miss Donovan but we have to follow procedures that are tried and trusted, ' he replied, looking at the female agent raising his eyebrows.

'You may be interested to know that Colm MacDiamid is no longer Chief of Staff in Dublin, it would appear he has retired to care for his sick wife. I wonder if he thought of that when he was screwing you in the office and elsewhere, Miss Donovan.'

'I have no idea but one thing is for sure, he won't be screwing me, as you so eloquently put it, in future. I'd kill him first, the cowardly bastard,' said Mairead.

'Well I have to say we are unhappy with the way you decided to stop working for us but these things happen;

however we will be keeping an eye on you and the boyfriend, so make sure you behave yourself and keep out of trouble. If you are contacted by any member of the IRA, past or present, call me immediately on the usual number, is that clear Miss Donovan?'

'I will you can be certain of that,' she replied.

'I will have you driven home now and you will not hear from us again but you can rest assured we will be watching you,' said the man in a threatening tone and ending the meeting.

Mairead wanted to be dropped off at a supermarket to get some shopping and this was done without any conversation between her and the female driver. Once inside Tesco's, she relaxed a little and filled her basket then walked home with the aim of feeding her baby.

Liam Reagan returned home after work at the golf club tired and hungry and just wanting to relax with his girlfriend and their baby in front of the television.

'Darling what have you been doing today?' he asked casually, whilst fiddling with the TV tuner to get the early evening news.

'Apenas algumas compras no supermercado - just some shopping at the supermarket,' she replied, in her recently acquired knowledge of basic Portuguese.

'Very impressive, love,' said Reagan. 'I'm struggling a bit with it at the moment but I will get there I'm sure.'

MI6 decided to put a tail on Mairead Donovan and watch her every movement becoming more and more convinced she had not told them everything; they already had her address and intended to find out the identification of her boyfriend and the father of her baby. Strictly speaking, this operation should have fallen to MI5 because it was taking place on UK territory and therefore outside their jurisdiction.

In London, at the weekly meeting of the security services, this latest issue was raised. The first to speak was Sir Claude Foster of MI6.

'Good morning, gentlemen, I have to tell you our informant within the IRA in Dublin disappeared temporarily, but has since contacted us and is, in fact, now living in England. She fled fearing her own life because of her affair with the Chief of Staff. He also has now left his post and gone into semi-retirement, another source tells us, to look after a sick wife. The whole bloody lot of them are sick if you ask me,' said the director general of the secret intelligence service.

'What do you intend to do with her now?' asked the Minister of Defence.

'Well, she has provided us with some useful stuff including the proposed operation to kill the Home Secretary, therefore giving us the opportunity to change the location of the event and increase security on all key members of the cabinet. To answer your question, sir, just let her lie low but keep discreet surveillance on her and see what happens. She has recently had a baby with her current boyfriend and enquiries are going on to establish his identity,' continued Foster.

'Sir I really must protest at this blatant MI6 activity on the UK mainland; this is our role entirely,' said Sir James Overton of MI5, the Counter Espionage Service.

'I fully appreciate your concern, James but this young lady is already an agent of MI6 and I don't believe anything is to be gained, in the short term, by handing her over to your service. You must remember the Prime Minister has given me total authority on this whole issue, in agreement with the both the Home and Foreign Secretary's so my decision stands. Is that clear gentlemen?'

'Sir Claude you have my directive to continue your activities but if any other person or persons come to light during this operation, you are to inform MI5 and they will take over this role, with the exception of the young lady and her boyfriend. If and when arrests are required, this then becomes the province of Special Branch and Commander Collins here. If we do it any other way the defence lawyers will have a field day in court, citing incorrect procedures and all the rest of it,' concluded Michael Deakin MP, the Minister of Defence.

The meeting broke up and the various heads went back to their respective departments and the Minister of Defence reported directly to the Prime Minister.

'Prime Minister, sir, I have just come from the weekly Defence Intelligence meeting and the usual old divisions over jurisdiction have reared their ugly heads once again. I can't help feeling, at times, if all this is a hindrance to good progress on this whole issue of the assassination of the late chief constable as we have not made a great deal of progress in catching the perpetrator,' said the Minister of Defence.

'But, Michael I gave you total authority over this and you have to stamp on them if this continues.'

'I have made that abundantly clear to them this morning, sir, but if it continues then may I suggest you have them in and reinforce this directly. You know they see us as ministers just passing through and wondering whether we will win the next general election. They are professionals and see us as rank amateurs, which in a way I suppose we are.'

'Just so, Michael but we have a far more ranging manifesto than they do so we must reinforce the command structure, they work for us directly and of course the security of the United Kingdom and the sooner they realise that the better. They will do as they are told. Please arrange a meeting with the heads of MI5 and MI6 for tomorrow morning. Is there anyone else you would like me to include?' asked the Prime Minister.

'No, sir the rest are fine and fully understand their respective roles, including the SAS and Special Branch. Do you want me to be present?'

'No, Michael that won't be necessary, I will deal with this once and for all. Thank you for telling me.'

The following morning the Prime Minister met with both the heads of the Security Services and laid it on the line that co-operation was essential and if there were any further difficulties with this then their premature retirements would be accepted. For the last two years the Prime Minister had secretly discussed the possibilities of combining both services into one; who knew if this could still happen in the future.

It didn't take MI6 long to establish who Mairead Donovan's boyfriend was and suddenly the name Liam Reagan rang a bell; this being mentioned by MI5 following Alan Conlon's interrogation at their centre at Dorking in Surrey. They didn't know if he was the killer of Sir Frank Cooper the late Chief Constable of Northern Ireland but it was a distinct possibility.

Intensive but discreet background checks were being made about Reagan using all the resources available, including unofficial contacts with the Irish Garda Special Branch in Dublin and the Special Branch in Northern Ireland; the old pals act being used to its full potential. Results were soon forthcoming and action against Reagan was imminent. MI6 decided to give Reagan some space, with the intention of allowing him the opportunity of implicating himself further. The pressure from Downing Street was mounting by the week.

Phone taps were placed on the flat he shared with Mairead Donovan and their baby and surveillance was on twenty-four hours a day. Further enquiries into both their bank accounts and also the college they were studying Portuguese at, produced predictable results. The young couple were keeping their head above water financially and managing to save a little each month. With only him working now, this saving was severely reduced. The fact they were both learning Portuguese indicated that this was their likely intended future destination.

There was no way MI6 was going to let them go to Portugal and if they tried to make a run for it, they would both be arrested under the Prevention of Terrorism Act, designed to fast-track terrorist offences in the UK.

By the next weekend Liam Reagan had secured a possible job in a golf resort near Faro on the Algarve. It would appear from the response by the owner that an interview was a mere formality. 'The convenience of the internet,' he muttered logging off his laptop.

When Mairead came in from shopping, he told her the good news about the job in Portugal, adding that the golf club owner had informed him of accommodation available nearby at a subsidised rent and is available immediately. 'Oh, darling when can we go?'

'I have to give a month's notice at the club and renew my passport at the Irish embassy in London, so soon after that we are off to the sun and a new life. I have accepted the position and the interview should be no problem at all as I have the experience required, plus I'm good at figures, so a possible manager's position in the future with a bit of luck love.'

MI6 monitored all this via GCHQ computer intercepts and so they decided to strike within the week. It was imperative that Reagan did not get away; far better to arrest him here than have all the usual trouble with extradition from Portugal later.

That evening Liam and Mairead went to bed early as she had a bad cold and their baby had been playing up during the day; she was exhausted but elated at the thought of Portugal.

At 6am the next morning, the front door came crashing off its hinges and the police stormed into the flat waking up most of the neighbours. Detective Chief Inspector Richard Walters of the Metropolitan Police Special Branch entered the bedroom and confronted the pair, still in bed. The raid was so quick they had no time to get out of bed let alone make any form of escape.

'Liam Reagan, I am arresting you on suspicion of murder under the Prevention of Terrorism Act of the United Kingdom. You do not have to say anything but anything you do say may be used in evidence that you later rely on in court, do you understand?' said the inspector.

Liam Reagan just nodded and Mairead started to cry, her hopes dashed in an instant.

Reagan was taken to London by an armed, escorted police car and placed in the cells under high security at Paddington Green Police Station. Mairead stayed in the flat with her baby and a representative of MI6 soon arrived.

'Hello, Mairead I'm sorry it has come to this but we believe your boyfriend is the killer of the late Chief Constable of Ulster. If there is anything you can tell us to help with these enquiries it will be of help to you and him in the long run. We have substantial evidence to suspect Reagan and we intend to fill in some gaps before he is charged. At the moment he is in police custody and you are unable to visit him but will be able to later. In the meantime stay close to this flat. I have no problem with you going out shopping and any baby clinic visits you have to make. If you try and make a run for it we will get you and throw away the key, is that clear? I hasten to add you are under surveillance and will remain so until we decide otherwise,' said the man, without compassion.

Mairead was totally devastated and unable to stop crying; she had to phone her mother in Dublin but decided to compose herself first. Her first concern was for Liam but there was nothing she could do about it at present.

In Dublin, Julie Donovan was equally distraught for her daughter's sake and offered to come over to England immediately.

'Oh, mum I would really like some help here, I don't know what to do. The baby has colic and I am not getting much sleep and what with all this I don't know which way to turn. Please help me!'

'Darling I'm on my way just as soon as I can get a flight to Gatwick or Heathrow. Have they said anything about charges against you?'

'No I haven't broken any laws that I know about, so hopefully not. Please come soon, please mum.'

'Now don't you worry and be sure to look after that baby now. I'll be with you as soon as I can, my lovely daughter,' replied Mrs Donovan. 'Holy mother of Jesus, what is happening to my family, what have I done to deserve this?' she said out loud, whilst packing clothes into a case and looking for her debit card to draw some cash to help her daughter.

The following afternoon Julie Donovan caught the Shuttle from Belfast to London Heathrow and the train to Brighton arriving late evening, exhausted and hungry. Her daughter met her at the station and they caught a taxi to the flat. Mrs Donovan looked after the baby whilst Mairead cooked some food for their dinner. After dinner and the baby put to bed, mother and daughter sat down for a long talk, not realising the flat was bugged by the security service.

'Now tell me, Mairead, did you know Liam was a suspected murderer?'

'No. mum not at all. I was convinced he was just a low ranking member of the IRA and nothing more. Like me, he just wanted to get away from it all and have a better life,' replied Mairead cautiously, believing now that the flat could be bugged.

'Well you are in a right old pickle now, my love, the question is what are we going to do about it?' said Julie, sipping her wine and lighting a cigarette.

'I don't know, mum, I really don't know what to think. I know Liam is not a murderer, he is just not the type, is he?' she lied.

The next two days passed in a whirl for Mairead and she was denied any contact with Liam Reagan by the police, not even a phone call.

Reagan was held by the police in custody whilst investigations were carried out and had his statutory custody time extended by a magistrate to allow for further investigations. It was obvious now to him that the police and security services had ample evidence to send him to jail for a very long time. It was clear that some information had come to them by informers within the IRA and he realised he was done for. MI6 interviewed him extensively, along with MI5.

'Mr Reagan,' said the senior MI6 agent, 'we have enough evidence to provide you with accommodation at Her Majesty's pleasure for a very long time, possibly permanently, in fact it's very unlikely you would ever be released. You would die in prison!'

'Well there's not much I can do about that is there, so you might as well bang me up now,' said a dejected Reagan, slumped in a chair in the interview room.

'Not so fast, Mr Reagan. It's possible we may be able to do a deal and go some way to help you get a reduced sentence. I can't say a pardon because we think you murdered the chief constable of Ulster and that's not pardonable under any circumstances you understand.'

'What do you want from me then?'

'First I want a full confession regarding this murder and then as much information as you can give us about IRA activities in Ireland and on the mainland. Only then can I evaluate the usefulness of this data to put before a judge in chambers with regard to sentence. In fact, turning Queen's evidence,' replied the senior agent.

'I can't give you much information at all because I only played a small part in the movement and had no planning input at all. I can only reveal the names I know but you probably have them anyway.' said Reagan.

'Try us, Mr Reagan,' replied the agent.

'Most of them are pretty low in the organisation but there is John O'Hagan, Sean O'Rourke, Alan Conlon, Colm MacDiamid, and of course Mike Lenihan, an American who trained me in Galway. I believe Lenihan was a former member of the US Green Berets; how he was recruited by the IRA and where he is now I have no idea.'

'Keep going, Mr Reagan. We need more than that, I'm afraid, if there is any hope of leniency by the courts,' said the agent, lighting a cigarette but not offering Reagan one.

'Well, there is an office in Dublin set above a dry cleaners off O'Connell Street and it has regular IRA visitors from all parts of north and south of Ireland, you know meetings and such like. I went there regularly to see MacDiamid for instructions. It's a main hub of operations but I imagine that secret papers are stored elsewhere because they have been raided by the Garda many times but nothing of importance has ever been found to my knowledge.

'The main thing I was to be involved in was the proposed assassination of the British Home Secretary at a place called Woolwich, South London I believe. MacDiamid wanted me to hit him with an M60 machine gun but it would have been a massacre and I was having no part in it. That's why Mairead, Miss Donovan, and me escaped to England and now I'm here,' said Reagan.

'How did you intend to get such large weapon and ammunition into place in an area where there is already good security in operation? Woolwich contains a large army base and that's where many ceremonies take place, Mr Reagan, hence your mission,' continued the agent.

'That's right but I wasn't the person moving the gun. It is apparently already in place and ready to go,' said Reagan.

'Where is this gun located, Reagan?'

'I genuinely don't know. I really don't and further more I have no idea who is responsible for this side of things,' continued Reagan nervously.

Without warning the agent left the room and was gone for about half an hour but returned with some tea and biscuits.

'Right I'm going to leave you now but I expect the police will want to question you further. Rest assured, Mr Reagan I will be back and I expect more from you when I return. Think on it!' said the agent, getting up and making for the door.

Liam Reagan was left alone for the rest of the afternoon but had a meal brought in and some materials for washing and general hygiene including some fresh underclothing. A television was supplied for him to watch and during the late evening he called for the custody sergeant.

'Yeah what do you want, Reagan?' said the sergeant.

'I would like to see the gentleman who was here this morning talking to me, as I have something I want to discuss with him.'

'I'll get the Special Branch inspector in.'

'No, I said I want the man I saw this morning. I won't talk to anyone else. Is that clear Sergeant?'

'Suit yourself, I'll see what I can do,' said the sergeant gruffly.

Chapter 29

Mairead Donovan carried on as best she could with all her dreams for the future shattered; her mother was a really good shoulder to cry on and this helped her and the baby a great deal. What will happen next is anyone's guess she thought.

Meanwhile, in the ministry of defence, there was relief at last that an arrest had been made and that the security services seemed to be working together along with special branch. Michael Deakin MP, the Minister of Defence and with overall authority for the whole investigation, albeit an unusual appointment, worked earnestly and conscientiously with the heads of the security services and police to bring the whole affair to a conclusion; if only to get the Prime Minister off his back.

The morning meeting commenced with him being briefed by MI6 with additional information gained by MI5 from informers both in Ireland and Britain.

'Sir,' said the head of MI6. 'We have in custody, a Liam Reagan of Dublin who has admitted to membership of the IRA and given us names and some locations of republican activity. There has been no admission of murder but we are at an early stage in the investigations at Paddington Green Police Station so please bear with us on this. I will keep you informed as to any new developments.'

Sir James Overton of MI5, the Counter Espionage Service, continued, 'Minister, we have set up a search in conjunction with the police and army of the Woolwich area. The fact that the hit was to take place close to the barracks provides us with the opportunity to search all premises and houses within five hundred yards of the parade ground. The figure of five hundred yards came after discussions with army weapons experts from the School of Infantry. If nothing is found we will of course extend this as far as reasonably practical, no stone will be left unturned.'

'Thank you, James. What information have we had from informers that might be relevant to this investigation?' asked the minister, sipping his tea.

'It may well be relevant, minister the fact that Colm MacDiamid has stood down from the position of Chief of Staff, or indeed forcibly removed; at this stage we simply don't know but enquiries are continuing. Our informant is a disgraced former member of the Garda CID who was jailed for an assault on a senior officer. However, he is very low level and we are cultivating him at the moment, the best may be yet to come,' concluded Sir James Overton.

'Minister, as you know, Reagan gave us the name of an American ex-Green Beret, who apparently had a big part in training the IRA at the camp the SAS destroyed in Galway, his name is Michael Lenihan, whereabouts unknown at present but his name has been passed to the CIA for investigation. We are expecting them to come up with something but you know what they are, they want information from us but are not very forthcoming

413

the other way round, especially with extraditions and the like. Personally, I'd rather deal with the Russians than them at times, even though they are our so called allies and brothers in arms,' added Sir Claude Foster, with a Gallic shrug.

'If you need more time holding Reagan let me know and I will talk to the Lord Chancellor and see what can be done. For God's sake don't let him go until we are sure one way or the other, gentlemen,' said the minister.

The phone call to MI6 came through from the custody sergeant at Paddington Green High Security Police Station just after 9pm and was handled by the duty officer, who in turn contacted the senior agent at home.

'We have had a request from the subject you are investigating. He says it's important you see him as soon as soon as possible, he will speak only to you in person,' said the duty officer over the phone.

'Ok thank you I'll deal with it straight away,' said the agent ringing off.

The agent made his way to the police station and after producing his identity card was shown to the cells holding Reagan.

'Mr Reagan I understand you want to see me.'

'Yes I do. I want to confess to the murder of the Chief Constable of Northern Ireland; I shot him with a rifle on the golf course at Broughshane on the specific orders of the IRA. I then made my way to a safe house and later back to Dublin, managing to enrol in the university there to study classics. I was diagnosed with cancer of the bowel and underwent extensive surgery and follow-up treatment including chemotherapy and the like.

'The IRA insisted I carry on with further work for them, even though I had some time to recover; they never take no for an answer. I have told you all I know with exception of yet another training camp in Donegal near Creeslough and one in Libya but I don't know where, just bloody miles out in the desert, at least four hours by road from Tripoli,' said Reagan.

'Well, Mr Reagan you have at last come to your senses and confessed, bringing us some closure on this issue at last. We knew we would get our man one of these days because we always do; the IRA is full of informers and people who turn Queen's evidence to save their miserable skins. The question now is what we do with you. The law requires you to stand trial and receive justice in due course and that's what will happen. However it is possible that because you have helped us we might be able to reciprocate in some way but I can't promise you understand,' said the senior agent.

Later that day the Special Branch took up their questioning procedure in correct textbook fashion and all interviews were taped.

The Prime Minister in Downing Street greeted the news with elation and eagerly awaited a full report from both heads of the security services. The full showcase trial that was to follow would show the world that Britain would not tolerate terrorism under any circumstances and would indeed impose the harshest sentences for those found guilty. He would undoubtedly boost his chances at the next election, he thought in passing.

The next day, Liam Reagan was formally charged with the murder of the Chief Constable of Ulster and appeared at Horse Ferry Road Magistrates Court. He was automatically indicted for trial at the Old Bailey and remanded in custody to Belmarsh Maximum Security Prison in South London.

It was two weeks before he was allowed a visit from Mairead and their baby and the hour-long visit seemed to go so quickly they had barely time to say all the things they wanted to each other; the close presence of prison officers throughout the visit was no help at all.

Back at the flat in Brighton, Julie Donovan tried to talk Mairead into going back to Dublin and live with her until things sorted themselves out one way or the other. 'Mairead, you will never see Liam released from prison, the British will make damn sure of that, they will show this statement to the IRA and any other terrorist organisation who goes up against them. They can be completely ruthless, much more than other countries in the civilised world when they are pushed.'

'But, mum I love him and have his baby. Won't they take that into consideration?' she wailed.

'Not a chance, darling. Not a chance in hell. Let's go home and time will heal things for you. Liam is finished for good you know,' continued Julie.

'If I go back home to Ireland, the IRA will be after me soon enough that's for sure, mum.'

'Not if I have any say in the matter. You just leave them to me, my girl. I'm not afraid of those bastards to be sure,' said Julie pouring the tea.

Julie took the morning flight to Dublin with the intension of going to the IRA command and putting her daughter's case directly to the Chief of Staff himself.

416

Although she didn't know exactly where the chief was based she managed to locate him by judicious enquiries among the local community.

When she arrived at the office above the dry cleaners George Collins, the Chief of Staff of the IRA, invited her in and asked her to sit down. 'What can I do for you, Mrs Donovan on this fine, sunny day?'

'I'm sure, Mr Collins, you are aware that Liam Reagan has been arrested and charged with the murder of the late Chief Constable of Ulster. It's obvious he will not see the light of day again, certainly not in our lifetime anyway. My daughter used to work for your predecessor, as you also know, but I must add she went away with him out of pure love for the man and no other reasons. She had nothing to tell anyone because she was never in a position to be in possession of any incriminating facts about the IRA. Your predecessor naturally kept all that to himself and quite rightly so, in my opinion; she was just the office girl and nothing more.

'When Reagan decided to flee he did it, as I understand, because he feared for his own safety and, naturally, Mairead wanted to go with him; she has since had his baby, a girl. What I want from you is the guarantee that she will not be harmed if she comes home to her rightful place in Ireland. She tells me that Reagan has been interrogated by the British but they have asked her nothing, simply because they understand she knows nothing. Are you in a position to give me that guarantee, Mr Collins? If so, you will not hear from either of us again because she will get a job somewhere and rebuild her life, hopefully with a new man. How about it, Mr

417

Collins?' she concluded with passion in her voice and a tear in her eye.

'Mrs Donovan you put me in a very difficult position because normally the act of desertion from a post is viewed very seriously by the movement and the punishment is severe in most cases; I'm sure I don't have to tell you that. You have put to me a strong case; I will, however, have to discuss this issue with my colleagues and get back to you. I will indeed stress to them the impetuousness of young love and that she realises she has made a mistake. Leave it to me, just give me your phone number, that's all I require and I will be in touch soon. Thanks for being honest with me, Mrs Donovan,' he said, showing her the door.

Julie Donovan walked down the road to the bus stop, shaking and breathless after her ordeal with the chief. 'Fingers crossed,' she mumbled. It wasn't until she got home that the middle-aged grandmother switched off the small recording device she had hidden in her underclothing. On playback the complete conversation was loud and clear, every word captured. She shuddered at the thought she might have been searched, if the device had been found, her death would have been immediate.

The next day, she deposited the tape with a solicitor with the instructions that if she disappeared he must take it to the Garda, along with the attached sealed letter. 'Holy Mary, Mother of God you're getting to old for this sort of thing,' she said aloud once back in the safety of her front room.

Mairead Donovan just carried on as normal, certain that MI5 or MI6 had her under surveillance; her mother had left her some money to tide her over whilst she was away in Ireland.

The following Saturday, Julie Donovans phone rang soon after 9am; it was the Chief of Staff of the IRA.

'Mrs Donovan, good morning to you. I trust you are well?' he said without preamble.

'I'm fine and yourself?'

'I said I would come back to you following our conversation recently and I have some good news for you. I would like to meet you at the main bus station in Dublin at 12.30 today if that's OK?'

'Yes of course I'll be there. Where shall I wait?'

'Just near the news-stand and you will be contacted. I must stress you must come alone is that clear?'

'Thank you, Mr Collins. I'll be there without fail.'

Julie Donovan arrived early and just stood by the news-stand, reading the headlines of the displayed papers. Right on time there was tap on her shoulder.

'Please come with me, Mrs Donovan,' said the young man, leading her gently away by the arm in the direction of the car park.

The blue Ford Galaxy contained two men, one she recognised at George Collins. 'Please get in, Mrs Donovan, 'said Collins with a smile, after winding down the window.

As soon as she settled into her seat the car moved off immediately; not a word was spoken for a tense few minutes.

'Well now, we are alone again, well almost,' he said nodding to the other man. I have to tell you that following the meeting I told you about, it has been agreed that your daughter can safely return home without fear. There is however some conditions she must abide by; please take note and pass them on to her. If she is contacted by anyone other than friends or family she must report this immediately to me. She must also not talk about the IRA and her work to anyone under any circumstances, Mrs Donovan. I must stress this point; failure to comply will result in her untimely death. Please be warned, as we will be watching her and any breech of these conditions will bring dire consequences! Do you understand everything I've said, Mrs Donovan?'

'Yes indeed, Mr Collins and thank you for your kindness and consideration. I will pass this onto Mairead as soon as possible. You have my word she will comply to the letter as she wants to put this whole thing behind her and concentrate on bringing up her baby girl, the lovely little thing.'

Julie Donovan had earlier decided not to carry another recording device; she simply didn't want to chance her luck a second time. She was dropped off at the bus station and made her way home to the Dublin suburb of Blackrock.

That evening, she telephoned Mairead in Brighton to give her the good news that she was free to come home, stressing she could stay with her in the spare room until she got settled again. Secretly, Julie Donovan was looking forward to playing the doting grandmother on a much more permanent basis, therefore allowing Mairead the freedom to get a job.

Mairead Donovan was glad, in a way, she could go home but at the same time very sad that Liam would be

420

incarcerated in prison for many years, if found guilty, as he had admitted his guilt. Prison was inevitable she knew.

During a visit to him in Belmarsh, she told him of her decision to go back to Ireland and live with her mother. 'Liam, mum has told me the IRA have given me a pardon, in a way, so I can go back and look after our daughter, Annie, so she can have a good life and future, but I'm so sad to leave you here, really I am, darling,' she said crying and biting her lip.

'Well there's nothing I can do about it, love. I'm stuck here for God knows how long and they said the trial could be months away yet. There is one hope that a deal might be made with the courts because I have given them some information but not much I'm afraid because I simply didn't have any stuff of real importance. Go back, Mairead but write to me often, my love, and don't forget to send pictures of Annie so I can see her progress as she grown up,' he said, choking up as the visiting time came to a close.

Mairead made her way home to Brighton and began to pack up the few items she had, then contacted the airport for a reservation for a flight to Dublin. She decided to contact her MI6 handler for permission to return to her homeland. They agreed, with the proviso that she was to let them know of any information of IRA activities that may come her way.

Julie Donovan picked up the phone as soon as it rang, it was Mairead.

'Mum it's me. I'm coming home and have a flight booked for tomorrow, landing in Dublin at 4.45pm. Will you be able to pick me up?'

'Of course, darling is everything alright with the baby and all?'

'Yes, fine, mum, don't worry, it will great to be back home at last. I have been to see Liam and he agrees it's best if I come back and be with you. He's sad but accepts all that has happened and already he has met other IRA men in the prison. Not sure if that's good or bad really but there you go I suppose,' she said with a tremor in her voice and on the verge of tears.

The British Airways flight left on time and the journey to Dublin was over quickly, with the baby asleep all the way. Mairead, not a good air passenger was glad it had been a smooth flight.

Mrs Donovan met her daughter and granddaughter at the arrivals area after they quickly got through immigration and customs without incident. The car was parked close by and the journey to Blackrock took about 35 minutes as the traffic was light on that Sunday evening.

A couple of days later there was a knock at the door and Mairead opened it thinking it was a neighbour who was due to come round to see the baby.

'Hello, Mairead,' said the taller of the two men.

'Hello, who are you?' she replied, with a cold shiver going down her spine.

'I think you know who we are. Can we come in as it's pouring out here?'

'Yes I suppose so,' she said, standing aside.

When they went into the living room, Mairead picked up her baby and pulled her close to her chest.

'Well, Mairead, this is just a visit to emphasise what the Chief of Staff told your mother recently; the conditions we granted you for the freedom to come home after your desertion with Liam Reagan. I have to inform you that any breach of these conditions, however small they may seem, will bring upon you the most severe retribution possible and leave your daughter without a mother. Is that clear, young lady?'

'I hear what you say and of course I will obey. You must remember I worked for the movement; I was put forward for the job through a friend and did it to the best of my ability. The IRA principles are engraved on my heart and always will be. One day there will be a united Ireland and the war will be over,' she replied forcefully and with passion, or at least she hoped it appeared that way.

'OK, Miss Donovan we will leave you now but you will be watched from time to time and checks will be made on you through a variety of sources, so please comply with our instructions and all will be well with you and the baby. By the way, what's her name?'

'Annie, her name is Annie and she currently keeps me awake most nights and sleeps during the day; if you have children you will know what I mean, gentlemen,' she replied, trying to lighten the atmosphere a little.

'OK, Mairead just behave yourself and all will be well and you will have no trouble, I doubt though that you will be offered a job with us,' he said with a smile.

After they left, Mairead made herself a cup of tea and sat down, still shaking a little at the chilling warning she had just received. When her mother returned from shopping she decided not to tell her of the ordeal and let sleeping dogs lie.

Chapter 30

In Belmarsh Prison, Liam Reagan was called to an interview room to meet two men from MI6.

'Mr Reagan as you know full-well the situation you are in, I do not intend to go over all these matters again but rather concentrate on what you can tell us further about your dealings with the IRA,' said one of the men, without introduction.

'I have already told you all I know and have nothing further to add. I spoke about O.Hagan and O'Rourke as well as the American, Lenihan at the training camp in Galway. Oh and about Conlon, a complete tosser if there was one,' he replied with a shrug.

'You might be interested to know that O'Hagan and O'Rourke along with Conlon are all dead; as a matter of fact, several others have fallen by the wayside it seems in the meantime. However, several other evil bastards have risen to the calling and taken up the challenge for the lost cause you all fight for, Mr Reagan.

'We have a couple of options for you, Reagan. The most obvious is going through the courts and a long time at Her Majesty's pleasure, or the possibility of a deal whereby you provide us with a lot more information in exchange for a clemency consideration,' said the senior agent.

'I have told you all I know, you must believe me. There is nothing more I can tell you no matter how much you keep asking,' he replied.

'Listen, Reagan. If I had my way I would have you taken out and shot in some local woods, just like the lot you used to work with, you murdering bastard!'

Liam Reagan was startled by this outburst from the agent and thankful he was in a civilised country, or that threat would have been carried out without a second thought.

'Mr Reagan, for one last time, what more can you tell us?'

'Nothing. I have nothing further to add because I know absolutely nothing other than what I've already told you and the police,' concluded Reagan in complete despair.

'See you in court, Mr Reagan!' replied the agent and his partner, getting up and banging on the cell door for the officer to let them out.

It was three months before the court case started at the Central Criminal Court, otherwise known as the Old Bailey, and lasted just three weeks with all the evidence being heard for the prosecution and defence.

Reagan was found guilty, resulting from a unanimous decision by the jury and he was sentenced by Mr Justice Hegarty to twenty-five years in custody. His next accommodation was Frankland Maximum Security Prison in County Durham.

Back home in Dublin, Mairead Donovan was shocked when she read about the court case in the newspapers and the subsequent verdict. She cried for three days but Julie helped a great deal by giving her and the baby support and lots of encouragement for the future. If she wanted to visit him in future, Julie would supply the fare costs and money for accommodation.

Secretly, Julie Donovan was pleased it was all over and now life could return to some form of normality for them both. Fortunately, the IRA never again came near or by and that was fine by her. The tape she had deposited with the solicitor in Dublin would remain there until her death and this wish was clearly stated in her will.

In the months ahead, Mairead Donovan started to go out with friends and began to enjoy life again whilst watching her baby grow up fast. She finally managed to get a job in a manufacturing plant, as a secretary, and began to earn a good, steady wage thereby paying her way at home. One of the managers seemed nice and clearly took an interest in her by asking her out for dinner one evening. Julie Donovan was very happy in her active role as the doting grandmother.

In Frankland Prison Liam Reagan settled into the routine of prison life and managed to get a position teaching some of the inmates to read and write. He often wrote letters for them and read the replies from their families. Because he had been accepted into Trinity College Dublin he managed to get a place on the Open University course reading classics to pass the time and which would lead to a degree. He doubted though he would ever be able to use the qualification in due course. Prison did, in fact, have its drawbacks.

His best course of action, he decided, was to keep a very low profile and just get on with his studies, hoping that in the future he might be transferred to an open prison with a better confinement and an easier regime. He realised that release was at least fifteen years away so there was no point in worrying about that. Life would be more acceptable if his stomach pains had not returned, accompanied with the occasional bouts of diarrhoea. Had the cancer returned? he wondered.

In London, at a meeting, the heads of security were jubilant with the success of catching the killer of the former Chief Constable of Ulster. The Minister of Defence was the first to speak.

'Good morning, gentlemen, I have to offer my congratulations to all who played a part in bringing this sad state of affairs to a successful conclusion. The killer is now behind bars and will remain so for many years. I also offer the Prime Minister's express congratulations to the SAS for "Operation Cobra"- for those of you who are not sure, that was the code name given for the raid on the IRA training camp in Galway whereby they managed to remove some prominent figures of the terrorist movement from this planet, unfortunately losing one of their own in the process.'

'Minister,' said Sir Claude Foster of MI6, 'I wanted to clarify the position with regard to a possible clemency deal with Reagan for information received concerning IRA activities. On deep questioning he clearly has nothing to offer and as a result I felt we had no obligation to intervene in the legal process. Would you agree that was the right decision?'

'Yes, Claude, in fact the Lord Chancellor said it would have been difficult after he had been formally charged anyway; the law has its process and changes can present many problems. If a clemency deal had been struck and it got into the press God knows what would have happened, so all's well that ends well I suppose.'

'Sir, I would like to offer some recent information gleaned from our investigations. We have picked up some gossip from the pubs in Kilburn regarding a possible bombing campaign on the mainland, quite likely in Manchester. I will keep you posted as to further developments,' said the deputy director of MI5.

At that moment a messenger knocked, came into the room and handed an envelope to Commander Paul Collins of the Special Branch.

'Gentlemen, I have some welcome news. The police have discovered and removed an M60 machine gun with one hundred and fifty rounds of armour-piercing ammunition from a flat in Woolwich with three men arrested,' announced Collins obviously pleased.

'Excellent news, Commander, wouldn't you agree gentlemen?' replied the minister.

'Sir is there any progress in the pursuit of the American, Michael Lenihan, the instructor at the camp in Galway?' asked Brigadier John Chalmers the Director of Special Forces.

'John the latest I have is that the Foreign Office has asked the CIA and FBI to investigate his whereabouts but so far nothing has come back to us. Perhaps it's time to jostle them up a little, leave it to me and I'll get back to you at the next meeting,' replied the minister.

The meeting broke up and The Brigadier and Lt Colonel George Berryman the commanding officer of the

22nd Special Air Service Regiment went to the Special Forces Club in Hans Crescent behind Harrods for lunch and a well earned drink.

'Well, George what do think of it all?'

'I suppose it has come to a successful conclusion but I have one concern that part of our operation went a little adrift, in as much as we lost a man and never killed all the protagonists. As you know, sir the subsequent investigation found Captain Rodd had not followed orders to the letter and failed in some simple procedures therefore compromising the raid, at least in part. It is a great loss to the regiment that he went back to the Black Watch and has since left the army altogether and subsequently joined the family beef farm in Perthshire. Sergeant Jones has also left and returned to serve his remaining time with his parent regiment the Royal Green Jackets in his current rank. I was sorry to lose both these fine soldiers, sir,' replied Berryman.

'George I am pleased to inform you, unofficially so far, that you are being considered for promotion to full colonel in June this year and to be given, if successful, the position of defence attaché at the British Embassy in Madrid, how do you feel about that?'

'That is the last thing I want. Rosemary would never want to live in the heat of Madrid and a desk job at the embassy would drive me mad with boredom. All those bloody diplomatic parties and being at the beck and call of the Ambassador; not for me, sir I'm afraid.'

'George this is a promotion for you and of course an increased pension at the end of your service. Think about it, my friend,' said the Brigadier.

'If the army cannot offer me anything other than that, I will resign my commission and take Rosemary on a world cruise as we had always planned when I retire, sir,' replied Berryman.

The Brigadier was despondent at this reaction as he had personally recommended Lt Colonel Berryman for the promotion and posting in the belief that it would be a fitting end to a distinguished army career. What the Chief of the Defence Staff would say now was anyone's guess as he had already agreed this with the Brigadier. Clearly if Berryman was ordered into the post he would resign.

George Berryman returned to his regimental HQ in Hereford somewhat saddened his career had apparently stalled close to the finishing post. That evening he discussed with his wife Rosemary what the Brigadier has proposed with regards to promotion and the posting to Madrid.

'George you know I can't live in that heat, I hated it when we were in Singapore for two years, it never did my asthma any good at all.'

'I know, darling and that is exactly what I told him, plus my opinion of the desk job kowtowing to the ambassador day after day; any job too difficult, oh just give it to the military attaché. That sort of thing; no not for me! I feel early retirement coming on. I'll just wait and see what happens and then act accordingly I think, love,' he concluded.

The sudden, fatal heart attack that killed Brigadier John Chalmers, the director of Special Forces, at the ministry of defence, came two months later and that night Lt Colonel Berryman's phone rang at 9pm. It was the new Chief of the Defence Staff.

'Colonel Berryman I'm sorry to disturb you this late but John Chalmers has died suddenly from a massive heart attack and I want you to take over immediately as acting director of Special Forces. This is almost certainly going to become permanent in the rank of Brigadier on the normal two year cycle. I know you were unhappy about the Madrid job and I do understand. Who would you recommend to command the regiment as your successor?'

'Sir, this has come like a bolt out of the blue. Er... you have caught me on the hop. I suppose the best man for the job at Hereford is Major Alan Stevens, a very experienced officer and he would be my first choice. He has the necessary courses behind him and the authority of command. Sir, he's your man,' added Berryman with a tinge of excitement.

'Right, George, or should I say Brigadier, can you come and see me tomorrow morning at my office in the MOD? I will arrange the clearance for you now and advise the Prime Minister and Minister of Defence accordingly of your appointment,' replied the Air Marshal, Sir Roger Knightly.

When he told Rosemary she couldn't make up her mind if she was pleased or not, the thought of the world cruise, but at the same time she would be the wife of a Brigadier and all the trappings that went with that. The jump from Lieutenant Colonel to Brigadier was rare but not unheard of, George assured her over dinner.

Ten days later, the British Embassy in Yemen was stormed and taken over by armed rebels. The new Brigadier and the SAS were going to be busy yet again!

Extensive enquiries had taken place in America and finally, ex-Master Sergeant Michael Lenihan was located by tracing his insurance and driving licence applications.

The fact that he had not committed any crimes on US soil and was not wanted by the police was waived by the authorities at the request of the British Government investigation into terrorist activities against the crown. The British wanted to question him and the FBI allowed this, provided they were present throughout.

At 9am the knock on his door at the trailer park near Leavenworth did not come as a complete surprise; he had been expecting it for sometime...